Aleph

Aleph

Storm Constantine

IMMANION PRESS
Stafford England

Aleph

By Storm Constantine

© 1990

2nd Revised Edition 2012

http://www.stormconstantine.com

Cover by Ruby

Interior Layout by Storm Constantine

Set in Palatino Linotype

IP0032

An Immanion Press Edition

8 Rowley Grove

Stafford ST17 9BJ

http://www.immanion-press.com

info@immanion-press.com

ISBN 978-1-907737-35-0

Books by Storm Constantine

The Wraeththu Chronicles
*The Enchantments of Flesh and Spirit
*The Bewitchments of Love and Hate
*The Fulfilments of Fate and Desire

*The Wraeththu Chronicles (omnibus of trilogy)

The Artemis Cycle
*The Monstrous Regiment
*Aleph

*Hermetech
*Burying the Shadow
Sign for the Sacred
Calenture

The Grigori Books
*Stalking Tender Prey
*Scenting Hallowed Blood
*Stealing Sacred Fire

Silverheart (with Michael Moorcock)

The Magravandias Chronicles:
Sea Dragon Heir
Crown of Silence
The Way of Light

The Wraeththu Histories:
*The Wraiths of Will and Pleasure
*The Shades of Time and Memory
*The Ghosts of Blood and Innocence

Wraeththu Mythos
*The Hienama
*Student of Kyme

Chapter One
Mireway Pools

'Oh Goddess! Damn! Damn!' Corinna Trotgarden jumped backwards, clutching her right hand then shaking it wildly.

'You alright, C'rin?' Hollis Backwater dropped his tools and hopped from tuft to tuft across the mireway.

Corinna was still dancing with pain. 'It's not much. Dammit, one of those mean whipthorns got me right in the palm!'

'Not much? Here, let me look.'

Corinna held out her hand obligingly. She and Hollis had been repairing the mireway boundary fence since dawn. A flash storm the day before had uprooted a plaisel bush and hurled it at the fence, causing a gap in the defences. The damage had been greater than they'd anticipated, but there was no way they wanted to come out again later.

Mireway Pools, in the south of Freespace territory, was an unwelcoming location of blood-crazy whirball nits and corroding acid-puddles; nobody went there unless it was unavoidable. The place had its advantages, however. It was unlikely that scavenging leapdogs or stray smooms seeking easy meat would cross the Mireway to reach the settlement. Also - although it was rarely alluded to for fear of tempting fatal agencies - the Pools were a more than adequate defence against any unwelcome visitors from the south.

The Freespacers tried to convince themselves they had travelled too far for pursuit to be a real possibility, but they still harboured a consensual, superstitious fear that, one day, someone might come and hunt them down in their sanctuary.

The cruel thorns of the fence were an illustration of both their anxiety and their desire to maintain their freedom.

Hollis was peering at the injured hand. 'Can't see any trace of a splinter in there, C'rin, but you'd better get it seen to. Seems to be swelling.'

'Let's get cracking, then. I'm damned if I'm coming out here again this season.'

'You sure you can work with that?'

Corinna sneered, her scarred face twisting to dramatic effect.

Hollis shrugged. 'It's your infection, Trotgarden.' He jumped back to his tools. 'Here, take this.'

Corinna caught the thrown hammer in her left hand. 'It's nearly done,' she said, knocking in a nail.

The thorns writhed and steamed in the mid-day heat, and the Pools exuded a none too refreshing odour behind them. With luck, they'd be finished in half an hour. Privately, Corinna fretted about the thorn-wound. It would mean being handicapped for several days; not time that she could afford. There was so much she wanted to do - not least because manual labour eased her mind of other stresses that she'd dragged with her from the south.

The Freespacers had only been rooted in the patch of land they'd named Freespace Town for a couple of moons-arc. Always reluctant nomads, they'd tried to settle places before, but never successfully. What might appear to be a promising location initially, generally presented a host of problems as time went on; stealthy, unseen, local predators picking off their meagre herd of stock animals, irrigation supplies being contaminated by sour-water leaks so that everybody got sick, shifting ground - a common phenomenon in the north it seemed - undermining all attempts at settlement. It was as if the land possessed a sentient objection to human life, throwing up obstructions to keep the Freespacers moving. The new site, however, appeared to be suitable and had, so far, presented no major problems. It was rich in edible plants, situated near to water and could be easily defended, if necessary. Gradually, the Freespacers were daring to suppose they'd found a place to call home.

Corinna could remember how, on the journey north, she had lost patience with her friend Rosanel Garmelding's tireless insistence that they would eventually discover some paradise plot. As time went on, the majority of the travellers, whatever they had believed at the outset, became disillusioned, and their concept of paradise undoubtedly underwent severe change. And yet, despite their cynicism, most people believed that, with the benefit of a few years' hard work, Freespace Town could be crafted into a shape approximating their original dreams.

By the time the fence was secure, Corinna's hand was throbbing in time to her heart-beat headache, and the flesh was turning purple. Hollis kept on wittering about it, which Corinna found irritating because, although whipthorn slash was inconvenient and painful, it was never really dangerous. They remounted their dank-beasts and set them splashing for home. Corinna knew that most of Hollis' concern was because he'd developed a pointless fondness for her. He'd been making this obvious for several moons-arc now; a phenomenon that Corinna found rather surprising. She felt that over the last two years, since they'd left the marsh, she had evolved into a hard-bitten and difficult creature. In her more charitable moments, Corinna would admit these characteristics were perhaps only superficial. Hadn't she been likable and easy-going once? Nowadays, when she was around other people, her old self went into hiding and sent out the defence persona, which bristled with sharp words. Most of the time, she bitched Hollis into the ground yet, in spite of this, he worshipped her. No matter what she said to him, he had a way of making a joke of it, or else - even more infuriating - would ignore it. Was it the status he wanted - to be able to call himself the partner of Corinna Trotgarden? He couldn't desire her, surely? And yet, she noticed his hands always hovered to touch her, fluttering around her but never landing on skin. She wondered what perverse part of his nature found her physically attractive.

Although her body was fit and lean - perhaps the only thing she was proud of - she felt her face had been ruined, made hideous, by its scars. Corinna knew Hollis was a generous, caring person, attractive and, to many people no doubt, desirable. He could probably take his pick of the Freespace women and receive a favourable response to his advances. This knowledge invoked the worst demon of all in Corinna's heart: did he pity her? She would prefer it if he was only status-seeking.

Corinna was aware that the Freespacers regarded her facial scars as marks of honour. She despised this concept deeply. True, she'd received them during imprisonment for crimes which, through a slight distortion of facts, could be termed as being of a political nature. Privately, Corinna considered her participation in past events to have been entirely accidental. Certainly, it had lacked bravery, valour, or even political conviction. The Freespacers had had to flee the comparative comfort of the southern marshes because of their disagreement with the policies of the women who held power in the major southern city, Silven Crescent. Corinna had been a casualty of that conflict of ideas. She and her fellow Freespacers had fled the marsh, escaping what they considered a cruel and unjust regime. They knew its prime mover, Yani Gisbandrun, was dead, but there had been plenty of her followers left alive, eager to pursue the woman's demented aims, and continue the matriarchal dictatorship that had been her life's work. The Freespacers were farmers, who for generations had familiarised themselves with the landscape of the marsh and had become used to those static conditions. Now, they were floundering in alien conditions, and many of the skills they needed to establish themselves had to be hastily relearned, often through trial and error. The availability of usable water, for example, had been taken for granted, which had led to the failure of many attempts at settlement.

Corinna had confided in no-one the truth of what had happened to her in Silven Crescent, and it gave her a strange kind of comfort that she possessed this hidden knowledge, for all its vileness. Apart from the scars on her face, there were other wounds too, both physical and mental, that Corinna kept secret. These were the injuries that she felt had rendered her emotionally functionless. The Freespacers, unaware of her inner pain, seeing her only as a heroine of war, wanted her to be a figurehead for them; something she'd had to fight in the early days. She wanted none of that; no leaders, no possible matriarchs. If the pioneering group couldn't thrive as a non-hierarchical society, then it might as well sink into the Mireway and be thoroughly destroyed by whipthorns. They hadn't come all this way to repeat old mistakes. Corinna gradually had to admit to herself, however, that human beings found it difficult to function without some kind of pecking order, someone at the top to take responsibility. She couldn't decide whether this was an innate trait or learned behaviour, but still hoped it was the latter, and that it could be unlearned.

Artemis was a big world, and there was so much of it uncharted by human hand. Freespace literally had the world at its feet. There was so much potential, and Corinna sometimes feared opportunities would be missed because of petty human dilemmas. She had vowed not to compromise her principles, not to take a commanding role, no matter how much it was thrust upon her, yet it was difficult to avoid at times. She was a planner, an organiser and, in the face of what she considered her ghastly disfigurement, wanted to be admired for her efficiency and creative skills. Having Hollis fawning over her did not help, whatever his motives. It only reminded her of how much she'd lost.

Chapter Two
On Africa Plate

Zy Larrigan was not a happy man. Not only was he having to escort his lover, Kitzuki, to one of her damned company functions within the hour, but she was not being at all sympathetic about his new commission. Did he want to leave Africa Plate for a while? Yes. Did he want to work again? Well... Yes, of course he did. Did he want to court danger on a back of beyond world, peopled by cultural Neanderthals? No, he did not, and neither, he felt, should Kitzuki expect him to. So she hadn't actually voiced the complaint that, unless he took the job on, he would soon be living off her income, but the message was there anyway. He'd learned to detect it during previous episodes of financial distress. 'It's too much to ask anybody,' he was saying. 'I'm not qualified to handle diplomatic incidents.'

Kitzuki had lost patience. 'So get another job, Zy. Quit moaning, will you!'

'I'm not moaning. This is rational objection. Do you think I'd be worrying if I could just get work somewhere else? You know the score.'

'Don't I just!' Kitzuki, more used to functional chic than official ceremonial garb, looked uncomfortable trussed into an evening gown comprised mainly of turquoise wire and feathertrim. She was perched awkwardly on the edge of Zy Larrigan's most comfortable recliner, knees together, feet splayed out, waiting for him to put the finishing touches to his own regalia. Her thick, black hair was tweaked and stretched into incredible coils, making it impossible for her to scratch her head, which was itching madly. Why did Zy have to be such a hopeless case? He wasn't a loser genetically, she was sure. There was no way she'd have taken up with him otherwise. He was just sloppy, and lazy. Now, he would ruin the evening by wearing that face; a mask of pinched self-pity she loathed. He knew she abhorred these ritual functions as much as he did. Usually they endured the situation, supported by mutual wit. Tonight, she felt that would be out of the question. 'Anyway,' she said, flexing her fingers together in an attempt to dispel stress, 'I think the job sounds kind of... interesting. I'd like to take a look around that place myself.'

Zy snorted disparagingly. 'Yeah, of course you would!' He frowned into his vanity screen. His holographic image grimaced back. He was host to a recently-kicked expression, and attempted to modify it. 'I suppose it's a secret wish every female has inside them; woman power and all that.'

Kitzuki hissed. 'Don't be maddening, Zy! That's not what I meant at all. I just think it would be interesting, like I said. They say that world hasn't changed for hundreds of years. If I went there, I'd feel like an archaeologist or something. Aren't you even a little bit curious about it?'

'Intrigued beyond measure. Naturally.' He sighed. 'The truth is, no-one else would touch this job, Kitz, so it comes down to me.' His voice took on a martyred tone. 'Clearly, I am expendable.'

'Well, if you hadn't been such a naughty boy, you wouldn't have to be treading so carefully nowsabouts, would you! It's your own fault you can't turn it down. Right?' Kitzuki made a tutting noise and shook her head, smiling; her exquisite, porcelain features crinkling up. 'You have no choice, Zy. It's either get on with the job or quit it.'

'I can't quit. As you know, I took out another credit extension recently. I still don't think it's worth risking my life for, though.'

Kitzuki shrugged. 'You're exaggerating. Astracruise wouldn't be going in there unless it was safe. They have their customers to think of. You're just making excuses.'

'I am not...!'

Kitzuki had heard enough. She knew Zy well enough to be aware that if he had reservations about this job it was not because he feared for his life. He had travelled across a hundred worlds alone. It was altogether to do with another aversion; a distaste for the inhabitants and their way of life. She stood up and interrupted whatever exclamation Zy was preparing to make. 'You ready? I want to get this over with.'

'Enjoy it tonight,' Zy said. 'It might be the last time we socialise together.'

Kitzuki rolled her eyes. 'Oh, please ! Don't give me that garbage, Zy. You don't believe that.'

'I know men are a threatened species where I'm going, that's all!' Zy took one last glance in the screen, and flicked his white-blond hair out of his eyes.

'I'm really not looking forward to this,' Kitzuki said, her voice tight, making it clear the evening was going to be a trial for her in more than one way.

'Right. Furthering your meteoric ascension within D&K really hurts you, doesn't it? How terrible. I pity you.'

'I do what I have to do,' she replied, which was more than a slight accusation. 'Let's go.'

The reception was only walking distance away. Zy's apartment was a central address in the fashionable New Latin district of Africa Plate. He'd over-reached himself the previous year, taking out the lease on the place but, because being in the right surroundings meant so much to him, he didn't consider it an undue sacrifice. New Latin was simply the place to live at the moment. All the most celebrated people had apartments there; it boasted the best consumer galleries, and the entertainments complexes of all the most influential companies. Zy, cushioned among these illustrious neighbours, bloomed within the designer under-statement of his personal space. The orbital state of Africa Plate was segmented into several dozen boroughs, each of which had a group of artists, under the patronage of the Interior Design Guild, employed specifically to imbue the decor with their inimical and exquisite marks. New Latin was serviced by a collection of designers who espoused the Post Terran style, embracing an almost Spartan, neoclassical purity and simplicity - colours of pale biscuit, faded terra-cotta and ochre, with a hint of faintest cerulean blue. Zy adored these surroundings. A walk down the public gallery, amid the cool, soothing statements of architecture and colour, could restore the worst of his humours to gentle contemplation.

By contrast, Kitzuki lived downside, in Carabanda, spurning Post-Terran chic, in favour of the baroque intricacy of Neo-Byzantine. Zy was given to panic attacks and claustrophobia in her apartment, and avoided walking through the borough when he went to visit her.

They promenaded down the vast public gallery of Tosca Plaza, where raw starlight shone down onto giant, hybrid palms, which were dwarfed by the sheer size of the space they occupied. Cafes, bars and curio shops, all outfitted in the bare Post-Terran style, lined one side of the plaza; the other open to the stars, but for the seemingly-fragile, polarised barrier of sheer polycrystal. Other residents of Africa Plate were ambling slowly across the sward of tan and ochre reproduction antique carpet, towards appointments of their own, mingling with Plate visitors, who were faster and noisier presences. Visitors were always recognisable by their tendency to point at things, their swivelling heads anxious not to miss anything of interest. Kitzuki marched like a princess, her coiffure trailing nodding wires, tipped by featherbursts and glittering beads, her stiff, shiny skirts catching starlight. People moved from her path. People turned to look at her, and also at the handsome escort walking by her side. Both she and Zy stared straight ahead. They were used to this attention.

Zy knew Kitzuki was impatient with his complaints about his job. She believed he could have eased himself into a more comfortable and less demanding position years ago, had he not repeatedly fallen foul of his employers. He blamed bad luck for this, never himself. He was a prospector for Astracruise Pleasurelines; a galactic tourist company, whose resorts were to be found upon 236 worlds. The job itself sounded like a dream to Kitzuki who, as project coordinator for a pharmaceutical company - albeit an embarrassingly successful one - envied Zy's ability to move around the galaxy without having to pay his own travel fees. She marketed new products; drugs from exotic sources, milked from newly-discovered plants, animals and insects. Materials from a hundred distant worlds passed through her hands and across the design screens of her staff, bringing with them that peculiar excitement invoked only by the alien and intriguing, but she would never be the one to discover and harvest these magicks herself. She would never forage through jungles, beneath a distant star, uncovering miracles, treasures, or unspeakable wonders. That was the job of the company agents, glamorous people with rough skins and piratical charisma; explorers, alchemists, pioneers. Kitzuki was only a business woman, excellent at her job perhaps, but who would turn her ankle the minute she stepped out of a cruiser onto bare rock. Zy might work for a tourist company but he shared in the freedom of the explorers. He actually trod alien soil, travelled over it alone, and often witnessed things never seen before by another human being. He seemed oblivious to the romantic connotations of his trade, however, and scoffed at her wistful envy. 'You save lives, give people highs,' he'd once said. 'I help steal their money, that's all.'

Whenever a previously unclaimed potential site presented itself, Astracruise whisked one of its prospectors off to calculate where, when and how a thriving tourist attraction could be engineered. Zy had been off duty for nearly a month now, fretting because he'd fouled up on his last job. Tardiness and inattention to detail had allowed another company to stake first claim on an idyllic moon. Astracruise had simmered with disapproval, punishing him by silence. Zy had been forced to gnaw his knuckles as, daily, his house monitor informed him of the slow descent of his credit balance. He had even considered risking humiliation by approaching a rival operation and asking them for work, although he was aware that his reputation had established him as a less than desirable commodity.

Then, even as Zy had been scanning his accommodation contract for escape clauses, his comms unit had whispered into life, and the commission had been offered. The relief had possessed an almost holy intensity. *Forgiveness! Another chance! Oh thank you, thank you!* Further examination of the details, however, had caused him first to grin in disbelief, and then frown with apprehension. He was being directed to a world that had been estranged from the galactic community for hundreds of years; only political upheaval had instigated its re-emergence. Its name had become a byword for the unhinged rantings of fanatical beliefs: Artemis.

Artemis, heroine of a thousand moon-silvered legends of sacrificed youths and bloodthirsty Amazons, was a huntress goddess. Her other aspects included that of the Eternal Virgin, Diana, who shunned the contact of men; patroness of a multitude of radical women's religious cults across the known galaxy. There were even shrines to this misanthropic deity on Africa Plate. After receiving his commission, in a spirit of mounting frustration at his misfortunes, Zy Larrigan had felt compelled to visit the nearest of these shrines. He perceived this as a kind of preliminary research, but in truth he really wanted to look upon the face of the monster he must meet and decide whether or not he felt up to it. Artemis the goddess and Artemis the world amounted to the same thing, ultimately.

An affluent branch of the Revised Dianic Mysteries had a temple in New Latin itself. It was there that Zy Larrigan began his orientation exercise. Naturally, no man was allowed within the temple, so a certain amount of deception was called for. Zy detested religious fanatics of all persuasions and had no qualms about robing himself up in the Revised Dianic fashion, in order to gain access to the fane. He was of slight build and pretty enough to pass for female if he chose. In fact, as he observed other women making their way to the temple, he was probably prettier than the majority of devotees. After a few minutes loitering outside, he was able to attach himself to a group of female pilgrims from off-Plate, and walk sedately inside. Nobody penetrated his disguise, which was perhaps very fortunate under the circumstances. He doubted whether the devotees of Artemis would actually abandon themselves to murdering blood-lust at finding a man on their premises, but a hundred lesser unpleasantnesses sprang to mind.

Like all buildings in the borough, the temple was Post Terran in design, simply and classically adorned. The interior was completely white and devoid of any seating. The only concession to luxury was a thick, cream-coloured carpet underfoot, which was intended to uphold the silence rather than provide comfort for any worshippers. At the end of the room, merciless beneath a crop of withering spot-lamps, a representation of the Goddess presided over her fane, within an invisible haze of smokeless incense. Irreverently, Zy decided her stern expression was one of severe constipation.

A handful of women were sitting cross-legged on the floor before this disinterested idol, rocking and crooning ecstatically, lost in the cosy hum of meditation.

Zy stood at the back of the white room, hovering on the fringe of the pilgrim group. He reviewed, in the lap of the Goddess herself, what he knew of the world that carried her name. He remembered, from childhood, that Artemis had been one of the planets ringed in red on the star maps he and his peers had studied on their school consoles. The red rings had meant only one thing; prohibited. Like all the kids, he'd been fascinated by this concept and curious to uncover the secrets of the red-ringed planets. He and his friends made a list of all they could find on the star maps. They had scoured encyclopaedic study files for information, gradually piecing together a largely fictional picture of these forbidden worlds. Artemis had been one of the most impenetrable, hugging her secrets to herself, as if she had been scoured from the public information files to conceal a hideous crime. Because of this, Zy and his friends had concocted their own history for the place - lurid and blood-soaked - which was why it had stuck in his mind. The encyclopaedic notations had revealed nothing more than a scant outline.

Artemis had been colonised by a group of political feminists and their supporters three hundred years before and, after some kind of social disruption, the settlers had shunned virtually all communication with the rest of the colonised worlds. A great silence had come. The Artemisians had guarded their territory against outsiders, utilising an ancient contract that the Galactic Habitational Working Party had countersigned for them centuries past, granting them exclusive rights to the landmasses. Back in those pioneering days, enterprising people could virtually buy whole worlds for their own use.

After this excision from the galactic community, whatever events took place upon the sparsely populated surface of Artemis were dramas enacted without a wide audience. A few traders had maintained minimal contact with the planet, and they gleefully reported tales of extremist behaviour; madness, burnings, cannibalism. Zy knew now that these reports had been merely legends, because the star-lanes were rife with their own mythology, but perhaps some of them had been rooted in fact.

Zy Larrigan, despite his pretensions and affectations, was not a person easily scared. He had travelled over many strange, uncharted worlds during the course of his job, usually alone. He had been in danger before, but considered himself enough of a survivor to cope with most of the situations he was likely to encounter. It was simply a residue of that childish wonder then, that thrill of mystery, the scent of smoke and burning flesh that had filled his fantasies, causing his misgivings now.

The *people* of Artemis were female; all of them. Males had

been relegated to a debased position somewhere alongside, if not below, domestic animals. Popular opinion declared that, even now the planet was turning towards the civilised worlds once more, Artemisians hated men exclusively.

Zy was experienced in his field, despite his failures, and he was aware of many worlds hidden within the spirals of the galaxy where human societies had evolved that were very odd indeed. Some of them he had experienced firsthand. However, prompted by a deep instinct in his gut, he far from relished the thought of treading Artemisian soil. Although he thought he knew his reasons, there was something else; something he was unable to define. A nebulous unease.

He had stared hard at the pristine enamelled features of the Goddess and tried to fathom what mentality the craziest of her daughters might espouse. Eventually, he had turned away, discouraged. The Goddess would not divulge her secrets to him. Not yet.

From the moment Kitzuki stepped inside the pale and high-roofed foyer of Dee and Kelly's entertainments complex, she slipped with ease into her corporate persona. It was all kisses, perfume breath and delighted musical exclamations.

'My dear, how wonderful to see you again! You look marvellous!'

Zy hovered in the background, collecting cocktails and nodding at people, wandering around the lacquered cavern and casting a critical eye over the few examples of ancient Terran sculpture, tidily secreted into niches, illumined by dim UV lamps. The only people he knew there were colleagues of Kitzuki's, most of whom they both despised. Therefore, it was with a mixture of horror and relief that he noticed the unmistakable figure of Silas Calico, lounging in a doorway. Silas' lanky body was clad in clinging garments of dull gold and black, his long hair teased into a riot of braids. He wore a predator grin from ear to ear. Doubtlessly smelling blood, he was lazily assessing the crowd of glittering, twittering socialites, perhaps wondering how best to exploit the situation to his gain. Silas was not a regular presence at these functions. Zy slid across to him.

Although Silas Calico was ostensibly in the same business as Dee and Kelly, he concentrated on a decidedly alternative end of the market. The avenues and boulevards of Africa Plate were his company headquarters, the lean, star-burned hustlers of deeper alleys his project staff. Some of his operations were undoubtedly of questionable legality. For this reason, it was surprising to find him at this function, although he probably earned far more than any of the D&K people did with their legitimate status. Kitzuki had introduced Zy to Silas, in the early stages of their relationship, five years before. Silas had immediately communicated his interest in initiating a relationship with Zy that was rather more than platonic.

'He is more than a brother to me,' Kitzuki had said, meaningfully to Zy.

Confused but intrigued, Zy had offered little resistance, and Kitzuki had supervised this bizarre courtship, with the benevolent yet detached air of a mother cat watching its kittens tear at each other in mock battle. At the time, Zy had been extremely puzzled by her motives, and also by her choice.

Silas Calico came from a sub-culture utterly alien to Zy and Kitzuki; they could barely understand its patois. Then Zy had learned just how far back Kitzuki and Silas went. A long time before, she'd spotted Silas in a nighthaunt of dubious reputation, and had wanted him immediately.

'He was unique,' she told Zy, 'so different to all I knew, in many ways.'

She'd wanted excitement, but had ended up falling in love; the enduring kind. Later, it seemed, she had gone hunting for the two of them; Silas had refined her appetites to demand unusual gratification.

Bemusedly, Zy had gone along with their games, telling himself it was a temporary diversion. Now, here he was, five years later, still deeply entrenched. He did not want it any other way. Careers had diverged as age advanced, Silas slipping further into a darkness Zy and Kitzuki could barely penetrate, but personalities still resonated sweetly.

'What are you doing here?' Zy asked in a stage hiss.

'Kitz asked me,' Silas replied in a similar deliberate whisper, grinning.

'No!'

'Yes. You know how it is with her. Keeps tryin' to make me legit. Got some scheme or other; some blubber-chin for me to ape at. Never works, but keeps her happy. So...' His grin widened. 'I hear you're travellin' again soon. Why'd you not tell me right off?'

Zy shrugged. 'Only found out a day back. You're difficult to locate, you know. There's a message on your memo. Several messages.'

Silas pulled a face, his ropy muscles contorting his features into a clown's pathos. 'Sorry. Never there when you need me, huh? Bet Kitz has been down hard on you 'bout the knuckle rap of last work, yeah?'

Zy shook his head. 'No. She gave me a lecture when I got home and then kept quiet. You've been off-Plate, I take it?'

'Here and there. Here and there. Is it right you're headin' for Artemis?'

'News travels fast. Yes. And no comments please!'

Silas laughed out loud. 'Ah, the bitchin' of Momma Destiny! You and Artemis'll find it cruel to be workin' partners. Never were a woman's man, were you, Zy. You and Kitz only crack it out because she's got more dick in her pants than you.'

'How empathic of you to point that out,' Zy replied dryly, glancing round quickly to see whether any of the other guests had heard it.

'It's true. Wish I could be with you. Kill to see how you handle it.'

'I'm glad you find it so amusing. It could be dangerous, I think, in that place.'

'No way! From what I heard, the sweet sisters of Artemis

want in, community-wise. They'll be syrup on your chin, Zy. Don't worry.'

Silas was a compendium of social information. Usually, his observations on the disparate cultures of the galaxy were infallible. Zy automatically relaxed.

'So, when are you leavin'?' Silas asked, intercepting a circulating refreshments trolley and loading his hands with sweetmeats.

'Day after tomorrow. I'm being briefed come morning. I gather Astracruise has big plans for Artemis.'

Silas chewed thoughtfully. 'New market, virgin territory. Lotsa room, few people. Ideal.'

'Theoretically.'

'So bring me a souvenir.'

Zy smiled thinly. 'Don't I always?'

Kitzuki breezed up, having relaxed into her role and nodded at all the right talking heads. The formal gown had magically become malleable, graceful. She kissed Silas' cheek. 'Glad you're here! I expected you not to turn up. Lots of people want to meet you.'

'Shows you're into marketin', Kitz.' Silas flicked a wry glance at Zy.

'Hmm. Zy told you about his new job?'

'Yeah. He'll get his feet dirty on this one.'

Kitzuki linked her arm through Zy's protectively. 'No he won't. He'll get round them. They'll all end up loving him.' She kissed his nose. 'Because he's just so lovable.'

Zy wriggled away. 'Stop it, Kitz. People are watching. You make me sound like some kind of fluffy pet.'

'I hear they like fluffy pets on Artemis,' Silas said, 'especially ones in the shape of a man. You'll be fine. Soooo lovable!' He laughed loudly, causing heads to turn, and Kitzuki smothered a giggle, which came out as a snort.

'Look, just drop it,' Zy said.

Kitzuki attempted to mollify him. 'Oh, come on, Zy! How can you fail? They're all just peasants there. Isn't that right,

Silas?'

'Cave women,' Silas agreed. 'No technology to speak of, political unrest, the works. Place is a mess, Zy. Get in there and scoop up land by the flyer-load. They don't know their toes from their tits, I heard.'

'You won't be able to call us!' Kitzuki said, with some alarm, having only just realised it. 'Zy, I shall worry about you!'

'Why? You just said the job would be easy,' The whole business was starting to annoy him.

'You watch the report on the public net about that place?' Silas asked.

Zy and Kitzuki both shook their heads. They considered the public net vids beneath their notice.

'Hardly any of the planet is populated. Weird laws or some shit like that. Anyway, there was a revolution. Can you believe that?'

'Really?' Kitzuki said. 'How fascinating. How historical. What happened?'

'Yes, well this is all very interesting,' Zy interrupted, 'but I shall be having my fill of Artemisian history tomorrow. Let's talk about your work instead, Silas. That should be entertaining.'

Silas grinned at the waspishness. 'OK, OK, but I'll say one last thing. Folks'll flock to see the crazies of Artemis, Zy. Astracruise'll be currency drunk. Could be your lucky break at last.'

'The luckiest break will be your neck if you don't can it,' Zy said, but he knew Silas was right. Artemis was ripe for the picking and if he did a good job this time, came up with some innovative and appealing ideas, his fortune might well change for the better. Tomorrow, he would study the briefing data thoroughly. This time, things were going to go smoothly. After all, he was a professional. *Brace yourself, goddess,* he thought. *I'm coming for you.*

Chapter Three
The Tent of Windteasel

The danks scrambled awkwardly onto dry ground and loped through a stand of plaisel trees, a loopier and more languid strain than that found further south in the marshes. Freespace Town was revealed beyond them, crowned with heat haze. Corinna reflected that to call the rambling sprawl of hastily-erected cabins and low, sway-backed tents a town was perhaps rather an exaggeration.

The settlers had been experimenting with various forms of architecture; wood, baked clay bricks and woven reedstraw being the different materials available. Initially, many people had envisaged the actual construction of the town as being the main project of settlement, but experience had taught them otherwise. Food and water came first. Which rivers and pools were safe to use? Which new plants were in accord with the human digestive system?

The further north they had travelled, the more widely spaced familiar food-crops had become, the bulk of them dwindling altogether eventually. Now, entirely new varieties of flora and fauna had to be examined, catalogued and warily tested. Sour-water was the worst hazard they'd had to educate themselves about. Seemingly crystal-pure springs and streams turned to virulent poison for what had appeared no reason at all. It was purely by accident that a child had discovered the cause.

Ellie Clackbrake had come running to her parents, chattering excitedly about seeing long pieces of slime tying themselves together in the river and squirting out black stuff.

Adults strode to the scene quickly to investigate and discovered that a northern species of mollusc were conducting their mating rituals underwater. The secretions emitted during their stately copulation were the cause of the disastrous outbreaks of gastric disruption, which at times had halted the progress of the group completely.

As with many of Artemis' crueller aspects, sour-water's effects were painful, but rarely lethal to humankind. This was especially fortunate for the refugees fleeing blindly, with no knowledge of the land, into uncharted territory.

Now, Hollis insisted on dragging Corinna directly to the nearest healer. The Windteasels were a marsh family that Corinna had had very little to do with back home, mainly because their isle had been situated at least fifteen lope-leagues from anyone else's estate. The Windteasels had always enjoyed a reputation of eccentricity and weirdness. They had never exactly shunned the company of their fellow human beings, but had definitely not encouraged it. A dark, sallow clan, they had hollowed out a niche for themselves within the pioneering group as healers, diviners, Wise People. Because of their reserved and dignified nature, and their self-imposed lack of close friends, Corinna harboured a deep regard for the Windteasels. She felt she and they had much in common.

The family were still living under canvas, next to a half-constructed two-storey house of white squeal-wood, unvarnished and fragrant, which Quality Windteasel and his eldest daughter, Softly, had been reverently working on for over a moons-arc now. Corinna had often passed the site at dusk or dawn and heard the skin-prickling melody of Softly's high voice and her father's low, vibrating hum as they worked virtue into the wood they handled. As far as Corinna knew, none of the other Windteasels ever offered to help with the work, or were asked to. Other families instinctively withheld offers of their own assistance.

'One day, one day' Corinna said. She was leaning rather drunkenly on Hollis' arm, more than a little crazy with whipthorn toxin.

'What?' he asked.

'That house,' she replied, waving her left arm towards it. 'It will become... a nucleus. In hundreds of years' time, when Freespace is a city the size of Silven Crescent - which it will be - people will walk here and see the house dark with age and smiling and sagging, but still proud, and the people will say that's the House of Windteasel. It has been here from the beginning.'

Hollis smiled and adjusted his grip on her arm. He wasn't sure he could share Corinna's optimism.

Farris Windteasel, youngest son of the clan, was skulking beneath the far wall of the tent when Corinna Trotgarden came inside leaning on the arm of Hollis Backwater. He was in disgrace. His mother, Elvinia, had been studiously ignoring him for most of the morning; a difficult task for her because, despite his waywardness, Farris was her favourite child. She had asked him to seed some skin-pine cones. He had done so without question, but used a knife contaminated by sick-apple juice. The seeds were now useless for her purpose. Had it been a deliberate sabotage on his part or an act of stupidity? It was impossible to tell with Farris. In her heart, Elvinia wanted to believe he did not set out to be troublesome, or even disobedient. He was absent-minded, just forgot things, and was very shy. To others, who alluded to Farris' behaviour when it affected people beyond the family, Elvinia would maintain that he had been born under a sour star. He was not responsible for his actions.

Farris had grown up with this rather gloomy explanation and now accepted it, and life's cruel ironies, as his natal affliction. He was some four years younger than Corinna making him seventeen years old. In some ways, he felt much younger - the awkwardness of extreme youth still clung to him stubbornly yet in other ways far older. Like all the Windteasels he was dark of eye and hair, yellowy-dark of skin. If he had given himself any love, he might have been beautiful. As it was, he hunched and sulked and merely looked skinny, sharp and mean-spirited. Elvinia tried desperately hard to drag him into the world of light, but whilst he was content to bury his head in her skirts, he would not be affected by her attempts at education.

She worried about him.

He worried that he would live forever.

Farris looked up with genuine interest when he saw the visitors included Corinna. There were people within the community who held a certain fascination for him, and she was one of them. Although they had never spoken - a requirement, in fact, because Farris generally disliked people after he had talked with them - he admired her wild, slightly barbaric appearance and steely, fist-gripped power. Although she had grown her hair back now (Farris could remember when she had returned to the marsh, shorn, with her scars still livid), it had never regained the sleekness it once had. Now, it resembled a smoom's mane; tangled, startled, and of many subtle colours. Her scars made her look angry all the time. Perhaps she *was* angry all the time. Each cheek had been scored twice. Sometimes it looked as if she had painted furious lines there.

There was another girl with the Freespacers, named Gick, whom Corinna had brought out of Silven Crescent with her. She too had been scarred and shaved, had even lost her ears to the disciplinary knife, but in every other way, Gick was different. Elvinia found Gick an irritant and said she was crazy, whereas most people just considered her a fool; amusing most of the time but occasionally annoying. Farris often tailed Corinna and Gick when they were together, never getting too close, just observing. In privacy he would mimic Corinna's loose-limbed stride and Gick's careless yet emphatic hand gestures. Occasionally, he thought about how he might actually work towards some kind of communication with these women. Because they were different - and he suspected most of their differences were kept hidden - he felt an affinity with them. As far as he knew, neither of them had noticed him yet, for which he felt grateful. Being invisible meant he could observe more efficiently.

Now, Corinna was here with the Backwater boy, who was behaving in a distinctly proprietorial manner towards her. Farris had no affinity whatsoever with Hollis' kind - the typical young Freespace male; confident, stepping up beside the women without trepidation, building, creating, giving orders when it was necessary and not just taking them. Farris found this new, liberated man image somewhat contrived. Could Corinna Trotgarden possibly be fond of such a person? Farris wondered about it uncomfortably. He had noticed how much time Corinna had been spending with Hollis recently.

Corinna folded to the floor, trying to sit, but flopping, and Hollis held out her arm to Elvinia Windteasel. 'Look,' he said. 'A whipthorn.'

Elvinia wiped her hands on her trousers and went to have a look. She cleared a path through the tools of her trade; the tent was really too small to accommodate her equipment, never mind her family. She'd been blending healing mixtures over a smouldering fire outside, the smoke of which had quickly drifted into the tent, filling it with a sweet and stinging fog. Her latest project, recently perfected (she hoped), was a new and quicker antidote to whipthorn slash. Mudberry poultices, the usual remedy, were efficacious but took several days to heal the wound. She was delighted by this unexpected opportunity to test the new mixture so soon. 'Hmm.' Elvinia poked the wound. She would be diplomatic about this. Some of the Freespacers were squeamish about trying out her newest potions. 'No splinter in there.'

'That's what I thought,' Hollis said. 'Swelling though. Quite badly.'

'Yes.'

Corinna sighed and looked as if she was about to make an abrupt remark but couldn't manage it.

Elvinia rubbed her face for a few more moments,

humming to herself, as if in deep thought and then went outside the tent to fetch her mixing pot off the fire.

Hollis looked at the pungent, bubbling liquid with distrust. 'What's that? Haven't you got a mudberry poultice?'

'Well, I think we should try this,' Elvinia replied. 'It's new, but I'm certain it's a better way to treat whipthorn than mudberry poultices. It's taken internally and fights the toxin that way. You know mudberry takes a few days to completely clear the infection? Well, with this, Corinna'll be fine in an hour or so.' She hoped that was a correct assumption.

'Worked on danks then,' Hollis said mordantly.

Elvinia shrugged. 'Seemed to.' She offered Corinna a spoonful of the stuff. It evidently tasted foul judging by the way the girl's scars writhed. 'I wonder if that's enough?' Elvinia mused with an alchemist's curious detachment. 'Maybe just a little more. I don't think it will harm her.'

'How well have you tested this stuff?' Hollis was beginning to sound worried. 'Perhaps a mudberry poultice is a better idea.'

'Don't panic, Backwater. It's not toxic. Here, Corinna, just another mouthful.'

'You'd make an excellent animal doctor, Mistress Windteasel,' Corinna said shakily, wiping her mouth.

Elvinia nodded. 'Animal doctor, midwife, physician and witch, that's me. Got anyone better around here?'

'Yeah, your daughter Zeta when you're too old!'

Elvinia laughed good-humouredly. Nobody but Corinna Trotgarden could get away with a remark like that with her. 'Want a drink?' she asked. 'I have some very good plaisel tea brewing.

Corinna settled herself on the bundles of matting more comfortably. 'Mmm, OK. We'd better not stay too long, though. My mother has decided to hold a celebration tonight. It's Meonel's birthday and I promised to help her get the food ready.'

Meonel was Dannel Trotgarden's second husband,

Corinna's stepfather; although some might argue that he was married to the eunuch Shyya rather than to Dannel. Because of the influence of Silven Crescent, many of the marsh marriages had been a biological rather than emotional institution. In many cases, individuals had turned to their own gender for affection. It was clear that, even now, many Freespacers did not feel entirely comfortable having their taboos ripped to shreds. The liberation of men was as disorientating for males as if was for females. Meonel had never wanted contact with women, yet the marriage of Dannel and Meonel was one of the most successful Corinna knew of. Their friendship had become one of the deepest and most supportive kinds.

The hot drink consumed, Corinna stood up and flexed her hand. 'You were right, Elvinia, your new method does seemed to be far quicker than the poultices. Just tingles now. Very little pain.'

'Reckon I'll start bartering the stuff then,' Elvinia replied. 'No need for people to come to me now for whipthorn slashes.'

'It'll leave you time to work on the pollen-gripe and melody itch then,' Hollis said, standing up. 'And the multitude of other ills this land throws at us! Thanks for the tisane, Elvinia.' He nodded in the direction of Farris at the back of the tent. 'Good-day to you both.'

Chapter Four
Dannel

The Trotgardens' new home was as far removed from their farm estate at Vangery Isle than Dannel could imagine. Still, it was theirs and nobody could take it away from them, other than truculent weather spirits. Used to the imposing pile of her old residence, Dannel couldn't help feeling the long, low four-roomed shack was rather flimsy. It smelt good, for they had used Gomery balmwood to build it, and the pungent reek of incense filled the air when the night-fires were lit - and almost choked people when the sun shone on rain- moistened timbers.

Nearly all the new plants and trees they had discovered had been named after the person who'd found them. Leto Gomery had an almost fanatical interest in different woods. He graded them for their durability, perfume, and for the indefinable quality of allowing themselves to be worked successfully by human hands. As well as being thoroughly acquainted with the timber itself, Leto also studied the foliage, buds and fruits, working with the healers to assess their properties, watching the way animals treated each species. He maintained that nearly everything you needed to know about a tree could be learned by burning its sap or resin. One good sniff could tell a trained nose whether there was poison present, whether the wood was friable or pliant, whether parts of the tree could be used for food.

Dannel was not so sure if this method was reliable. She usually waited to see what results other people obtained before trying any new food stuffs. The long journey had taken a toll on her statuesque frame. She was still a hefty size but decidedly more nimble than in the past. The first few months' travelling had been a nightmare for her; a nightmare of heaving and struggling, panting for breath, always feeling cold and uncomfortable. She had watched her daughters, Bolivia and Corinna, and her son Orblin, leaping from raft to raft, running thigh-deep through marsh to catch stray danks, pulling boats from mud-patches, and generally illustrating to the miserable Dannel just what a fit body was capable of. Her offspring had never seemed down-hearted; it had all been a great adventure to them, even Corinna, who to all intents and purposes had become completely strange. Dannel felt she hardly knew the girl now.

Sighing at the memory, pleasurably, because it was just a memory, Dannel settled herself comfortably by the window to shell balm-nuts. It would be quite some time before the Freespacers could manufacture glass for themselves, so nearly everyone who'd built dwelling-houses used skins, cloth and wooden shutters to keep out the cold. The season was mild at present. Dannel didn't look forward to the time when they'd have to burn lamps all day because the air outside would be too icy for the shutters to be kept open. People had been trying to discover other methods of admitting daylight to their houses. She'd heard that the Tendaughters had been experimenting with reed-pad membranes, stretching the carefully removed underskins of the large, flat leaves and fixing them to frames. So far, it had been found that the skins had a very short life, but if a way could be found to preserve them, they certainly let in sufficient light. Perhaps it wouldn't get too cold in this land in winter.

Now, it seemed not to matter. The sun was shining, her house was emitting a pleasing fragrance, and tonight her family and friends would gather to celebrate Meonel's birthday. It was lucky she'd bothered to keep a record of the days on the journey north; hardly anybody seemed to bother with that now. Dannel still missed the assistance of her old cook, Gabriel, but now he had set up home for himself with some of the other men once bonded to the Trotgardens. Gabriel was a free man and although Dannel had considered asking him to prepare the meal for tonight, she felt that would be trying to cling to the past. The celebration would hold far more meaning if she had prepared the food herself.

At first, Dannel had thought the house would be far too small for the six of them, having been used to the space an affluent farm afforded. Most of the time, though, everyone was out working at some task or another, often only coming home to sleep. She loved the peace this gave her, allowing her to potter about her little abode, free of responsibilities and worries. If she broached the subject of materials they were lacking, Corinna or Bolivia would say, 'oh, don't worry about that Dannel!' Invariably, one of them would come home with something approximating what they required the next day. She sensed their almost patronising concern about her well-being and did not resent it. Her beloved Vangery was gone. Life required a new perspective now so that she was not immersed in grief.

In Vangery, Dannel had been a great matriarch of one of the most influential families on the marsh. Now, she felt like a coddled grandmother, even though she was not that old nor had grand-children. Thoughtfully chewing a sweet balm-nut, she allowed her mind to dwell for a moment on what might have happened to her old home. Was it open to the elements now, already sinking back into the cruel and beautiful marsh from which it had sprung? Or had new people from Silven Crescent come to work the shemble-frack and wild rice fields, bringing their technology with them? Although it provoked the slightest twinge of possessive jealousy, she really hoped the latter was true. Her family had laboured too long, and with too much love, for Vangery to decay. She prayed that whoever lived there now cared for the place as much as she had done.

The front door opened with a squeal, interrupting her nostalgic reverie. Corinna breezed in, trailing the Backwater boy, and came to muss Dannel's hair and kiss her forehead.

'Really, Corinna! I'm not an animal!' Dannel said, embarrassed that Hollis had seen it.

Corinna laughed and helped herself to a handful of nuts.

'Stop it! They're for tonight!' Dannel put the bowl down on the floor.

Corinna pushed a nut into Hollis' mouth.

Dannel narrowed her eyes. 'What's wrong with your hand?'

Corinna flapped it vaguely in front of her mother's face. 'Oh, I had a whipthorn slash, but the old witch Windteasel has invented a new remedy and, look, it's perfectly OK now.'

Dannel took the hand roughly and studied it. 'Perfectly? Looks sore to me. How do you feel?'

'Fine. Just fine. Don't worry about it.' Corinna turned to Hollis. 'Dannel worries about everything. It's her hobby. She hasn't got used to not being able to throw her weight around yet, and believe me there used to be quite a lot of it to throw around at one time!'

'Corinna, you're a shrew!' Dannel said, resuming her shelling.

'And you brought me into the world, mother dear! Hollis is going to stick around and help. Want to tell him what to do? We have to let her have these little concessions now and again, Hollis. Just bear with her.'

'What needs doing, Mistress Trotgarden?' Hollis asked quickly, to stem any further remarks Corinna might make.

'You can chop those musk-leaves over there, if you like. You staying to eat with us Hollis?'

Hollis sat at the table and began sifting through the leaves. 'If that's alright, Mistress Trotgarden; I'd like to.'

'Who else have you invited?' Corinna asked, sitting on the table. Her question was careless but she was studying the blade of the knife she'd picked up far too intently.

'Your old friends, of course,' Dannel replied. 'Meera, Gick, Rosanel...'

'No-one else?'

'Not Carmenya, if that's who you mean.' Dannel sounded sharp, causing her daughter to look up.

Corinna shrugged. 'Just wondered.'

'Did you want me to ask her?'

Another shrug. 'I didn't say that.'

'I didn't think the atmosphere would be too sweet, if Carmenya was here. Neither Meonel nor Rosanel feel comfortable in her presence. You know that.'

Corinna sighed and spun the knife in the air, catching it deftly by the hilt. 'Don't upset yourself, mother. I doubt if Carmenya would have come if you'd asked her, anyway.'

Dannel didn't reply to that, but had to show her displeasure in some way, and shook her head gravely.

There was a whole history to tell of the friendship between the Trotgardens and the erstwhile General, Carmenya Oralien. Years ago, Carmenya had been one of the most esteemed of Yani Gisbandrun's personnel. Dannel had known her for many year, from long before Carmenya had possessed such a position, and had experienced only the slightest of qualms when Carmenya had asked for Corinna to become part of her entourage in the city. At seventeen years of age, Corinna had left the marsh for the delights of court life, in Silven Crescent. Carmenya detested malekind exclusively and had seen fit to educate the young Corinna in the ways of city women. They had been lovers until Corinna fell foul of Gisbandrun. Even though Carmenya had decided to leave the city and throw in her lot with the Freespacers, her relationship with Corinna had never been re-established. The fact that interest remained on Corinna's side was, to Dannel, painfully obvious. Carmenya kept away, maintaining all contact with the Trotgardens to occasional, electric frissons, always to do with necessary work, and after which, Corinna's scars would burn red, and her temper would be shorter than usual.

It was clear Corinna thought that now the Freespacers had settled themselves, her family and Carmenya Oralien could attempt to mend their rather dilapidated friendship. Corinna was undoubtedly the only person who desired this.

The atmosphere was a little strained in the room after this exchange. Hollis frowned at the musk-leaves, his ears red. The Freespacers enjoyed gossip, as any community does. Everyone knew about Corinna and Carmenya, even about how Carmenya had maintained her loyalty to Gisbandrun, to the extent of helping take Corinna into custody back then. Carmenya was not a popular member of Freespace, but as she was strong, capable and willing to work as hard as the next person, her presence was tolerated.

Hollis did not think that Carmenya had any true friends here. It made him uneasy the way Corinna always reacted when the woman was mentioned. Now, he felt uncomfortable to the point of agony.

The tension was broken by the arrival of Corinna's brother and sister, Orblin and Bolivia. Orblin had grown into a handsome youth, sharing Corinna's lighter colouring. The dark, intense Bolivia had mellowed since leaving Vangery, more with the rigours of the journey north than age, but was still a heavy-browed, dashing-looking creature. She and Corinna sparred continuously. To outsiders, their mutual insult sessions were plainly embarrassing. Confidantes of the family knew the sisters' arguments were merely performances, that both of them enjoyed immensely.

Corinna smiled toothily at their arrival and threw her knife, which flew with a satisfying thunk into the doorframe between them.

'Corinna!' Dannel screeched.

Orblin laughed, extracted the knife and threw it back.

Corinna ducked and the blade embedded itself in the wall

'You are animals!' Dannel declared. 'All it takes is one little accident!' Her face had gone crimson.

Corinna hopped from the table. 'Oh stop fussing, mother,' she said, wrenching the knife from the wall.

'Put that down, or Goddess help me, I'll throw you all out, and Meonel, Shyya and I will celebrate alone!'

The threat was empty, but Dannel's children knew when they'd pushed her far enough. Corinna discreetly put down the knife.

Bolivia was smirking, one eyebrow virtually through her hairline. She poured herself a mug of water and drank, daintily. 'The dam's nearly finished,' she announced. 'If all goes well, our esteemed engineers should have running water in Freespace soon.'

'For each house?' Dannel asked.

'Well, it's not worth it for this hovel, is it?' Corinna interjected.

'You planning on building us a new Vangery within the next few months, then?' Bolivia asked, acidly.

'Meonel and I have plans, as it happens,' Corinna said. 'In fact, we approached the Tendaughters about it the day before yesterday. Their place is coming on fine. We offered our labour in return for theirs when they've finished. This is a community, remember. We help each other.'

'You didn't tell me about this!' Dannel said.

Corinna sauntered over and hugged her. 'We were going to discuss it tonight actually,' she said, in appeasement. 'Meonel was going to indulge in a little more rooting around today. Make a thorough assessment of what other people are building. Naturally, we are planning on constructing a palace for you, mother!'

'Gick was up at the dam today,' Orblin said. 'Carmenya was with her.'

Corinna narrowed her eyes at her brother.

'These musk-leaves are chopped now,' Hollis piped up in a deliberate voice.

'I've had some meat smoking in the shed out back,' Dannel said. 'Fetch it, Corinna, will you.' She eyed her son fiercely. He pulled a sour face.

Chapter Five
Silven Crescent

A large flock of wading birds swept in from the marsh, honking mournfully as they circled the highest spires of Silven Crescent. Behind them, the sky was gold and pink, fading to a magnificent mazarine blue where stars proclaimed a thousand new legends. Zy Larrigan looked up at the stars, his bags by his feet, the oily smell of the spaceport fighting with the numerous odours of this new, virtually untouched world. He was impressed. Artemis might be peopled by psychotic females and their invertebrate subordinates, the men, but the scenery was fantastic.

He picked up his luggage and sauntered towards the gates, where tall women carrying guns in aggressive poses supervised the off-world visitors filing rather tentatively into the city. Regular patronage by off-worlders was still something of a novelty for Artemis and her population. This was demonstrated by the awkward way in which visitors were dealt with. There was still a strong instinct to treat every stranger as a potential threat or as unruly animals with unpredictable habits.

And here I am, briefed to convince these harpies they need tourist resorts! Zy thought rather glumly.

There was a pile-up at the gates. Artemisians had not quite got the knack or organisation required for a smooth-running customs kiosk. Zy had been stunned when Astracruise had equipped him with official papers, testifying his identity. Papers? He'd believed it a publicity gimmick until he saw the wooden shacks and primitive wire around the edge of the spaceport. No identity verification via iris or genetic print here, that was clear. It was quaint. Kitzuki would love it.

In the customs office, a surly creature stood behind a rough trestle table serving as a desk. She snatched the papers from Zy's outstretched hand. Zy grinned wolfishly at her. He had never seen such a brute in all his life; male or female. The hair was hacked off short, the bulky body encased in stiff leather armour that creaked as if in pain. Zy was amused. Could the Artemisians really be like their popular image off-world? Surely this woman must be in costume and on duty here for the benefit of visitors seeking local colour.

The official frowned short-sightedly at his papers. 'A resort prospector? Are you sure you're in the right place, Mr Larrigan?'

'Quite sure,' Zy answered, smiling benignly, charmed by the archaic title she had accorded him. 'I think you'll find everything in order.'

The woman continued to pore over the antique hieroglyphs, her mouth moving as she read. All of Silas' and Kitzuki's predictions appeared uncannily correct. These people were tribal.

'Is everything OK?' Zy asked, inserting the right amount of indignant impatience into his voice. He felt the performance had outlived its entertainment value.

Stonily, the woman handed him back his papers, without saying anything.

'Well, thank you. I'll be on my way, then.' Zy said with strained politeness, nodding in complicity at the discreetly intrigued group of people waiting behind him.

Moments later he had stepped out onto the true soil of Artemis. Before leaving Africa Plate, Zy had studied all the available data on this world. Fragments had been drifting into the galactic databanks for a couple of years now; the veil was beginning to lift. And what did it reveal? Startling, colourful and bloodthirsty events, perhaps nearly as garish as those Zy had imagined as a child. Through utilising this history,

Astracruise might transform Artemis into the biggest theme park humankind could ever imagine. Since the almost unmentionable demise of the late self-styled Dominatrix, Yani Gisbandrun, (Was she *serious*? Zy wondered), the government of Artemis had decided relations with other worlds should be rekindled. In the past, it had been argued that the risk of contamination from unsavoury cultures might damage the Utopian glow of Silven Crescent, her sister cities and the marsh. Now, however, in the light of recent political events, nobody had the gall to call Artemis a Utopia - at least not out loud. The aims and dreams of the first settlers had been systematically disassembled over hundreds of years, so that the current society bore no resemblance at all to the intentions of the past. Women had travelled with their children to this world, in order to start from scratch; to shun the heartless, materialistic society of the so-called civilised worlds, to shun technology and become in touch once more with the primal forces of nature. Tripping out with the Goddess. A feeble fantasy, Zy thought. But, perhaps it had worked in the beginning.

Yani Gisbandrun had been both the product and initiator of hysterical beliefs – matriarchal rule taken to risible extremes - which had turned the society of Artemis into a grinding, medieval dictatorship, where men, as a species, had been wavering on the brink of virtual extinction, and women had rapidly been falling victims to Gisbandrun's paranoias. Nobody had been safe. Luckily, Gisbandrun herself had to be included in that count, and had been mysteriously dispatched one hectic, surreal night, several years ago, by the male rebel leader, Elvon L'Belder. L'Belder had not hung around to take control and, in fact, was generally believed dead himself. Rumours had filtered out of Artemis of how, when he'd burst into the city intent on murder, he had somehow been changed into something other than human. There was no precise specification to indicate the exact nature of this change, but Zy felt it all reeked suspiciously of star-lane fabrication. Other rumours suggested L'Belder had actually been some form of alien life, although Zy had examined the records now available and had uncovered no evidence of that. To all accounts, L'Belder had begun his career as some kind of librarian, which hardly suggested a man composed of heroic fibre, never mind an alien being. It was likely Gisbandrun's followers had killed him. Reports indicated he had actually committed the dirty deed of dominatricide in one to one combat with Gisbandrun. Unlikely - but romantic all the same.

Legends such as these were of immense use to Astracruise. Zy wondered whether the Artemisians would permit a costumed reconstruction of these historical events to be staged regularly for tourists. Now the small population of Artemis had a government of a semi-military nature, only because Gisbandrun's generals had more or less been forced to take control when she'd fallen. Roping in several high-ranking priestesses from the Temple to lend a more passive note to the proceedings, the generals had elected themselves into various offices.

Governing Councillor in residence at the time of Zy Larrigan's arrival was Eugenia Gulding, an unimaginative creature generally, but favoured for her soothing predictability and common-sense. Astracruise had enjoyed several communications with the government in Silven Crescent and had assured them they were sending an envoy of unimpeachable suitability for the task. Zy, humbled by recent failures, had promised to secure his company the tourist rights to the entire planet. Admittedly, this was not as ambitious as it sounded.

Artemis was, for the most part, unexplored and it would require years of intensive study before the best areas could be determined and exploited. It was known as a world of marshes but, in actual fact, the fertile and eerie marshland covered only a small portion of the main continent. Brief aerial forays had revealed vast forest tracts further north, stunning, tortured mountain ranges and even a peculiar lavender-coloured desert to the east. Island clusters punctuated the southern ocean, perhaps concealing tropical havens where holiday-makers could walk virgin sand and believe themselves to be alone. Artemis was a well-developed world as far as topography, flora and fauna were concerned. Like many before him, Zy Larrigan had wondered why there were no dominant intelligent lifeforms on Artemis other than the interloping humans.

Zy stood for a while on the edge of the street. After the synthetic air of Africa Plate and the star-liner which had carried him here, the brisk breezes, heavy with a thousand, living scents, made him feel dizzy. Even as a seasoned prospector, it still took him a while to acclimatise to being planet-bound once more. The city designers of the Plate would be astounded by Silven Crescent, Zy was sure. A multitude of clashing styles prevailed in this downtown area; the horizon being a hastily-scrawled mess of sharp roofs, chimneys, and abrupt gaps. Buildings were made of stone and wood, and there was little evidence of designer landscaping - one of Africa Plate's most celebrated features, and a distinction prevalent on most civilised worlds he'd visited. Here, rank, scrawny grasses clamoured for purchase through the stones of the street, crisped by dry mud. Astracruise's first task would be to modernise the space-port and its abutting areas. Tourists would be put in a sour mood from the start of their trip otherwise.

After a few minutes of wondering how he'd manage to find his destination, Zy established that the quaint carts, hauled by the most ugly beasts he'd ever seen, (rather like a combination of camel and mule), were in fact public conveyances. He waved down a vehicle driven by a shock-haired young woman smoking a pipe, and asked to be conducted to the governmental building on Palace Hill. He had learned no-one liked to refer to it as a palace any more.

The female Artemisians were still not sure whether they ought to feel guilty about Yani Gisbandrun's fascist tendencies, or disappointed because she had failed to realise them. The male Artemisians remained too uneasy to do anything but keep their heads down. Although the government now advocated equality (of a sort), the majority of those in power still harboured an instinctive antipathy towards the male of the species. However, they were aware that in order to benefit from being part of the galactic community, oppression of any form was out of the question. The sexes existed alongside each other in wary alliance, with which neither felt comfortable. No-one had suggested the Artificial Insemination centres should be closed down and, recently, financial incentives had been introduced for men to become donors. Heady reunification did not seem a possibility for the near future.

Silven Crescent exhaled its evening perfume, and Zy Larrigan reclined in his carriage and took in the sights. Not many men were visible upon the streets, and most of the women he saw were dressed in functional, featureless clothing; leggings and tunics. The overshot upper stories of dark, drab buildings virtually concealed the tiny shop-fronts he passed. What he took to be some kind of factory or workshop was little more than a blank box of stone. As the cart drew nearer to Palace Hill, however, the surroundings became more attractive. Trees lined the roads; houses were garlanded with flowering vines. Well-dressed women walked socially in the dusk, arms linked, and heads moving in animated conversation. A few of them noticed Zy's passage and stopped to stare, haughty expressions of surprise on their faces. It was obviously unusual for a man to be seen travelling freely in these parts. Zy huddled down in his seat. If Astracruise had had any sense, they'd have sent a woman to undertake this job. Zy was unsure how he was going to compensate for the unfortunate handicap of his sex. He would have to work twice as hard to secure the claim.

Palace Hill had been virtually rebuilt since Elvon L'Belder had brought his strange, vengeful power to the city and nearly destroyed it. The tasteful residences of the more well-to-do, who inhabited the district, were constructed of pale stone that looked as if it would be warm to the touch. Very little remained of the old palace itself, but modern extension wings had been built in the same antique style. Apart from the difference in colour of the stone, it was difficult to tell which were the new sections. All signs of the legendary evil fire, which had raged and consumed, had been meticulously scrubbed, scraped or painted away. The result was that Palace Hill looked uncommonly clean; more like a model of a town than somewhere where people lived. It had been renovated very quickly too.

Zy was conducted to a rear gate of the governmental building. He had expected more lengthy argument to justify his presence, but apparently he was expected. Without fuss of any kind, one of the guards on duty accompanied him into a courtyard and spoke with someone through a reception window. Moments later, a slim young woman came out, smiling - if rather guardedly - in welcome. She shook Zy's hand firmly, and escorted him into the building. The guard, obviously well-briefed, wished him a pleasant stay and returned to her post. A girl was summoned to carry Zy's luggage, about which he tried to protest. His remarks were ignored.

As he walked beside his new escort down a dark corridor, Zy covertly examined her. She would have been attractive, but for the hideous scars which scored both of her cheeks; two each side. In a way, they resembled claw marks. She also had an odd, swaying gait that reminded Zy of a professional model, but in this place was probably more indicative of some genetic abnormality. The luggage carrier struggled behind. He did not look at her.

'I am Layna Minnders,' the guide told him. 'I'll be here to help you during your visit. If you'd like to freshen up in your room first, General Verspatch and General Glossling are looking forward to you joining them for dinner later.'

'I don't think I'm familiar with those names,' Zy said, removing a notefile from his pocket and touching a few keys. 'Ah, here we are. Apparently, my company have been dealing with a Verity Blackreed.'

Layna Minnders frowned; a graciously gentle expression.

'Ah yes. Verity was to have met you, Mr Larrigan, but unfortunately she has been called on business to one of our sister cities. I apologise for this inconvenience.'

'No inconvenience, I assure you. She is not, after all, a personal friend of mine. And please, let's not be formal. Call me Zy.'

Layna Minnders smiled thinly and inclined her head. 'This way, please.'

Zy was conducted up a wide flight of stairs, along further dim corridors of polished wood, and into a modest apartment, clearly reserved for visitors to the building. It was not as palatial as he'd hoped, although warm and filled with comfortable-looking furniture. The atmosphere, however, was oppressive to his senses, fond as he was of Plate interior design. He disliked the thick drapes and rugs, all of dark colours. This effect was partially alleviated by an open fire crackling in a black grate, but the naked energy of the flames made him feel uneasy.

Layna Minnders dismissed the luggage-carrier, and produced a tray laden with a ceramic pot of the local beverage, silver-tea, cups, and a plate heaped with great slabs of what appeared to be cake. Laying out the crockery on a table, she pointed out the amenities of the room; where the bathroom was to be found, where Zy could store his clothes.

'How long do you think this will take?' she asked, sitting down on a stool by the fire, and tucking her long dress around her legs. She poured tea, holding back her hair with one hand.

'This visit or the prospecting in general?' Zy asked, settling himself into a plump chair on the other side of the fire. He accepted the offered cup and portion of cake, wondering how he was going to consume it. Neither hot drinks or sticky confections were really to his taste.

Layna shrugged. 'Well, both, I suppose. Many of us are concerned that Artemis might be spoiled by a...' She barely suppressed a grimace, '...a tourist company.'

Zy raised his hand. 'No, Layna Minnders, do not worry.

Astracruise make sure that the natural beauty of the countryside is not interfered with in any way. Our hotels and chalets always blend perfectly with the surroundings. We have been known to disguise memorabilia shops as trees in some cases!'

'How reassuring!'

'We aim to please.' Zy smiled, privately wondering how the unspoiled beauty of Artemis would fare once the big boys of commerce started their heavy descent on the place. It would annoy the mineral pirates - free spirits, hardly more than criminals - who shunned the corporate cartels: they'd probably been harvesting the other side of Artemis for centuries unmolested.

'In response to your question,' Zy continued, 'I expect I'll discuss things with the Council for a few days and then head off into the wilderness to take a look around.' He took a tentative bite into the cake and was relieved to find it quite pleasant.

'I'm sure nobody wants a resort too near to Silven Crescent!' Layna said, her voice sharp with alarm.

'Naturally, but not too far that you won't make some kind of profit from it, huh?'

Layna turned her head away and stared, blinking, into the fire. 'I think you'll find we Artemisians have a different view of what is profitable to you and your kind,' she said.

General Verspatch was a stolid woman of middle age, while General Glossling, though younger, presented a more waspish, bleached mien. Both kept their distance from Zy Larrigan, treating him with distant civility and undisguised suspicion. Layna Minnders had accompanied him to dinner, leading him through a maze of dimly lit, tapestried corridors, to a wood-panelled dining-room. Candles adorned the table, another fire burned high, fuelled by fragrant logs that released a piny tang into the air. The generals were already seated, waiting, cromlechs of stiff leather among the glitter of silver cutlery.

Zy reflected Layna Minnders was not typical of the Silven Crescent resident in general. The generals clearly disapproved of being sent a man to deal with and also did not hide that they doubted his ability to do a worthwhile job. Layna obviously did not trust the motives, or claims, of his company, but neither did she treat him condescendingly. She was a trained diplomat, of course, so perhaps she really felt nauseated having to be pleasant to him.

The meal itself was exquisitely prepared and very appetising. Zy could find no cause for complaint there. Local cuisine, obviously, promised to be a feature of merit in his report.

The women waited until the final course had been cleared to broach the subject of business, all talk until then being of an awkward and superficial nature. As waitresses in trim, floor-length uniforms brought round a tray of liqueurs, both generals lit long pipes filled with an acrid smoking-herb, and General Verspatch opened the discussion.

'You have several champions in the Chambers, Mr Larrigan,' she said. 'There are people who feel Artemis should join freely with other worlds in the realms of commerce and... entertainment. I am not so sure. We have managed perfectly well until now. We have everything we need here.'

'I'm sure you have,' Zy responded carefully, 'but is it fair to deny your children the chance of interaction with other cultures? Just think of the unimaginable experiences awaiting them out there.' He waved vaguely at the ceiling.

'It is because we have thought of those *unimaginable experiences* that we are reluctant to get involved,' General Glossling said.

Unfortunately, because of the recent history of Silven Crescent, she could not voice the usual complaints. She was well aware of how a knowledgeable off-worlder could tear them apart now, and embarrass her severely into the bargain.

Zy smiled widely. 'The universe is not such a bad place, general. We have heaven as well as hell out there, you know.

Perhaps you should go and see for yourself.'

Glossling shuddered visibly. 'No thank you! I have more than I can cope with here! Tell us what your company plans to do.'

Zy cleared a space among the remaining crockery. He liked to illustrate his claims with graphic gestures. 'We shall survey the land - probably just on this continent to begin with - and when we've found a suitable site, we'll build a vacational village. That's what we're specialising in at the moment. Letting holidaymakers experience the world they're visiting with as little interference as possible. We'll use local materials for the construction and local personnel as staff - if, of course, that's acceptable.' He produced a plastivellum brochure from the case he'd brought with him, which vividly portrayed other Astracruise triumphs. 'See here? That's a tropical resort on Aidra Phen 105.' He passed the brochure round. 'See how it blends into the surrounding scenery? We avoid garishness and commercialism whenever possible, unless the location lends itself to such measures, of course.'

The generals grudgingly assented that the Aidra Phen complex was most aesthetic and sympathetic with the land.

Layna thumbed through the brochure. 'What's this?' she asked. 'Pleasure Palace on Storax Trine. By the Goddess, what a lot of lights!'

Zy deftly whipped the brochure from her hands and secreted it back in his briefcase. 'Yes, well, you can examine it later, Madam Minnders. That's not the sort of project we envisage for Artemis, so I don't want to waste your time now on such things.'

Layna smiled and poured Zy another measure of the fiery liqueur. He was grateful she didn't pursue the topic.

By the time he went back to his room he felt quite light-headed, as much from the effort of persuasive sales-talk as from the effects of the wines and liqueurs he'd consumed. Layna Minnders walked him back to his door. She was quiet and seemed introspective.

'I'm not looking forward to tomorrow,' Zy said. 'I was thinking earlier that it would have been better if Astracruise had sent a woman for this job. Am I up before all of them in the morning?'

Layna smiled, but he didn't find it encouraging. 'Don't worry. It'll just be Gulding and a couple of her aides.'

'Just! Is she another old hatchet?'

Layna raised her eyebrows and Zy apologised. 'I think you'll find Eugenia Gulding far easier to deal with than the two 'old hatchets' you met tonight, Mr Larrigan. Good night. I trust you'll sleep well.'

'Thank you. Oh, one more thing. Could you arrange for another bottle of wine to be brought to my room?'

Layna Minnders paused for a moment. 'If you think that's wise, I suppose so.'

'It's wise. I'll have a clearer head in the morning if I steam it up tonight.'

Layna did not share Zy's amusement. 'Really! An unusual recipe for clearheadedness. Still, if you're sure, I'll see to it.'

She walked off down the dimly-lit corridor, a lonely, poignant figure. Zy had found that, since the shock value of her scars had worn off, he'd begun to see her as a very attractive creature. He stared after her wistfully for a moment before giving himself a mental shake. 'Remember, remember these are not women as you understand the word,' he told himself and went into his room.

The wine arrived very shortly afterwards, though Zy suspected Layna had had it watered. Whatever. It didn't matter. Silas had generously donated a supply of the leisure-drug Mangine for his trip, and he washed down a couple of capsules with a glass of wine. Relaxing on his bed, waiting for sublime experience to unfold within his tired mind, Zy extended his senses to try and get a feel of the place. Mangine investigated the corridors of his mind with gentle, twisting fingers, creating doors where there were none, activating his imagination. He experienced a profound feeling of being isolated from the world of women here, but it was not uncomfortable. He was a witness, nothing more. This detached observation darkened considerably, as a serious sense of imbalance pervaded his consciousness. It was uncomfortable, like sitting in a draught outside a door concealing a horrible experience soon to be faced. Presentiment blossomed within him; effusive, dark blooms as beautiful as they were disconcerting. The world beyond the city spread out, a landscape in his mind, shadowed and moving, blistered by lesions of light, and an aching sense of unendurable loveliness. Concealed within this wonder was a sense of threat. There was a voice in his head, silky and suggestive, whispering, 'Oh, there's something odd here, boy, and it's waiting for you.'

Zy sat up, blinking rapidly, to dispel such delusions. He must remember to have a stern word with Silas about the quality of his Mangine when he returned to civilisation. He had clearly been given part of a faulty batch to be infected by such paranoia. Anyway, even if there was something dangerously mysterious, beautiful and unseen out there in the world, Zy wanted no part of it, unless it could be successfully utilised as a tourist attraction. He sighed, put his arms behind his head and lay down again.

'Let's just get this job done and get out,' he said aloud, reaching for the wine bottle and swigging from it liberally. 'Let's just get the hell out.'

Chapter Six
Meonel's Party

Meonel Trotgarden, soothed by Dannel's strong, bitter ale, leaned back in his chair and regarded, with satisfaction, his birthday gathering. Not even the thought that his thirtieth year was creeping uncomfortably close could taint his pleasure tonight. Across the table, Rosanel Garmelding sat nursing her cup, listening attentively to Bolivia's anecdotes of what had occurred at the dam site that day. Rosanel's dark, smoky hair was haloed in the mellow light and she looked far younger than she had for months. Still a sulky beauty was Rosanel, appearing too sophisticated to be a part of their rough community. Meonel knew it was a misleading appearance because, like everyone else, Rosanel was not afraid to get her hands dirty, but he still felt that Milady Garmelding would look and feel more at home in the court at Silven Crescent. She'd adapted well to her new life, considering how much she'd lost.

The Garmeldings had been an influential family in Silven Crescent, and Rosanel, being the last of her line, had been the mistress of her ancestral home. Not only had she lost her position and her wealth, but also her lover. Rosanel had been a political crusader, caught up in the hurricane of all that had happened, and she had been obsessed by the rebel leader, Elvon L'Belder. Corinna had once said that Rosanel had cared more for the man than she had for his beliefs. Perhaps Rosanel regretted that now. If she'd not got involved with L'Belder, she would doubtless still be lady of her domain in the city. Was Freespace really worth as much to her? It was, after all, Elvon's dream, not hers. Poor Elvon. Meonel suppressed a sigh. He too should have been part of this gathering, sitting at Rosanel's side. But it was best not to think of L'Belder. Meonel knew that if the man still lived, he could no more sit easily at this table than stop the world turning.

Meonel had not actually seen with his own eyes what had happened to L'Belder all those years ago - only Corinna and Gick could admit that privilege - but he'd certainly seen the Greylids, the creatures L'Belder had turned to for help. When he'd been forced to leave Silven Crescent and seek sanctuary in the marsh, fate had decreed L'Belder should find refuge at the Trotgarden Estate of Vangery. Fate had also decreed that Corinna should involve herself in L'Belder's causes; seduced, (in perhaps the same way Rosanel had been), by L'Belder's persuasive words. She'd been marked by a dark finger before she'd even left Vangery to join Carmenya in the city.

Should we have stopped her leaving? Meonel wondered. Would things have been any different, then?

L'Belder, along with his wild beliefs concerning society, had been obsessed by the idea that a native Artemisian race was concealed within the forests of Ire and Penitence, on the borders of the marsh. To most people, the Greylids were no more than a subject of fairy-tales, but L'Belder's faith in himself - and his convictions - had been unshakable. Meonel still wondered whether it was this strength that had somehow caused the Greylids to exist, because L'Belder had certainly found them. Meonel and Shyya had been with him; they'd seen. Now, it was a matter they never discussed. Caught up in the mundane business of everyday life, Meonel could sometimes almost believe it had never happened. It was, perhaps, better that way.

Next to Rosanel, Corinna, more than a little intoxicated, was trying to stab Orblin's splayed fingers on the table top with her meat-knife. The only person Meonel loved more than his step-daughter was Shyya, but he and Corinna were no longer as close as they had been. A vivacious girl had entered Silven

Crescent; an abused scrap had escaped it. She kept her silence; never purged herself of the past, never even complained about it. Did she confide in anyone nowadays? Did Gick have that privilege? Somehow, Meonel could not imagine that. Gick was far too abrasive a person for Corinna to open up to, he was sure. How about Hollis? He was around a lot these days. Yes, how about Hollis? He had never seen Hollis and Corinna touch, not even in friendship, but he was certain the boy wanted something closer than mere companionship with her. In return, Corinna teased Hollis and kept him at arm's length. No, Meonel doubted whether Hollis was Corinna's confidante. That meant she had no-one. Too chilly a thought for this happy occasion.

Meonel let his eyes wander further down the table. Next to Orblin, the priestess Meera was arguing some metaphysical point with Hollis Backwater - an argument that had been circling to mutual enjoyment for over half an hour. Meera was a stern-looking, patrician woman who, Meonel considered, took her faith far too seriously nowadays. Perhaps it was the only thing she had to hang on to, now she had lost the security of the city temple. The further north they'd travelled the swifter Meera's sense of humour seemed to have fallen from her, like a shed skin, into the marsh. She was not crusading enough to actually berate the Freespacers out loud for their apparent neglect of worship, but Meonel guessed she was disappointed the Goddess Parthenos had lost her allure for them. This was hardly surprising, really. It was likely most Freespacers associated the Goddess with Silven Crescent and the tyrannical regime that had oppressed them. How could anyone feel truly comfortable entreating a power embraced by the city women? He couldn't. When he thought about it, the only time the Goddess' name was heard nowadays was when used in an oath.

Next to Meonel, Shyya, Gick, and Sander Tendaughter - who had dropped in when he smelled meat cooking - were having a happy time gossiping about other Freespacers. Shyya was probably the only person Meonel never had to worry about. Despite his mutilation, which had occurred when he was very young, after a bizarre fertility rite at some settlement in the north of the marsh, he was the most well-balanced, serene individual Meonel had ever known. If anyone was distressed, they could find comfort in talking to Shyya. He was already a legend among the Freespacers, not just because of his smooth, tawny skin, lithe body and sculpted face, but because of the light in his dark eyes. Soothing light. It was incredible how anybody of Shyya's age could possess such wisdom; he was not that long out of his teens. Shyya sensed Meonel's attention on him and lifted his head. The eyes said, 'And later, I will give you your real birthday present,' before looking back at Gick, who always demanded complete attention from the people she spoke with.

I am lucky, Meonel thought. *We are all lucky.* He refilled his cup with wine and felt himself fill up with a warm rush of pride for all of his people. It had been hard being literally ripped up from the roots and expelled into the limbo of Artemis' wild north. Nobody had expected it. Nobody had been properly prepared, but they'd had the vitality to survive and to enjoy their survival. Perhaps the elders of the marsh had wandered, bewildered, behind their children into the wilderness. It had certainly been the children who had sustained them. In Vangery, Meonel had never taken much notice of his son. Now they had discovered, almost to mutual surprise, that they had a relationship. Meonel was young enough to be a friend to Orblin as well as a father. It still gave him a start that was almost chilling when the boy caught his eye and smiled at him, offering a window onto the pile of maturing emotion he held within. It was still difficult to look upon Orblin as part of his flesh. The boy had bloomed freed from the marsh. Obviously, he was a plant that did not need roots. Shreds of musk-leaf and wild potato in cream littered the table top, as well as liberal splatterings of grease from the smoked antelope steak. The meal had been a triumph.

Dannel reposed, with flushed face, grinning in contentment. She caught Meonel's eye and raised her cup to him. In that moment, both were aware, they had at last come home.

Dannel knew that, although their marriage was perhaps nothing like it should have been, she and Meonel were very happy. They liked each other. They were friends. It hadn't always been that way but the troubles that had beset them in the past, together with Shyya's insidiously harmonising presence, had brought them together. Meonel was far younger than Dannel. She had purchased him when he was sixteen from a travelling trader, (whose main commodity had been man flesh). Still raw inside from the death of her first husband, Corinna and Bolivia's father, she had promptly married Meonel, in the hope of filling the aching hole in her heart. It had been a big mistake. Meonel was feral; he hated women, hated confinement and repulsed all Dannel's attempts to domesticate him. She had tried hard in the beginning to forge some kind of relationship with him; she had been patient, tried to be loving. In some grotesque, best forgotten, way he had eventually fathered Orblin. Later, she resigned herself to the fact that husband number one was never to be replaced and had bought Shyya for Meonel, hoping that at least one of them could find happiness. It was probably the best thing anyone had ever done for Meonel, although it had taken him a while to realise it. All those hard times of the heart, though, seemed unreal to Dannel now. The Trotgardens had closed ranks against greater difficulties. Now, she felt, they were very close indeed.

'So Sander,' Meonel said, filling a gap in the conversation, 'how is the Tendaughter residence coming along? Corinna told me you'd nearly finished it.'

Sander wrinkled his nose. 'The house is virtually built, yes, but we have a lot to sort out. Mother wants running water and proper heating of course. I've heard her muttering about a generator. She's even had the babies out searching for ores.'

'We told you we'd help,' Corinna said, granting Sander a warm smile.

At one time, which seemed millennia ago, they had been as good as betrothed to each other. Sander still had a tendency to blush youthfully in Corinna's presence.'It would be appreciated,' he said, and turned again to Meonel. 'Have you found a site for yourself yet?'

Gick butted in before Meonel could speak. Meonel was not sure whether he liked the girl or not. 'Stop looking Trotgardens! I've found it! It's really you! It's fabulous!'

'Oh, do stop gushing, Gick,' Corinna said with abrading cool. 'What do you mean?'

'Well you know I've been helping out up at the dam?'

Everyone nodded, because she wasn't going to continue until she got a response. 'There's a track up there that leads into the crags.'

'You aren't suggesting we build up there, surely!' Bolivia exclaimed, who had seen it.

'Listen. I know it looks difficult from the lake site, but it could easily be widened, and there's a superb mountain meadow up there. Stream, waterfall, fertile pastures, the lot. I can just see a new Vangery sprouting there. You must see it!'

The Trotgardens were wary.

'Think we should have a look?' Meonel asked Corinna.

'Are you two the committee on home-building?' Bolivia asked acidly. 'What do you think, Dannel? And let's hear Orblin's and Shyya's thoughts, shall we?'

'Won't hurt to survey,' Orblin said.

'And it would be quiet up there,' Shyya added. 'I've been meaning to explore that area for a while. Haven't had time. It has a good feeling.'

Dannel was reassured by Shyya's remarks. She trusted his instinct. 'I think Corinna and Meonel should take a look first,' she said, knowing the pair of them had set their hearts on the Home Project. 'If they think it's suitable, we can all go and see it.'

Bolivia smiled sourly into her mug and took a drink. Dannel still had the last word in this family, whatever other authorities had been removed from her.

'That's settled then,' Corinna said. She raised her mug. 'Let's drink to tomorrow.'

'A proper home!' Dannel added.

Mugs clacked together and the hope was solemnised.

Chapter Seven
The Women's Room

'We are not quite as provincial as you think, Mr. Larrigan,' Eugenia Gulding said, a remark carefully spiced with condescension. 'We are not stupid; neither are you. Artemis has had her problems over the last few years. This is the reason why I, personally, think we should spread our wings a little more. Perhaps we have become too subjective - certainly too feudal - left to our own devices here. It has been made clear that the intentions of this world's first settlers have not come to be, so we might as well do away with their restraints too.'

'One of those being interaction with other worlds?' He knew that to be true.

Gulding inclined her head. 'Precisely. As a matter of fact, Yani Gisbandrun had dealings with off-worlders throughout her reign. Less than savoury characters I feel.'

'Really?' Zy had known that too. Pirates and slavers, mainly. The civilised worlds had looked on Artemis as a planet-sized mental institution and had fastidiously kept their distance. Objectively, half of the stories that filtered out into the star-lanes must have been gross exaggerations, if not more than half. That still left a sizable portion of truth.

Having looked around him on this visit, Zy could still detect phantoms of those times hanging around. If the Artemisians could have seen how they were regarded outside their own atmosphere, they might be too affronted to continue any business with off-worlders. Their name was synonymous with ignorant craziness. Far from what they believed, the galactic community was not a grinding, patriarchal dictatorship, and Zy doubted whether it had been even when Artemis had first been settled. Crazies had rooted here, and crazies had spread their odd notions along with their genes. Their intentions might have been noble, but they had only bred murder and oppression. Now their descendants assumed they were doing everybody a favour by extending friendly overtures. If only they knew. He wished for a cruel, brief moment that he could enlighten them, but realised it would not exactly benefit his cause for being there. People outside only wanted to exploit Artemis, not rejoice because they were at last being accepted by her residents. How could these people be so deluded? No, delusion wasn't the word. Innocence was.

Eugenia Gulding's office was at the heart of the Governmental Building. The attentive Layna Minnders had accompanied him there before noon. They had passed down sunlit corridors, red carpet underfoot. At one point, Layna had paused before the turning into a short passageway, where heavy, barred doors could be seen at the end. 'Some of this place has not been rebuilt,' she'd said in a curious, toneless voice. 'I like to think it never will be. I think we need some kind of reminder.'

'So what lies that way?' he'd asked. 'The torture chambers of the late Dominatrix?'

'Merely her old apartments,' Layna had replied without changing her tone. 'What's left of them.'

'Hmm.' Zy repressed a shudder; not unnerved by a breath of icy air, or the presence of ghosts, but merely Layna's voice. The tone of it chilled him, invoking the echo of bitter memories. They were not his memories either. Perhaps he'd overdone the Mangine last night. He shivered and decided he would not like to investigate this area of the building further.

Eugenia Gulding's office was panelled in warm, dark wood. The high, narrow windows were leaded and overlooked a pleasant courtyard where flowering plants were laid out in ordered ranks between pathways of yellow sand. General Gulding sat in a throne-like chair at the head of a glossy table, between a pair of younger women and in front of an unlikely display of scarlet flowers and exuberant lichen fronds. Sunlight fell flatteringly onto the general's fading auburn hair and onto her hands clasping each other on the table. Her face was in shadow. Smoke from a domestic incense burner hanging from the ceiling curled indolently in the air.

One of the other women was biting her nails, leaning back in her chair with what Zy could only infer was an assumed posture of nonchalance. Layna Minnders introduced him, and General Gulding bade him be seated without rising herself. The other two women were announced to be Alouine Crestick and Welma Barbarel.

Alouine was a heavy, masculine creature with a square, healthy-looking face and short, black hair, perhaps forty years old or so, while Welma was a younger, skinnier, more nervous woman. She'd been the one biting her nails. Her cropped hair was so blonde, Zy could almost see her scalp through it. Both women wore simple uniform; plain, grey coveralls. Not exactly glamorous sirens, Zy thought acidly.

He put his briefcase on the table and sat down, Layna dropping gracefully into a chair on the opposite side. As before, he'd outlined his company's plans, with a little more detail and suggested that he'd really have to take a look around before he could tell them anything more definite. 'You understand that photographs and written reports are all very well, but I need to assess the actual ambience of the place, the fall of the light, the quality of the air to decide the best possible places to...er... utilise.'

'You make it all sound very artistic, Mr. Larrigan,' Welma Barbarel said.

He smiled at her sarcasm. 'Far from it, madam. People will be spending considerable amounts of money with Astracruise for the privilege of visiting Artemis. We are merely making sure they will get their money's worth. What might seem like romantic fancy to you is hard business to us.'

'Of course, I should have realised.' She savagely lit a

cigarette, of some pungent, native herb, and stared out of the window, exhaling furiously.

Zy caught Layna's eye. She shrugged, but didn't let the smile spread further than her eyes. Perhaps he could have told them then that the prospective tourists would flood to the little world more to examine the eccentric inhabitants than to appreciate the beauty of its countryside. That was when General Gulding made her pronouncement on the Artemisians spreading their wings.

Alouine Crestick produced a map of Silven Crescent, the marsh and the surrounding area to about two hundred miles' radius of the city. This, in fact, encompassed the Artemisians' entire knowledge of their world. Zy found it incredible that nobody had disobeyed the government's directive and explored further. But of course, he realised, they must have done. They wouldn't be human otherwise. The ones that disobeyed just weren't around anymore. Artemis had been populated by humans for roughly three hundred years. It was inevitable that some of them had headed off somewhere else, especially during Gisbandrun's reign. He realised it would prompt an adverse reaction, but in the interests of his company, he had to voice his thoughts.

'Do you have any knowledge of other occupied territory?' he said. 'I'll have to know because I can't go staking claim to land that's already been boundaried by someone else.'

'What do you mean?' Welma Barbarel asked.

'I think we all know,' General Gulding said calmly. She smiled at Zy. 'I thought you understood that we Artemisians made it a policy not to take more than we needed from this world. Our entire settlement is as outlined on the map here.' She gestured towards it.

'Yes, yes. I appreciate that. But what about the possibility of people breaking away from your settlement, or even other off-worlders arriving? All I'm asking is if you've had any intimation of this.'

'How could we have done?' Layna Minnders said, having

been silent until then. 'We never go outside of our boundary.'

'And the only people who've ever 'broken away', as you put it, are the odd escaping...' Welma looked nervously at Gulding, '...the odd few men who've disagreed with some political view or another. It's doubtful anybody could survive beyond the protection of our civilisation. We have reason to believe there's some very hostile territory out there. They'd have no knowledge of the land or what dangers might exist.'

'True, but people have been known to survive such hardships before in human history.'

'I don't really think it's a problem, Mr. Larrigan,' General Gulding said. 'Obviously I can't really speak for potential off-worlders, but as far as - personnel - from our community, I think there's little chance of finding any number of them likely to object to your plans.' She laughed dryly and the other women followed suit.

Zy didn't think they found the idea as laughable as they'd like to have him think, however. It annoyed him. There was no way he wanted to be blissfully sweeping over the land, only to be sniped at by territorial refugees from the city. If they knew something, for his own safety, they should tell him. Perhaps he could speak to Layna about it later. She seemed more approachable and sympathetic towards him than anyone else.

'Well,' Zy said, closing his case and beaming round the table. 'There's not much more to discuss at the moment. If it's o.k. with you, I'll take off tomorrow and survey the land. I've brought my own transport with me, if you could arrange to have it cleared at customs. The only thing I'll need is food supplies. Obviously, you won't be able to supply me with a guide!'

General Gulding nodded thoughtfully. 'It would help you considerably if we could issue you with comprehensive maps of the continent. I apologise that we can't, but it's been decided that at least two Artemisians should accompany you. After all, you might well need the protection. It would be rather reckless for you to head off into the unknown alone, wouldn't it?'

'General Gulding, I can assure you it's a situation I'm used to. I have very sophisticated equipment on board my flyer, which will be more than adequate to see to my safety. I never take risks.' He did not relish the thought of having to be cooped up with any of these women.

'All the same, we would look upon it as a courtesy if you would allow my two assistants to travel with you.' General Gulding made it plain he had no choice.

With wilting spirits, Zy looked at Welma and Alouine, who stared stonily back. Sighing inside, he stood up. 'Very well, although it might be a little cramped for three of us. My flyer has never carried more than two before and I doubt whether I'll be actually leaving it very often.' He smiled rather thinly at Gulding's assistants. 'I'd advise you to bring some kind of entertainment with you. I won't need any help with the survey and, like I said before, there won't be much tactile exploration involved. Time, more than safety, is the pressing factor there!'

'It doesn't matter,' Welma Barbarel said. 'I'm just looking forward to seeing more of Artemis. How can that possibly be boring?'

Gulding uttered a chuckle. 'Years ago, you could have been arrested for saying that, Welma.'

Welma grimaced. 'Years ago, it would have been unlikely we'd be having a tourist company prospecting the place. Times have changed. Personally, I welcome it.'

Zy felt a stirring of respect for Madam Barbarel. Perhaps she wasn't quite as objectionable as he'd first thought.

'Anyway,' Alouine Crestick said, 'we would like to bring plant samples back to the city, make charts of our own, survey the animal life. I don't see why only you should benefit from this trip, Mr. Larrigan.'

'Fair enough,' Zy said. He was willing to make some concessions. 'Meet me at the spaceport after breakfast tomorrow.'

Layna accompanied him back to his apartments and

suggested that perhaps he'd like a tour of the city for what remained of the afternoon. Zy was anxious to use the communications facilities at the spaceport, to transmit a message for Silas and Kitzuki. He'd be long gone into the wilderness by the time they received it, but it was a superstition he had, contacting them before heading off into unknown territory.

Layna told him there was communication equipment within the palace he could use. 'Not as up to date as you're used to probably,' she said, 'but we can bounce information off Gypsy Satellite towards the nearest constellar orbital.'

'That should be sufficient,' Zy replied. 'As long as I can get a message through somehow.'

'Family?' Layna asked.

'The nearest I have to it now. My lovers.'

'Oh. I see.'

Zy kicked himself inside. He'd used the plural. Mistake. Layna looked disgusted.

After he'd sent a brief, carefully-worded message on its way back to the Plate, Zy agreed to Layna's earlier suggestion, although what he'd seen of the city below the watermark of Hill affluence the previous day had weirdly offended him.

A dank-drawn carriage awaited them outside, in a lesser courtyard of the Palace. Layna had dressed herself in a fur coat; the season was turning towards chilliness. Zy found himself wishing it was Layna accompanying him on his exploration trip rather than the stony Gulding assistants. He felt they would have got on together rather well. He told her so.

'I don't think I'd enjoy it,' she replied.

'Whyever not?' Zy asked. 'Alouine and Welma seem to be looking forward to it. Have you no sense of adventure?'

Layna pulled a sour face. 'Mr Larrigan, I have had adventures that would cause you to go prematurely bald! No, I happen to like the routine of my life now and have no wish to disrupt it.'

'Are you afraid of what might be out there?'

She fixed him with a cold stare. 'Very little frightens me now, Mr. Larrigan.'

Her expression and tone silenced further teasing on his part. He remembered the scars on her face, that he'd so quickly grown used to, and that they were not natural features. Indeed, Ms Minnders must have tales to tell.

The carriage bowled cheerily down the slopes of Palace Hill towards the markets. Layna pointed out landmarks of interest to which Zy responded in a monotone. He was beginning to feel weary, and his thoughts kept turning wistfully to the pouch of Mangine he'd secreted in his room; one dose of that could restore his humour, even his interest in life, whether it was tainted or not. He wished Layna Minnders would shut up. Her world was beginning to bore him severely.

'So what's the real story about the escaping man-slaves, then?' he asked abruptly.

Layna was silent for a moment. 'I'm not sure if I understand what response you want from that remark,' she said at last.

'Well, it's obvious the old general and her cronies were tale-spinning a little. A lot of people must have left Silven Crescent over the years. Where are they? Does anybody know?'

'There is nobody. Or if there was, they're dead now. Men couldn't survive without women.'

'Biologically, maybe not,' he replied coolly, sensing there was more than that in Layna's remark. 'But I'm not convinced every female here is as anti-male as that. It's possible women and men left the city together, isn't it?'

'I'm puzzled as to why you're pursuing this point. Surely, you'll see for yourself soon if there is anyone out there.'

'I'm just curious that's all. I can't believe nobody ever wanted to investigate beyond your territory. People just aren't like that.'

'Your people, maybe not.'

'Artemisians were 'my people' too once. Don't forget that.'

Layna sighed. 'I wish you'd get it into your head why

people came here. They were disgusted by the way the human race was raping the galaxy, taking and spoiling and using. Artemis was to be treated with respect. The people who first came here believed in that firmly and brought their children up the same way. You talk as if our territory is small; it isn't. It would take a lifetime to explore the marsh. When you have seen it, you'll understand. It isn't just a flat expanse of swampy ground. It's a fascinating wilderness. If people really lusted for exploration, they'd have more than enough to cope with there, and that's precisely where the more pioneering-spirited Artemisians went...' A frown crossed her face.

'Yes?'

'You'll see, that's all.'

Chapter Eight
The Valley

It had not been Farris Windteasel's intention to follow Meonel and Corinna Trotgarden that day. He'd been squatting idly outside the family tent, sleepily absorbing the morning ambience of Freespace, when he'd been woken up by the unmistakable abrasive drawl of Corinna Trotgarden's voice. He had seen them coming through the drooping plaisels, dappled with light and kicking up dust. Both of them were dressed in the functional brown and green garments typical of the settlers, both adorned with small flamboyances characteristic of Trotgarden; a family renowned for its style. Corinna was wearing huge earrings, and Meonel had a multi-coloured scarf over his green-gold hair. They could have been mistaken for brother and sister, sharing as they did a particularly tall and rangy look. Meonel also had several animal tails hanging from his belt, and Corinna had a grimacing face painted on the back of her shirt. Farris stood up like an eager dog as they sauntered past him, but hadn't been noticed.

Corinna waved a hello over her shoulder to Softly Windteasel, who was coming home with a barrel of dank-milk from the Tanteberrys.

'Where are you two off to?' Softly had asked.

'To the dam,' Meonel had answered. 'Gick's found us a meadow to build on, or so she says.'

'We're just going to check it out,' Corinna said.

'Good luck then,' Softly said. 'Can't say I'll be sorry to be living in a real house again myself.'

The Trotgardens made noises of agreement before walking

away.

Farris peered round the edge of the tent, watching them leave.

'What are you doing?' Softly asked him severely. 'You're a creep, Farris. Don't ogle people like that.'

Sneering in response, he scampered away, ostensibly going nowhere near the Trotgardens, but still heading uphill, in the general direction of the dam.

Freespace had settled itself under the shadow of a huge crag, whose red rock surface was virtually indistinguishable from the profusion of plants and trees digging their roots into its crevices. The site had been chosen primarily because of the protection the crag afforded, coupled with the fact that a small waterfall cascaded into an open-topped cave nearby, providing a pool of sweet, clear water. Later, the mountain lake had been discovered, its size more suitable to the Freespacers needs. Using what equipment they'd managed to haul north with them, they would soon be able to supply themselves with both hydroelectric power and a much-desired sewerage and water supply system. Not every marsh family had elected to join the Freespacers in their flight but, including those people who'd fled from the city and those who'd joined up with the group later on, Freespace consisted of over four hundred individuals. It would take time to build enough accommodation for them all.

Farris paused under the exposed roots of a northern threadwood, looking down onto the canvas roofs of Freespace town. He had no particular love for it and was unmoved by the care lavished on the site, the tidiness of its meagre dwellings, the attempts at enlivening the place; humorous slogans, rough paintings on the sides of huts and tents. He felt like an outsider. All these people were doing something together, and he was not part of it. At least at home, on the marsh, he'd been able to sneak off and enjoy being alone without anybody noticing it. Here, the desire for solitude seemed to be regarded as aberrant behaviour, as if he should always be throwing himself into the community like everybody else. He couldn't. On those occasions when he tried, it merely felt contrived and embarrassing.

There was no discernible difference between his own upbringing and that of his sisters and yet, while they now fitted in with nonchalant ease, moving slowly away from the isolation the family had preferred back on the marsh, he squirmed and wriggled and sweated his way around the edges of society, sometimes looking for a gap to sneak through towards the warmth, sometimes just howling in his head like a smoom afraid of fire.

Farris sighed and scrambled upwards, his toes digging into the gravelly path. Sometimes, he'd dream of arms around him, breath in his face, the long heat of a closely held body, but it was always a faceless body. He tried to put an identity to this fantasy: Corinna, Meonel, even Shyya, of whom he was slightly afraid. None of them fitted, but oh, how his body ached for that contact. He was sure once he knew the face of this person, the dream would become reality.

'An impressive site.' Meonel nudged an efflorescence of garnet-wort with his foot as they stood at the edge of the lake. Young mountains reared sharp walls on three sides of them, multi-coloured in the brilliant light of Artemis' two suns. The air up there still had an edge of chill in it, perhaps rising from the lake or down through the twisty corridors of mountain passes. Corinna was not cold, just aware of it, but rubbed her arms anyway. Across the water, they could make out the shapes of people working, hear distant shouts and the wooden stamping of primitive machinery.

'It's beautiful here, really beautiful,' Corinna said. 'Kind of isolated though. Do you think it would be a good idea to try and build this far out from Freespace?'

'Think it will be isolated for long?' Meonel asked cynically. 'No, we shall merely be the first of many, I think. Let's take a look at Gick's meadow, shall we? She doesn't appear to have remembered her appointment with us.'

'OK, which way?'

Meonel squinted round the rock walls. 'Place looks pitted with path-ways. She said to the left, didn't she? We'll just walk that way.'

There wasn't much of a path to follow. All the mud-tracks made by the Freespacers skirted round the right side of the lake to where the mountain river tried to spill over the cliff beyond. Caves which had once looked out over the water were now dark tunnel mouths beneath it. Grasses and reeds grew right to the lake's edge, and Corinna could see them waving beneath the water, dying. Whatever natural pathways the local animals had made had been submerged as the water level rose, so Corinna and Meonel had to clamber over rocks for much of the way.

Corinna wondered how Gick had found this supposed perfect meadow. She also wondered how accurate her report had been that the pass which led to it could be effectively widened. That might be so, but a road would also have to be built around the lake. It would take months just to get the site ready, never mind to start work on the house.

'Here!' Meonel called, some way in front.

Corinna scrambled up to him, wiping her face on her sleeve. Chill forgotten, the scramble had made her sweat. There was a sandy, narrow pathway winding up into the mountainside. 'Could easily be widened, my eyes!' Corinna said, resignation rather than anger colouring her voice.

'It's not as narrow as it looks, C'rin,' Meonel answered. 'It winds a lot, see? Come on.' He was already striding into the rock and was lost from sight after only a moment.

'Hold on!' Corinna hurried after him.

Once the first corner had been turned, the walls became damper, sprouting acid-green ferns and patched with dark crimson lichen. It was almost dark in there and the smell... Corinna inhaled deeply. Perhaps it came from the lichen or the ferns, or even the rock itself. Never had she smelled anything so intoxicating, yet so subtle; not the heavy scent of fleshy flowers or the sharp tang of tree sap; something else. Indescribable.

'Corinna!'

She heard Meonel's voice echo and realised she had stopped walking and had closed her eyes. Narcotic perfume perhaps? She gave herself a shake and hastened forwards.

Round another corner, Meonel was examining the rock wall. 'Take a look at this,' he said.

'A cave...'

Meonel shook his head. 'No. It's an alcove.'

'Yes, very nice. We'll be able to sit here and catch our breath on the way home from Freespace every night.'

'Does it look natural to you?'

'What's natural?'

'It looks human-made to me... or something-made. It's been carved out from the rock.'

'Don't be ridiculous. Someone else would have noticed it. Gick, for one. She may act like a complete infant, but she's sharp. She would have realised.'

'If this is the same path she followed, of course...' Meonel stared at Corinna for a moment and then raised his eyebrows.

Corinna looked more carefully at the rock. 'It's hard to tell, Meonel. It may just look artificial. There could be any number of reasons why it's here. Who could have done it, anyway?'

'We may not have been the first to run from the marsh, C'rin.'

Corinna shrugged. 'Whatever. It looks ancient anyway.'

They began to walk again, but more slowly, side by side. 'I've been on the lookout,' Meonel said. 'Ever since the marsh. You and I both know, C'rin, humans are not the only residents of this planet.'

It was the first time he'd mentioned this subject since they'd had to leave Vangery. That he, Shyya and Elvon L'Belder had encountered the remains of an intelligent, indigenous species on Artemis was no secret, nor that L'Belder had coerced that race, the Greylids, into helping him combat Yani Gisbandrun. However, either because of respect for the Greylids, who prized their privacy and had little interest in human affairs, or because the recollection made him uncomfortable, Meonel rarely alluded to them. As far as the Freespacers knew, they were the only human beings on Artemis who were sure of the Greylids' existence. Corinna realised she should have known Meonel would have been prospecting for further evidence of old Greylid settlements, or even current ones, if it were possible they lived beyond the forests of Ire and Penitence. She looked at Meonel warily wondering, if she spoke now, whether he'd say any more. She knew it was a touchy subject with him and didn't want to scare him off.

'We were told they'd come from the realm of the Lord of Rocks,' Meonel continued, as if thinking aloud. 'That could conceivably be mountains - these - whose foothills dwindle into the forests. There's so much we don't know, which I think the Greylids themselves have forgotten. It's all wrapped up in myth with them, symbol and metaphor, rather like our own history, I suppose.'

'That does seem to be the way information is handed down,' Corinna said carefully, to show her interest without interrupting.

'Indeed. Something cataclysmic happened on this world, something which wiped out intelligent life, but for the Greylids, who'd been greatly altered both physically and mentally before that happened. Why? How? Are there important things we should know about that, things that might affect us? After all, humanity has not fared terribly well on Artemis either, turning upon itself as it did. Imagine, if we found sizable remains of settlement, some clue as to what occurred all those centuries ago.'

Corinna considered this unlikely. She caught his eye. 'Goddess, Meonel, do you really think that's possible? Here?' She didn't want to be more specific.

Storm Constantine

Meonel shrugged. 'Well, as you said, that alcove looked ancient, even if it was deliberately constructed. Little likelihood of finding another Greylid community here, I'm sure. Somebody would have come across something by now. Oh, I don't know. Perhaps I'm being over-imaginative, seeing things that I want to see. Let's just keep an open mind until we've had a good look around.'

They followed the winding path upwards. Meonel had been right - it wasn't as narrow as Corinna had feared, but occasionally fallen rock would block the way and they had to fight for passage through waist-high tangles of a prickly shrub they'd never seen before. Further along, a creature the Freespacers had hurriedly named a spider-lizard had spun a thick, clinging nest from wall to wall, in which young lizards peeped and crawled. The lizards were a placid, harmless species, curious and friendly to humans. It had been discussed whether their webs could be utilised by the Freespacers - for their properties of durability and adhesiveness - and domestication of the lizards themselves had been considered. The female lizard stood on a ledge of rock above the nest, tasting their scent in the air with her tongue. Neither of them wanted to harm the nest, which blocked the path like a dense curtain, sequined with glittering insect husks.

'Climb,' Meonel said. The female lizard watched them with interest as they hauled themselves past her. Corinna wondered whether she appreciated the gesture.

Meonel was investigating a hole in the rock. 'I can see light further on,' he said.

'Fine. Shall we just drop back onto the path now, please?'

'No, let's go up here. It might be a quicker way.'

'In which we could happily lose ourselves.' Corinna was already following him.

'What's that noise? Stop.' Corinna put her hand on Meonel's ankle.

'What noise?' Meonel asked.

For a moment both were silent, then Corinna shook her

head. 'Nothing. It's gone, whatever it was. Did you feel the vibration?'

Meonel shook his head. 'Must have been from the dam site.'

'Mmm, must've been.'

They emerged once more into stinging sunlight. 'Mirrors,' Meonel said, but it wasn't quite that. The rock around them reflected the light from a million crystal points. It took them a while to see where they were. 'Paradise meadow,' Meonel said in an awed murmur. He strode out into the lush blue-green, mossy grass leaving Corinna to linger at the rock wall.

Gick had been right; the place was beautiful. Almost an accident of nature, a sumptuous wound between the mica-starred cliffs, the valley sloped gently down for at least two lope-leagues, towards an indistinct cluster of trees in the distance. Corinna could hear the faint chuckle of water. It seemed too good to be true. Why then did she feel so nervous, reluctant to move her body away from the rock? The place was almost too peaceful, somehow watchful. *Is it just another reminder of the past that I mistrust whatever appears benevolent?* she wondered and steeled herself to join Meonel, ankle deep in grass ahead of her.

'So what do you think?' he asked her.

Corinna rubbed her gritty palms on her trousers. 'Great place for a day out; idyllic. But where's the access Gick told us about? Apart from that little tunnel we just used there doesn't seem to be any easy way in here.'

'Could be beyond the trees.'

'Would Gick have come that way? Surely that's leagues away from the dam. In the opposite direction in fact.'

'I don't know. We'll find a way. Let's take a look around.'

'OK.' Corinna decided not to voice any objections. Meonel seemed to have picked up her slight reserve about the place and there was an irritable edge to his voice.

As they walked down the valley, Corinna couldn't resist glancing up at the towering cliffs on either side. How would it feel lying in bed at night knowing those great things were looming over you? She shuddered and tried to rationalise her misgivings. Perhaps it was a kind of claustrophobia, a fear of being trapped. She had good reason to feel that way, didn't she? Something about the glittering cliffs must have triggered a memory of Silven Crescent.

A shallow stream cut through the meadow, which Corinna suspected might just be seasonal, or even a result of their dam-building. Meonel pointed out the sand and stones at the bottom of the channel. 'Water has run through here for years,' he said. They had walked into the shadow of the left-hand rock wall. Here, the cliff was pitted with dark openings of various sizes.

'Lairs for carnivores,' Corinna said.

Meonel stared at her keenly. 'Somehow, I get the impression you're just thinking up excuses for us not to build here. Why?'

She shrugged. There was little point in lying. 'A feeling, that's all. I don't feel comfortable.'

Meonel swept his hand out towards the sunny grass. 'Can't you imagine it, though, a strong, wooden house? We could dam the stream, make a pool, fence the meadow into fields. Come on, C'rin, you have to admit it's ideal.'

'There's still the problem of access.'

Meonel shook his head. 'Normally, I'd trust your instincts; you know that. This time?' He sighed. 'C'rin, I get good feelings from this place. It's as if it's been waiting for some family to come and make a home here.'

That made Corinna shudder again. She thought, *Yes, perhaps that's what I'm afraid of.*

'If we don't claim this place some other Freespace family will,' Meonel said. 'Then you'll regret being so... stupid about it.'

She sighed. 'Perhaps you're right. I'm just feeling jumpy. We'll see what the others think, shall we?' She harboured some hope her mother or Shyya would be sensitive enough to feel wary about the place too.

They had almost reached the trees. Meonel pointed out threadwood, Gomery balm, amber-oak; all the most useful woods for building, burning, resin extraction. Corinna felt easier once they were among the trees, perhaps because their foliage obscured the sight of the cliffs. Tiny scrub-deer bounded away from them as they pushed through the undergrowth. Corinna swiped at thorny tendrils of milk-flower with a broken stick.

After they had been poking around for quite some time, Meonel suddenly stopped dead and said, 'Just look at that!'

Ahead of them, the thickly-clustered trunks thinned abruptly to leave a perfect circle of short, deer-nibbled grass. Sunlight fell down into the shaft between the trees like a curtain of water. To the left, a black finger of rock poked out onto the lawn from the dense foliage; the cliffs feeling their way into the wood. Corinna felt her skin prickle. Meonel strode out into the sunlight, turning round, hands on hip, nodding appreciatively. Corinna leaned against an amber-oak. It filled her with inexplicable dread to see Meonel standing out there. He looked so unprotected, so spot-lighted, so unsuspecting.

This is crazy, she thought. Not once on the journey north had she been prey to unrealistic fears; she was not a superstitious creature. She had been the one to comfort Rosanel, who had been a little jumpy now and then, especially at night, when large animals had roamed the shadows beyond their fires. Rosanel had told Corinna that, ever since she'd found out about the Greylids, she couldn't help feeling they must be watching the Freespacers' progress. Corinna had laughed away such fancies. She had never felt unseen eyes upon them, other than curious smooms and leap-dogs.

Thinking of animals, she wondered whether she ought to bring her two felids up here to see if they picked any unusual vibrations up. If the felids felt at ease in the valley, then Corinna would fight her reservations as being lingering fears of the city. She was just about to join Meonel in the glade, when he suddenly dropped his arms rigidly to his sides and said, 'By the Goddess, I don't believe it!'

Before Corinna could reach him he'd darted off towards the black rock. She stepped out onto the grass and looked up. Between the trees, she could see the black stone sloping back towards the main cliff, naked of clinging vines, moss or even the tenacious lichen that tended to cover everything on Artemis. She could see Meonel clambering upwards, his head tilted back. Above him, a huge cave mouth yawned silently over the highest trees. That alone was disconcerting, dark and hungry as it looked, but what froze Corinna's flesh was the fact that the finger of rock issuing onto the turf was cut and sculpted, to form a wide, shallow staircase winding up to the lip of the cave. It couldn't be natural; it was too regular, too smooth. Corinna wanted to call Meonel back, but was afraid to make too much noise. These steps had been hidden here for the Goddess knew how long. Could it be possible they were still used? Corinna sprinted forward, more afraid of being alone than concerned for Meonel's safety. She followed him up the stone steps.

Chapter Nine
The Cave

Farris crawled over the warm, spiky rock along the edge of the valley. It had been easy to follow Corinna and Meonel from the lake undetected. At first, he'd considered catching them up, walking with them. After all, there was no reason why he shouldn't, other than having to make conversation, at which he didn't particularly shine. But what an unbearable sweetness it would be to walk and talk with the tall, handsome Trotgardens; heroes of the Freespacers. Farris held no similar regard for anybody else; it was a naive and exaggerated worship. Then he'd visualised the impatient expressions on their faces if he'd announced his presence. No, he wouldn't be welcome. He wasn't even sure what motivated him to tail them, other than a dimly-recognised fantasy they'd notice him and invite him to join them. He kept just out of sight, always one curve in the path behind them.

When he'd reached the point where the Trotgardens had climbed out of the way of the spider-lizard nest, it had confused him for a moment or two. Where had they gone? He could still hear their voices faintly, although it was obvious they hadn't gone through the web. The female lizard had stood shifting her weight from side to side, somewhat agitated by the presence of all these humans. Her young had gathered together in a corner of the nest just below her perch, peeping in alarm. The lizard herself indicated the way Corinna and Meonel had gone. Turning her head from Farris to the narrow path above her, she stamped her wide, clawed feet and flicked out her tongue, gathering scents to identify whether any of these strange, upright creatures were hostile. Farris nimbly climbed up the rock and it didn't take him long to come across the low tunnel, still trickling stones from the Trotgardens' passage.

The discovery of the valley had delighted him. He'd been happy to let the Trotgardens stride out of his sight so he could investigate the caves in the cliffs. One of them had particularly taken his fancy. It had a dry, sandy floor and natural shelves where someone might climb and hide and dream. He silently claimed it as his own and hopped up to the highest shelf, huddling under the rock. All it needed was some lichen fronds strewn around to make it more comfortable. He could bring things from home to furnish it; a pan for water, dried meat to chew in the dark, perhaps a blanket for warmth. Here, he would be able to escape everyone else. If he needed company, he could try to tame some of the animals; perhaps a spider-lizard or a leap-dog pup. Lost in such pleasant reverie, it never occurred to him the Trotgardens might be there prospecting for territory of their own.

Considerable time had passed when Farris crawled out of the cave and jumped down into the grass below. The shadow of the cliff had lengthened. Scampering out of the gloom, he ran to the stream, lying down full length on the grass to put his face into the water. A risk maybe; there was no guarantee it wasn't sour, although he felt the valley was far too benevolent to poison him with sourwater. *I love this place*, he thought, almost ecstatic, rolling onto his back and throwing out his arms and legs into the sunlight. *This place, I think, loves me.* He was filled with joyful sensations that were partly erotic. He could feel the great weight of the cliff walls looming over him, pressing him down into the soil until he was dissolved into it, part of the valley itself, willingly helpless as the shadow of the cliff crept towards him.

After a while, he rolled onto his stomach and peered through the grass stalks at the distant wood. It was easy to see the flattened trail through the meadow the Trotgardens had left behind them. Farris considered they might be searching for building woods, although it wouldn't be easy to haul stuff back through the tunnel and down to the lakeside. Perhaps he should try to catch them up now. It was obvious from their trail that they hadn't come out of the wood yet, although there might be another way back to Freespace on the other side of the forest. It wouldn't hurt to find out and, anyway, Farris wanted to investigate the wood himself. He felt that at least he'd have something to say to the Trotgardens if he ran across them now. Surely, they'd have been as impressed with the valley as he was. Would they be angry if they thought he'd followed them, though? His sister had called him a creep. Wasn't it rather a creepy thing to do to follow people? *Don't be stupid*, he told himself. *People are crawling all over the hills by the dam. People may have come here before, lots of them. There's nothing strange about me being here too.*

He jogged through the grass towards the trees; a longer distance than it appeared. There was no sign of the Trotgardens, although once in the wood, their trail was very easy to follow, Corinna having smacked a wide path for herself with the stick. Farris could hear no voices. In fact, the whole wood was unusually quiet. Occasionally, a bird would flap among the branches out of sight, but there was no song of animal calls as one would expect. A haunted wood? Now Farris imagined himself dancing in moonlight with pale wraiths, running through the trees, surrounded by flying gossamer shapes, empathic to him alone.

Eventually he came to the glade where the stone steps led up the cave. Almost crying out with excitement, Farris ran towards the cliff. What was this? Would Corinna and Meonel be at the top? The steps were wider than a woman's stride and halfway up, Farris paused to catch his breath. He looked down at the glade, shining in the lengthening shadows. Could this be a Greylid path? He'd heard the stories, as had all the Freespacers, of how Elvon L'Belder had discovered the strange, hidden, alien race and been given their power. However, he had to admit there was no particular feeling of life around here, either alien or human, but someone had once carved this stairway - that was undeniable - and it was far more thrilling to think it might have been hewn by Greylid hands rather than those of earlier human fugitives from the south.

Reaching the mouth of the cave, Farris pressed himself against the cliff face and gazed out above the trees. There was only a narrow ledge to stand on and a stiff breeze plucked at his hair, blowing it into his eyes. The view was breathtaking. On his left side, the forest suddenly plummeted downwards as if the valley floor had been sliced away. Folds of rock, in bizarre patterns like petrified water, curved down on either side of the trees to a distant plain, where the smoke of Freespace Town could be seen drifting past the concealing cliffs. In the far distance, beyond the plain, Farris could see the purple smear of other mountains. He followed the ledge around the cliff for a while, past the cave mouth, discovering another flight of steps, these far steeper and narrower than those he'd climbed up. They were moss-covered and swathed with milk-flower thorn braids, descending swiftly into the sloping forest below. It was obvious that someone had recently cleared a path for themselves down to the trees. The moss was smudged and flattened, the briars kicked aside. Corinna and Meonel must have gone this way, undoubtedly considering this torturous path a quicker route back to the town than retreating through the valley.

Farris turned back to investigate the cave. It appeared dark and forbidding, the lair of unfriendly beasts, its steeply rising floor disappearing quickly into utter blackness beyond the opening. However, because he loved mystery and was not easily frightened, Farris willingly scrambled inside on hands and knees. The rock was warm and smooth beneath his fingers. Above him, the roof of the cave was hung thickly with crystalline straws, so perfectly formed they too appeared human-made. The walls that he could see were as smooth as the floor. Farris lay on his back on the rock, tilted towards the opening, staring up to where the crystal spears disappeared into darkness. He would have to bring some kind of torch with him next time so he could investigate further. Even though he could not see very much, the place felt enormous around him; a maze of hidden chambers, rock-bound lakes and cathedral halls. It had the calm, stately atmosphere of a temple. The Freespacers had no temple, offering their thanks to the Goddess under the open sky, dancing and singing together round a central fire by the light of the moons. Farris was well aware that their celebrations were more a social than religious activity. Now, perhaps, he had a temple of his own. He pressed his fingers hard against the rock. This whole place was a miracle; the valley, the forest, the cave. It was as if it had been created solely for him; all that he could ever want. Nearly all.

Farris closed his eyes and held his breath. He could feel the atmosphere of the cave soaking into his flesh; nurturing, comforting, vibrating with strength. For a brief second, light flashed across his inner vision as if someone had lit a torch beyond his closed lids. A needle of pain lanced through his head, gone before he could even cry out.

Farris opened his eyes and sat up. He was convinced he could hear the echo of some kind of vibration, which had faded before he could identify it. He shook his legs against the stone. Goddess, they felt numb and the numbness was creeping higher, claiming his thighs, his groin.

I need to move, he thought, *I'm getting cramp.*

He tried to kneel, wobbling precariously, suddenly aware that unless this sensation dissipated he was more or less immobile, helpless and alone in the cave.

Don't be stupid! he admonished himself, struggling to rise. *Get up and out of here!*

It was impossible.

With a whimper, he fell back against the rock, alert for sensations of fear. Nothing. Just the peculiar numbness. Perhaps he had trapped a nerve somehow. Time stood still. Then, his insides began to churn. This was not an unpleasant feeling, exactly, but very strange.

What's happening to me? Suddenly his lower body jerked as if pounded by unseen fists, his legs shuddered against the rock floor. An indescribable, delicious agony swept up his body like a spectral wind. It was an embrace, an overwhelming phantom of sheer desire, quickened by harrowing, obsessive love. His spine arched; he spasmed, spontaneously experiencing orgasm that was as excruciating as it was ecstatic.

Crying out, he slammed his hands against the floor, delirious with pleasure, lamenting the sensation's passing even before it left him.

He wasn't sure how long he lay there, recovering, panting on the stone floor. His mind was a blank, but for the simple, single thought that he'd been blessed with a divine gift. He did not question why, did not dare to, for fear of offending whatever power had possessed him.

Gradually awareness of time crept back into his mind. It was getting late. He could hear the mournful evening cries of birds outside, below, in the trees. He swallowed painfully, aware that all numbness had left his body, which felt drained, yet suffused by a delightful languor. Gingerly, he got to his feet, ignoring the uncomfortable sensation of viscous fluid adhering his clothes to his skin.

Outside, the quality of the light had changed. Farris knew he'd better start making tracks for home, and quickly. He must have been lying there longer than it seemed. The rock had become cool beneath him and the voice of the wind outside was a querying moan.

Farris hurried from the cave and was sliding down the steep steps to the forest before he even realised his skin was beginning to prickle with subliminal fear. Farris prided himself on never being afraid, but he didn't look back once as he plummeted down through the forest, ripping his clothes on thorns, choking on clouds of lichen dust. 'I will be late, I will be late', he chanted to himself, banishing the thought, the image, that high above him, unseen, the cave roared at the sky.

The Warmth, the Warmth has come! I felt it moving, a raw blaze over the rock. I felt the thoughts, the feelings; all that chaotic jumble. And it woke me. Yes. How long have I been away in the other land of nowhere? It feels like only yesterday the sky was turning above me. Oh, but I'm not complete, not any more. I remember now. Vague, it is, vague. Something missing. I smell for it in the land and the land has changed. Time has moved on without me. Desertion, sleep. But now the warmth has come. I must become fully awake. It is Time, and I am once again swimming the stream of it.

Chapter Ten
The Heart; the Heart's Desire

It had taken Corinna over half an hour to get Meonel out of the cave. Even as she'd called to him from the place where the light from outside still reached, confessing, 'Meonel, this place is creepy. Let's go. Please!' he'd been merely an echo from the darker regions beyond, making enthusiastic noises and exclamations of delighted surprise.

'Corinna, you should see this!'

Oh, no thank you. She'd instinctively hugged herself, hopping from foot to foot as if cold, avoiding looking upwards into the sinister palisade of ancient stalactites.

Meonel appeared to be utterly unaffected by an atmosphere Corinna could only experience as dank and forbidding. Even the steps outside had been unpleasant to walk upon, her imagination conjuring pictures of alien forms lumbering upwards over the same stone, dragging an etheric miasma of oddness behind them. This cave was just a culmination of the bad feelings she'd been picking up ever since they'd set foot in the valley, as if the feelings themselves emanated solely from this place.

'Meonel!' She called him. Why was he so stupid as to go venturing into the darkness? Anything could lurk there, anything. 'Meonel!' This time more shrill, garnished with fear.

He didn't answer.

'Damn you, damn you,' she muttered under her breath and went to the cave mouth, gazing out over the vast slope of trees to the left. If anything, her paranoia was worse standing there. She felt she was being watched. Typical. A quick, furtive glance over the shoulder into nothing. 'Bad place, bad place,' she murmured, shaking her head and clutching herself harder.

Carmenya's voice in her head said, 'Only old stone, C'rin. Look, it can't hurt you!' and there was an image of Carmenya behind her eyes, slapping the stone and laughing.

Corinna made a mewing noise to dispel the image and rubbed her face. Odd she should think of Carmenya like that; for so long she'd suppressed such daytime fantasies. She uttered a bitter, silent laugh. Fantasy! The fantasies of Corinna Trotgarden confined to happy, girlish friendship. Nothing else, ever, no! Don't think of that! She made another anguished noise and called Meonel again. If he didn't come now, she'd leave, damn him, leave him here alone and run home. Run, run, run. A prickle of imaginary cold agitated every hair on her body, making her uncomfortably aware of her flesh. She edged towards the open light, almost weeping with anger at her stepfather. Insensitive bastard!

A blast of wind caught her full in the face as she stepped from the shelter of the cave, making her eyes brim and spill. She groped blindly for a moment, feeling the world tilt beneath her feet. *Get out of here! Get...*

'Corinna, where are you going?' She felt Meonel's hand roughly grab her arm, pulling her back. 'That is not the easiest of ways out, dear!'

Corinna blinked rapidly and the world swam back into focus. No, it wasn't. She'd nearly ventured over a horribly steep incline blanketed by wicked thorn. 'Eyes running,' she said.

'Phenomenal place, that,' Meonel said, unperturbed by his step-daughter's near accident. 'I wonder who used it and why.'

'The way it felt to me I wouldn't be surprised if it was used for child sacrifice,' Corinna said.

Meonel shot her a quizzical look. 'My, we are being female and sensitive today, aren't we!' he said, an attempt at jocularity.

Corinna would normally respond to like tone. Today, she merely shrugged. 'Perhaps you shouldn't knock it, Meonel. I'm telling you I've been feeling bad about this place since we got here. You must be a brute not to sense it. Aren't you the expert on alien encounters?'She knew how to wound his vanity.

Meonel actually stopped to take stock of the place, an expression of irritability crossing his face. He felt nothing; she could tell.

'Can we go back now?' she said, already poking around for a way down through the trees.

Meonel sighed. Corinna usually shared his interest in exploration. It was unlike her to be so edgy. All the way north, they had veered off from the main party on any occasion when an interesting feature in the landscape had presented itself. Together, they had charted the journey, adding as many details to the map as possible, sharing an unspoken agreement that, once settled, they would set about exploring as much as possible of these northern lands. Corinna had actually said, on numerous occasions, that she firmly believed the Freespacers should not be bound by old conventions espoused by the city women, especially that of not venturing into new territory. 'This world of ours is a marvel,' she had said, 'and I want to cram as much of it into my lifetime as possible.' Today she was peevish and wanted home. Picking his way down the forest behind her, Meonel wondered if her instincts weren't correct, and if he wasn't the one at fault not to heed them.

Gick was waiting for them at the cottage. From Dannel's harried expression and Gick's exaggeratedly uncomfortable pose, it was clear she'd been there for some time and had been irritating Dannel into the bargain.

'Where have you been?' Gick demanded, jumping up when Corinna and Meonel opened the door.

'Well, we did spend some time looking for you,' Meonel said, 'But then managed to find your valley ourselves when you didn't show up.'

Gick snorted loudly. 'Didn't show up? Are you kidding? I waited for hours at the entrance to the trail and there was no sign of you! I've been wandering around the dam all day hoping you'd show your faces.'

After further remarks on both sides, it was soon established that the valley Corinna and Meonel had explored that day was not the one Gick had found herself.

'I don't know why you didn't see me,' she said grumpily.

Nor why you didn't see us, Corinna appended silently. Her jumpiness had increased. Why couldn't Meonel see the implications? Surely, they had been meant to find that valley today. Something had prevented them meeting up with Gick. Surely. Surely? No, that was crazy.

'Corinna, are you all right?' Gick asked.

After breadlemen, a meal to which Gick's unexpected presence had added a certain stilted atmosphere, Corinna asked her friend to go for a walk. She desperately needed to talk and although Gick could be abrasive, annoying and far too voluble, she was also someone Corinna trusted implicitly. They had been through so much together; their friendship bond was insoluble. However, Corinna was aware that under different circumstances, they might have disliked each other intensely. Trickster and bitch were personae that resonated fairly well, but the faces they tried to keep hidden, those of bitterness and bewilderment, were completely out of tune. Sometimes, looking at Gick, Corinna felt the girl was a living reminder of all the bad times she'd ever been through. The very things that made them close were deeply painful. Corinna knew Gick must feel that way too occasionally.

As they walked away from the Trotgarden cottage together, Corinna thought, *When, when, when will all that be over?*

Artemis was enjoying one of its most lovely evenings. The moons hung radiant in a perfect sky, and the horizon was aglow with vivid colours as the second sun dropped below the horizon. All around the town the astounding silhouettes of gigantic trees were stark against the sunset. The air was not too cool, fragranced by a hundred aromas of earth and plant, alive with the night-calls of birds and animals, only half of which had been identified or even yet seen by the Freespacers. From a nearby hut came the sweet, wistful melody of a woodflute.

'So, what's on your mind?' Gick asked carelessly, kicking up leaves.

'I had the weirdest feeling today, Gick. It was completely new yet it brought back so much.'

They had come to the edge of the dwellings where arbour lizards raised flamboyant tufts to the sky and sang their sad songs. Corinna sat down on a tuffet and stared at the sunset.

Gick remained standing. 'I thought something had happened. You weren't a bitch once over dinner.'

I don't feel like laughing, Corinna thought, and didn't.

Gick sighed and squatted down beside her. 'So?'

'That valley we found, and the cliffs and the cave. All that. I hated it Gick. It was... It was, oh Goddess, this sounds so ignorant, but it was *evil,* or at least that was how it came across to me. Meonel felt nothing. Am I going mad?'

Gick was quiet for a moment, stirring soil with a sharp twig, swirls and swirls. She jabbed the dirt and the stick broke. 'C'rin, we have our scars, yeah?'

Corinna blinked in reply, her gaze flickering away from the cruel marks on Gick's face, similar to her own, and the place where Gick's ears had been cut from her head, hidden beneath her shaggy hair.

'Yes, we both have our scars.'

Gick squirmed uncomfortably. 'What I mean is, all that happened to us, it must have affected us in all kinds of ways. Let's face it, none of it was natural. People aren't meant to suffer that kind of torment...' She shrugged helplessly.

'What you're saying is, I've got some kind of mental problem stemming from what happened in Silven Crescent,' Corinna said in a flat tone. 'I can understand you thinking that, but why should it manifest now, just as we're getting settled? I've been fine all the way here: optimistic, strong, fairly happy.'

'That's just it. We *are* here. We *are* getting settled. Maybe you had no time to dwell on past events before. It was all travel and worry about getting food and shelter, worry about possible pursuit from the south. We had no time...'

'Have you felt anything then, Gick, anything different since we came here?'

'No.'

'Then...?'

'It was just a suggestion. The other explanation is that you're damn right and Meonel is a dank-ass. There's only one way to find out.'

'Go back. With you. I was afraid you'd suggest that.'

'I didn't. You beat me to it! Got any other ideas, though? You have to set your mind at rest, C'rin. These people *need* you and you *can't* fall apart on them.'

Corinna smiled at the sarcasm. 'OK, but not yet. I need a few days to get all objective about it.'

'Anytime.'

'You won't go up there by yourself?'

Gick looked up sharply at the urgency in Corinna's voice. 'No, why should I?' She shook her head. 'Sometimes, C'rin you are one weird lady.'

'I know. Bear with me.'

Gick sighed and smiled. 'Well, I've done that before and I sort of trust your judgment.'

'Thanks Gick.'

'Any time.' Gick got up to leave. 'I'm shattered. Are you staying here awhile?'

'I think so.'

Corinna watched Gick saunter off between the huts before settling with a sigh to watch the sunset again. Already she felt a little easier inside. Perhaps Gick was right and it was just some kind of air bubble from the past surfacing in her mind that had made her so jumpy today. Maybe. We'll see.

And now I must pull from the stone, pull through. More than a winged thought, more than a feeling; I must kindle form for myself. I stretch out beyond the stone and there are a multitude of sparks glittering far below, a multitude of jumbled thoughts and desires. I want the warmth again, the living heat of their crude machines. I want to touch it. Too long alone, I must measure my actions. Too long alone, but I always knew they'd come back...

Meera the priestess sat cross-legged before her roughly-made altar. It was time for her nightly meditation. As usual, there were many things for her to ponder on, problems to be solved for Freespacers who'd arrive at her hut in the morning for advice. She smiled to herself, lighting a candle to sanctify the atmosphere of her crude little home. This was a very different procedure from her regular devotions back in the city, where she'd walked the solemn, majestic halls of the High Temple and worked her magics in comfortable and well-equipped chambers, aided by her sisters in the priestesshood. Still, the Goddess' work had nothing to do with external surroundings; that was just for human comfort. Perhaps it was an important life-lesson for her to learn how to operate alone and without the ceremonial props of the temple. It was hard for her. She wondered why no other priestesses had fled the city, why she had to be the only one. Goddess knows, more were needed.

In times of stress - and there'd been many on the journey north - the people had turned to Meera for reassurance and, if the truth were to be faced, miracles too. Now, she'd set about organising training for any young people who were interested in the spiritual path, but the half dozen or so who seemed most suitable, had to spend more time on mundane matters than esoteric ones at present. They found it hard to focus their inner powers, having to concentrate so much on day to day concerns, tasks which were often physically exhausting. Meera's only help must come from the Goddess herself. She'd supposed she would feel closer to the Lady out here in the wilderness, but so far she'd only become closer to humanity. Another lesson?

Meera sighed. Perhaps soon, matters would clarify in her head.

Closing her eyes to shut off the most distracting aspects of the outer world, she concentrated on sensing the path of the moons as they began to glide up through the sky for their graceful, nightly promenade. The priestess sucked in long, even breaths, sinking effortlessly into the preliminary stages of deep trance. Silently, she began an invocation to the Goddess, Parthenos, Lady of Artemis, visualising her with arms outstretched to embrace the whole world and all that lived upon it.

Let me feel you, she thought, opening herself up, seeking that distant divine spark that was always tantalisingly visible but so beyond contact.

Suddenly, Meera was suffused with heat, which took her breath away. Her head jerked up from her chest. She gasped, opening her eyes quickly, fearing her candle had ignited something in the hut. But it wasn't fire. Her rough blankets, her simple pots, her jumble of clothes all seemed to glow with a vague, blue light. Almost beyond the edges of perception, a faint threnody as of a far choir raising their voices in praise reverberated through her inner ear. She felt a bloom of joy uncurl within her heart. Her whole body was comprised of glowing petals, opening, opening, revealing an unbearable splendour.

Tears ran down her face. She raised her arms, laughed through the tears. At last the prayers had been answered. The vigil was over. 'Lady, you are here!' she cried.

Meanwhile, the erstwhile general of Yani Gisbandrun's military force, Carmenya Oralien, tossed and wriggled on her narrow bed. Her sleep was pervaded by startling dreams, snatches of amplified conversation as if heard through a partial faint, brief phrases of music, laughter, the sound of clinking glass.

She awoke with a start, breathless, already sitting up in bed when she opened her eyes. Her body was drenched in sweat, immediately cooling. For a moment she dared to wish there was someone with her now, someone to talk to, someone to make things go back to normal.

Am I ill, sickening for something?

Strong moonlight fell across her shivering body. Normally she found it soothing but tonight it seemed intrusive, harsh. She went to the makeshift window, planning to fasten the rags that served as curtains more securely. Something caught her eye outside.

She squinted, drawing the curtains to a crack, feeling somehow vulnerable. Across from her own shack, just a short distance away, a wavering figure was limned against Gabriel Lammeran's tent. It shone, it faded, it swelled, it held out its arms to Carmenya where she peered rigidly from the window.

A woman, tall, glowing, like a silver lady come from the moons.

The apparition made a vague gesture, as if of farewell, before drifting off between the listing tents and shacks of northern Freespace town.

Carmenya heard a felid yowl nearby, fretful. She gulped air. Had she seen that? No, a dream, hallucination. She was still half asleep. That was it. Or had it been some poor girl sleepwalking? Yes, yes, that was likely.

Carmenya fastened her curtains tightly together and sat on her bed, staring at the shuttered window, for quite some time to follow.

It may have also been a coincidence that Rosanel Garmelding, once a leader of the rebel force in Silven Crescent, should have woken up convinced she'd heard the voice of her lost lover Elvon L'Belder urging her to get out of bed. 'Come on, Ros, there's still work to do,' he'd said, in that irritable, harried tone he'd used sometimes when things had been particularly rough for them.

'All right, all right, I'm coming,' she'd answered, before realising she'd been asleep. 'Elvon!' she'd hissed, quickly sitting up in bed, but the room had been empty of presences, empty of ghosts, empty even of memories.

Chapter Eleven
Speed Lady

The Astracruise flyer, Speed Lady, was a scintillating arrow soaring above the marsh. Glancing out of the side port, Zy could see a vast herd of brindled oxen browsing through the shallows, their backs supporting ditch-cranes who pecked at insect parasites in the thickly furred hide. The marsh gleamed like a vast lake of liquid silver, dotted here and there with spinneys of leaning trees, odd saurian-looking humps of rock, and lawn islands where the old farms of the marsh families still stood, now worked by women from the city.

Good scope for a floating hotel with daily excursions into the marsh. Plenty of exotic wild-life around and how about a chalet bar on one of those weird back-bones of rock?

Zy already had ideas, but of course they were still too near to Silven Crescent here. He picked up his pocket viewscope from the ledge under the sloping front visor, and flicking it into life, gazed through it at the horizon. Marsh, marsh and more marsh for as far as the eye could see. There was a strange topographical phenomenon just a little further on, though, where the land plunged abruptly downwards as if the whole continent had broken in two and half of it had sunk. He requested Speed Lady to increase her velocity and, as the flyer soared over the cliff, he sucked in his breath at the amazing vista of sparkling waterfalls plunging hundreds of feet into a reed-tasselled lake below. What a site! Still too close, though? Hmm.

He scrabbled for his notefile among the detritus of cigarette packets, fast-food wrappers and crumpled worksheets on the ledge. *Must tidy the little lady up some time,* he thought, activating the notefile. *Worth taking a bit of data here.*

His employers must decide whether the site was too close to the city or not, but personally Zy considered it perfect for a graceful, facility-packed floating hotel that only the richest of galaxy travellers could afford to patronise. There'd be other places more suited to economy chalets, he was sure.

He told the flyer to carry out the appropriate scans and connected his notefile to the flyer's intelligence so she could sort the data out into an easily readable form. The Speed Lady was completely trustworthy; she'd carried out more surveys than he had. Zy requested a north-westerly course and slithered out from his seat.

Behind him, in the main cabin, he could hear the murmur of female voices; Alouine Crestick and Welma Barbarel, busy assassinating his character, no doubt. This was going to be a long journey. Flexing his shoulders and trying to stretch his arms in the cramped cabin, Zy squeezed past the jutting knees of the women and manoeuvred his way to the coffee dispenser. He considered that this little bird just wasn't built for three, especially when two of them were great hulking Amazons like these. Graceless monsters, the pair of them, he thought. And why the hell had they needed to bring all that garbage with them? As far as he'd been told, they were there simply to keep an eye on him, for his own safety as well as that of the women of Artemis. Now, they sneakily bring on board all this equipment for gathering plant and soil samples. They were using Astracruise's flyer and his good will to further their own investigation of their planet. How convenient for them.

Zy swallowed a Mangine capsule along with the bitter, synthetic-tasting coffee. He pulled a face. Might as well stay up front. The women had fallen silent when he'd barged in and were now appraising him with steely faces.

'Ladies, you're such good company,' he said, and saluted them with his plastic cup.

Their expressions didn't change.

He rolled his eyes and ducked back into the control cabin.

The flyer skimmed along with ease, untroubled by its extra load. Zy sat down and patted the warm styroskin above the control pad. 'Good girl,' he said. 'You're doing fine. Which is more than can be said for me!'

'Talking to yourself Larrigan?'

He turned around and saw Alouine Crestick wedged in the doorway. 'Yeah, I have to talk to somebody. What can I do for you?'

'We think it would be best to land the craft on the next sizable isle. We could all do with some exercise.'

They'd only been travelling for half a day and, for Speed Lady, at a comparatively leisurely pace. Zy decided to be awkward for the sake of it. 'Well, that's tough, Ms. Crestick. You wanted to come along. I'm not going to waste time while you and your lady friend stretch your legs. If I set you down on the next isle, you stay there and I carry on without you. That's a promise. I'm working to a time limit, remember; your government's as well as my own company's. You don't want me on this planet and I don't want to be here, so let's make this trip as brief as possible, huh?'

'You are an objectionable stripe of piss, Larrigan,' Alouine Crestick said, and stomped back to her friend.

Zy smiled and slumped down in his seat. They'd only been away from the city for a few hours, and already all attempts at civility had broken down. 'Fuck 'em,' Zy thought and settled down to a Mangine-vision-filled snooze.

If he'd been alone, Zy wouldn't have set the flyer down at all, but for a minimum of exploratory forays to get the real ambience of the place. There was plenty of room on board for a single person to be perfectly comfortable. However, what with the women and all their equipment, he knew he'd have to comply with Alouine Crestick's suggestion sooner or later, just so they could get some proper sleep. Speed Lady was generously equipped with bivouac supplies and was capable of constructing an impenetrable safety net around herself and the sleepod for as long as they needed it. Nothing hostile would be able to break through it. It was an unavoidable nuisance, but nothing could be done, so he was philosophical enough to put up with it and get on with the job as best he could. He estimated leaving the marsh's vicinity sometime the next day, heading due north. Then, distanced enough from the Artemisian civilisation, he could take more time looking around.

Even as he drifted into dreams, Zy was wondering how long he'd be able to put up with the women before things got really nasty.

Welma Barbarel woke him abruptly from a troubled sleep some hours later. He started violently when she touched his shoulder and for a moment couldn't remember where or what he was. An instant of complete estrangement from reality. Odd. He wriggled up in his seat, mouth bitter from Mangine residue. 'Yes, what is it?'

'The flyer's stopped,' Welma said. 'We thought we should wake you.'

'What do you mean?' Zy brushed back his hair and leaned forward. Dammit, the woman was right! Speed Lady was hovering effortlessly at a standstill only a hundred feet above the marsh. Had he kicked some directional pad in his sleep or something?

'Lady, what the hell are you doing?' he asked.

The console monitor was a disquieting mess of fuzziness but, after an insulting pause, responded to his queries. It didn't shed much light on the situation however. The flyer, although responsive to vocal interrogation, had no voice of her own, and fluttered a series of garbled messages across the screen.

'What is this?' Zy muttered.

'What's the matter with it?' Welma Barbarel asked. She sounded frightened.

'Just go back and sit down,' Zy replied, in a voice calmer than he felt. 'It's OK. Just a quirk. Must be something to do with data collection.'

This seemed to satisfy the Artemisian who ducked back into the main cabin.

'Lady, come *on!*' Zy whispered. He transferred the controls to manual and the ship responded immediately, sweeping forward once more. How peculiar.

He interrogated the computer, but all it would say was, 'Direct command input.' It wouldn't specify what the command had been or how it had received it.

'You take your orders from me, my little silver beauty,' Zy admonished, wondering, with dread, if there was some awful bug lurking in the flyer's computerised depths. It had never happened before and he'd been partnered with the Speed Lady for five trips now. He must have knocked something or even muttered something in his sleep; it was the only explanation. He hoped.

They set down for the night on an uninhabited isle. Speed Lady, exhibiting no further irregular behaviour, shook out the sleepod from her side and erected her glowing security net. The women insisted on going for a run round the island and Zy was happy to let them. Hopefully, some native beast would attack them, thus relieving him of their unwelcome company. No such luck. Half an hour later, they returned, with glowing faces and a little more *joie de vive* than usual. Zy asked the flyer to create a portal in the net to let them back in.

The suns were setting in multi-coloured splendour, dying the surrounding water deep red and violet. Zy sat on the grass, smoking an off-world lotus-herb cigarette, leafing through the photo-reconstructions Speed Lady had made of the prospective site they had passed earlier. He'd also asked for a printout of all transactions for the day, and had been presented with an astounding array of hieroglyphs which clearly depicted the occasion of Speed Lady's abnormal pause. Once they'd landed, he'd checked all the systems as best he could but had found no irregularity.

Welma Barbarel came and squinted over his shoulder,

hunkering down behind him. He had no fear that she'd be able to understand what he was looking at.

'What went wrong today then?' she asked.

'Nothing went wrong.'

'Then why are you worried?'

'I'm not.' He sidled away from her. These macho women upset him, almost as if they were likely to break out in fits of hysterical violence any minute. He also realised that they were every bit as intuitive as the women he had as friends far beyond this backwater world.

'You had the flyer on auto-heading. Why should it have stopped?'

'And what the hell do you know about it?' Zy asked, getting to his feet and slipping all the papers back into a folder.

'Don't think we're stupid just because we don't have all the benefits of sophisticated equipment like you do!' Welma said, folding her arms and assuming a stubborn expression. 'If there's something wrong, I think you should tell us. What would happen if there was some kind of fault again when you were out cold in drug-land? I think you should tell Alouine and I more about the running of the flyer, don't you? For your own safety, surely, if not for ours.'

He had to admit she had a point, although he had no fears that Speed Lady would act up again. However, it was impossible to be too careful, and once away from the marsh, they'd all be in unknown territory. He raised a placatory hand. 'O.k., you win. I don't know what happened today, but I have a feeling I must have said something in my sleep that the computer thought was a command. It's voice activated, you see. Whatever garbage I came out with must have confused the system. It's the only explanation. These survey flyers have unimpeachable records for reliability and I happen to know this particular girl quite well. It must have been my fault.'

'But you can't be positive.'

'No,' Zy conceded reluctantly. 'I can't, which is why I'll give you two some instruction tomorrow. It'll help to pass the time anyway, won't it?' He tried a winning smile.

Welma sighed and shook her head at him, before retreating smartly into the sleepod.

Zy couldn't face sharing sleeping quarters with the women and wrapped himself up in a silver sleeping bag on the grass. For a while, he lay staring beyond Speed Lady's exquisite tapered nose at the deepening sky. 'Goodnight, you weird little world,' he said and, taking the precaution of popping another Mangine capsule beneath his tongue, turned on his side to prepare for dream-crowded sleep.

The marsh chittered its night language of insect, plant and animal voice around him, and Speed Lady's svelte body clicked faintly as she cooled beneath the moons. Deep in her blinking, whispering depths, the flyer's synthetic brain listened to a wavering signal borne on the motionless air. It came from the north.

Chapter Twelve
The Companions

Northwest, the land began to dry out; the silver puddles and spear-shallows becoming flats of long, yellow lichen-grass, pointing east away from the wind that sliced down from the western mountain range. Zy was astounded to learn that these mountains had no name, and immediately termed them Larrigan's Back, making a notation to such in his cartograscan. The women clearly didn't know whether to be outraged at such effrontery or amused. They said nothing, but crowded into the control cabin to use Zy's viewfinder, exclaiming to each other over new features of the land that, until now, they would never have imagined.

Speed Lady had been behaving herself ever since the incident further south, but Zy couldn't help feeling his little flyer was merely biding her time before springing another unwelcome emergency on him. He hoped it was paranoia rather than instinct that prompted such feelings. As he had promised, Welma Barbarel and Alouine Crestick had received preliminary instruction as to the controlling of the Speed Lady. It seemed this simple act of capitulation on his part had lessened the women's need for antagonistic defence, or perhaps they were simply getting used to having him around. Whatever the reason, relations had eased between them all, although they could still hardly be termed congenial. That suited Zy fine. He had no wish to cultivate friendships with the women. However pleasant they attempted to be, they still grated on his nerves.

There was so much to investigate in this land. Zy couldn't help feeling more and more impressed by what he saw, nor, he had to admit, prevent a developing fondness for this little world. Animals they encountered had never learned to fear humanity and, if approached cautiously, appeared to regard the travellers with the same amount of curiosity as the humans felt for them. On one occasion, a pair of carnivorous feline smooms had approached them as they rested within Speed Lady's protective cocoon for the night. Zy was amused by their yowling conversation, which sounded uncannily as if they were swapping remarks about what they'd found. One of them was even brave enough to try and sniff the net, but was rewarded by a repulsion force that sent both animals high-tailing it swiftly into the trees.

Zy had also been mystified by the effects of certain insect bites. Although some of them could inflict very painful wounds, others had saliva which actually contained healing chemicals, thus speeding the recovery of the host animal's flesh after the parasite had fed. 'It's astounding,' Zy said, 'and so polite!'

Welma Barbarel told him about the floating forests of Ire and Penitence. 'There,' she said, 'you might find the fauna and flora less accommodating. The insect bites in those places can be fatal.'

'Luckily, I don't plan to cite them as locations for resorts,' Zy responded with a smile.

'You really think Artemis will attract tourists, then?' Welma asked. 'I wouldn't have thought we have much to offer the galaxy-roving sophisticates of your worlds.'

Zy shook his head. 'You must not think so badly of us, Ms. Barbarel. Most people would look on this place as a paradise, and treat it as such. We're not the marauding bunch of hooligans you seem to believe we are.'

Welma shrugged, looking anxious. 'I just wish things could stay as they are, or at least that we could investigate this world ourselves.'

They had been out from Silven Crescent for nearly two weeks now, a period longer than Zy had envisaged. Neither had they travelled as far as he'd hoped, mainly because their landings had become more frequent. So many enticing locations presented themselves that he felt he had to experience them first hand. Also, the women spent a considerable amount of time collecting plant samples. The flyer cabin was virtually full of bulging bags and boxes, smelling like a greenhouse. Zy didn't mind this. He was quite happy to sprawl out on some rocky shore and lose himself in a Mangine dream while Welma and Alouine hunted round niches and crannies for new plant life. In fact, he realised, they were spending more and more time on the ground, just looking around. Several times they had also landed on occupied isles, where they were courteously welcomed by the farming communities that lived there. Alouine Crestick had advised against explaining to people, in too much detail, exactly what they were doing out on the marsh, so Zy told the farm people he was an off-world historian gathering information about Artemis. This gave him an adequate excuse for collecting as many local stories as people were willing to recite to him. It was the first time he came across the term Greylid and, although his natural scepticism more or less decided for him such creatures could not exist, the simple fact that nearly everybody he interviewed knew some tale or another about them made him begin to question such a rigid view. Could it be possible Artemis still harboured vestiges of an earlier race? Hard evidence was non-existent. The Greylids seemed like fairy folk; retreating and ghostly. More likely to be myth, of course, but one particular girl impressed Zy with her account, in which she believed implicitly without embarrassment, of coming across a strange being on the marsh, in full daylight, who gave her what appeared to be some kind of sweetbread.

'And did you eat it?' Zy asked, aware of his cynicism reflected in the girl's eyes.

She shook her head. 'Would you?' she responded, quite rightly he felt.

The creature, conveniently concealed in ragged robes, had marched off smartly once she had accepted the gift. She had not seen where it had gone to. When she got home, the gift, which she had stowed in a pocket, had vanished.

Zy recorded many such stories; the marsh seemed full of them. Apart from arousing his own curiosity, he felt the tales would help to spice up the Astracruise advertising brochures once the resorts were completed. It was customary to insert a little local legend into such literature.

At the northern edge of the marsh, they passed over the last settlements, a more primitive culture than that of Silven Crescent and her perimeter conurbations. Welma told Zy the people practised a very ancient form of religion there and did not recommend a landing. From what he could gather, these communities were virtually separate from Artemisian culture; another fact the government in the city had neglected to mention. Zy felt, that for this reason alone, they should at least try to contact these settlements. It was only fair they should be advised of what was being planned for Artemis. But the evident discomfort this suggestion generated in his companions eventually impressed Zy that it might not be a good idea. He would simply write it up in his report and let someone higher up in the Astracruise structure deal with it, someone more suited to diplomatic activities.

Now Speed Lady had skimmed over an invisible boundary and they were flying above uncharted country. He had expected the women to be diffident about treading this alien soil, but he'd been wrong. They were so eager to become acquainted with it, the original reason for their being there seemed to have been forgotten, and the more paranoiac of their precautions concerning rogue settlements had lessened considerably.

They had set down for the night on a wide ledge of rock, overlooked by the foothills of Larrigan's Back. Alouine was building a fire; the travellers had become accustomed to doing this most nights now. It created a cosy yet stimulating atmosphere; civilisation might as well be nonexistent this far from the city.

Welma came to sit next to Zy against Speed Lady's warm hull, bringing him a mug of silver-tea brewed over the fire. He reflected that, contrary to whatever expectations he'd had, or decisions he'd made, he and the women were beginning to get along pretty well now. He saw in Welma an inquisitive intelligence and great undeveloped capabilities, while the brusquer Alouine possessed an almost grinding streak of practicality, a gift for problem-solving. Basically, they were beginning to regard each other as fellow human beings rather than adversaries. The exploration of the terrain and their mutual interest in all they discovered united them in a sense of wonder. Plans for returning to the city had become very vague; Zy wondered whether the three of them would just keep on travelling until, he thought with a wild thrill, they found something completely fantastic.

As if picking up Zy's thoughts, Welma sighed and said, 'Sometimes, I wish we didn't have to go back.'

'You don't. I can leave you anywhere,' Zy said lightly, sipping tea.

Welma laughed forlornly. 'I wouldn't let myself. I'd say no, I know I would, if you really offered that.' She didn't sound too happy about that.

Zy thought he'd probe further. 'I was under the impression all you Artemisians were happy in your womblike environments. I'm surprised you even want to leave.'

Welma sneaked a glance to where Alouine was preparing the evening meal. 'I've just come to love all this open space,' she said. It's so wasted. We should use it or at least *be* in it.'

'You will, shortly.'

'No.' Welma fixed him with a stripping stare. 'You will. Not us. If we come after you, we shall be like danks trotting at your heels, doing what your people tell us and where. I know this.'

Zy sat up straight. 'Welma, you're so short-sighted! Astracruise will be looking for smart employees to help run these places. Apply now. I could put a word in for you and who knows where that could lead.' He raised an arm to the sky. 'Star travel, working on other, distant worlds. Why moan about waste, when your own life is so narrow?'

Welma continued the stare. He could see her arguing with herself; loyalty to all that Artemis stood for against the urge for adventure and freedom. 'I'm not sure our government will allow us to do things like that,' she said. 'I'm also part of that government, being in Gulding's staff. I have to set an example.'

'That's just stupid!'

She shrugged again. 'Perhaps. I've not grown up with your freedom. We were always told that your kind of liberty leads to excess and destruction. No, I'm not stupid. I know this is true, but I can also appreciate it allows limitless opportunity. What is worse? A constrained society relatively without corruption, or an uncontrolled, chaotic society that allows every person to do as they wish? Not all people out there can be bad, I know, but it's such a risk to let their ways infiltrate our culture. I can see the reasons against it, can't you?'

'I can see them, certainly, but I can't agree with them', Zy said, although he didn't think the universe to be the black and white place Welma thought it was. 'Personally, I would rather have the free choice to fight tooth and claw in a human jungle than live without fear like a tame dog, incapable of and prevented from making my own life decisions.'

Welma flushed. 'Well, as I've always been a... a *tame dog*, perhaps I don't know any better.'

He had offended her. 'You choose your shackles, Welma,' he said carefully. 'Given the chance, all human beings snatch at freedom. It's a desire that goes back in our gene pool far further than any decrees by Artemisian governments. You just have to wake up and realise it.'

'You're determined to make me doubt, aren't you!' She sounded amused rather than angry.

He shrugged. 'Come now, if your people's way is right, there would be no room for doubt, surely?'

She digested this statement with unconcealed agitation.

'What you're trying to say is that people should do what they want to whenever they please. How can that be right? We need the law, restrictions upon people's activities, otherwise there'd be total chaos. Nobody would be safe. Doubts and questions about this come from personal greed, or selfishness. We have to fight to contain them and learn we can't have our own way all the time.'

'Believe that if you wish,' Zy said. 'But with true freedom there would be no reason why your personal, selfish desires need be detrimental to anyone.'

'Really? What if I wanted to kill someone?'

'And why would you want to do that?'

Welma made an abrupt gesture with one hand. 'Any reason, oh, I don't know, I wanted her house, her lover, more power.'

Zy raised unconsciously triumphant fingers. 'There you have it. Power. Power, and material and emotional possessiveness. Free yourself from those outmoded concepts and you no longer have a desire to kill. The only acceptable power is that from within, not that held over anybody else.'

'It would only work if everyone felt like that. It's impossible.'

'Perhaps. We can only live by giving example.'

'I don't believe you live like that.'

'Oh I do... He grimaced. '*Sometimes.* You can believe that or not. Each one of us is comprised of many different personalities, Welma. Some of them are more likable than others. Currently...' Zy waved a hand at the surroundings, 'because of this lovely country, good, clean air and blissful days of relaxation my spiritual self is out in force.'

'I wish I could say the same. All the things you find so moving only serve to fill me with discontent.' Welma shook her head. 'You certainly give me much to think about, Mr. Larrigan.'

'Good.'

Chapter Thirteen
The Imperative

The following morning, Speed Lady lifted into a thin mist and headed northwest once more. Zy, sprawling in the control cabin with his feet up, considered the flyer seemed a little sluggish that day. Imagination?

Welma, forever the confirmer of his worst suspicions, put her head around the door and said, 'Are we shaking or vibrating or something? The flyer doesn't feel right somehow.'

'Could be the weather,' Zy answered, the best reason he could think of at the time. He made a few brief interrogations of the computer. 'Everything seems fine,' he said.

Behind him, he could hear Alouine grumbling from the cabin. Of the two, he definitely preferred the company of Welma. Not just because she was younger and more attractive to look at, but because she was without doubt the more intelligent and adventurous. He'd got used to the fact that they both tended to stomp around like heavy youths, supposing it was something to do with their military training.

Welma brought him a beaker of coffee and asked if she could use the videoscan in an attempt to penetrate the mist.

'Go ahead,' Zy said, amused by the way the woman squeezed into the spare seat, furrowing her brow and stroking keypads as if she'd been doing it for years.

The computer graphically presented a picture of the surrounding countryside on Welma's screen. Zy knew she loved the novelty of his machines. 'Oh look!' she said, pointing and looking up at him. 'To the west, there. Wouldn't that make a good location for you?'

Zy leaned over to take a look. He saw yet another of Artemis' picturesque lakes, flanked by cliffs and waterfalls, but this one was unique in that it embraced a series of large islands, like gigantic stepping stones. The water around them was virtually hidden by wide pads of water plant sprouting flowering heads on long stalks, the blooms as wispy as if made from exotic feathers. He increased the magnification on the picture. Soon, the graphics were detailed enough to reveal the dark green velvet of moss carpets, the snowy banks of resting ditch-cranes - a smaller species than those found on the marsh, whose long, white tails trailed behind them like peacocks'.

'Looks wonderful, Welma,' Zy said and she smiled in self-congratulation.

It was a good idea to let Welma near the scanners, Zy thought. She'd probably picked up far more than he would have done, simply because it was so exciting for her to use them. 'Let's head west, then.' He issued a few corrections to the computer.

'It does look perfect, Mr. Larrigan. Perhaps I shouldn't have pointed it out to you,' Welma said mischievously. 'Now I expect you'll fill it full of hotels on stilts with lights and things.'

'Naturally. Stop complaining. You'd have never laid eyes on the place but for Astracruise.'

The flyer began to sweep around towards the site, lifting momentarily above the mist where the suns, Shamberel and Guimo, poured down their searing heat. Soon, the mist would be burned away and then, Zy decided, the three of them could have a holiday beside the new site. Then Speed Lady began to shudder; once at first, like a flea-bitten cat, and then repeatedly, as if suffering a hail of bullets, or worse.

'What's wrong?' Alouine had hauled herself into the cabin.

'Get back!' Zy snarled. 'With your weight up front as well as ours, we'll be nose-deep in mud soon!'

Alouine looked too alarmed to let his insult affect her. 'What's wrong, Welma?'

'I don't know.' Welma looked questioningly at Zy who

was frantically whispering short commands at the computer, his hands flying over the flight console, seeking errors.

'It doesn't want to go west,' he said. 'This is crazy. Like before... maybe.' He switched to manual, which took much more effort than it should have. Twice, Speed Lady ignored his request, her computer refusing to surrender control, like a ravenous dog hanging on to a raw bone. 'You bitch!' He slapped the console and the flyer dipped alarmingly, tilting the world.

Alouine covered her face with a yelp and Welma gripped the edge of the videoscan, her eyes wide, her mouth gaping in a silent scream.

The flyer herself was howling like a mad woman as he turned her towards the west. All suppleness had left the controls. It felt as if someone had poured syrup in the works. They flew headlong towards the lake, too low, the dark fern-shrouded cliffs growing larger and larger in their sight, Speed Lady screaming towards them as if on self-destruct. Swearing and praying out loud, Zy wrestled with the controls, his palms almost too wet to be of any use, his passengers silent with dread, staring straight ahead, doubtlessly visualising their own deaths with excruciating detail.

Then, with a sigh, Speed Lady dipped obligingly to the right, tilted her wings a little before coming obediently to rest on the largest island. The only sound other than that of her sighing engines shutting down was of rasping breath. The three travellers did not speak for over a minute.

'Let's get out,' Zy said at last, pulling himself together.

Obediently, trusting him because that was all they could do, the women followed him out of the flyer, jumping down onto the spongy, fern-carpeted moss, too shaken to take in the delicious scent of the place or the enchanting sights.

On the ground it was more beautiful than the videoscan had implied, but the travellers were far too disorientated and scared to take any pleasure in it.

Zy walked to the edge of the island, looking down onto a

slim beach of blue-grey sand. He squatted down, took deep breaths.

'What are we going to do?' Welma Barbarel had come up behind him. 'Do you know what's wrong with the flyer?'

'That's my problem!' he shouted, angry because he did not know the answer.

'Hardly! We're stuck here too!'

'I'm not getting in that thing again!' Alouine had stomped up to join them, her voice gravelly with fear. 'So much for your wonderful technology, Larrigan. Danks and skippers are much more reliable.'

Zy jumped up. 'Then why don't you, Alouine Crestick, go and catch yourself a couple of danks and fuck off back to your damn city. I don't need your crap remarks!'

'That might be a good idea,' Welma said.

'What?'

'Well, I mean, if the flyer is irreparable, we'll have to get back somehow, won't we? Surely, we could catch ourselves a few danks and then head back to the marsh. Someone there will have a skipper we can hire to get us back to the city.'

'I've seen no danks around,' Alouine said, clearly annoyed that Welma hadn't backed up her attack on Zy.

'Danks are everywhere on Artemis,' Welma said.

'How can you know that?' Zy was too exasperated to be more acidic.

Welma shrugged. 'I've been keeping records of the animals we've passed. Even when the herd animals are completely different to those of the marsh, there are still groups of danks around. We passed some yesterday evening, just before we landed. They can't be far away.'

'Hmm. I'll check the flyer over first. It seems as if the malfunction was caused because Speed Lady didn't want to fly in the direction I'd chosen. This is impossible, because the computer can't make that kind of decision, unless it's to avoid danger, and even then it would have told us the reasons. However, I think I've heard of something like this happening before. I must have accidentally set some failsafe co-ordinates on a north-south axis. There are tests I can run.'

'You check your flyer over as much as you like, Larrigan,' Alouine said sarcastically, 'but you're a fool if you trust it again.'

'Nonsense, it must simply be because of an error I haven't picked up yet. I'll run the tests from the manual. Anyway, if it is stuck on a north-south axis, there's no reason why we can't just turn round. The chances are, we'll be able to fly back to the city yet.'

'Not with us on board you won't!' Alouine cried. 'That thing nearly killed us.'

'Don't dramatise the situation!' Zy snarled back. 'Speed Lady wouldn't have crashed. It only looked that way. You saw how gently she landed.' He was confident he'd worked the problem out now.

'You're a fool!' Alouine said acidly. 'I obviously care more for my life than you do for yours!'

Zy threw up his hands and marched back towards the flyer.

Welma hurried after him. 'How about if Alouine and I take your inflatable raft and paddle to the lake's shore? We could look around for danks in case your theory doesn't work.'

Zy paused, hands on hip. 'And how do you know I have an inflatable raft?'

'I looked over all the equipment,' Welma answered defensively. 'I wanted to know what emergency supplies we had with us. Caution saves lives.'

Zy shook his head. 'OK, but be careful. I expect you also found the weapons in the hold. Take a couple of the Schecks. We don't know for sure whether we're alone out here and, like you said, caution saves lives.'

Welma ducked a nod, smiling, and went to unload the raft.

Zy watched them with cruel satisfaction as Welma and Alouine struggled to inflate the thing. He did not intend to offer help. Ride back on danks indeed! What did they think he was?

Eventually, left alone, with only Alouine's noisy complaints reaching him from the receding raft, Zy hopped back into the flyer. He ran every test the manual listed, but as before could find nothing out of the ordinary. As a precaution he followed the instructions for resetting the flight director program. All seemed in order. It had to be some mistake he'd made himself which had caused the aberration. He checked and rechecked the systems just to make sure.

Satisfied he'd removed whatever fault haunted Speed Lady's synthetic mind, Zy decided he might as well take a thorough scan of the area while the women were away, and video as much of it as possible. It really was a remarkable find. He had more than enough material for Astracruise to work with for now. To the west, vertebrae of Larrigan's Back dominated the horizon, dotted with tenacious forests clinging to the sheer cliffs. To the north, a wild plain with untold scope for development, led to a shadowy clump of hills and russet foliage. Through his viewfinder, Zy ascertained the dark growths were man-sized lichen clusters. Clumps of tall, spreading trees crowned each of the hills like ill-fitting wigs. Zy caught the occasional metallic gleam of water falling, moving dots that may have been some kind of antelope. To the east a wide, ancient river, mimicking a miniature marsh in places, spread its tussocky landscape to meet the hills sweeping round in an eastwards curve. Trees and giant lichens were virtually indistinguishable from each other, draped as they were in moss-vine and hag-moss. Zy could already visualise organised dank treks and skipper rides in this place. It seemed perfect; vast and beautiful. He looked around and saw that the cranes had glided over to investigate the flyer, a slow-moving, graceful mass of long necks, sword-like pearly beaks and floating, gauzy plumage. There just had to be a market for exporting those birds; any wealthy person would welcome them ornamenting their garden lawns. The cranes clustered like ladies in extravagant ball-gowns, without fear, as Zy pushed his way through them. Back onboard, he set a southwards course into the computer; it did not appear to object, assuring him everything was in order and ready to fly. All he had to do now was wait for the women to return, which meant he probably had time for a nap; one Mangine capsule, one cup of coffee, one prostration upon welcoming, mossy sward.

Welma woke him much later in the afternoon. He surfaced, twitching, from a disturbing dream that left a haze of fearful uncertainty in its wake, even though the details faded instantly. Welma's face was red, and Zy realised the sunlight was far fiercer than it had been of late. His head swam as he sat up.

'Fool,' Welma said. 'How long have you been unconscious out here? It's a wonder your brains haven't baked dry.'

'Only a moment or two. Did you find the danks?'

Welma pulled a face. 'Saw them. They don't seem as tractable as southern danks however. They ran off as soon as we approached.'

'Ah well, don't worry too much. It looks as if the flyer will be OK for a homewards journey.'

'Are you sure?' Welma asked anxiously.

'Yes. Look, if it will make you feel better, we'll keep to a moderate speed and height, and take it in turns to supervise the flight deck. If possible, we should endure the discomfort and not make any landings till we get back to the city.'

'No landings? We'll be terribly cramped.' From her expression, Zy wondered whether she was thinking about having to endure Alouine in such close quarters, as he was.

'I know. But the fewer stops and starts we can bear the better. It's only a precaution. I just want to get back.'

'How long will it take?'

'Oh, only a couple of days if we keep cruising. Let's face it, we've been up and down and side to side, all over the place.'

'We haven't come that far out of Silven Crescent territory then.'

'Not really.'

'Will you come back another time, go further?'

'Someone will.'

'Oh.' Welma looked crestfallen.

'Just consider all we've talked about,' Zy said.

Speed Lady lifted into the sky, effortlessly and smoothly. Zy breathed a sigh of relief. All was going to be well, but some damn service engineer was going to pay for this! Could have killed him, killed them all, and how would Astracruise have looked then? The moment he got back to Silven Crescent he was going to transmit a message to his headquarters and complain. Kitzuki and Silas would be amused by the tales he'd have to tell them when he got home.

True to his word, Zy kept Speed Lady aloft as darkness fell. Predictably, Alouine had plenty to say about discomfort. She was too tall to stretch out in the cabin now it was three-quarters full of plant samples.

'So junk the leaves and the racks,' Zy suggested reasonably. 'You can always come back for more, surely?'

Both Alouine and Welma objected vociferously to that suggestion, eager as they were to exhibit their discoveries to their colleagues, but it successfully silenced their complaints about available room.

Halfway through the night, in utter darkness, while Zy was taking his shift up front, Speed Lady stopped dead. 'Ah shit, what now?' he groaned, tentatively asking the computer what it was playing at. There was no response, only the familiar insulting buzz from the monitor, a scrambled mess of lines. 'You fucking bitch!' He was aware of a frisson of fear making his heart beat faster, the almost sentient scrutiny of the flyer herself. She was waiting, watching his reaction. *Don't be stupid*, he told himself, and tentatively stroked the pads that would revert control to manual.

Almost imperceptibly, Speed Lady edged forward. This reminded Zy of a time, on some distant world, when he'd ridden a particularly unpredictable horse, whose high-stepping, delicate progress had felt as if it might disintegrate into a mad, death-defying, full gallop at any moment. Similarly, he now knew he was not in control. *Maybe I should land*, he thought, *maybe I should have listened to the women and gone hunting danks with them. Maybe this is the end. Like hell!*

He accelerated the craft forward, or tried to. The engines whined, fighting whatever commands were being given, but speed did not increase. *Take her down, down*, urged a small, plaintive voice in Zy's head.

'OK, you win,' he said out loud, and eased the nose down. Speed Lady would have none of it. She bucked, shuddering backwards; an impossible manoeuvre.

Zy closed his eyes, sensing movement in the cabin behind him, the murmur of voices. He tried to ease the flyer down once more, and at first she seemed to slide towards the ground. He heaved a sigh of relief, but it was short-lived. Without warning, the flyer flipped right over. Zy was thrown against the front visor, white light exploding before his eyes. He heard a cry of pain, it could have been his own, Welma's or Alouine's, before being tossed backwards to land disjointedly against the cabin wall. Outside, the sky was alive with bright, flying stars. The flyer had accelerated beyond all reasonable speed, shuddering, shrieking in perverse delight as her engines strained to respond. Zy virtually fell onto the control console, his hands groping for some way to take control. His nose began to bleed, whether from his previous fall or unbearable pressure, he couldn't tell. Looking up, he saw the northern hills swaying crazily towards him, with such unbelievable speed, it was like a videodisc on fast-forward.

This isn't real, he told himself, time stretching bizarrely as the inevitability of their fate zoomed towards them.

Alouine and Welma had crowded into the cabin behind him, shouting questions in harsh, frightened voices.

Zy didn't know the answers. He kept quiet, hands racing over the console, trying any combination to break the senseless acceleration. The flyer gulped distance, covering ground at twice, three times, her cruising speed. And faster still.

In desperation, Zy did the only thing possible, an act that might prove even more disastrous than allowing the flyer her head. He stabbed the emergency land sequence. That should cut all engines at once and switch to glide mode.

In defiance, the flyer uttered an alarmingly sentient roar, lifting her nose higher so that the hills disappeared and all that could be seen from the ports were streaking stars.

In one last desperate movement, Zy tried to wrench the controls back to the south. *Nothing will work,* a calm voice said inside him, *nothing.*

Behind him, he heard Welma say in a wistful voice, 'Who's doing this?'

This was the first time he even considered an outside agency could be responsible. It was also the last time he ever heard Welma speak.

Moments later, the flyer, torn by conflicting commands, groaned shudderingly as her engines expired. There were one or two seconds of utter stillness, before Speed Lady, as if seeking to destroy herself in a weird kind of religious fervour, flung herself into the dense foliage ahead.

Chapter Fourteen
Rock Visiting

Meera knew something mystically important was happening to her. Admittedly, she hadn't yet had a repeat experience of what she was now sure had been a divine manifestation, but the spiritual residue was still with her. She was filled with the certain knowledge that something huge and powerful had visited her, something that was beginning to affect the entire community.

Nightly, she prayed to Parthenos - half garbled hysteria - thanking the Lady for her beneficence, her presence. The abject worship was interspersed with pleading questions: 'I have to know more, Lady, in order to do thy work.'

Parthenos was not forthcoming.

Meera was fairly sure other people had been blessed with similar encounters to her own, simply because of the increasing amount of Freespacers who were seeking her out to discuss matters of personal insight, revelation and faith. No-one, however, even under direct questioning from the priestess, would openly admit to having had a religious experience. This mystified and vexed her. Surely, they should all be sharing this new knowledge? Surely this was the consummation of their persecution and flight. Of course, she reasoned, they were Chosen. It was probably this conviction, which must have been apparent in her face, if not her voice, that prevented any of the Freespacers from telling Meera anything in detail.

She was told nothing about the disorientating dreams, the feeling of unseen presences among the huts and tents, the sudden pangs of a bizarre spiritual ecstasy that would shoot into unsuspecting minds during mundane labour, causing people to lift their faces to the sky seeking confirmation of ideas that faded to mere teasing fragments in seconds.

The Freespacers had necessarily developed into a highly practical people, feeling, with a certain amount of self-importance, that they had left all superstitious follies behind them in the city. The experiences puzzled and embarrassed them; they had come to look upon the Goddess as nothing more than an archetypal abstraction. This had been one of Elvon L'Belder's philosophies; he had believed all gods to be essentially self-generated by their devotees. Rosanel Garmelding, who considered it her vocation to perpetuate L'Belder's beliefs, had recently been emphasising this theory to anyone who would listen to her. She wanted to keep him a spectral figurehead for the group. The information only confused people who were finding it very hard to remain objective about their experiences.

Rosanel herself thought she knew exactly what was happening. She too had undergone moments of skin-prickling, sensing the presence of unseen eyes. Usually, this occurred in her cottage, late at night or first thing in the morning, but on one occasion it had actually occurred in the presence of others. She'd been out with a group of Freespacers, helping to dig the channels, which would eventually house water-pipes, and could have sworn someone tapped her bent shoulder. Looking round, no-one had been behind her, and the people she was working with didn't appear to have seen anything out of the ordinary.

'Who did that?' she'd demanded, unnerved.

Eyes had swivelled away, heads had shaken.

The Freespacers shrank from admitting they had all experienced odd things over the past few days. Thus, Rosanel felt she alone was suffering these phenomena, and the cause behind them was obvious to her. Elvon L'Belder had come back. Naturally, because of his mutated state, he did not want to shock his followers by a blatant appearance. Rosanel understood this and began to talk to him out loud whenever she was alone, convinced L'Belder was always within hearing. She had not yet actually seen him, despite constant pleas, and was sensible enough to keep what she knew to herself, but most nights as she readied herself for sleep, maintaining the fastidious, bedtime toilet rituals typical of a high-ranking city woman, she would feel the man's presence as strongly as if he stood beside her. Sometimes she could swear she caught a hint of his personal scent. When the day came for L'Belder's triumphant physical return, she could step forth as his partner, as she'd always been. Her wise reticence would be rewarded then, she was sure. The Freespacers were not quite ready for the miracle of L'Belder's return; he would wait patiently until they were. Meanwhile she would prepare the way for him as best she could, reminding everyone of all that he done for them, all that he stood for, perhaps mentioning that, if he still lived, his appearance might be a little odd, even frightening.

Many people, during those first few days after Corinna had visited the valley cave, commented on Rosanel's irritating persistence in this matter, her inability to see how much she was boring everyone with her constant paean to L'Belder's greatness.

'Anyone would think he was some kind of Messiah,' Leto Gomery commented, with exasperated cynicism. 'Why won't the woman just shut up and get on with her work.'

Shyya was undoubtedly the only person who understood Rosanel was, in fact, doing exactly what she considered 'her work' to be. The Trotgardens were perhaps the least affected by this sudden supernatural surge. Meonel had talked to the rest of the family about the building plot they had found, and many cosy conversations drifted around the breadlemen table about what they would build and when. Orblin even drew sketches but, mysteriously, no-one made any move to visit the valley again.

Corinna was so relieved by this, she dared to hope the subject would be forgotten and a new, more practical, site would soon be discovered. She herself was frantically seeking such a place, scouring the tributary valleys above the dam, whenever she got the chance. All the time, she was uncomfortably conscious of the first valley waiting and watching, as if it knew, with calm certainty, she would have to visit it again. Coupled with her fears about the place, was the rising acknowledgement that a very strange atmosphere indeed was beginning to invade Freespace.

Corinna discussed this with Gick. 'You know what you said about me having the time to get all worked up about past experiences now?' she said. 'I get the feeling you were right, and that's it's an affliction affecting everybody. Can't you feel it?'

Gick, who had suffered one or two painful revelations herself, nodded glumly. Like everyone else, she was reluctant to confide in anyone about what she'd experienced, feeling that if she spoke of it out loud she would appear foolish or, even worse, somehow dirty. 'We never went back to your valley,' she said.

Corinna glanced up at her friend and recognised, with shock, an expression of deep need. 'I hope you're not suggesting there's any connection...' she began.

But Gick cut her off. 'You said you wanted to go back. That was days and days ago. Are you that afraid you won't face up to it?'

Corinna thought, *Goddess, I think she needs to see that place more than I do. It's her fears she's talking about, not mine.* Suddenly, the valley did not seem such a terrifying place to her, as if its influence had passed her by to lay its fingers on other, unsuspecting minds. 'We'll go tomorrow,' Corinna said.

Since finding the valley, Corinna had been spending less time with her friends, other than Gick. Hollis Backwater was the most affected by this sudden distance. He was sensible enough to realise that Corinna had more than her fair share of problems, and that she was wary of forming physical relationships, if not downright repulsed by it. He did not understand why exactly, but was encouraged and comforted by the fact that Corinna didn't appear to look on anybody else, who found her attractive, more favourably than him. He'd discussed it with his mother Tuscany, who'd wisely told him not to push Corinna, as it might force her to reject him completely.

'Give the girl time,' she'd said. 'Think back to the day she returned to the marsh, skinny as a stick, bald as a marsh hen with her face all cut up. Think about what she went through to get that way. She needs careful handling does that one!'

Hollis listened to his mother's words, although he often had to fight an urge to visit Dannel. He wondered whether he should tell her of his feelings for her daughter, and that he wished to set up home with Corinna. Perhaps Dannel could persuade her daughter for him. Of course, there was always the Oralien woman. He suspected that Corinna was waiting for Carmenya to notice her again, and perhaps rekindle their relationship. What a waste! Carmenya had little to do with any of the Freespacers, and she clearly had no interest in Corinna anymore. Hollis felt the only living creatures Carmenya had any love for were herself and her dank beast. Now, Corinna was shunning all her friends. Whenever Hollis called round to see her, she was out. Prudently, he'd started paying Orblin and Bolivia more attention, but they treated his careful enquiries about their sister with amusement.

Orblin had worried him considerably one evening, when he'd let up on the teasing long enough to say, 'Look Hollis, if you really fancy C'rin this much, it's a mistake to show it. I know her, and I don't think, if she ever decides to take up with anyone, it will be someone who's obvious about it. Know what I mean?'

Hollis did, and stopped pestering them, but it didn't stop the longing.

The day Corinna and Gick set out to investigate the valley was drizzly and overcast. Gick arrived at the Trotgarden cottage early in the morning, well swaddled in animal skins and carrying a stout staff and a lantern. 'Might as well do this properly,' she said, brandishing the staff.

Corinna let herself out of the cottage. She hadn't felt it necessary to tell any of her family where she was going, although, at one point in the sleepless night, she had considered asking Bolivia to come along, before deciding against it because of unreasonable fear for her sister.

It had been a vile night for Corinna. Whenever she'd closed her eyes, she'd been assaulted by images of Silven Crescent, dominated by reminders of Carmenya Oralien. Remembering Silven Crescent, she had visualised the house Carmenya had installed her in; the servants, the street, the trained trees against the garden wall (as cut and constrained as she had been), and the long nights she had spent in Carmenya's company. The memory of their conversations more than those of lovemaking made Corinna feel bereft. One shared moment of laughter meant so much more than the most intimate of caresses. Why did it have to start hurting again? She had made herself get used to the fact Carmenya no longer wanted any contact with her, for whatever reason, whether of distaste or guilt. On the journey, she had seen Carmenya nearly every day; here in Freespace, over a week could go by before she caught sight of her. Why should she start thinking about the woman now?

Corinna and Gick clambered up towards the dam, wiping moisture from the ends of their noses and lashes. Gick had bound up her untidy mop of hair against the wet and, occasionally, when her hood moved, Corinna could see the ugly scars on the sides of Gick's head. It was easy to forget about that; Gick disguised the fact well. *Better her ears though, than... No, don't think about it, don't. Gick has inner ear infections because of it; she suffers. It's just as bad, isn't it?*

They emerged onto the wind-gusted plateau, where the dam lake surged and slapped as if governed by tides. It was too early in the day for anybody to be working, and the wooden constructions on the far shore, dark with moisture, looked debilitated and rotten. The drizzle had intensified to rain - curtains of it. Puffed-up banks of purple cloud gloated behind the farthest mountains.

'Oh hell,' Gick moaned, wiping her face.

Corinna was precariously sliding her way around the left side of the lake, hoping to find the entrance track again. It would be typical if she couldn't. Aware of Gick's persistent grumbling, louder expletives advising of when she slipped in the mud, Corinna eventually came across a steeply sloping pathway resembling the one they'd followed before. Listing dwarf threadwoods disguised the opening, which she could have sworn hadn't been there the last time. *Stupid! The rain's caused them to lean over, that's all. Must I read mysteries into everything?*

'Come on!' she called, waving back at Gick who had fallen some way behind, the front of her coat orange with mud, her face clay-streaked and sour with discomfort. Waiting there, Corinna studied her own position. There were so many outcroppings of rock around the lake, it was quite possible someone sitting further up might not notice two people this far down. Quite possible. *You see*, she told herself, *no mystery as to why we didn't meet up with Gick that day, no mystery at all.*

Once in the high-walled pathway, the two women were protected from the elements somewhat. The strong wind tended to carry the rain right over the gully; only the occasional squall landed to soak them.

'This would be a problem to excavate,' Gick said.

'That's what I thought,' Corinna answered, 'It's solid rock here, but Meonel fell in love with the place. Perhaps you will too.'

'Hmm. Maybe it won't seem such a ghostly place to you today either.'

'That's what I hope. Ah, here...'

They had come to the spider-lizard nest. All the lizardlings were crouched against the rock, close to their mother. Gick chittered out a greeting and the adult lizard extended her neck and expanded her ruff a little in curiosity.

'Nice neighbours, anyhow.' Gick had a fondness for spider lizards. She'd tried to domesticate an injured lizard she'd found on the trek north, but the injuries had been too severe and the animal had quickly died.

They climbed up the side of the gully, following the path Corinna and Meonel had discovered, which today was treacherous and slippery. The lizard extended her neck further to watch the humans' precarious progress as they entered the narrow tunnel that led to the valley, Corinna was once again alert for odd changes in atmosphere. Perhaps it was Gick's loud complaints that dispelled any such fancies.

Eventually, they scrambled out into the valley, Gick thumping Corinna in the back for kicking stones in her face.

Corinna ran a few steps backwards, arms outstretched. 'Well, this is it,' she said. 'Welcome to Death Valley.'

The rain had lessened now.

Gick came out from the shelter of the rock wall. 'Impressive,' she said, nodding.

The grass and moss were flattened and silvery from the rain, the cliffs slick and black. 'It's larger than the place I found and would be easier to build on, yes, because there's less rubble around. Running water too. I can see why Meonel thought it was perfect.'

'But do you feel anything... well... peculiar?'

'Do you?'

Corinna paused for a moment. All she could feel was wet and wind. It was as if the weather was masking the atmosphere of the place - or the valley was deliberately masking itself. Alternatively, she might have been wrong before. She hoped that was the explanation. 'I'm not sure. Let's head towards the trees.'

They began to march through the wet grass. 'I've been thinking about Carmenya a lot,' Corinna blurted after a while. She'd wanted to say something along those lines ever since

Gick had called for her that morning.

'Oh,' Gick responded, aware all that was required was a prompt.

'Yes. It seems odd because I haven't thought about her for ages, not in... well, certain ways anyway.'

'That must have been tough for you, C'rin. The woman's a beast, an unfeeling beast. I've never been able to work out what made her come along with us. She loved the city so much and all it stood for. If she'd done it for love, for you, I could understand it, but there seems no other reason. She looks older nowadays, don't you think?'

'I haven't looked that closely, haven't had a chance to. I wish we could speak, there's so much unsaid, important things.'

'I think it's a bit late for that, C'rin. You really should forget about her.'

'Like I had to forget about Shyya and Elvon L'Belder, huh?'

Elvon L'Belder had left quite an impression on the Trotgardens; Shyya and Corinna had both been romantically involved with him, at one time. Corinna had also harboured a few desires for Shyya herself, which she'd once told Gick about.

'I haven't had an easy ride either, you know,' Gick said. 'Do I have a lover? No. Don't get maudlin, C'rin.'

'I can never have anyone that way now, you know that. At least you have the choice if the situation ever arose.'

'OK, OK,' Gick said, painfully, inwardly kicking herself. Sometimes she forgot about Corinna's hidden physical scars. Apart from Corinna herself, Gick was the only Freespacer who knew about them. Corinna had more than her fair share of admirers, but they all thought her frigid and aloof, once their advances were snubbed. Gick would have happily set up house with any of them, but people who found Corinna attractive rarely had time for Gick. Gick sighed, reflecting on life's mordant unfairness.

In the distance, the wood appeared drab and forlorn, its

leaves downturned against the rain, displaying grey-brown surfaces.

Gick pulled a face. 'I think I understand something of your aversion now,' she said, eyeing the dark, thick undergrowth.

'The last time we were here this was a charming place,' Corinna said without conviction. 'Don't let the weather put you off. What repelled me had nothing to do with dismal leaves or rain.'

They pushed into the waist-high tangle of geeley-stalk, stiff moss and dwarf threadwood. Occasionally they came across an unfortunate small animal impaled upon a geeley thorn. The plant was carnivorous. Corinna was unsure of which direction to take. After all, she and Meonel had wandered around this place with no particular purpose in mind. However, if they kept the left hand cliff face more or less in view, they must eventually come across the stone steps leading to the cave. Gick was beginning to query, only half in jest, if Corinna had not dreamed the whole thing.

Then the clearing appeared through the dripping foliage ahead of them. 'Here,' Corinna said. 'It's here.' She pushed her way through and, without pausing, stalked over to the stone steps, which were shiny and slippery-looking, black as jet.

'Amazing,' Gick said. She staged a shiver. 'You're right C'rin, it is kind of spooky, all this carving being here. It's indisputable, isn't it, that someone built this, someone or...' her voice dropped to a theatrical hiss, '...some*thing*.'

'Quite,' Corinna responded dryly, trying not to let Gick get on her nerves.

Quick-lichens had sprouted on the stone, encouraged by the damp weather. Corinna and Gick were forced to use their hands for support as they climbed up. Halfway, the rain began to fling itself towards them in true ferocity, helped by an irresistible, icy wind. Corinna was relieved when they reached the cave mouth. Gick set about lighting the lantern, and Corinna was not loath to let her lead the way in. By lamplight, the cave was revealed in its true splendour. Clusters of quartz spangled the walls; the stalactites were straws of glittering ice, blue at the heart interspersed, here and there, with pendulums of red-veined, white stone, as if mottled with blood. Corinna wasn't sure whether it was Gick's constant stream of exclamations that dispelled any morbid atmosphere, but it was only the memory of fear that made her nervous of venturing beyond daylight, nothing more.

Various lightless passages led off from the main chamber, one of which, quite far back, was wider than the rest. Gick ventured inside it, lantern held high, her free hand feeling along the walls. Corinna thought it was undeniable these passages had been hand-carved in places.

'These are niches!' Gick exclaimed. 'Perhaps they were for lights, you know, candles or something.'

'That's possible.' Corinna was now experiencing a natural claustrophobia, deeply aware of the darkness beyond their meagre light. She wondered how far she'd have to suffer before it sounded reasonable to suggest turning back. 'Keep the floor lit, Gick, for the Goddess' sake,' she said, fearing they might tread in something unpleasant or, even worse, encounter some kind of drop. Apprehensions could so easily give way to panic, she realised.

'How do you feel?' Gick asked over her shoulder.

'OK. How long do you think we should keep going?'

'I reckon this will open out soon, don't you? It's got to lead somewhere.'

Precisely, wittered the voice of Corinna's inner fears.

The walls had become glossy; not with damp, but as if they'd been polished. Corinna took a deep, shuddering breath. Perhaps they should go back now. It would be stupid to go too far alone. Better to return later with more people and explore the caverns in numbers. Yes, that would be safer. 'Gick?'

'Yes?'

'I think we should head back now.'

'Why? Not scared are you?' Gick's laugh was the most irritating sound Corinna could imagine under the circumstances.

'No, it's just that... Goddess! What was that?' Corinna lurched forward, grabbing Gick's shoulders and causing the lantern to swing wildly. Within the glass, frail light flickered perilously.

'What was what?' Gick squawked. 'Look out, you idiot, you'll have us in darkness!'

'Ahead. Up there. Lights!'

'Where? I can't see anything.'

'It was there...'

Both of them squinted ahead, into impenetrable blackness.

Did I imagine that? Corinna wondered. Red, green, red, green; quickly - a burst of colour gone before she could cry out.

'Just an after-image from looking at the lamp, C'rin,' Gick said, but she didn't sound as confident as she had before.

'I don't think we should go on,' Corinna said.

Gick hesitated a moment. 'Perhaps you're right. It would be sensible to come back with more people. I think I'd feel safer. Goddess, C'rin, it must be your nerves infecting me.' She croaked another high, irritating laugh.

At that moment, Corinna realised with horror that they were both frightened stiff. The fear had crept upon them unawares. She also knew it was imperative not to speak of how they were feeling until they reached daylight. If they did, they might panic each other so much, they'd gallop blindly into another tunnel by accident. Corinna couldn't imagine a worse horror. *We must pretend we're calm*, she thought, slowly. *Just walk back. Don't think about the darkness behind us.*

Turning to face the way they'd come, Gick handed Corinna the lantern. The darkness ahead was absolute. Corinna dared not voice the fear that perhaps they'd passed turnings in the blackness, lost their way.

'Get going,' Gick said, with false heartiness, prodding Corinna in the back.

'OK.' Corinna only took one step before an incredible bolt of searing light engulfed her head with excruciating pain. She couldn't cry out, couldn't move, paralysed with agony. Gick's worried enquiries seemed to come from the other side of the world. A great booming echo filled her ears, industrial, sounding similar to the wooden machinery at the dam, but so much bigger, so much more alive. The walls of the passage seemed to vibrate to its rhythm.

Gick had the sense to grab the lantern, before it fell from Corinna's grasp. Asking no more questions, she pushed past Corinna and literally dragged her up the passage, ignoring any sounds of distress. Gick couldn't hear the booming noise. To her, it felt as if the dense blackness was whistling, thronged with unseen eyes. She didn't know what had happened to Corinna, but realised the only priority was to get out of that place, and fast. Questions and examination could come later, in safety, in daylight.

Panting, stumbling, splashing through shallow puddles, Gick hauled Corinna along the interminable weaving passage, never pausing until they reached the greyness of the main entrance chamber. She uttered an uncontrollable cry of relief as she saw the light ahead. Corinna could barely walk and was virtually scrabbling along on her knees. Gick didn't let her go until they were well out of the cave. An icy wind gusted along the rock ledge, and Gick put her head down between her clasped knees to regain her breath. Corinna was making odd sounds, little howls, writhing in a helpless huddle on the rock. Gick lifted her to her feet, glancing back into the silent depths of the cave. It was still in there, whatever it was; watchful and cunning. Gick felt safe out here in the open. She was sure they wouldn't be pursued into daylight.

Corinna's neck was warm and wet. Gick pulled her hands away, lifted the hair, stared without comment at the thin ribbons of blood still seeping from Corinna's ears. 'You were right,' she said, and now her jaw was shaking.

Corinna said nothing, but slowly put her hands to her face.

By the time Gick had virtually carried her down through the forest, she was only half-conscious.

Chapter Fifteen
Lady Down

Zy came back to consciousness feeling as if he'd been dismembered, sewn back together and then strung up somewhere to slowly fall apart again. He opened his eyes to flickering green, realising, after a few minutes of dazed study, that he was looking through leaves. A painful attempt to move told him he was hanging in the foliage of a fallen tree that rocked dangerously with his movement. There was no way of telling how far from the ground he was.

We crashed, he thought, remembering, and then tried to call out to the others. Even speech was an agony. He was so relieved when the angry-looking, battered face of Alouine Crestick appeared between the branches that he began to weep aloud.

'Hold still!' Alouine ordered, gently parting the leaves. 'Can you tell if anything's broken?'

'I'm all broken!' Zy replied.

'Well, I can't leave you there,' Alouine decided and grabbed him beneath the arms, ignoring his cries of pain as she eased him out in a hail of torn twigs.

The crash had created a raw crater of bleeding sap, exposed roots and peaty soil in what appeared to be a thick forest of lichen trees, whose untidy, lacy appearance was relieved in places by grand sentinels of a more deciduous nature; such as the tree Zy had landed in. The air was thick with disturbed spores, dusty on the tongue, strangely sweet.

Even as Alouine was dragging him over stumps and through bundles of ripped fronds, Zy was aware that soon his wounds would be covered in powdery dressings, which might, or might not, be toxic. There was a buzzing in his ears that reminded him of Kitzuki's voice, as if heard through static. If he called out, would she hear him, send help? The hallucination seemed more real than pain.

The remains of the flyer were scattered a short distance away, having gouged a passage through the foliage. Alouine, panting heavily, managed to get Zy propped up against a ragged stump; Speed Lady had taken the rest of the tree with her, her battered nose still mostly intact, buried in a cradle of leaves and branches, streaked with yellow liquid from burst sap bladders.

'Speed Lady,' Zy mumbled, miserably. 'Speed Lady.'

'Save your grief for yourself,' Alouine replied, leaning down to brace herself on bent knees. She coughed, wiped her face, which, through a sizzling haze, Zy could see was gashed badly. Blood dripped off her square chin. 'Can you breathe alright?'

Zy wriggled, winced, nodded painfully.

'Any idea where you're hurt bad?'

He shook his head. It was impossible to tell.

'Stay there a while. Get yourself in order, Larrigan. We can't stay here long. I have to see to Welma.'

He watched her stooped form stagger over to where Welma Barbarel lay moaning in a bed of lichen. Her raised knees were all that could be seen from his position; the trouser legs wet and dark with blood.

Alouine made soothing sounds, squatting down beside the injured woman.

She is strong, Zy thought. *She is so strong.* He closed his eyes for a while, tried to regulate his breathing and discern where and how he might be injured. Alouine may have retrieved the medical pod from the flyer. If she hadn't, it was essential they found it. He dozed, deliriously, dreaming of safety, home, friends. He dreamed Kitzuki came tramping through the lichen, looking for him. He dreamed Silas lifted him in his arms as if he were a child.

He awoke to reality, and a kind of clarity. Alouine was still kneeling beside Welma. Zy looked down at his body. His clothes were ripped, mostly missing altogether. His arms, legs and chest were badly scratched. Some of the cuts looked deep enough to need stitches. His jaw, neck and upper chest were a core of white-hot pain, although he was relieved to find he could still move all his fingers. It was vital he had access to the medical pod.

'Alouine!' His voice sounded absurdly weak, considering the urgency of his request.

The woman looked round.

'Help me up!'

She straightened up, pressing one hand to her side and came over. 'Sure you're up to it?'

He nodded. 'Only one way to find out.'

She shrugged, pulled a face through a mask of blood and placed strong, square hands under his arms. Between them, they pulled his body into a precarious standing position. Zy's sight was obscured by spinning motes of light. It felt as if his head had detached itself from his neck and was soaring up above the trees, but at least he was on his feet, despite the waves of nausea lapping through his body. 'The medical pod. Did you find it?' he gasped.

Alouine shook her head, eyes narrowed. 'No... Larrigan, you're in bad shape. I think...'

'Think nothing,' he said, feeling for support behind him. 'We're all in bad shape. We need the med supplies. Help me over.'

He had already tottered round to face the wreck.

Alouine put an arm around him. 'I've dragged some stuff out already, she said. 'We're lucky - the envirotank is still intact.'

'Should be,' Zy grunted. 'It's designed that way.'

'Thank Goddess, then! I used water from that on Welma, and a few rags. But it won't go far, won't last long.'

Zy didn't answer. That much was obvious.

After considerable effort, they reached the crumpled cabin section of the flyer, debris spilling out of its tortured casing like entrails. Alouine helped Zy struggle through the wreckage. It seemed incredible that such a sturdy construction as the flyer had once been could now resemble no more than a screwed up piece of plastic. Zy thought it was a miracle they'd all escaped alive, but then his memory of the last moments before impact was a blank. Had Speed Lady tried to pull up at the last minute or was it just because they'd landed in trees the damage hadn't been more severe?

They found the pod after having to clamber painfully over the spiky remains of the plant sample racks. It was still secured to a section of bulkhead and had to be manoeuvred through a tangle of twisted metal struts.

Alouine virtually had to carry Zy back to the clearing, the pod clutched beneath her free arm. She watched with growing misgivings as he rummaged through the contents, crazily talking about stitching her face. 'I'm trained to do it,' Zy insisted. 'Hell, Crestick, think what you've just been through. A little pricking here and there isn't going to make it feel worse is it?'

She relented grudgingly, wincing away from Zy's bloodied, shaking fingers. He kept blinking as if his vision was fading. It was not reassuring. *This is his fault*, she thought, and wondered why she didn't feel as mad at him as she should. Welma was unconscious, and there was no way of knowing how badly damaged she was herself. That would come later. And where, in the Goddess' name, were they?

'This cut is deep,' Zy said, dabbing antiseptic gel on the wound. 'Think you've broken ribs?'

Alouine shrugged and winced. Maybe. 'I'll fix you up,' she said.

'Be careful.'

'Now, you're worried!'

Zy smiled weakly and lowered himself back to the ground.

Alouine Crestick had never touched a male body before. It was like dealing with an alien species; bone close to the skin, hard muscle. His chest looked mutilated to her; no breasts. Her military training, all those years ago, had included basic medical skills. She was fairly sure Zy had a broken collar bone, and strapped him up the best she could, using ripped lengths of cloth from what remained of his clothes. She had been lucky enough to find several items of clothing in the wreckage. They would need them to keep warm.

'We'll have to be careful with the painkillers and antibiotics,' Zy said, as Alouine deftly stitched his wounds. 'Supplies are low. Give two of the red capsules to Welma.'

Alouine snipped off the final suture and sifted through the plastic containers in the pod. 'These? What are they?'

'Should fight infection.'

'Her legs are gone. Broken, anyhow.'

'Have you splinted them?'

'Of course. Much as I could.' She paused. 'Larrigan...'

'I know. I know,' Zy interrupted her. He clearly didn't want to hear what she had to say. Thoughts of their immediate future must be filling him with despair. Only a steely will kept despair at bay in Alouine's heart.

Apart from her legs, Welma's injuries didn't show from the outside. Then a couple of hours later, she began to pass blood uncontrollably, lots of it, her breathing became very shallow, and her skin took on a bluish hue.

Zy had been trying to rest and recuperate his strength but, prompted by Alouine's worried noises, forced himself to crawl over to where Welma lay. It was a stranger lying there, a broken puppet. He remembered the conversation he'd had with her about her future. Neither of them had envisaged anything like this. From her appearance, it seemed Welma had very little future. Zy pumped her full of the last of his Mangine, telling himself he didn't need it as much as she did. Mangine changed reality, distanced the mind from the body, and conjured dreams, which Zy hoped would be pleasant ones in this case.

'What are we going to do?' Alouine asked, her voice cracked with hysteria. Her short hair was matted with blood; she'd been running her hands through it constantly.

'Maybe one of us should try and find help. Take a look around.'

Alouine turned on him. 'Are you mad? Where? This is a wilderness!'

'We have to do something!'

'What, though?'

'I don't know! Just look. What else can we do?' He tried to emphasise his words with a hand gesture, causing him to wince in pain.

'Then I'll go,' Alouine said. 'I'm in better condition than you.'

'You don't know that.' He sank down on the lichen. 'Anyway, what if you don't come back?'

'Afraid of being left alone, are you?'

'Yes. Wouldn't you be?'

Alouine gently stroked Welma's damp, pallid face. 'We can't move her.'

'Then we wait,' Zy said.

'What for? Till we starve, go septic, die?' Alouine groaned, and eased herself down. She was looking progressively sicker with each passing minute.

'No, until she does!' Zy said, pointing at Welma.

As if she'd heard him, Welma moaned softly and shivered beneath her meagre covering of soiled sleeping mats.

'We could save her, someone could,' Alouine said, in a dazed voice.

'Who? Where? There's a good chance we'll follow her soon. Do we know what's wrong with us? No.'

'I ache too much all over to be able to decide.' Alouine rolled painfully onto her back. 'We should never have tried to use the flyer again. We should have looked for danks, like

Welma said. We should never have come with you.'

Zy made a spitting noise and lurched shakily to his feet.

Alouine stared up at him. 'What are you doing?' she asked.

'One of us has to take a look around,' he said, and with considerable effort, began to limp off between the trees.

At some point, one of them was going to have to decide what to do, where they should go. From here, the southern plain was not even visible because of the dense foliage. Alouine had told him she'd found Welma crushed beneath the fallen plant sample racks. Zy had so far refrained from pointing out that if the women hadn't loaded up the cabin that way, Welma wouldn't be so badly injured.

He slowly followed a gently sloping animal path up through the lichens and ferns, pausing every few moments to muster strength. Perhaps from higher up, he could make some decisions about where they could go. The ground was moist and spongy beneath his feet, fragrant from recent rain. Luckily, it was not too cold.

He came to a flat rock poking up from the foliage and eased himself down onto its sun-warmed surface. It would be easy to lie here and die, he thought. How had this happened? It was unprecedented in Astracruise history. The flyers were thought infallible. Well, if he ever got back, he'd be able to enlighten them about that. And yet... He remembered Welma's last words before the crash. Had someone been tampering with the flyer's controls externally? If so, why and, more pertinently, who? He had to admit he had a strong conviction there were people around somewhere, not too far away. This feeling was not induced by what Welma had said, but by his sensing a certain ambience in the air, which suggested human habitation. It was a knack he'd picked up during the survey trips he'd made on other worlds; sometimes it became a necessity for survival. He did not feel completely alone, as if, should he climb the next hill, he would see smoke curling into the air or the huddle of buildings. City refugees? Almost certainly. Had it been them tampering with his flight controls? Surely not. Not even Silven Crescent had technology sophisticated enough to do that, and its refugees must have even less. So what was the explanation? Half of him hoped he'd never find out.

He wondered, if they found people, whether they'd be friendly or hostile. It would be better if he and Alouine could wait until they felt stronger before seeking help, but he suspected they were too injured to delay. If hostility was encountered, agility might be a life-saver, and Zy felt far from agile at present. Like Welma, both he and Alouine might have suffered internal injuries that were already putrefying away inside. Their supply of antibiotics was small. Surely, anyone they came across could only feel sorry for such pathetic casualties as he and the women. Wouldn't even the most vicious individual feel moved to help them?

Yes, but this isn't the universe outside, Zy reminded himself. *This is Artemis, and if the people out here are escapees from the cities, they will undoubtedly feel extremely bitter and unsympathetic towards anyone from the south.* As a man, he might stand a better chance, but Alouine and Welma, dressed in their Silven Crescent uniforms, were unmistakable enemies. Perhaps he'd better try and salvage some clothes of his own for them, if any remained unshredded after the accident. What a mess!

They were right, he thought. *Dammit, they were right.*

He could not help but feel responsible for what had happened, no matter how he tried to tell himself they were nothing more than victims of fate. He was certain he'd have to watch Welma Barbarel die. If he'd been more wary and abandoned the flyer, as the women had suggested, by now they'd be chasing danks, losing their tempers with each other, but alive and whole. What if Alouine should die too, leaving him alone? What if there were no people anywhere near here, and the impressions he was picking up were just figments of his imagination?

He lay back on the rock and closed his eyes, fighting

despair, but too weak and wracked with pain to resist.

'Larrigan. Here.'

He opened his eyes. Alouine was hunched over him, holding out a battered plastic cup. He must have fallen asleep.

'The coffee machine still works - for now.' She looked terrible.

'We have to find more water.'

'There's plenty of it about.' She eased herself down onto the rock beside him. 'We have to talk, Larrigan.'

'Talk, fine. Argue? Not interested. I hurt too much.'

Alouine sighed. 'Welma thought that someone was... well, interfering with your flyer.'

'I heard that. It was the last thing I remember hearing before we crashed.'

'I didn't mean that. She had a feeling about it before then.'

Zy struggled to sit up. 'Really? Did she say who she thought it was?'

Alouine shrugged uncomfortably. 'Hell, yes. There's no point in keeping quiet about it now. A lot of people left the city when Gisbandrun fell. They headed north. There's no reason why they shouldn't be around here someplace.'

'But they had no technology, surely!'

'Well, we're not sure about that. Some pretty strange things happened at that time...'

'Such as?'

Alouine pulled a face. 'Well, it's hard to say. What I saw firsthand was this: when that terrorist L'Belder came back to the city, he... Oh, this sounds ridiculous!'

'Anything to do with the legends about him being somehow... inhuman?' Zy prompted.

Alouine looked faintly embarrassed. 'You don't believe that, obviously.'

'It seems farfetched, but I have an open mind. Enlighten me.'

'All I can say is that what happened in Silven Crescent was like nothing I'd ever seen. The palace blew apart and everything was filled with this strange vibration that was actually light - or perhaps sound. Does that make sense?'

'You saw L'Belder?'

'No. I was outside the palace at the time. I just saw people go crazy. Everything went crazy.' She laid a bloodied hand on his arm. 'Larrigan, those people who left the city, they were followers of L'Belder. Is it possible he went with them?'

'Why ask me?'

She shrugged. 'You come from another world. You might understand these things better.'

'Sorry, my world, for all its otherness, is pretty mundane. Anyway, I thought you people were sure L'Belder was dead.'

She lowered her eyes. 'That's the official story. He just disappeared.' She looked up. 'But no-one got out of that place unseen, Larrigan. No-one.'

'What are you telling me?'

She turned away. 'Oh, tell me I'm mad or something, but I can't help thinking that, if L'Belder did go after his people, then they must have powers that we don't have. Perhaps powers that could influence your flyer's computer.'

Zy was silent for a moment. 'I can't believe you people just closed the file on all this and tried to forget about it!'

'You think we should have gone after them - the people who got away?'

Zy sighed. 'Yes, no, oh, I don't know. You should have got off-world help before this. And you should have been straight with us from the start, told us everything.'

Alouine looked surprised. 'I thought you people knew about L'Belder. We sent a report on it to the galactic administration.'

'Alouine, that report describes L'Belder as a librarian! There's no mention of him being... alien in any way. It says that he and his supporters fired the palace and he slugged it out with Gisbandrun. That's all. Nothing out of the ordinary... so to speak.'

Alouine sighed. 'Oh, I see. Still, some of our people talked about it with the off-worlders that came. It wasn't approved of, but Gulding didn't try to stop anyone telling the truth if they wanted to.'

Zy pulled a rueful face. 'True. The trouble is, we thought it was all fairy-tales, or trader talk. There was nothing in the official report. It seemed too *unlikely*... Anyway, thanks for telling me.'

'That's OK. I suppose you're right, though. I should have said something sooner. But it's not a subject we're encouraged to talk about, exactly.'

'You don't say!' Zy was too weary to be annoyed. Would that knowledge had changed anything anyway? He wouldn't have believed it. He'd have just kept on flying - wouldn't he? Still, it was a relief to know there might be people around. Aliens or murderers - there was still a chance they'd offer help. 'Well, if you think your refugees are around here someplace, we'd better start looking for them,' he said. 'We need assistance, and one of us needs it fast. Your friend.'

Alouine was silent for a moment and then she said the single word, 'No.'

Zy stared at her.

The woman's face was bleak. 'No, she doesn't,' Alouine said in a choked voice. 'Not now.' Her big, bony face worked against the grief, which she'd been containing so well, and then gave up the fight. 'Welma's dead. She just died.' The wide shoulders jerked, but there was no sound. Alouine buried her face in her knees, but she didn't throw off Zy's wary, comforting arm.

'In that case, we have to move,' he said. 'Now.'

He looked over his shoulder at the rising path behind them. 'We'll go that way.'

Chapter Sixteen
The Lover

Farris had struggled with the fighting twins of fear and compulsion for two days after his first visit to the cave. He knew, with no shadow of scepticism, that he'd been touched by something alien; alien in its literal sense. The cave he'd discovered was not empty, and it had to be faced that the Freespacers were not alone in this territory. Strangely, he did not think of Greylids, but of occult essences. Life without flesh.

After that first occasion, as he'd plunged hectically down the steep thorn-paths, fleeing from the cave, he'd visualised himself bursting into the family home, panting and trembling. His mother would ask abrupt, anguished questions, before which he'd be speechless. The awful truth, however, would eventually come to light, and he would suffer the shame of it.

And yet, by the time he'd reached the outskirts of Freespace, his hammering heart had slowed, his breathing had become regular. With relief, he'd found he could hide what had happened to him.

That night, he'd vowed never to visit the cave again. Whatever had happened to him there must not be repeated. It was too intimate, too powerful. He had a fear of being absorbed into something vast and unfathomable. Soon, when he'd recovered from the experience enough, he would tell others, perhaps his mother, that he'd encountered something inexplicable, something that lived without flesh. Then, it would be out of his hands. If it was not a secret, he could never be drawn back there against his will.

At night, in dreams, his subconscious replayed the

experience. The delight gnawed at his soul and, in the morning, at his convictions. He had a hunger inside him that was part curiosity, part unashamed lust, part yearning for affection. His dreams had been haunted by phantom lovers, whose faces could never be seen, but who left live scent on his waking body and the echo of tender words. This was the seduction of the presence in the cave.

Natural fear of the unknown warred with his desires; it took two days for the courage and the weakness to combine. He'd taken the route through the forest, avoiding the area of the dam aswarm with Freespacers. He'd climbed in a daze, repelling all thoughts of what he was approaching. Rain lanced through the trees, soaking his clothes. His eyes were full of water, lashes dripping; hot and cold. His fingers gouged the mud and fern-tangled peat; his feet scrabbled. It felt as if a fine wire was hooked around his heart, reeling him in.

He hauled himself onto the rock shelf outside the cave and lay on his belly for a few moments. His flesh throbbed with exertion. He felt feverish, weak, dizzy. The wind threw fistfuls of heavy rain onto his back. It was a desire for comfort, more than anything, that encouraged him to crawl under the shadow of the rock.

The relief was instantaneous. He sat, shivering, on the sloping floor of the cavern, rubbing life back into his icy, scratched fingers. Water dripped off his hair. He wiped his face with his hands, scraping the moisture away. As a precaution, he'd brought a knife with him. He removed it from the sheath hanging from his belt and placed it on the rock beside him. He knew the knife - a kitchen implement - was no defence against whatever lived in the rock, but its fine edge reassured him. It was a totem rather than a weapon. Then he lay back and waited.

Eventually the words came - voiceless - softly entering his mind. *You resist me. You mistrust me...*

'No!' he said aloud. A ghost finger touched his face. He reached up, but there was nothing there.

I cannot harm you...

'What are you?'

An invisible hand caressed his neck, feeling inside his clothes. If he closed his eyes, he could imagine....

'What are you?'

Whatever you want me to be.

'Are you alive?' Hollis sensed laughter and, as if in response, something pinched the skin on his throat. He instinctively raised a protective hand, but there was nothing to brush away.

Felt that, didn't you?

'Show me what you are!'

You decide that. Close your eyes and make me real. I will come to you in whatever form you choose.

It was too tempting an offer. *My lover has no face,* he thought. *My lover has no sex. Who are they?*

He had closed his eyes. When he opened them, a smoky shape was standing against the light. It held out shadow arms to him, laughed a shadow laugh. Then it came towards him.

Farris had spent most of his time in the cave after that. Down below, in Freespace Town, a maelstrom of emotion and bizarre events splashed across the collective mind of its people, but to Farris it was all an erotic adventure, with the faceless lover who could be male or female, exquisitely skilled in the arts of love whatever form he chose for it, and who said to him, 'Soon, soon, I shall be with you in flesh.'

This was his treasured secret, his sanctum. In the limbless embrace of the shadow, he felt like a priest, a prophet, whose cries of ecstasy turned to petals as they fell from his shuddering lips. He sought pain, rendering. He sought dominion. And it was all offered to him without question. It knew his mind, telling him his inner thoughts. He felt no violation at this, but merely took it as a cue to speak of his fears and doubts. The shadow lover listened. The shadow lover told him strength would be his. He believed it.

Then, one afternoon, when he entered the cave, the atmosphere inside it was different. He stood for a moment, trembling with fearful outrage. He knew. Someone had been there, in his temple, and recently too. He closed his eyes, and a flickering image of Corinna Trotgarden's face passed through his mind. She had been there. He tried to control the possessive anger this invoked, the immediate furious thought: *How dare anyone come here! How dare they!* He told himself it was senseless to think that way. Perhaps Corinna's visit presaged fulfilment of the shadow's promise. *Soon I shall be with you in flesh.* Corinna. Perhaps it had summoned her for him. He could not bear to think his shadow lover had enticed the girl there for its own pleasure, betraying him in that most cruel of ways.

'Where are you?' he cried, and his voice echoed emptily.

Then, another picture message. Corinna had not been alone. She'd brought someone with her.

'Where are you?!' More urgently.

Farris scrambled up the sloping floor, towards the back of the cave. Multiple images cascaded through his mind. Whoever had been there hadn't respected the Presence; they'd been carelessly curious, bringing their loud, human voices to mar the sanctified stone. They had forced the shadow to retreat down one of the tunnels, like a frightened animal. How dare they do this! He braced himself with his hands against the smooth lip of the largest tunnel, sending out a silent call with his mind. All he could feel, though, was Corinna, the remnants of her shuddering spirit essence. He ran one hand along the cold, slick walls and an echo of the girl's agony ran up his arm in a warm, almost erotic current. Here. Here. In the dark, the moist and breathing dark. Too dark to see.

Breathing heavily, Farris ventured forward, his feet paddling in water. It was the first time he'd ever investigated any of the tunnels; the shadow had always been waiting for him in the outer chamber before. Now, he could feel it calling for him, from deep within the rock. Its messages were crazed, filled with panic.

Here is a beginning and it is a spiral, no starting point, no finish, only eternity. A paradox. What is infinite becomes bigger in my sight, and I have always been part of it, only not realised, not stopped to feel it. Oh, I am coming home and fast! And I hear you, sense you, become you in a transcending rush that will open all their eyes. What is coming? Yes. Yes. I can feel that. Part of you? Is it?

Farris was no longer sure which were his own thoughts. Eventually, in the darkness, he sensed the tunnel was opening out into another large chamber. He could hear the echo of his breathing. It did not matter whether his eyes were closed or not; the blackness was absolute.

Look at me.

Behind his lids, red and green light pulsed softly. Farris opened his eyes. Before him, a tremulous effulgence, that had no true source, hung in the air. Within its intense core, a shifting shape described geometric patterns in acid colour. His skin became laced by a lattice of green radiance. 'Is this your true form?' he asked. He was not afraid.

The light pulsed, like a heartbeat, its core taking on the shape of a translucent, pulsing organ. *There is a response. Soon. Feel it. Resistance. But a response. I must describe its form.*

Farris felt as if strong hands were gripping his shoulders. The shadow had never been so urgent before. 'What is wrong? Did they hurt you?'

No, she is mutilated. Mistaken. I. Wrong message. It caused her discomfort. No receiver. Blanked. Wrong message. She is not the one for restructure I. Other purpose. I have to impart. Now! Heed me!

'I don't understand!' Farris said. He was afraid the shadow was trickling away from him, losing cohesion, the appearance of sanity.

Have to learn now. You. Heed me.

'Learn? Learn what?'

In response to his question, white sparks began to fly off the core of light. They passed right through his flesh, leaving a heat like the tracing of a spectral feather. It felt like being tickled; from the inside out. Farris laughed out loud, and the light flickered rapidly in reply. A picture came into his mind; then another and another, too fast for him consciously to assimilate the information. His head began to ache.

Learn now. No pleasures. Learn time.

'It hurts! Stop!' Farris pushed his fingers into his eyes, as if to prevent the insane parade of images cutting through his mind. He felt intense heat, smelled blood, smelled burning metal. Impossible.

A sudden wave of vertigo sent him slamming onto the rock floor, where he rolled and writhed, curling his limbs, extending them, crying out with pain.

A learning. Yes. Brief. Pleasure later. See this!

Farris screamed in horror. He was a metal bird, high above the world, flying fast as a star, and falling down, down...

Chapter Seventeen
The Assembly

'She'll sleep now.' Elvinia Windteasel dried her hands and turned away from the bed where Corinna lay. Only Dannel was in the room with them, a narrow, low-ceilinged place, crammed with the two beds shared by Corinna and Bolivia, strewn with the sisters' clothes and belongings.

Corinna had been brought home some time ago, before lunch, by a harried and incomprehensible Gick, who wittered on about haunted caves, and could not explain coherently why Corinna was bleeding from her ears, why her eyes were so bloodshot and why she could not speak.

Luckily for Dannel, who would probably have ended up knocking Gick to the floor in frustration, Shyya was in the cottage that morning, sitting at the family table, teasing out strands of hag-moss wool the Freespacers used as twine. Exhibiting his natural calm, he methodically tidied away his work before deftly running his hands over Corinna's face, pausing to feel more thoroughly beneath her jaw and ears. Then he stood up and quietly suggested Dannel should send for Elvinia Windteasel.

'But what happened?' Dannel had insisted, 'Did she fall? Was she attacked? What happened, Gick?'

'I don't know!' Gick had replied with equal heat.

'Just send for Elvinia,' Shyya interrupted. 'Now.'

Gick jerked her head in assent. 'I'll do it.'

Prior to this, Shyya had attempted to interrogate Gick himself, perhaps the only person possessed of the required patience. What he learned disturbed him deeply, as it served to confirm vague suspicions he'd been harbouring ever since Corinna and Meonel had found that place. He'd known something strange was stirring, affecting Freespace with a peculiar atmosphere, but whatever it was concealed itself from all of Shyya's psychic efforts to penetrate it. He couldn't identify it, and therefore couldn't empathise enough to communicate, on any level.

Meonel had been twitchy lately, although Shyya doubted whether Meonel himself was aware of this. On one occasion he'd spoken briefly, as if embarrassed about having such thoughts, of how he suspected there had once been a Greylid community nearby. When Shyya asked him for more details, he shied off the subject, saying it was all conjecture and that he needed more proof.

Shyya couldn't pick up any vibrations recognisable as Greylid in origin, but as his knowledge of the alien race was so slim, he was prepared to admit he might be wrong. He needed to speak to Corinna as soon as possible, hoping she could give him something to work on.

As he and Dannel laid the girl on her bed, she'd moaned and gibbered, pawing air as if delirious.

Elvinia had arrived within minutes.

'What's wrong with her?' Dannel asked.

Elvinia shook her head, raising a winged, black brow. She sighed. 'Nothing.... well, nothing that I can ascertain. There was bleeding from orifices, that was all, but as to what caused it...' She shrugged. 'It seems to have cleared up by itself. There are no other external signs. Her eyes are normal, her aura feels more or less sound, if a little psychically disturbed...' She glanced at Dannel, in what Dannel could only interpret as a furtive way.

Dannel felt her face flushing uncontrollably, conscious of Elvinia watching the redness rise up her neck. *Is it something I've done?* Dannel wondered, a brief tickle of paranoia making her feel guilty. She had never forgiven herself completely for sending Corinna to the city. 'What is it you're not telling me?'

she asked gruffly, hoping the answer would still be 'nothing.'

Elvinia put down the towel she was twisting in her hands, cast a nervous glance at the bed, the sleeping girl. 'I don't know how to say this.'

'For the Goddess' sake, don't give me that!' Dannel hissed, looming forward. She was still an impressive size.

Elvinia leaned back. 'You don't understand. I may be breaking her confidence...'

'What the hell do you mean? If there's something wrong, I have to know! I'm her mother! Corinna has no secrets from me!'

'I wouldn't be too sure of that,' Elvinia replied, a little too sharply. 'How much do you know of what happened to Corinna in the city back there?' She jerked her head in what she hoped was a southern direction.

'Not all of it, obviously,' Dannel replied stiffly. 'Corinna doesn't like to speak of it. That's understandable, isn't it? We could all see the scars on her face, the shaved hair. I know what you're implying, Elvinia.'

'Do you?'

'Yes, of course. Don't think I haven't thought about it or not worried about it. Corinna's mental health...'

'No!' Elvinia broke in. 'That may be part of it, Dannel, but not what I was referring to!' She scraped a hand through her hair. 'Hell, I have to tell you. You may know already, but... Dannel, she... Corinna has been... mutilated in places other than on her face. Did you know about this?'

Dannel's expression confirmed what Elvinia feared: she didn't.'What do you mean, mutilated?'

'It must have been done some time ago.' Elvinia gestured. 'Down here. In males, they call it circumcision. In females it virtually amounts to a kind of gelding, removing any ability to feel pleasure, if you understand what I mean.'

Dannel had gone rigid, staring at the bed. Later, she would realise that this information explained a lot. 'Gick's ears,' was all she said, wondering how Corinna could have lived with this secret alone.

Elvinia answered, 'Yes... Like that. Gick's ears.'

'How could she not have told me?' Dannel was pacing round the living room of the cottage, shooting angry remarks at Shyya, who had resumed his work.

When Dannel had told him what Elvinia had found out, he'd been angry himself, but more because the two women had betrayed a secret Corinna obviously felt very strongly about, rather than the original mutilation. He'd known for a long time Corinna kept a lot to herself about what she'd been through. Now, he felt guilty because he knew some of it. 'The reason she never told you is because of precisely what you're doing now,' he said, his voice sharper than Dannel had ever heard him use it. 'She didn't want her condition made public. I know how she feels. I've been through all that myself, remember?'

Dannel winced inwardly as she realised her blunder. 'I'm sorry. You're right. I didn't think.' She sat down heavily. 'But I had to talk to someone. It's such a... such a dreadful thing to discover about your own child. I trust you, Shyya. I know you won't spread this any further.'

Shyya nodded. 'Naturally. One freak doesn't fill the wind with whispers about another, does it?'

'That's not what I meant. Don't twist my words.'

'OK. This is a waste of time, anyway. It's an old wound to Corinna. We should really be worrying about what happened to her today.'

Dannel nodded. 'I know. What worries me is that she might have had some kind of mental seizure. Sometimes, she just has that look in her eye, like she's leagues away and seeing something else...' She sighed. 'Part of me has been waiting for something to happen. After what Elvinia told me, well, I'm more concerned than ever about what's going on in my daughter's head.'

Although all the Trotgardens shared Dannel fears, it was rarely spoken of plainly.

Shyya shook his head. 'I don't think that's the case,' he said. 'At least, not this time. Gick felt something too, remember. Something so strange that our beloved, familiar little Gick didn't have the wit to be able to describe it. We have to talk to the whole of Freespace about this Dannel. The implications are immense. It might be our haven isn't as safe, or as idyllic, as we'd like to think.'

The Freespacers congregated, later that day, in the clearing of packed earth outside the priestess Meera's hut. It was an uneasy gathering, rumours having spread quickly round the settlement. At last, one or two people felt brave enough to start disclosing their own, recent experiences. The atmosphere was that of relief mingled with fear. Now, nobody felt they might be going insane, but in that case, what in the Goddess' name was happening?

Meera waited inside her cabin until everybody had settled themselves outside, within the ring of threadwoods. She loosed her long, brown hair and dressed herself in the only white robe remaining in her possession. So long since she had worn it. A relic of the past. She spoke to her altar. 'Now, we shall see,' she said, nodding.

Outside, Rosanel Garmelding was having a terrible time trying to keep her mouth shut. Meetings? Discussions? She could stand up now and tell them all the truth, dispel their worries, explain away their fears. But no. She had promised Elvon she'd wait until he felt the time was right for him to return. She had a feeling that would be soon.

Up in the cave, Farris sat open-mouthed while his shadow-lover stroked image fingers over his brain. 'You will bring them here!' he said, aghast. 'Why?'

Meera came out of the hut and sat down gracefully on the mat outside her door. Everyone else took her cue and arranged themselves on the ground, mutters flying round the ensemble in a low rumble. They were waiting for her to speak. She ran her fingers through her hair and said, 'Well, the sooner we get our meeting hall finished, the better, don't you think?'

There was a chorus of subdued laughter.

Meera cleared her throat, and tapped her mouth with steepled fingers for a moment or two. Then she looked up and smiled once more. 'I know you have all been very worried recently,' she began, 'and have brought those worries to my door. I've tried to help you as best I can, but you must admit you've all been very reticent about what's really been upsetting you.' Here, she risked a benignly admonishing glance from beneath her brows.

The audience shifted uncomfortably. She had them in the palm of her hand.

'However, I understand how confusing it's all been, for me too, as I'm ready to admit, but now, perhaps, some of our questions are about to be answered.' She was performing another of her priestessly glances, when Gick stood up defiantly. All eyes turned to her.

'There are no answers yet, Meera, only more questions!' she exclaimed, her face flaming with the attention she was attracting. 'I can see where you're trying to lead this discussion, but I think all the evidence of what happened today should be presented first.'

Certain members of the gathering made noises of agreement; heads turned this way and that to gauge opinions.

Meera displayed her open palms and shrugged. 'If it will make you feel better to get it off your chest, Gick, then by all means do so.'

Gick was furious that Meera had managed to make her appear foolish. She began a stammering account of all that Corinna had told her, leading up to the events of that morning. She struggled to find words capable of describing what they had experienced in the cave. Her impassioned stumbling probably impressed her fellow Freespacers far more than a disciplined, clear account would have done. 'So you see,' she concluded, 'it's obvious there's something up there. We don't know what, but it's very powerful.'

'Indeed,' Shyya added in a clear, loud voice, even as Meera opened her mouth to reply, 'and it's something that has been making its presence felt among this community for several days.'

'Well, boy,' Quality Windteasel said, 'you, more than any of us, can sense a way around these things. What do you think it is?'

Meera was fighting off a feeling of annoyance that her religious authority appeared to have been bypassed. 'We will listen to everyone's opinions,' she said, in a tone indicating that she did not have much faith in Shyya's testimony.

Shyya inclined his head to her and smiled, indicating, just as clearly, he knew what she was thinking. 'I'm sure our priestess is aware none of us has any clear idea of what we are facing,' he said. 'Discussion will help, naturally, but in the long run, we can't put off having to face this thing outright. After we've heard what everyone has to say, perhaps we can begin to judge whether we have something hostile on our hands, something benign, or simply something that we cannot understand. I can't tell you what it is. I don't know. It's beyond my ability to penetrate. However, we all know humanity is not the first race to inhabit this world. I think we should bear this in mind as we listen to what our friends have to tell us.'

Shyya's speech elicited a round of applause.

Meera was aware of thinking how she should have begun along such lines, even if her inner conviction still assured her it was none other than the Goddess herself, the spirit of the world, manifesting up in the cave and down among her children in Freespace. People needed nudging in certain directions; acceptance of divine miracles was one of them.

One by one, at first hesitantly, but with greater confidence as each tale was recited, the Freespacers took turns to stand up and disclose their stories. There was talk of ghost-like apparitions, strange atmospheres, feelings of being watched, inexplicable movement of objects, bodiless voices and, to

Meera's heartfelt relief, one or two instances when the person concerned experienced spiritual revelation.

Rosanel sat and listened, without commenting. She did not volunteer to stand up and tell them what she'd felt and sensed, but she digested what she heard with great interest. Greylids! Naturally. Perhaps Shyya was right, and Elvon had bought his adopted people with him. It was possible. She wished she could openly support Shyya's suggestion, as she had a distaste for the direction in which Meera was trying to steer people's opinions, but her loyalty to L'Belder remained intact. *Be patient*, she told herself. *They'll know soon enough.*

The stories left a silence in their wake as everybody considered them.

Orblin Trotgarden was the first to break it. 'So,' he said, 'is it agreed some of us should go up to that cave and investigate?' Despite his brave words, he did not sound particularly eager about the idea.

'Perhaps we'd be wiser just to avoid the place!' Leto Gomery said with a laugh, nodding his head to his nearest neighbours. A few people echoed his laughter, albeit nervously.

Yaschel Tendaughter raised her hand. 'I, for one, think we should seriously consider whether we should even remain here in Freespace,' she said. 'Is it worth risking such danger? Perhaps we should up camp and move on. Let's face it, we're old hands at that!'

Several people agreed with her.

'But we've done so much!' Bolivia Trotgarden exclaimed, thinking of all the work she'd put in on the dam. 'Are we going to run like frightened danks before we've even investigated? No-one has actually been hurt, after all. Elvinia could find nothing physically wrong with Corinna...'

'Yes, but she was still hurt in some way, even if not physically!' Hollis Backwater pointed out. 'Perhaps it's a little early to say she wasn't damaged permanently. There may be delayed effects.'

Bolivia didn't like to be argued with. 'Rubbish!' she said,

but could offer no further support to her stance.

The argument for investigation against flight was pursued for over an hour, as different members of the community gave their opinion.

Meera, watching this debate with rising irritation, because she wasn't asked for her own opinion often enough, realised the matter would have to be decided by vote. If these fools voted to leave Freespace, then she alone would stay behind. No way would she jeopardise her chances of enlightenment just because of ignorant fear.

Then Meonel Trotgarden, who had been unusually quiet, stood up and called for silence. 'I think we're all over-reacting,' he said, in his most chilling, reasonable voice. 'May I just summarise?' He waited politely for permission. 'Thank you. Now it seems to me we have several camps here.' He held out his fingers to count them off. 'Those of us who feel there is something supernatural afoot, those of us who suspect Greylid interference and, I believe, one or two of you who still think it's all in our imaginations.'

Here, the Freespacers laughed out loud. Sander Tendaughter, who was one of the sceptics, made an embarrassed gesture as everyone looked at him.

'No need for laughter,' Meonel said, 'They may be right. Now, some of you feel concerned enough to want to avoid further risk to life and limb, and have suggested we all move on. I can understand this concern, but feel we owe it to ourselves, especially those of us who have worked so hard to turn Freespace from a camp into a town, to do at least a little more investigation before we start panicking or making major decisions. I'm afraid I must agree with Hollis here that we have no real proof that whatever is interfering in our lives cannot severely harm us. However, evidence suggests that only the cave and its immediate environs offer any real danger. No-one in Freespace has experienced anything injurious. Therefore, if any of us are prepared to take the risk, I think we should investigate the caves thoroughly. I, for one, am prepared to do so. Anyone else can line up right here!'

Meonel sat down to another round of applause but there were no immediate offers.

The first came from the back of the group, where Carmenya Oralien was standing alone, leaning against a threadwood. 'Well I guess you can count me in!' she said loudly.

There was a strangely tense silence, but Carmenya maintained a smile, as if unaware a greater part of the gathering did not feel particularly warm towards her. It was the first time she'd spoken.

'Well that's sensible. You're certainly somebody whose sensitivity isn't likely to be affected,' Gick said, perhaps voicing what everyone was thinking. Her voice, in the silence, was horribly clear and sounded more spiteful because of it.

Carmenya shrugged. She had too few allies to take offence.

Shyya, who was watching Carmenya carefully, said, 'I'll go with you,' looking the woman directly in the eye.

She favoured him with an expression which, to someone less discerning than Shyya, might have appeared contemptuous. Shyya, however, was quite aware that Carmenya was reluctantly grateful for his gesture.

'Me too!' Hollis Backwater called out, sensing a course of action which might sway Corinna's opinion of him.

'Well, four is enough to begin with, I'm sure,' Meonel said. 'We'll go up there tomorrow morning.'

This more or less concluded the meeting for the time being. The Freespacers began to talk quietly among themselves, discussing what they had learned.

Shyya was still watching Carmenya, who was standing with folded arms, frowning above the Freespacers' heads. He was thinking about the loneliness of Carmenya's life, and what courage it must take to face it every day. She was intelligent enough to recognise she trailed a leaden weight of past beliefs and actions behind her, the ropes of which many Freespacers took great delight in renewing as often as possible. However subliminally, the libertarian Freespacers did not want Carmenya to forget her old allegiances. Someone had to take at least some of the blame for the loss of their old homes. Shyya wondered sometimes why Carmenya didn't just pack up and go back south. Probably because she wouldn't be wanted there either, he concluded. Whoever thought I'd end up feeling sorry for her?

Suddenly she caught his eye and he glanced away quickly.

Rosanel harboured no doubts that the investigators would find nothing. Elvon L'Belder wouldn't reveal himself to them before she'd seen him herself. Of this, she was quite sure. And she was convinced they were quite wrong about the cave. He was everywhere.

After the meeting, Meera beckoned Rosanel into her hut. She poured them both a mug of ale. 'Well, they've certainly made their minds up, haven't they!' Meera said, taking a long drink.

'Investigation won't hurt,' Rosanel replied cautiously.

'Investigation! Ros, for the Goddess' sake, can't anyone see the possible truth here?'

'What do you mean?'

'I feel wary of speaking outright, even to you.'

There was a certain tone in Meera's voice that alerted Rosanel to the possibility she might not be alone in knowing the truth. Meera stared at her meaningfully. Both women were waiting for confirmation of their hopes.

'I think we both have an idea about what's really happening,' Rosanel said carefully, to test the ground.

Meera stared her in the eye. 'Perhaps we do,' she said softly. 'Something we've all been waiting for without knowing it.'

'Yes,' said Rosanel, her face lighting up.

Meera smiled widely. 'Something we had to leave the city to experience.'

'Yes,' Rosanel breathed. 'Oh yes! Thank you, Meera!' She

hugged the priestess, relieved that someone shared her convictions.

Meera gently pushed her to arm's length, putting a finger to her friend's lips. 'Hush,' she said. 'We must only wait.'

Chapter Eighteen
Liaison

Corinna opened her eyes with a start. 'What?' she said aloud. The room was silent, the cottage beyond it felt empty. For a moment, she could not remember what had happened earlier. Had she overslept? There were blankets over the window, and what little light came into the room was mellow.

There was a feeling of late afternoon, the sound of insects whirring by lazily outside. Both Corinna's felids were lying across her legs, fast asleep. She eased their sleek bodies aside and sat up, her head reeling for a moment. It felt as if she'd been drunk. Not only was her head spinning but her mouth was dry, her limbs aching. It took her a moment or two to balance herself when she stood up.

Dressed only in her night shirt she went cautiously into the living room, thankful to see several full jugs of water on the table. Lifting one of the jugs, she took a long, satisfying drink, wiped her mouth and then thoroughly stretched the muscles of her neck and shoulders.

Ah, that's better. Where is everybody? It must be slightly later in the day than she'd guessed. The light outside was that of early evening. *Am I ill?*

She rubbed her forehead and a picture of Gick's startled face flashed in front of her eyes. The cave! Nausea came back momentarily. She had to lean against the table. Goddess, what was up there? Had the others gone to see? She supposed Gick must have said something to her family. No, they couldn't have gone there. They mustn't. But why wasn't Dannel here preparing breadlemen? Where were the men? Why was everything so quiet?

'Oh, the stupid little fool!' Corinna exclaimed out loud, convinced Gick had persuaded her family to take a look at the cave. Didn't she realise the danger?

Corinna hurried back into the bedroom and began pulling on her clothes. As she dressed, the conviction became stronger within her. In her mind's eye, she saw Meonel examining the cave walls, a curious expression on his face, Dannel looking puzzled, Bolivia taking rock samples, Orblin climbing down tunnels, and Shyya? Shyya would open himself up to that thing, right up, and it would swamp him.

'No,' Corinna muttered under her breath. 'No, no.'

She knew she had to stop them.

Outside, Freespace seemed too quiet. Had the whole town gone up there? She began to run towards the dam path, realised it was much quicker to go up through the forest and doubled back to run alongside the red cliff.

So blind, so single-minded, so affected by what she had seen earlier that day, Corinna ran straight past the trees at the back of Meera's cottage, not even noticing the large gathering of people sitting talking, out front. Corinna was a blur beyond the plaisels. The Freespacers did not notice her, either.

The sloping forest was beautiful in the early evening light. All the rain clouds had passed and mellow sunlight fell down through the high branches. Corinna, however, was not in the frame of mind to appreciate it. She scrambled and panted her way up the slope, tearing ferns up by the roots as she sought handholds on the rockier parts. By the time she was half way to the cave, her chest was tight with pain, her heart beating so deeply, it felt as if it might burst and stop altogether. She did not slow her pace, however, still driven by the conviction that all her family were walking into extreme peril. Startled birds screamed in displeasure as she crashed through the undergrowth and splashed up stream-beds, seeking the quickest route. If anyone coming down the slope had run into her, it was likely they'd have fled in fright from such a wild-eyed, demented-looking creature.

She had hoped to intercept them in the outer chamber of the cave, but when she reached it, there was no sign of anyone being in there. Goddess, that meant they must have gone right inside! Down the passage! Possibly lost!

Almost sobbing, and oblivious of any danger to herself, Corinna pelted into the cave, slipping on the slick, stone floor. She scrabbled blindly for the passage she and Gick had followed earlier in the day, forgetting the darkness and the terror she had felt. Her family were in there. She would kill to protect them. Nothing scared her now. She didn't even notice that the dark wasn't as intense as it had been, or the insidious warmth coming from the glossy walls of the passage. She simply kept moving, her breath rasping, her heart still beating hard from the exertion. She could not stop.

Suddenly, there was a sharp sound, followed by a brief, dying cadence as of choral voices. Then silence.

The sound halted Corinna in her tracks. She had to put her head down, catch her breath. Her limbs were shaking as her heart pumped wildly to supply them with energy. *Goddess, my chest hurts! What the hell am I doing here?* She stood up, leaning weakly against the passage wall. *Am I crazy?*

Her senses reasserted themselves. It was as if she'd woken up from a dream, a dream which had commenced when she'd come to in the bedroom at home, a dream filled with paranoiac dread for her family.

They're not here. They never have been. I am going crazy!

Corinna wondered whether, in fact, she had ever left here with Gick. Was waking up at home and the flight through the forest part of the dream, too?

'Gick!' she called, without much hope.

'Co...ri...nna!' The answer was echoing and sibilant.

Corinna was not sure whether she'd heard it or not. Had it been her imagination? 'Gick, is that you?' She realised she was hugging herself, realised too that she could see her arms. Light was coming from somewhere. From further down the passage?

Wet hair hung in her eyes. There was water underfoot.

Still hugging herself, Corinna splashed towards the light. *Am I afraid? I can't feel anything. I should be afraid, surely.*

A voice in her mind whispered: *this is what you came for. This. Should have come the first day. Invited. Too craven, cowardly, gutless, that's what. Should have faced your fear. Not real fear, no. Knowledge, that's all, and Corinna Trotgarden is afraid of knowledge. Isn't she?*

Corinna shook her head and struggled on towards the light. Someone was here, evidently. Someone from Freespace? Somehow, she didn't think so, yet they'd known her voice, called her. What was in this place?

She came to where the passage opened out into another cavern; the source of the light. Red, green, red, green. Greater concentrations and effulgences of these colours were pulsing here and there, as if electricity was being turned on and off. *What is this?* The sheer strangeness and weird beauty of it obliterated any fear Corinna might have felt. At first, there was no sense of threat, nor any sign of someone being in there. She stood for a moment on the threshold, just looking around at the display of colours. A natural phenomenon? Was this what she'd been terrified of? There was still no sense of menace, or even watchfulness, as if whatever agency moved the light was merely intent on its own being; a kind of choreography.

An intense desire to enter the light flooded through Corinna. She was fed mental images of warmth and comfort, which banished apprehension as thoroughly as the compulsion to return had banished her fear. Gingerly, she took a step forward. There was a shudder, very much like earth movement, and the light contracted abruptly into a single, condensed sphere, retreating to the far side of the cave. Was it some kind of creature?

Then there was movement. Something appeared to solidify and step forward from the clustering pulses of colour. Corinna was too surprised to move. She said, stupidly, 'Gick?' even though she knew it couldn't be her. What or who was it then? There was still no sense of menace, only a kind of horrified curiosity. *No going back now*, she thought, and there was relief in thinking that. Whatever happened, it was necessary and ordained. This feeling was very strong.

A figure materialised from the light. It came towards her. Corinna began to laugh, but it was short-lived. However familiar the figure might be, there was something undeniably odd about it. 'Farris? Farris Windteasel?' she said. 'What are you doing here?'

'We go tomorrow, then,' Carmenya said, striding along beside Shyya as they left Meera's cottage.

'Seems best,' Shyya replied. 'If there is anything up there, I'd rather meet it in daylight, wouldn't you?'

'Sounds as if there's blessed little daylight up there from what Gick said.'

'Yes, it was pitch dark when I saw it.' This was Meonel, stalking rigidly a little in front of them. He could not conceal that he loathed this woman.

Shyya felt embarrassed, as if he had to carry the conversation for both of them. He could tell Meonel was hoping Carmenya would be finished off by whatever lurked in the cave. This thought was so strong, Shyya was sure Carmenya must be able to pick it up herself.

'At least my firearms are still in working order,' Carmenya said, provoking a sneer from Meonel, which signified just how much use he thought such weapons would be. 'What do you think it is up there?' Carmenya asked.

'Like I said at Meera's, could be anything,' Shyya answered. 'We're such blind little creatures. It might be some kind of Greylid activity, but I doubt it. From what we learned, they prefer to keep away from the mountains. Do you remember, Meonel, what they told us about the Lord of Rocks and all that?'

'Legends,' Meonel said abruptly. 'It was probably something historical, dead kings or something, mutated into fairy tale.'

'Surely it would be a good idea to examine all you learned from those people now?' Carmenya suggested tartly.

'I don't see how it can have any bearing on this,' Meonel replied with equal stiffness.

Shyya wanted to tell him not to be such a fool, but realised forgiveness would be a long time in coming if he contradicted Meonel in front of Carmenya.

'Anyway, I respect the Greylids' privacy,' Meonel continued, a remark Shyya felt sure was aimed at him. 'What we learned in Vez'n'Kizri should go no further.'

'Not even if it helps save lives?' Carmenya said.

'There's no real evidence that what's up there is hostile, or even dangerous,' Meonel said. 'It seems to me, we've just stumbled on something we don't understand.'

'But ignorance is dangerous.' Carmenya would not be deterred.

'If you're that curious, why not trot off to Ire and Penitence and ask the Greylids for yourself?' Meonel snarled.

'Sometimes that idea does seem most attractive,' the woman responded, smiling wryly at Shyya.

He felt it would be betraying Meonel to smile back, but did so anyway. 'You might have made an important point,' Shyya said. 'Perhaps we should ask the Greylids about this, rather than take unnecessary risks.'

'Don't be stupid,' Meonel replied. 'You know they don't want us back there. I'm sure we were barely tolerated before.'

Carmenya accelerated to walk beside Meonel. Shyya was awed by her tenacity. 'Meonel, have you thought about how, if we're successful here in Freespace and eventually spread, one day the Greylids are going to have to accept they share this world with another intelligent species? How will they be able to keep in hiding forever? OK, they're so evolved and so ancient, but it seems to me they must have grown lazy and stupid to want to retire from the world so much. If they possess such vast knowledge, surely it's their duty to share some of it with a younger race; teach us, whatever.'

'You think humanity is ready for something like that?' Meonel snapped. 'Imagine if Yani Gisbandrun had been privy to such knowledge. Think about it! It's not inconceivable there will be other Gisbandruns in this planet's future.'

'I thought it was our vow to make sure there isn't.'

'Carmenya Oralien, don't be such a child. We won't live forever.'

'Neither did Yani.'

'This argument is fruitless,' Shyya said. 'Let's just take a look tomorrow and then decide.'

'If we're still alive.'

'I'm sure it's not that dangerous, Carmenya,' Meonel said coldly. 'And you don't think so either, otherwise you wouldn't have volunteered.'

'True. I just like an argument.'

They had come to the Trotgarden cottage and could see Dannel, Bolivia and Orblin just going inside. Shyya felt it would have been polite to invite Carmenya in for breadlemen, as it was long past the habitual hour for a meal, but realised what an uncomfortable experience it would be if she was brazen enough to accept.

'Well, I'll see you tomorrow, then,' Carmenya said.

'Yes, early,' Shyya replied. 'Thanks for your support.'

Carmenya grimaced. 'Think nothing of it.'

Shyya was relieved Meonel ignored that cue.

Carmenya was just about to head off to her own dwelling when Orblin came running out of the cottage, Dannel in pursuit.

'Corinna's gone!' His voice was high with alarm.

Shyya and Meonel looked at each other in a moment of voiceless despair. *Where? Where has she gone? Where can we look?*

'She was sick. She was unconscious,' Dannel said lamely, wracked by the torment of wondering whether Corinna had overheard her conversations with Elvinia and Shyya earlier.

'Look, you go and round some people up, and I'll begin

searching,' Carmenya said. 'Don't worry, she can't have wandered far. Probably a bit disorientated.' She jogged off towards the cliffs.

Shyya was quite sure Corinna was not the least bit disorientated. He knew where she'd gone as plainly as if she'd left a written note. 'She's at the cave, Meonel,' he said. 'She's gone back.'

Meonel didn't have to ask how Shyya could be so sure. 'Then we're going too,' he said. 'Call the warrior woman back and let's get moving.'

'Farris?' Corinna went slowly towards him. The boy seemed to be in some kind of trance. Goddess, why hadn't Meonel taken any notice of her feelings when they'd first come here? Now someone else was involved; something which she might have been able to prevent, if she'd been taken seriously. Farris looked semi-catatonic, wraith-like, his eyes huge and round, dark as stones.

'Are you OK?' Corinna extended a hand, which the boy looked at as if he'd never seen one before. He didn't speak. She touched his arm. It felt as if all the hairs were standing on end. He began to tremble, his eyes bulging like a frightened dank's, staring past her. 'Did you call me?'

He looked at her then. 'My temple,' he said.

'Yes, I'm sure. Perhaps we'd better go now.' Corinna glanced at the soft glow at the back of the cave; it was as if something without proper form was coiled there, watching. She was wary of it, but did not feel threatened exactly. Putting her arm around Farris' shoulder, she began to lead him towards the passage. He went with her readily enough, but seemed dazed out of his mind. At the entrance, he began to struggle and tried to get away from her.

'Calm down,' Corinna said, attempting to restrain him. Goddess, what had gone on in here? What had he seen? 'Let's go home. Come on.'

Farris whined and writhed in her hold. 'Can't,' he gasped.

'Metal twisted. Hot. Blood everywhere.'

'Come on.' Corinna spoke more sharply, tugged at him roughly.

Farris kicked her.

Corinna cried out and pushed him against the wall. Behind them, the light had grown in intensity, more green than red. Farris' wild face was horrible in its illumination, almost bestial. She wondered whether she should leave him here and run, but now he was clinging onto her, his mouth stretched into a hideous grin.

'Farris!'

She tried to beat at his face, but his hands had come up to drag on hers. She could feel his hard fingers scrabbling at her eyes, digging into the sockets. Sick fear forced animal sounds from her throat. Was he trying to blind her? Then a stunning bolt of energy crashed into her head. Her eyes felt as if they were boiling. She could not move.

'See,' Farris hissed. 'See. See!'

And she did. Images - half formed - kaleidoscoping before her mind's eye - rushing greenery - nauseating sense of quick descent - impact - pain. Corinna howled and tried to pull away.

'See! Seee!' Farris cried, his voice cracking with hysteria and terror.

'Get. Off... mee!' Corinna had her hands about his wrists, struggling on two levels, as the images flooded her mind and vertigo her body.

Farris suddenly gasped and snatched his fingers from her eyes.

Corinna staggered back, bent double.

They were in darkness. Total. Impenetrable. An eerie sound; Farris sobbing. Blindly, Corinna groped towards him, aware that something had passed them by, visualising it retreating into the deeper passages of the cave system, swift and emotive as a banshee howl. As pain and fear subsided, certain knowledge settled comfortably into place, like falling feathers. Corinna reached into the darkness, finding Farris' warmth with her fingers. He fell into her arms, holding onto her so tightly, it hurt.

'It's alright,' she said. 'We must go. Come on.'

Farris didn't argue.

Supporting each other, they edged forward, feeling for the passage mouth.

Corinna and Farris were nearly at the edge of the sloping forest when they saw the bobbing lights coming towards them. They had walked in silence, but now Farris said, 'I knew they would come,' in a bitter voice.

'Don't be silly,' Corinna said. 'We need them.' She found she knew quite a lot about the way Farris was feeling now. Some of it resonated quite painfully within her. Ahead of them, she saw Shyya break away from the main group of Freespacers and come bounding up the slope towards her. A fleet of visions sailed incongruously through her mind, fragments of past events, tatters of old fantasies, accompanied by the clear, wistful sentiment: *he could have been mine once.* For the first time since she'd escaped the city, Corinna allowed herself to think, *He is beautiful. He is so beautiful.* But, whatever rogue emotions urged her otherwise, she knew this was not the time to push Farris from her and throw herself at Shyya, either physically or psychically. Her face must have been clearly displaying her unusual mental state.

Shyya looked quite worried. 'The cave...' he began.

Corinna shook her head. She walked past him towards the others, Farris still clinging onto her as if his sanity depended on it. 'No,' she said, 'not there. There's somewhere else we have to go.'

Chapter Nineteen
Rescue

They were facing the end, Zy knew this. They were sick. Alouine's face was swollen and painful. Bones were broken, infection settling there. He'd had to support her as they had staggered along. They'd found mountain-water; a cool gully, an overhang of rock free from draughts. Zy had fought against the urge to submerge himself in the pool, feeling he would only taint the water. Ripping up his last whole shirt for a rag, he cleaned himself down, carefully probing all the painful areas on his body with his fingertips. Perhaps a rib had gone, maybe two. He agreed with Alouine that his collar-bone had been damaged, and he was so bruised, it was getting too painful to walk now. His head ached interminably. Alouine was lying in the shade. Heavy rain the day before had made it impossible to travel in their condition. Against their better judgment, Zy had gathered ferns for a bed, so they could rest comfortably. Now it was too hot to move.

'This is delusion's Summer', Alouine had said.

They'd made pitifully little progress and Zy knew their condition was getting worse. Alouine lay there, defeated, weeping helplessly. The skin on her face was stretched and shiny, so painful to move she had to cry in a hideous, gulping way, her features virtually motionless.

'Here, drink some of this.' He had a plastic cup salvaged from the flyer filled with water.

Alouine drank carefully.

Neither of them bothered saying things like, 'we're going to die, aren't we?' because it seemed inevitable. They'd buried

Welma in a shallow grave and kept heading north, quite easily at first, until muscle-ache set in with a vengeance, the ground became steeper and all their wounds began to protest. They'd used all the antiseptic cream from the flyer emergency aid pod too quickly, plastering it on in a fever of dread, attempting to banish infection. Zy wished they'd been more sparing with it now. They'd also shared out the remaining antibiotics, but the supply had been insanely small.

If I ever get back, Zy promised himself, *Astracruise are going to get a law suit between the eyes for this oversight.*

Crash-landings and the need for attendant medical supplies were not regular problems for the company. Alouine obviously needed something for the wound on her face.

Zy lay down beside her, horribly conscious of how little he could do to help. 'This is my fault,' he said, for the hundredth time. 'I'm sorry.'

'No, we wanted to come,' Alouine replied, the usual answer.

That way they comforted each other.

Alouine muttered about how it had been her idea to bring the plant racks, the ones that had killed Welma. 'More my fault than yours about her,' she'd said, which Zy had negated with culpabilities of his own.

He lay with his arm across her shoulder, unable to offer more positive comfort than that. He watched the light grow dimmer beyond the overhang. Would they see another morning? Oh yes, he was sure they would. And another. And another. And then, maybe, unable to struggle further, unable even to reach water, they'd slowly die.

Sputtering torchlight illuminated the wreckage, as Freespacers picked through what was left of Speed Lady. 'Looks like there was a grave back there,' someone said. 'Too shallow. The smooms have excavated it. Whatever was buried there has gone.'

'That means there was at least one survivor,' Shyya said.

Corinna had scrambled over the tangled metal and was now holding the torch into what remained of the flyer.

They'd come straight away, following Corinna's command, as they always did, without question. No matter how much the Freespacers enshrined the icons of reason and logic, Corinna was still their archetypal prophetess, however subliminally. She had suffered so they might enjoy freedom. Sometimes, Corinna reflected cynically, that legend had its uses.

'We should wait until dawn to look for survivors,' Carmenya said. In the darkness, all that could be seen of her was the glow of her smoking-pipe.

Corinna was too hyped up to respond to the woman's electric presence yet. She was aware that might come later. 'I don't think we can wait. Look at the state of this thing. Whoever crawled out of here didn't crawl far, I think.'

Carmenya strode forward. Corinna could have reached out and touched her, if she'd wanted to. The woman poked her head into the flyer. 'Wonder where they came from? The city?'

'Looking for us you mean?'

Corinna and Carmenya looked directly into each other's eyes, for the first time in months.

'It's a possibility.'

'They had nothing like this.'

'Off-world help. Yani had her contacts, remember.'

'I can't believe they'd come after us. Not now. Why now?'

'Well, it seems immaterial,' Meonel said, dryly, behind them. 'If they did come looking for us, they crashed, and rather horribly.'

'There may be others.'

'Let's not get paranoid, ladies, please. Hopefully, we'll discover somebody alive and then we can find out.'

Farris came running down the hill through the thick foliage, crashing like a charging dank. 'There's some stuff back there, on a rock. Perhaps they headed up.'

'Towards Freespace,' Corinna said meaningfully.

'Perhaps we'd better go and see,' Carmenya decided, already heading that way.

The party mounted their danks and followed after Carmenya, who'd gone on foot, leading her animal behind.

Everything had happened so quickly, neither Corinna nor Farris had had time to think about it in any detail. Both had been fixed on the certainty that there were people in trouble. They knew in which direction to head, and how important it was to get a rescue party there as soon as possible. They did not concern themselves with how this knowledge had been mysteriously imparted to them within the cave; analysis could come later, after the people had been found.

Twenty Freespacers had galloped their danks south along the mireway, down Freespace valley, skirting the western flank of the mountain spur. Five lope-leagues down, Farris and Corinna had led them upwards, following trails they'd never seen before, as if pursuing a scent; certain, decisive, relentless.

Progress had been slower in the mountains. Sometimes the trail faded altogether; a faint, animal pathway, rarely used. Nobody doubted that they'd find something. Farris and Corinna were too sure, too urgent. Their faith in Corinna ran so deep, nobody questioned her knowledge.

Rosanel and Meera were not among the party. Both still absorbed in their personal beliefs, they felt the Freespacers were being given a sign, proof of whatever now haunted their lives wasn't hostile. They waited at home for the evidence to be delivered to their doors.

Dawn was beginning to lighten the sky when they found the rags beside the gully. Blood-stained. 'They're near here some place,' Carmenya said, looking round, rising from her hunter's crouch by the rags.

Shyya realised the woman was thoroughly enjoying all this. Carmenya didn't get much enjoyment nowadays.

Everybody raised their torches.

Corinna called out, 'Hello!' which echoed off the gully walls.

'Up there, look!' Farris pointed at the overhang.

A white hand could clearly be seen hanging over the edge.

Carmenya leapt up, taking the short path in a couple of strides. 'Bring a torch up, someone!' she yelled. 'Here're our survivors, or what's left of them.'

To Alouine Crestick, it was like waking into the past. Her commanding officer was leaning over her, barking orders. She'd slept too long. Were they out chasing renegades? Was the city burning? No, impossible. Carmenya Oralien hadn't been her commanding officer for over two years. Oralien was gone, gone with the rebels, a rebel herself, no longer existing in Alouine's world. Then who...?

Alouine gave voice to a feeble cry. Carmenya Oralien must be dead and now she had come for Alouine. A vengeful spirit. She painfully raised her arms against this vision. Death could not be like this.

No. Light, flickering light, flooded the little niche of rock.

'There're two of them,' Carmenya called down. 'A man and a woman. In bad shape too. The woman's game enough to squeal, but the man's out cold. Where's the healer?'

Zeta Windteasel scrambled up beside her, calling for her brother.

'What's the diagnosis?' Carmenya asked.

'Give me some time, will you! And some space!' Zeta shoved Carmenya away.

Farris scrambled past her, holding out a sputtering torch.

Zeta was making worried noises, the habitual accompaniment to any healing she undertook.

Farris squatted beside her. 'Are they both alive?' he asked.

'At the moment,' Zeta replied. Her job was made more difficult because the injured woman insisted on wriggling around. Zeta was unaware how frightening her appearance was in the primitive torchlight; witch-like and feral. Her wind-mussed hair looked like ragged black feathers, combining with her animal bone necklace and home-made clothes to make her look unnervingly savage and threatening.

Alouine was moaning pathetically, trying to move away from what she supposed were demons come to claim her soul.

'Just take a look at the man, Farris,' Zeta said. 'Concentrate on his neck, will you?'

Although Farris had been given rudimentary healer training by his mother, it wasn't often he was asked to use it. He was flattered Zeta wanted his help and couldn't summon up enough cynicism to brush it aside. Edging further under the overhang, he prised Zy's arms away from where they clutched his chest, running fingers, feather light, beneath the jaw and round the back of the neck. Zy moaned and turned his head. This man was not Artemisian, Farris was sure. He did not give off a familiar aura at all. As Zeta had suspected, there was swelling and heat within the muscle surrounding the collar bone. Farris shuffled back to rummage in Zeta's supplies bag, taking out a small pot of cooling unguent.

'Give him a couple of balm pellets if he can take them,' Zeta said, without looking up from Alouine. 'They should melt if placed under the tongue.'

Farris nodded and took some of the pellets from the bag. When he tried to open Zy's mouth to insert them, the man struggled back to consciousness, his eyes instantly alert and panicking, although he did not try to move. His face was almost comical in its mask of blood and dirt.

'It's all right,' Farris said. 'Don't be scared. Just let me give you these. They'll help you get well.'

'You found us,' Zy croaked.

Farris smiled. He had had no idea how the grateful response of a helpless soul could be so fulfilling to a healer. For the first time, he felt powerful among other human beings. At this moment, someone truly needed him. 'We found you. You're safe,' he said.

'Thank you. Are you an alien? No, you can't be, you're too beautiful,' Zy said and closed his eyes.

Carmenya had skidded down the rocks, back to the others where they waited, with anxious curiosity, for the healers to tell them exactly what they'd found.

Corinna mustered up the courage to stroll over to Carmenya who was standing, staring up at the ledge, with her hands on her hips. She hoped her stroll looked casual enough. 'Well?' she asked. 'What do you think?'

'Hard to say. They look pretty beaten up. Our suspicions seem justified, however. Think I recognise the woman.'

'Oh no!'

'She's with a man, though. They're huddled up together. Perhaps they were running too.'

Corinna shook her head. 'I don't know. I hope we're not too late, otherwise we might never find out.'

Meonel shouted up to Zeta. 'Can we move them?'

'We're going to have to!' Zeta called back. 'They've struggled this far. Loading them onto litters shouldn't do much more damage! Somebody get them ready!'

Corinna went to help unload and reconstruct the primitive stretchers they'd brought along.

'You look tired,' Shyya said and put his hand on her shoulder.

'I'm exhausted.' She put her hand over his own.

They held each other's eyes for a second too long, until Shyya smiled nervously and took his hand away. 'Are you going to tell me now, what it is that's going on?' he asked. 'And where does Farris Windteasel come into it?'

'I have no answers, Shee, not yet.'

'Not even an educated guess?'

She narrowed her eyes at him. 'An educated guess?' She shrugged, frowned. 'We've found an intelligent... thing. That's all I can say. What it is, I can't even guess at.'

Nearly every Freespacer was waiting on the edge of town when the rescue party returned. Dannel was at the front of the party, looking aggressive through worry. She had to be restrained from virtually picking Corinna up bodily and carrying her back to the Trotgarden cottage.

'Mother, I'm fine!' Corinna tried to insist, finally giving in and allowing Dannel to lead her home.

Elvinia came to take charge of the crash victims, installing Zy in the Windteasel tent and reluctantly accepting Yaschel Tendaughter's offer of a bed for Alouine. It irked her that she couldn't have both patients under her own roof, but there simply wasn't enough room. As it was, Farris would have to sleep on the floor so they could accommodate the man. She was itching to get to work on them, appraising Zeta and Farris' emergency repairs with a critical eye and finding there was nothing to scold them about. The Silven Crescent woman had worked herself up into an extreme state of panic, seemingly initiated by the fact that Carmenya had been the first person she'd seen when the rescue party had reached them. Well, that made sense, Elvinia thought cynically. She asked for Meera to be summoned to the Tendaughter place, because she knew the priestess was adept at calming people down, and sent her daughter, Softly, to make a more thorough examination of the woman.

Zeta still wanted to help, but it was obvious both she and Farris needed rest.

'You'll have plenty of time to lend a hand later,' Elvinia said. 'Now, go and get your heads down. No argument!'

Farris followed her to his room.

'You won't be able to sleep here,' Elvinia said, reaching to muss his hair; a gesture he ducked away from. 'You can use my bed.'

Farris nodded distractedly. 'How bad are they hurt? Will they live?'

Elvinia smiled at him. 'With you out of my hair, I might be able to find out. Now, off with you.'

'I want to watch you. It's important. Just a while. Please?'

Elvinia appraised him carefully. So strange the way they grow up before your eyes, yet you don't notice until it's all over. 'Just a few moments, then.'

Meonel and Shyya were bending over the bed, going through the injured man's pockets, examining what they found, which was very little.

'Trotgardens, out!' Elvinia ordered. 'There's not enough room for spectators - you can come back later.'

'Send someone for us if he wakes up. Immediately,' Meonel said.

Elvinia made an exasperated sound. 'Haven't you got eyes, man? I doubt whether he'll wake up for quite a while. Now, go away.'

She began to wash her hands in the hot water her husband had brought in. Quality Windteasel was already cutting away the remains of Zy's clothes with a razor-edged knife.

Meonel and Shyya reluctantly left the tent.

'Well, wash up, Farris, if you're going to stay,' Elvinia said.

Farris gratefully dunked his hands in another bowl.

Quality had begun to clean Zy's skin, as his wife approached the bed, damp hands raised like a priestess. She made a thorough inspection of her patient. 'This man wasn't born on this world,' she declared.

'I thought that too,' Farris said.

'Tie up his hair,' Elvinia instructed. 'Rinse it with briar-water first.'

Farris sponged the antiseptic wash over Zy's head. The hair was so fine, and such a strange colour, almost white. It still gave off a sharp, alien scent. The facial bones were also finer than an Artemisian's, the skin softer. Yet despite these apparently feminine characteristics, the unconscious body gave off a subliminal statement of absolute maleness; far more than any native man ever would. Farris couldn't help associating this sense of otherness with the shadow-presence in the cave. The shadow had brought these people here. Why? It hadn't divulged the reason to him.

Elvinia, concentrating on her work, kept a vestige of attention on her son, watching him covertly. He had surprised her considerably, done well. Had all her hope and attention begun to pay off now? He hadn't been around much recently. Perhaps he'd sorted himself out, without any help from her. She had never known him to show interest in another human being's welfare before. All his education in the healing arts had been accepted with stubborn reluctance. Now this. And the boy had skill. His hands had the healing touch, Elvinia was sure. She dared to hope the awkward, insular Farris had gone forever.

Because Farris was not an outstanding member of the Freespace community, nobody had thought to comment on the fact that he'd been with Corinna Trotgarden, when she'd come down from the cave with her mysterious instructions - neither had anyone mentioned it to Elvinia. She may not have been so relieved if she had known.

'I get the feeling we're being side-tracked,' Shyya said. He and Meonel were still in bed, late the following morning. They'd had barely six hours sleep but tiredness was elusive. There was too much to think about.

'What do you mean?'

Shyya wrinkled his nose. 'Not sure, really, but I've been lying here thinking about all that's going on, and how we're more worried about these people we've found, rather than what caused us to find them.'

Meonel sighed and put his hands behind his head. 'Nothing's convinced me yet, that what Corinna stumbled across in that cave is malefic.'

'Farris too, remember?'

'OK, whatever, but it helped those people didn't it? Why show Corinna and Farris where to find them?'

'Look, Meonel, I think you've convinced yourself that whatever is up there is Greylid work, whatever you say to

Carmenya or anybody else, and because of that, you think it's harmless. I'm not saying it isn't, but we don't understand it - that's what worries me.'

'So, what do you suggest we do?'

'A little analysis won't hurt. Corinna was frightened of the place when she first went in there, yet she was drawn back. Twice.'

'I think you can discount the time with Gick. That was merely a little analysis of C'rin's own.'

'But the other time?'

'She was disorientated, half conscious...'

'Meonel, she was called. She intimated as much to me. Now why?'

Meonel sat up, looking as if he wanted to wind the conversation up as quickly as possible. 'Whatever is in the cave could actually be a Greylid, for all we know. Their form is pretty mutable, after all. It saw someone in trouble and made sure we went to help. Corinna was scared at first because it was something unknown. That'd scare anybody.'

'You didn't feel it.'

'No, I'm not as sensitive, maybe.'

'I'd have thought anything remotely connected with the Greylids would tune in with someone who'd already had dealings with them, wouldn't you?'

'Shyya, you're grabbing in the dark. Making mysteries. I admit we need to tread carefully, but I don't see it as a threat. What is more threatening is that these people we've found may have come from Silven Crescent. They know we're here now.'

'You said that with menace, Meonel.'

Meonel shrugged. 'May be necessary, Shyya. Think about it. Can we ever let them go back?'

Chapter Twenty
Awakening

The Freespacers waited patiently until the following morning, when they began to converge on the Windteasel tent, as if awaiting some kind of prophecy. Because the rumour had got around that the man they'd found was not Artemisian, people were more interested in hearing what he might have to say, rather than the woman. The fact that Alouine appeared to be from Silven Crescent might also have contributed towards Freespace avoiding her.

Elvinia, however, was adamant that no-one should enter the tent, even to look at her patient from the doorway. Meera, she allowed inside, but she'd remained deaf to Meonel's entreaties that it was vital the stranger was interrogated as soon as possible. 'Tomorrow, maybe,' she'd answered, and they were the only words Meonel could get out of her.

In the privacy of the tent, she confided her thoughts about the injured man to Meera. 'He's woken up once or twice already, but hasn't said anything. He might look fragile, but I'll wager that man is strong as a brace of danks. He has a determined spirit.'

'I'd like to see him, Vinny,' Meera said.

Elvinia grimaced. 'I know you would. Who doesn't? Maybe. I'll take another look at him, and then... maybe.'

Zy opened his eyes, saw Elvinia Windteasel standing over him and said, 'Either you're the most beautiful sight in the world, lady, or simply an angel, and I'm dead. I hope it's the first.'

Elvinia smiled uncertainly. 'How do you feel?'

'Butchered. I suppose I owe you my life or something.'

'I suppose you do. Lie still. Let me take a look at you.' She inspected his dressings, examined his eyes and mouth.

Meera poked her head around the door-curtain. 'I heard voices. How is he?'

'Well, he's alive and kicking at least,' Elvinia replied.

Meera walked over to the bed. 'Think he's well enough to talk?'

'Soon. Let him get used to the fact he's alive first. And don't think I'll let you speak to him before anyone else, Meera. I'll be lynched!'

Zy couldn't lift his head from the pillow, but lay staring at the two women. They looked like terrorists or pirates, having the lean, furtive, hard-fingered appearance he associated with people of that type. In fact, most of his friends came from such ranks. Occasionally, he was still rather surprised to find himself out of that scene and nested in a fairly respectable job. Were these women refugees or off-worlders, doing a little looting of their own away from Silven Crescent eyes?'

Where you from?' he asked, reaching out to grab Elvinia's dangling trouser belt, to stop her from leaving.

'Why? What's it to you? Oughtn't you to be more concerned about your broken bones, boy?'

'I want to know whether I'm among friends, that's all.'

'That depends on what criteria you set for friendship,' Meera told him.

She reminded Zy of a bird of prey, and he noticed there was a hefty amulet round her neck, which spoke religion to him loud and clear. 'OK, you from off-world or not?'

The women glanced at each other. 'Maybe,' Elvinia said.

Zy exhaled a long, painful breath. 'You don't know how relieved I am to hear that! I'm in shit, sisters, stranded on this forsaken history lesson of a world. I thought I'd been picked up by a bunch of natives. Can you help me get out of here?'

'We'll have to speak to our people,' Meera said, smoothly.

'Who's your friend, the one from Silven Crescent, or at

least dressed as if she should be?' Elvinia asked.

Zy grimaced. 'She's no friend of mine, just a chaperone. She's from the city, but she's OK. We've been through a lot together.' He tried a dazzling smile, which he suspected appeared rather more menacing than he'd intended. 'How is she, by the way?'

'Mending. It's been traumatic for her,' Elvinia answered. 'City women aren't used to clawing their way up the life-path, after all.' She leaned over and quickly examined Zy's eyes once more. 'You're a tough one, I must say.' She rubbed her hands together fastidiously after touching him and went to call, 'Farris!' into the next room. 'I'll have my boy Farris fix you something to eat,' she said. 'Then, when you're rested, you can tell us all about yourself.'

'I'll enjoy that,' Zy replied.

'Thought you might,' she said.

After they'd gone, Zy lay blinking at the dim light. How long had he been here? Painfully turning his head on the pillow, he assessed his surroundings. For off-worlders, these people seemed to have built fairly permanent dwellings. Even though he was under canvas, it was clear, from the furniture and possessions lying around that it had been lived in for considerable time. There was little sense of impermanence about it. Where were they from? A handsome race, certainly, and too tanned for spacers. Mineral pirates? Maybe.

The door-curtain lifted, and a boy, presumably Farris, came into the room, carrying a wooden tray on which stood a single, steaming bowl. 'Smells good,' Zy said, trying to be friendly. 'Are you Farris?' Perhaps the boy would be more forthcoming than the women had been. Zy attempted to sit up, but it was too painful to move.

'I'm Farris, yes.' The boy put down the tray. 'Be still. I'll feed you.' He propped Zy up with pillows and then sat on the bed, beside him. 'This is soup,' he said, lifting the bowl.

Zy obediently opened his mouth, and Farris began

spooning it inside. A memory surfaced in Zy's mind: opening his eyes, wracked by pain, but filled with the almost spiritual relief of knowing he'd been saved. Farris had been the first person he'd seen; recalling his face brought back a taste of balm pellets to Zy's mouth. 'I remember you,' he said.

Farris didn't answer.

'Thanks for what you did.'

'Be quiet. Eat.'

'That's enough,' Zy said, after a while, turning his head away.

Farris leaned forward to wipe his face with a cloth.

'How long have I been here?' Zy asked. 'Who are you people? Where are you from? What are you doing here?'

'You talk a lot, don't you?' Farris folded the cloth and laid it on the tray with the half-empty bowl.

'Will you answer me or not?'

Farris shrugged. His face was in shadow.

'Well, seeing as I know your name, I'll tell you mine,' Zy said. 'I'm Zy Larrigan. I'm from a place called Africa Plate.'

'Do you want the bottle?'

'Do I what?'

'The bottle. To piss? Do you?'

Zy sighed. 'Listen, I have to get out of here,' he said. 'If not back to Silven Crescent and the terminal, then out in one of your ships.'

'One of our ships?'

Zy mistook Farris' bewilderment for reticence. 'That bad, are they? I'm not fussy.'

Farris raised an eyebrow, shook his head and stood up. 'I've been told not to answer your questions, or ask any. My mother and the others will see you later. You can speak to them.'

'The fact you're so cagey tells me just as much about you as the longest answer you can give.'

'I don't think so.' Farris smiled, which changed his appearance considerably.

'I meant what I said,' Zy told him, hopefully.

'And what was that?'

'The first thing I said to you. You're beautiful. Are men allowed to say things like that to each other where you come from?'

'I can't answer your questions, Zy Larrigan. Don't try to get round me. You can't.' Farris fetched a bowl of water, which his mother had left to cool by the door. 'I'll clean you up. You worked yourself into a sweat during the night, and I really think you ought to use the bottle.'

'If you insist.'

Farris' appearance of calm was a sham that, even in his panic, he was quite proud of. Already, the call was building up within him; insistent, demanding. He knew he would soon have to climb back to the cave and, as always, half of him was afraid of that, filled with repugnance. The other half, naturally, welcomed it. Strangely, what had happened there had brought him closer to his people; brought him closer to Corinna Trotgarden whom he admired. But he knew now that Corinna was not the one the shadow had promised him. He knew this simply because the person lying on his bed wore a face Farris felt he had seen before, knew well. Zy Larrigan lived beyond the stars and did not belong here. He was a doorway, summoned by the shadow. Looking down at this helpless man, Farris could not summon up the tingle of dread that accompanied all his fantasies of pleasure, tainting their sweetness with a jarring tartness. His common sense warned him that what he imagined was benevolence might well be simple manipulation, and that his welfare might not be that important in the long run. Couldn't this man feel it? Didn't he know? Apparently not. Ah, but he was hurt. Perhaps that was the reason. With a simple extension of his senses, Farris could feel every morsel of pain as if it was his own body that was injured.

Zy lapsed into a weary drowse as Farris cleaned his skin. The intimacies of nursing him did not feel sexual, but at the same time, it invoked a very intense feeling. Farris touched Zy's brow. 'Don't hurt,' he said and began to stroke the pain away, muscle by muscle. He drew it down through Zy's body and out of the soles of his feet, folding it into a black ball, which he dumped into a nearby bucket of water to earth it. His mother had certainly not taught him that technique. Nobody had. He'd just suddenly remembered it.

'Don't stop,' Zy mumbled. 'I feel better already.'

'I'll be back,' Farris said and took the bucket of water outside. He threw the contents high into the air, watching it splash down onto the packed soil outside his family's tent, where the pain it contained dissipated and became something else entirely

Chapter Twenty-One
Old Ties and New Plans

A town meeting had been arranged that afternoon. Decisions had to be made concerning how much the Freespacers should reveal about themselves to the strangers, and what action should be taken about the events involving the cave.

On her way to the gathering, Carmenya just had to stop by the Tendaughter place where Alouine Crestick was convalescing, and take a look at her. Yaschel was not as stringent about visitors as Elvinia was with the man, but then again, no-one had come around to see Alouine anyway.

Oh, reminders of the past, Carmenya thought. *No matter how hard I try to kick it away it just keeps coming back.*

Sander Tendaughter took her into Alouine's room - his own - which, like Farris, he had been required to donate. He told her about the woman's progress, what she'd eaten, what she'd muttered in her sleep.

Carmenya wasn't interested. She just wanted to look on the face of the past and see whether it had changed.

Alouine was groggily awake, her face pulled into a hideous rictus by the swollen wound. Elvinia's people had stitched it up and drained it, but it still looked angry. Around the livid wound, Alouine's face was unnaturally white and damp.

'Well,' Carmenya said, standing some distance away from the bed, 'who'd have thought we'd ever meet again under these circumstances.'

'You really got away,' Alouine mumbled.

'It hurts you to talk, so don't,' Carmenya said. 'Yes, I got away. We all did. We've done pretty well too. Was this what you were sent to find out? No speeches please, a single word will do.'

'No.'

'Well, that's a relief.' Carmenya didn't want to be sarcastic and wasn't sure why she was being that way.

'You haven't changed,' Alouine said faintly.

'I was afraid of that.'

Alouine Crestick had been a member of Carmenya's staff for several years. It all seemed such a long, long time ago. Alouine hadn't really made much of an impression on Carmenya back then, and it had taken her a while to actually recall the woman's name. Carmenya had hardly known her, hardly even spoken to her. Now, it seemed as if an old, close friend was lying there. Strange. A friend with whom she'd parted on bad terms, perhaps? She wanted to interrogate the woman, get answers, but it was clear from her condition that would be unwise, even cruel. One question, that's all she must ask, one question. Had anyone else asked it?

'We have to know, Alouine Crestick, what are you doing here in this part of the world?'

Alouine blinked at her. 'Zy Larrigan, the off-worlder...' she said.

'The man you were found with?'

'Yes. Is he... still here?'

'He's alright. In better shape than you, I gather.'

'Then ask him.'

'Hmm.' Carmenya tapped her jaw with impatient fingers. 'I'm asking you.'

'We were dragged here,' Alouine said, spots of livid colour beginning to bloom in her cheeks. 'Dragged.' She closed her eyes.

One question, that was all.

'Thank you,' Carmenya said.

The meeting was once more held out of doors so all the

Freespacers could attend. Some were panicking, haunted by persecution fears, suggesting again they should all pack up and move on quickly.

'I don't think that's necessary,' Meera told them calmly. 'From what evidence we have, it appears these people crashed here by accident.'

'It doesn't solve what we should do with them, though,' Meonel Trotgarden said, stating something nearly everyone must have thought about.

'Let's see what they have to say when they've recovered,' Meera replied. 'There's no need to panic.' She was wondering whether she should introduce the subject close to her heart. After all, what other proof did these people need? Parthenos was giving them a message, telling them to put aside old hatreds and embrace those considered to be enemies. Ruefully, she wondered whether she would always be the only one aware of the truth. Perhaps Parthenos expected her to guide the Freespacers towards a new spiritual path, without ever manifesting herself more clearly.

Since the two southern people had been found, there'd been no more strange events and no peculiar feelings hovering around Freespace. All that seemed to be over. What now?

'Corinna, can you tell us all exactly what happened yesterday?' Meera asked.

Corinna was sitting on the ground nearby, tufts of torn-up moss grass scattered round her feet. 'It's difficult,' she said, 'but I'll try.'

She related the events as well as she could remember.

When she'd finished, Meera said, 'Where is Farris? Shouldn't he be here?'

Elvinia looked around the gathering, a puzzled expression on her face. She was still rather shocked to discover her son's participation in Corinna's adventure. 'I told him to come,' she said. 'He's probably still back at our place.'

'Perhaps you should fetch him. We need to hear his story too, I think.'

Elvinia nodded and gestured for Softly to run off and find her brother.

Corinna alone knew this was a waste of time. Farris would not be at home. He was already back at the cave, where she should be now. The urge to run there right away was so strong. It was more than fascination, though that was involved. It was a need, a craving. She was not even convinced the light, whatever it was, might not be dangerous - her fears hadn't evaporated completely - but she had to find out more.

Someone was suggesting a party of people should go to the cave as soon as possible to investigate what was going on. Perhaps those who had offered before should continue with their plan.

Corinna spoke up. 'I don't think that's a good idea. We don't know what it is yet. The fewer people taking risks the better. I'm prepared to take the risk, and so is Farris. We will conduct whatever investigations seem necessary. After all, it does seem as if the thing specifically wants to make contact with us two, doesn't it? If it starts looking like anything is... happening... to us, then take whatever action you feel is best, but I think you should let us go ahead for the time being and just monitor us carefully. I'll tell you all I can.'

'Well, personally, I think that, as spiritual leader of this community, I should go along too,' Meera said. 'I think the bulk of you have forgotten the religious aspect of all this.'

'There is no religious aspect to it,' Corinna snapped quickly. 'We have no proof at all of that, and I think your presence would inhibit our investigations.' She knew she might be going too far in front of so many people, but Meera had annoyed her, to a point where she could no longer keep her feelings to herself. 'Also, Meera, you should be reminded there are no leaders in this community, spiritual or otherwise. We've left all that behind. Have you forgotten why?'

There was a palpable silence after that, but Corinna sensed most people agreed with what she said. Victory for the archetypal prophetess!

Meera looked stunned, but Corinna didn't relent. Just because they'd been co-conspirators back in the city, it didn't mean Corinna would go against her beliefs in the name of friendship. Meera should know that and respect it.

Meonel stood up to break the silence. 'I think we should go along with what Corinna suggests,' he said. 'For now.' He shot her a keen glance as if he suspected she knew more than she was letting on, and to advise her not to stick her neck out too much.

She nodded to him. Point taken, step-father.

'However, I think you should wait until we've spoken to the off-worlder before going back there,' he continued. 'You'll need to be armed with all the knowledge you can get.'

Tell that to Farris, Corinna thought, but reluctantly agreed to the suggestion.

Following that, a vote was taken, and the majority went along with Meonel and Corinna.

Softly Windteasel returned to say Farris could not be found.

'He's already back at the cave,' Corinna said, with even greater reluctance. 'And no, before you all get worked up, I don't think anyone should go up there and drag him back. Farris knows what he's doing, believe me.'

'It might appear so, Corinna,' Meonel said sharply and turned to Elvinia. 'However, when he returns, I suggest you tell him to stay in Freespace, like Corinna. They can go back together, after we've spoken with our off-world guest.'

Everything being more or less agreed, the meeting was declared closed.

As people began to drift away, Meera beckoned Corinna aside, mainly, Corinna felt, to let everyone see she wasn't going to take offence. 'I'm not going to apologise, Meera, if that's what you want.'

The priestess waved her comment aside. 'No matter. You have no faith, Corinna, but I don't hold it against you. Time will tell. Perhaps you are right, and a sceptical mind will be of more use for now.'

'Well I think so. What is it you want?'

Meera smiled. 'Don't be so prickly. I'm not about to lecture you. Just a suggestion. I think it would be a good idea if you took notes while you were up there, meticulous notes. Record everything you think, see and feel. Everything.'

Corinna nodded. 'That seems sensible. I'll start with what's already happened and write it while I'm up there.'

'Good. Do be careful, won't you?'

'Of course. Thanks.'

They embraced awkwardly, though Corinna felt there was an insurmountable barrier between them now.

Chapter Twenty-Two
Pillow Talk

'I'm wondering what exactly it is you're made of, Mr Larrigan,' Elvinia said, arms folded, looking down at him critically. 'I'm beginning to doubt it's flesh and bone. Two days ago, you were nearly dead, I'd say, now look at you!'

Zy was sitting up in bed. 'Maybe I look better than I feel,' he said. 'Although, I do believe my parents had me genetically engineered to be able to fight infection within my tissues more rapidly than most.' He shrugged, pulled a wry face.

Elvinia frowned, unsure whether to believe him. 'You'd have died if we hadn't found you,' she said.

'Most probably.'

'Well, I'd better warn you. People want to speak to you today, and I reckon you're well enough to face it.'

'Of course.'

'Be straight with them, Mr Larrigan.'

'I wouldn't dream of doing otherwise. And please, call me Zy.'

He thought it odd these people also used the baroque title of 'Mister' like the Silven Crescent women did. An affectation they'd picked up, maybe? He would have to be alert to idiosyncrasies of custom. Experience had taught him how communities could vary in their eccentricities throughout the galaxy. The fact that he hadn't seen Farris since his heavy-handed compliment seemed to indicate their sexual code was stringent, too. That wasn't unusual. He'd come across many cultures where the practices of the flesh had pursued very peculiar avenues indeed. Not everybody embraced the healthy ideals of Plate life, after all.

'So who are these people?' he asked Elvinia. 'Your leaders?'

'We don't have leaders,' she replied, bustling round the bed to straighten the coverlet, paw his pillows into place. 'But there are certain families whose guidance we trust. Individuals too.'

Families? Zy thought. They must be gypsy nomads, then. But that didn't exclude the possibility they were pirates. 'I'm no threat to you,' he said. 'Really.'

Elvinia peered at him closely. 'No, I don't believe you are,' she replied. 'Intentionally.'

Farris turned up again a short while before the visitors were expected. The reception from his mother was totally unexpected. Without raising her voice, and in a few concise statements, she made plain her discontent at his behaviour. 'What is all this business of the cave, Farris? I hear you've been dabbling around up there. How long has this been going on? What have you been up to?'

He was stumped for words.

Luckily, Elvinia left him no time to answer. 'You are a fool! Have you no sense of danger? Why didn't you tell me? What if something had happened to you?' She shook her head. 'I can't understand you, Farris. I thought I was beginning to, as well. I thought you were finally coming to your senses.'

He couldn't think of anything to say. The presence in the cave had been virtually non-communicative since he and Corinna had been there together. He felt it was waiting for something. Had its purpose been only to bring the off-worlder here? But, if so, why? Farris had begged for answers, for enlightenment about what he should do next, but no information had been forthcoming. Sheer exhaustion had driven him home, only to be confronted by a barrage of questions from Elvinia.

Fortunately, the arrival of the Trotgardens silenced her.

Farris retreated to a corner, in the main room of the tent, where he licked his emotional wounds and bathed himself in a pool of self-pity.

Elvinia, assuming the role of hostess, called Softly and Zeta in from outside and had them fix up refreshments for all the guests, pointedly not asking Farris to help.

Gradually, other people began to arrive; Yaschel Tendaughter, Leto Gomery, Meera, Rosanel Garmelding and Carmenya Oralien. Farris wasn't sure whether to be relieved or annoyed when Corinna pushed towards him through the animated throng, who were all discussing, in intense voices, just what they were going to say to Zy Larrigan.

Corinna squatted down beside him. 'Here, Farris, I've brought you a drink,' she said cheerfully. 'Are you feeling OK?'

He nodded and took the cup from her. 'Yes. You?'

'Fine. Fine. So, do you think we should go up there tomorrow?'

'Huh?' His puzzlement must have been obvious.

'Oh, you weren't at the meeting, were you?' She grinned. 'And nobody's told you, of course. We're going to make a scientific study of our new friend in the cave, and I fixed it so that you and I can get on with it without interference. Is that alright with you?'

'I guess so.'

'We'll have to work out a strategy.'

Farris couldn't help inwardly wincing at this. 'We can try,' he said, making sure his disbelief was evident in his voice. 'But I doubt if it'll work. The Presence has gone quiet since you went up there.' He gave her a significant look. 'Of course, it may be thinking... or something.'

'We'll see,' Corinna replied airily, ignoring any intended criticism. 'We have to hear what the off-worlder has to say before we can go back to the cave. Let's hope he comes up with something specific.'

'Who says when we can and can't go up there?' Farris asked indignantly. 'What's it to do with anybody else?'

'People only have our safety in mind,' Corinna replied carefully. 'It makes sense, Farris, if you think about it.'

'Hmmph.' He didn't want to get involved in some kind of community project, yet his autonomy appeared to have been whisked from beneath his feet.

'Shall I call for you in the morning if everything's to go ahead?' Corinna asked. Her expression showed she knew she'd offended him in some way.

'No. I'll meet you there,' he said.

'I'm not going to be in your way, Farris.'

She had no idea what went on when he was in the cave. 'I think this is all crazy. Why are they trying to understand what the Presence is? It's beyond them, all of them!'

'You don't like people much, do you?'

Farris gave her a piercing glance, without speaking, which she smiled at.

'Yeah, I understand. I really do.' She touched his arm. 'I'd prefer it if you believed that.' She tapped the scars on her left cheek, perhaps unconsciously or perhaps as an illustration.

Farris relented. 'OK.' He sighed and then jerked his head in the direction of Zy's room. 'I think they're closing in for the kill now.'

Elvinia was directing the way to the invalid's bed.

'Aren't you coming?' Corinna asked.

'No. Take notes for me. I'm sure you're good at that.'

She seemed surprised by his sarcasm.

'Well, you are the scientist, aren't you?'

She shook her head and jumped to her feet. 'Have it your way,' she said, rather stiffly.

Farris decided it was unwise to upset her further and offered her one of his best smiles. She grinned back uneasily. 'I'm not a crowd person, Corinna. I prefer it this way.'

'Fine. That's fine.' She waved her fingers at him and followed the others.

Farris bit the edge of his cup and watched her go. He badly wanted to be with them, but couldn't face Zy Larrigan with people around them. It would have to wait. If he could find the courage.

Zy watched tentatively, a rigid grin across his face, as everyone filed into the room. Elvinia introduced them all; the names were outlandish, and difficult to remember. No-one was smiling. Their spokesperson appeared to be the tanned, languid, fair-haired man named Meonel, whom Zy deduced immediately was no fool. It seemed sensible to address all remarks to him. 'So what do you want to know?' he asked, palms displayed in a gesture of openness.

'What do you think you should tell us?' Meonel asked in reply, folding his arms.

The question was a challenge, obviously. 'I'm not in your territory through any fault of my own.'

'Well, that's a start.' Meonel sat down on the end of the bed. 'Just what are you doing on Artemis? Off-worlders aren't a common feature here. And you were with a woman from Silven Crescent...'

'I'll start at the beginning,' Zy said. And did.

The Freespacers listened in silence while he related his complaints about his commission, beginning with how he'd fallen out of favour with Astracruise and the need to reinstate himself. He made them smile with anecdotes about his experiences in Silven Crescent, and became involved in his story, delivering several mordant impersonations of the women he'd had dealings with. Everyone in the room reacted favourably, and the atmosphere became more cheerful. People surrendered stiff, upright positions of defence and sat down on whatever surfaces they could find, huddling together in the confined space.

Then, Zy began to relate events occurring during his journey north, and the atmosphere changed again, to that of vigilance. 'So you see,' he concluded, 'things did not go entirely to plan, and here I am.'

There was a moment's silence during which people

swapped uneasy glances.

Then, Carmenya Oralien, who was smoking her long pipe as usual and leaning against the bound door-frame said, 'You mentioned the women suspected something from the north was interfering with your flyer?'

'Yes. I suspect now that they were right and that it was you lot.' He raised his hands in a placatory gesture. 'Oh, I'm not accusing anyone. I'm not saying you wanted us to crash. You just wanted the flyer, right?'

'Well, supposing you are right,' Meonel said carefully. 'Tell me how you think we could have influenced your flyer's computer when you were still on the marsh. The first error occurred only a short way from Silven Crescent, or so you said.'

Zy laughed. 'Oh, come on, you have all the sophisticated equipment, right? You must have been pretty surprised to find a craft of that advanced type in your trawl net!'

'Mr. Larrigan,' Meonel drawled. 'Just for your convenience, I'll dispel your illusions about us. We are not off-world pirates, as you seem to think. We are, to put it in terms you will understand, refugees from the City, from the time of the Devastation. We have no sophisticated equipment, very little technology at all, in fact. All we have are a couple of unwelcome visitors on our hands - who make us feel suspicious... and rather a large mystery.'

Zy was astounded. 'You mean, if it wasn't you fouling Speed Lady's works, then it had to be somebody else.'

'Precisely,' Carmenya affirmed quietly. 'And somebody quite close, wouldn't you say?'

Zy was puzzled. 'Well, I don't know what to say.' He screwed up his eyes, wagged a finger in concentration. 'Just a minute. Alouine said something.... That's it. You know about this L'Belder stuff, don't you?'

Meonel smiled. 'L'Belder stuff?'

'Yes. His followers escaped the city after he bumped off the Leather Lady. You must know that.'

'Well, yes.' Meonel narrowed his eyes. 'What point are you

trying to make, Mr Larrigan?'

'Apparently, Alouine thinks they've got some kind of - I know this is going to sound crazy - power. Alien power, or something. Now, I didn't believe this, naturally, but could it be possible these people are around? Could it have been them messing with the flyer?'

Meonel took a moment to raise his eyes skywards and take a deep breath. 'Sadly, Mr Larrigan, although your theory is ingenious, I must refute it. At this moment, you are looking at what remains of Elvon L'Belder's followers, and I regret we have little in the way of alien power here.'

'I'm disappointed.' Zy smiled. 'Well, was it true or not? Did L'Belder change? Was there any alien power at all?'

Meonel laughed. 'You said you didn't believe in fairy-tales!'

'I don't, but I do have an open mind. Why don't you just tell me - if there's anything to tell.'

Meonel looked stony. His people were silent around him, letting him handle the conversation. 'There is nothing to tell, Zy Larrigan.' He narrowed his eyes again, and stared at Zy hard. 'I wonder what's special about you. Were you brought here deliberately, or was it a mistake, even unintentional? This is what we have to ascertain.'

Zy wriggled uncomfortably. 'This is all very flattering... I think.'

Meonel stood up. 'Don't be flattered, Mr Larrigan. Be careful.'

'Of what? Is there anything to be careful of? I wish you'd be straight with me. I've told you everything.' He realised he could be in more danger now, injured and helpless, than when Speed Lady had been streaking to her destruction. These people knew more than they were telling him, he was sure. Were they really L'Belder's followers? Meonel clearly didn't want to speak about that in detail.

'Don't worry yourself,' Elvinia said into the awkward silence. She directed a scorching glance at her companions and went to stand by Zy's side. 'Just concentrate on getting well. You'll be perfectly safe here. You have my word.'

'But safe from what?' Zy asked, aware his voice had risen both in volume and pitch. 'What's going on here?'

Elvinia put a restraining hand on his shoulder. 'I think that's enough for today,' she said, firmly.

'I have to get back to Silven Crescent,' Zy said. 'I have to leave.'

Nobody commented on this statement. They began to stand up and make for the door-curtain. The last person to leave the room was a girl whose face he seemed to recognise, a girl whose face was scarred. She looked at him for a few moments before ducking beneath the curtain.

'Who was that girl with the scars?' he asked Elvinia. 'She seemed familiar.'

'Corinna Trotgarden. She was one of the people who found you.'

'I don't remember her from then...' Zy paused, looked up at Elvinia with what he hoped was a melting expression. 'Am I being kept here?'

'What do you mean?'

'You know what I mean. Am I?'

Elvinia reached out and stroked his hair. He knew she'd developed quite a fondness for him over the past couple of days. 'Zy, we have problems. I can't tell you more than that. Be patient. No-one will hurt you.'

'But when will I be able to leave?'

'I don't know,' Elvinia replied.

'I hope I can trust you.'

'I'm looking after you, aren't I?'

Zy shrugged. 'I know. It's just that this is another world to me. Do you understand what I mean by that? I don't usually come into such close contact with... please don't be offended by this... natives, during my work. You might find me rather strange.'

Elvinia laughed. 'We're all of us rather strange, in one way or another, believe me! You told us tales, alright, but wait until I tell you a few of my own!'

He smiled. 'I'd like that.' Paused. 'Elvinia?'

'Yes?'

'There's something I have to get off my chest. I've been lying here thinking about it.'

'Oh, and what might that be, Zy Larrigan?'

'I think I offended your son.'

'Who, Farris? I wouldn't worry about that. He's difficult to fathom - and relate to - most of the time.'

'It was rather more personal than that. I think I ran up against one of your social taboos.'

Elvinia frowned a little. 'I don't believe we have any! What kind do you mean?'

Zy shrugged helplessly, unwilling to expand on that.

'Oh. *That* kind,' Elvinia said. 'Don't worry, Zy. That's not a taboo. Remember we came from Silven Crescent originally.'

'Things can change.'

'True. But not in our case. Farris can be very odd at times. Please don't let it worry you.'

'You're not angry?'

'Do I have a reason to be?'

'No... I haven't seen Farris since. I just thought...'

'Yes well, he hasn't been around here much, as it happens.' Elvinia paused and delivered a meaningful look. 'Actually, I'm quite worried about him.'

'Why?'

'You're not supposed to be told, but...' She glanced at the door-curtain and then sat down beside him, leaning towards him confidentially, and speaking in a low voice. 'There are strange things happening around here. Very strange. Your being brought here is only part of it. Farris is involved. Frankly, I'm afraid he's in danger.'

'What kind?'

Elvinia screwed up her face in vexation. 'It's difficult to explain, but... Look, I'm only telling you this because it's obvious you will have more experience of this situation, given your job.' She sighed, clearly debating whether it was wise to continue or not. Then she shook her head, coming to an inner decision. 'It looks as if we've run up against something... well, there's a kind of strange thing. A creature, maybe. We don't know. It has *powers*.'

'Powers?' Zy exclaimed. 'Creature? What do you mean?'

'Hush,' Elvinia admonished. 'Keep your voice down.'

But it was too late for caution. The door-curtain lifted and Farris was standing there, his expression curiously blank and yet darkly intense. Elvinia physically flinched back against Zy.

She's afraid of him, Zy realised; a random, swift thought.

'Don't tell him, mother,' Farris said. 'You mustn't do that.'

Elvinia stood up. 'He'll have to find out eventually,' she said. 'And it looks like he's part of all this. His wider experience of... other life... could help us.'

Farris didn't reply. He directed a single, razor sharp glance at Zy, who felt a physical chill pass through his flesh. Then, he let the curtain drop and was gone.

Elvinia rubbed her face. 'Perhaps Meonel will explain to you,' she said, as if Farris' odd manifestation had not just happened. 'I'll ask him.'

'Please do,' Zy replied, and leaned back against the pillows. His heart was racing. He felt drained, and fervently hoped appearances were deceptive, and he had not crash-landed into a nest of lunatics.

Chapter Twenty-Three
The Study Begins

'It seems like we're having town meetings every few hours nowadays,' Corinna said to Shyya, on their way to yet another gathering.

'Perhaps people are beginning to enjoy all this turmoil and excitement,' Shyya replied. 'It's a bonding experience.'

'Isn't it just!' Corinna knew that one person, in particular, harboured decidedly caustic thoughts about the entire community becoming involved; Farris Windteasel. Few people made Corinna nervous like he did. She didn't know where she stood with him, whether she was regarded as friend or foe. His attitude seemed to vacillate from minute to minute. Sometimes he was as gauche as a pre-pubescent boy while, at other times, as knowing and cynical as Meonel. It was disorientating.

By halfway through the meeting, Corinna was beginning to sympathise with Farris' viewpoint. People were quite happily arguing about when she should go to the cave, and what she should do there, without bothering to ask her opinion. Every time she opened her mouth to protest, Meonel pinched her arm. What he was playing at, she couldn't fathom and, knowing Meonel, he was undoubtedly playing at something. This time, however, his manipulations were going over her head.

'I've had enough of this!' she hissed.

'Be quiet, step-daughter. It's therapy for them. They have to let off steam.'

'They don't know what they're talking about!'

'Of course they don't. That's why it's necessary. Sit still.'

'I feel like going up to the cave right now, whatever they think!'

'I know. But you have to sit here and let them see you sane and whole and brave. They have to believe you're going to march up there tomorrow, armed with their good advice.'

'Meonel, this is unnecessary.'

He shrugged and Corinna hunched down beside him, simmering.

When the meeting drew to a close, she realised she hadn't absorbed the majority of what had been said. She took a deep breath, stood up smartly, and said, 'Well, I'll be off, then. Wish me luck!' She considered it best not to look down at Meonel. Let him think what he liked.

Bolivia walked back to the cottage with her. 'When are you really going, C'rin?' she asked, trying not to appear worried.

'Immediately. I'll just get a few things together and then take off.'

'Are you sure you're doing the right thing?'

'No, but I haven't a clue what else to do.'

'Want me to come with you? I will, you know, if you need me.'

Corinna paused and put her hand on her sister's shoulder. 'Thanks, Livvy, but no. Farris will be up there. I won't be alone.'

'Farris, huh?' Bolivia said archly. 'Is there more to this than you're telling me? He's turned into quite a stunner, has that boy. Poor Hollis! He'll be heartbroken!'

Corinna laughed. 'Liv, if you think I've volunteered to expose myself to an unknown, unquantifiable power just to get a few moments alone with Farris Windteasel, no matter what a beauty you think he is, you're crazy.'

'Crazy things do happen, you know.'

'Yeah, all the time, but lust for Farris is not happening to me.'

'Might do you good.' Bolivia was still teasing and was unprepared for Corinna's sudden withdrawal. Her face had gone dark.

'You think I don't know that!' Corinna snapped and strode on ahead.

'Goddess, what did I say?' Bolivia muttered and ran after her.

Dannel hadn't bothered going to the meeting. She preferred not to think about what was happening and hoped it would all turn out to be a mistake. Didn't they all have enough to worry about without this? She looked up from her work with alarm when Corinna slammed into the cottage, wearing a face like a stormy sky. Bolivia wandered in behind, making helpless, shrugging gestures. Dannel shook her head and stood up, following her younger daughter suspiciously into her bedroom. She watched with rising unrest as Corinna started throwing a few clothes into a bag.

'What are you doing?' Dannel asked darkly. 'You're going somewhere again aren't you? Where?'

'I'm just going to be camping up at the cave for a while,' Corinna answered, steeling herself against her mother's reaction.

'On your own?'

'I expect Farris Windteasel will show up.'

Dannel bustled across the room and slammed her hand across Corinna's bag, preventing her from putting anything else inside. 'No!' she said, emphatically. 'Someone else can go, not you! Haven't you done enough for these people already?'

'Nobody's forcing me. I want to go. Mother, please take your hand off my bag.'

Dannel stood upright, arms folded belligerently under her breasts. She heard the front door close softly as Bolivia tactfully took herself off somewhere else. 'Corinna, don't do this to yourself, please.' Her voice was ragged with frustrated anger.

'I know what I'm doing. Somebody has to go and Farris and I have... well, we're developing a kind of understanding with whatever lives up there. I'll be alright. I wouldn't go if I didn't think that, honestly.'

'Maybe you're right, but at least take someone else with you... someone sensible!'

Corinna straightened up and glared at her mother. 'Someone sensible?' She laughed. 'Great. If I did that, I'm sure nothing remotely interesting would even happen! Who do you suggest? Meera? She's gone more loopy than I ever will! Yaschel Tendaughter? The thing up there wouldn't get a word in edgeways!' She shook her head. 'Someone sensible indeed! I told you, I wouldn't go if I thought it might be dangerous.' She lifted her bag and squeezed past her mother into the living room, heading for the food store.

'Wouldn't you?' Dannel followed Corinna to the door. 'You love danger, that's your trouble. It's almost a perversion with you.' She still hadn't told Corinna what Elvinia Windteasel had found out about her. Looking at this distant stranger, she realised she might never have the opportunity to do so. Every day, Corinna drew away from her. Every day, a little farther.

'Can I take some of this?' Corinna asked, holding out an antelope ham. Without waiting for an answer, she stuffed it into her bag, along with as many other supplies as she could carry.

Dannel didn't appear to have noticed. 'I'm worried about you, C'rin,' she said helplessly. 'At least talk to Shyya about it.'

'I don't want to talk to Shyya. I don't want to talk to anyone. I just want to go.' She hefted her bag onto her shoulder and bent to deliver a quick, faint kiss to her mother's cheek. 'I'll be fine. Someone will come up regularly to check on me, it's all arranged. Come yourself, if you can manage the climb.'

'I'll get Meonel to carry me up,' Dannel said, only half in jest.

Corinna laughed. 'That's more like it. I'll see you soon. Don't worry!'

Dannel watched her daughter stride away from the cottage, desperately trying to dismiss the dreadful superstition that it might be the last time she would ever see her.

All Corinna's family, and most of her friends, managed to intercept her leaving, just to wish her luck and, naturally, offer advice. Rosanel Garmelding had whispered something in her ear about 'give him my love'. Corinna was puzzled by this. Had Rosanel developed a fondness for the recently blossomed Farris, perhaps? How odd. Mind you, Corinna thought, people had been behaving oddly for quite a while now. Hollis Backwater hadn't shown himself, which Corinna found surprising. She realised she was quite disappointed he hadn't sought her out to say goodbye. Perhaps he shared Bolivia's idea that she was interested in Farris. How ridiculous! She liked Hollis a lot. Would he never get it into his head that she couldn't offer him more than friendship? If he knew the truth about her mutilation, he'd probably feel sick. She had no desire for him to know, not even to shock him into giving up his pointless wooing. Perhaps she'd neglected their friendship so much recently, his desire had fizzled out of its own accord.

Gick, however, was lying in wait, and was not prepared to be dissuaded from accompanying Corinna up to the cave site. Corinna was torn between appreciation of Gick's concern and outright annoyance that the girl was refusing to take no for an answer. Once, she would have said, 'yes, come along', and have been glad of the company; grateful too for the presence of another mind to corroborate what she might see, and to help assuage any fear. Now, there was no real fear left inside her, and she felt strongly that whatever waited up there waited for Farris and her alone. She was nervous, obviously, and hoped she was sturdy enough to weather whatever experiences awaited her, but she didn't need anyone else along.

Gick tailed her to the dam path, Corinna repeating assurances that yes, she would be fine, yes, she'd come out of the cave in the morning as promised, talk to Gick, talk to the others, yes, she had her note pad. Silently, she was raving, *yes, yes, yes, now just leave me alone!*

Reluctantly, Gick left her at the entrance to the valley pathway, and Corinna only looked back once. After she'd turned the first corner, it was as if Freespace were a million lope-leagues away. Corinna exhaled, long and slow. Her heart was beating fast in anticipation; her palms, armpits and upper lip damp with perspiration.

She took her time on the walk. The longer route hadn't been chosen to delay the inevitable. She merely wanted to find out whether she'd view the valley differently now she'd unveiled one of its secrets. It would be a relief to get away from the nest of anxieties incubating back at the town. Paranoia was setting in; a new debility and, she dreaded, a shattering one. Could Freespace ever feel the same as it had - brave, young and free - once it had stooped over the fearpot of conspiracy? Most people were convinced that the man and woman they'd found had been brought here by whatever lurked in the cave, and they were busily encouraging those who still harboured doubts to share their views. Hysteria had expanded this suggestion into the fear that the 'unseen power' might be uniting Silven Crescent armies and off-worlders, with the intention of leading them towards Freespace. Corinna wondered whether these suspicions could be correct, although Zy Larrigan had seemed straight enough. She would try to find out the answers to these mysteries herself. Getting worked up into a lather and high-stepping round in a tail-chase, bleating in fear, was one thing; taking a deep breath and investigating was another.

Corinna whistled a greeting to the spider lizard, who must have been getting used to interlopers on her territory, and leapt up to the hidden path.

The valley seemed as looming and vigilant as ever, but Corinna was relieved to find that it didn't spook her as much. She strode off quickly down the meadow, singing out loud, in a clear, defiant voice, to show she wasn't frightened. She knew she could only expect to be given a day without interruption. A single day; during which her family and friends would be frenziedly preventing themselves from charging up to check that she was all right. Corinna was no fool. She knew that fear for her mental health and constant supervision, albeit discreet, went hand in hand with her partial canonisation for the role she'd reluctantly played back in the city. It hadn't been much of a role really. Sometimes, she felt sick about it; she didn't deserve so much admiration. Sometimes, she wanted to stand up in front of them all and say, 'Look, I messed everything up back then. I was afraid. I was young, naive, meddling. I didn't realise the consequences of flirting with rebellion. I got caught and paid the price. They slashed my face, they shaved me raw, they gutted my sex. Then, then, as I was suffering my imprisonment, actually serving that bitch Gisbandrun because I wanted no more hurt, Elvon L'Belder came. He set us free. He engineered the circumstances that allowed Gick and I to escape. And we ran and we ran and we ran! No heroics. No fighting. I didn't want to fight. It wasn't my war. I just wanted home and peace and the marsh. I didn't really care! Understand me? Yes. Walk away and leave me. I'm just a girl, nothing else, not even that, just a vessel for a mind that's a shrine for a heap of memories that aren't even real.'

Some speech. At night, it shrieked through her fantasies. She wanted to smash the Freespacers' image of her. But in the morning, someone would come to her for advice, and it would feel good to be consulted, for her opinion to matter, and the night-time fantasies would skulk back to their sub-conscious lair to sleep the day through.

Tramping through the valley grass, Corinna sang louder to dispel these thoughts. They were not daytime preoccupations and she mustn't think them. *Think about what you're doing now.* Soon, she would enter the trees. Soon, she would see the slick, black steps leading up to the cave. She was nearly there. This is not a time to be thinking about the past. Then, there was a voice in her head; a familiar voice. Its tone was shrill and spiteful; an inner demon. 'Stamp on your thoughts as much as you like,' it said, 'but you know the truth really. One person is aware of what really happened in the city. Carmenya knows. And she is disgusted by you. She was there. You did nothing. She saw you run. That's why she keeps away.'

'So damn her!' Corinna shouted to the trees. 'I'm doing something now, aren't I?'

By the time she reached the stone steps, the sky had clouded over, and misty rain was filling the air with moisture. Quick lichens bloomed sluggishly. Soon their time would be over. What would winter be like here? Surely not like the marsh with its swift transition from balmy days to harsh storms, and its inhabitants' long incarceration against the elements? *Will I see it?* Corinna wondered. Time was measured differently now. Freed from routine, the Freespacers existed from day to day. She rarely heard people say things like 'in two moons-arc, this will be finished'. Now, they were likely to use the vague measurement of 'Some work in that yet'. When the suns sank, it was time to stop work because the light wasn't so good. People gravitated together to eat during the day, only because their stomachs were attuned to expecting food at certain times, but nobody kept a time-piece to arrive home for breadlemen at the exact minute. Corinna measured time in seasons, no way else.

'Goddess, don't let anything happen to change things,' Corinna said softly. 'Don't let the old ways catch us up. We were reborn. It's got to stay that way.'

She'd brought lamps with her, five of them. As she lit the first in the outer cave, she thought about how fortunate it was that the rocks in this area were so richly laced with veins of flashpowder. Otherwise, how would the Freespacers have managed when the stocks they'd brought with them from the south had run out? *We'd have made fire the long old way, of course. We are lucky.*

Lifting her lantern, Corinna paused for a while before entering the passage, taking time to have a good look around. The stone floor was smooth as glass; damp from wind-blown moisture. Was that because of age, or because countless feet had eroded it in earlier years? Greylids? 'Are you still here?'

Corinna whispered. 'Is it really you? Or something else...'

She ventured into the passage, noting now that moisture ran down the walls, probably from cracks in the rock above. If the rainfall here was anything like it was in the marsh in winter, this passage might well be impassable then. Corinna stood on tiptoes and lifted her light to the roof. The cracks might have to be filled, she thought. She rounded a corner, and soft pink light illuminated her path. *Well, here goes. Here I am. Are you expecting visitors?*

Farris was there ahead of her. She found him in the inner chamber, sitting on the stone floor, before a twisting morsel of gaseous light.

We accept this as if it is normal now, she thought. *Just look at that thing! What the hell is it? And yet, we're not afraid.*

She crouched down beside Farris and eased her bags off her shoulder. 'What's happening?' she asked in an exaggerated whisper.

Farris didn't seem surprised to see her. 'Nothing much,' he replied, in a normal tone of voice. 'I've listened a little. To the pictures.' He smiled. 'Are you here with permission, or not?'

She pulled a face. 'Shut up! I've brought blankets and food.'

Bolivia was right about him, she thought. She'd never considered him handsome or beautiful, but now it was as if he'd truly blossomed; a cavern flower, fey and delicate, perhaps brief. 'What are you picking up, then?' she asked.

'It's like I said; pictures. Old pictures. I think it's remembering, sharing its memories with me.'

'Can I see them too?'

'That's why you're here, isn't it?'

'I'm not sure why I'm here, why either of us are, for that matter.' Scrubbing at her hair, Corinna settled herself on the stone floor and put the lamp down beside her.

'Just relax,' Farris told her. 'Do a breathing exercise or something. Try to meditate. If it's going to speak to you, it will. Don't fidget, don't make a noise, and turn that damn lamp down.'

'I can't meditate if you're going to bitch at me!'

Farris turned his head, quirkily tipped it to one side, and smiled at her. That, Corinna decided, is a gut-kicking smile.

'Just listen,' Farris said.

Chapter Twenty-Four
Just Listen

The pictures came as softly as dreams. Corinna became estranged from her body; physical sensation was behind her. She was aware of other people around her, other entities. Voices conducted a measured conversation, swapping ideas. It was a verbal dance; innovative nuances on age-old philosophies. Corinna could not understand what was being said; the semantics of it were elusive, just beyond her grasp, but only a little way beyond.

A city gradually materialised around her, becoming more concrete with each passing thought. She walked. Narrow, winding streets curved steeply upwards all around her. Was this Silven Crescent? No, it was not that place. Silven Crescent could never have been like this, not even when it had first been built. The light was odd, shimmering off walls and paving stones as if they were all carved from living gems. Corinna sensed people around her, but their forms, unlike the city, were indistinct, mere phantoms. She felt she was walking with purpose, towards a predetermined destination. There were many bridges to cross over and, when she looked over their sides, she could see the sparkle of sunlit water, far below. This city was virtually no more than a complicated cluster of towers. Corinna felt she must be very high up. Bridges linked the towers above and below her. Looking up, she thought they were too slim and fragile to be safe.

Eventually, the body she inhabited stopped before a doorway. She knew this was a workplace and that it was familiar to her. She did not knock or have to use a key, but opened the door simply by running her fingers over a series of knobbly protrusions on the frame. Beyond, green light fell into a long passage through emerald-glass skylights. She walked along the passage and, at the end of it, into a low, airy room. Here, she saw a man relaxing in a strange device - part chair, part harness - that was holding his body erect, so he could work comfortably at the desk in front of him. He looked up and smiled when he saw her; a strange man. The planes of his face were all wrong; the teeth oddly long and curving, the lips too smooth. He wore coveralls of a faded, citrus colour. He said to her, 'Fesk was here last evening. He's made considerable advances. Come see. We're some way to understanding it all, at last.'

There were charts on his desk; stiff greenish parchment etched with purple marks. She had never seen this written language before, yet found she could read it.

'The sickness, it's genetic, you see?' The man tapped the parchment with a light scriber. 'But the alteration is so swift and, in an adult subject, almost magical. What have we got here?'

'If it's genetic, are we talking about deliberate meddling or, dare I say it, evolution?' Corinna's body said.

The man made a shrugging gesture, a procedure requiring far more wriggling than Corinna had ever seen in a shrug before. 'That's what we've yet to ascertain, I'm afraid, but - can't you see? - the implications are incredible!'

Corinna's body copied the wriggling shrug. 'It would seem so. Have we been so wrong all this time? Are the Wanderils not invalids as we've believed, but superior beings?'

'Look at this! Look at this!' the man said excitedly, tapping the charts. 'The evidence is inconclusive, true, but if Fesk's tangents are even only fractionally relevant, our whole world is undergoing some vast transformation!' He pointed to various glyphs. 'See this? Astrological fluctuation. And this? Abnormal plant cycles. This here? Migrations! And more of these Wanderils appearing all over the place. What does this suggest to you?'

'It suggests one of us is going to have to infiltrate their society, and obtain some first-hand information.' Corinna remembered saying this specifically, remembered the feeling of excited frustration, the juicy challenge of it.

'Not just that. We need subjects, Mollen, live subjects to investigate further.'

Mollen. So her name was Mollen. Who had she been? Or did she exist now?

Then there was a twisting in time and space. The identity of Mollen had undergone some change. Corinna possessed her memories. She was aware that she was participating in, or spectating upon, events that had occurred on Artemis perhaps thousands of years before. Mollen and her colleagues were native Artemisians, but obviously of a race that had preceded the mutated beings referred to as Wanderils. These mutants, Corinna knew, would eventually be called Greylids. Mollen had been seeking the Wanderil base, following them, trying to question them - always a difficult task; they were so vague. For a year, she had virtually lived with the Wanderils, charting their culture - eclectic to say the least - and studying their racial psyche. She had tried to catalogue their mutations, but there seemed no pattern. Physically, some were hideously deformed, but she suspected they could change these deformities at will. Some were so radiantly lovely, they were terrifying to look upon. Of these, it was said that their glance could turn a person to stone. Artemisians, like humans, had their legends. The Wanderils were not secretive, but simply difficult to comprehend. They spoke freely of the One God who had granted them the blessing of the Change. What was this One God? A scientist experimenting in seclusion somewhere? Possibly. The only way to find out was to follow and investigate.

Mollen wrote in her journal, 'This becomes more exciting all the time. I feel as if I'm following the River of Knowledge to its source. Soon, I will KNOW.'

Just how accurate these observations had been was frightening. The One God lived in a mountain labyrinth, far from the stilted cities of the marsh. Corinna regained her human modern-day identity and became merely an observer; a phantom in their time, unseen. A hundred thousand Greylids were living in the mountain, and Mollen was with them. She was in a dark chamber, deep inside the rock. Corinna watched as Mollen surrendered herself to the great change, casting off her clothes and her Artemisian flesh, as if without thought. Within a ring of robed Greylids, the One God manifested itself as an intense light and entered the body of Mollen; through her eyes, through her mouth, even through the pores of her skin. Corinna realised, with a kind of mortified fascination, that she was witnessing the most bizarre carnal coupling she could ever imagine. Was this what Elvon L'Belder had experienced? She watched, with growing horror, as Mollen's flesh was invaded. It was as if she was being sculpted from the inside out. Her facial features were contorted in agony, but her eyes were radiant with joy. She could not move. She could not escape. She could only endure what was happening. Her flesh was steaming. Corinna thought there might be blood. And the others just stood there, watching, as she was. But, unlike Corinna, they were part of it.

And then Mollen arose, from the ashes of her flesh: reborn, alien and terrifying. It was as if she was made only of liquid; the power of her will alone holding her into an attenuated, rippling shape. There were many others waiting behind her for the same privilege.

Now, winds howled and time blew a hurricane of seasons over the world. Corinna knew the lands beyond the mountain labyrinth had changed entirely. The stilted cities had sunk into the marsh and their people were no more. Whether they had expired from some natural calamity, left the area, or been totally absorbed by the Greylids was still unclear to her, but she was certain the Greylids were the only surviving people. Within the labyrinth, in a circular chamber of rock, shadowy forms glided around a pulsing globe of pink and green light. Inside the light, geometric shapes tumbled and spun, describing the mathematic reality of the universe. The figures had purpose. They were doing something. The rock walls of the chamber were translucent. Veins of darkness ran through this smooth, pearly lustre, suggestive of plant or animal life, and there were other strange scorings that reminded Corinna of electronic circuitry. Some of the Greylids were interrogating the light, others receiving impressions from it, still more feeding it with information. There was enough of Mollen's lingering presence in her mind for her to know this. Lightning flickers licked over the walls like blood through arteries.

Corinna wandered, an unseen phantom from the future, around the chamber. Just as she reached out to touch the walls, the rock around her shook violently, as if from an earth tremor. The Greylids were staggering around in confusion, and grasping for balance, as if suddenly they'd all become blind. The light went crazy. Corinna saw it shoot out beams of radiance that burned whatever they touched. Greylids were burning.

A voice cried out, 'There is division! The Moss King and the Lord of Rocks have bisected!'

Another voice called distantly, 'Hurry! The Lord of Rocks holds sway! We must leave. Quickly!'

And they did.

Corinna came to herself in the inner cave, breathing deeply, quickly. She instantly reached for the lamp, turned it up - despite a weak protest from Farris - and fumbled in her bag to find her notebook. She must write it down now, while it was still clear. She felt sure that the light, the Presence contained in this cave system, was some form of artificial intelligence, discovered, or even created, by the Greylids, which they'd been forced to abandon. Did it possess sentience, perhaps even consciousness? It knew the history of the Greylids, and obviously preserved some, if not all, of their memories, which could be accessed by anyone interacting with it. This would explain her experience of seeing through the eyes of Mollen, who was undoubtedly long dead.

After she'd finished writing, Corinna jumped up and went towards the light. It was quiescent, the size of a human head, resting just above the cavern floor. She bypassed it, conscious of what, in her mind, she'd seen it was capable of, and went to examine the further wall of the cave. Was this the same place as where she'd seen the veins and circuitry in her vision? She reached out and touched the rock. It was not illuminated now, and the chamber was too dark for her to be able to see much beyond the halo of her lamp. If the veins were deep inside the wall, it would have to be lit from within for anyone to notice them.

She felt a prickly heat, as if her hair was full of static, and turned round quickly. The ball of light was hovering just by her shoulder. She narrowed her eyes, trying to see mass within it. Impossible. 'Just what are you?' she asked it. 'Friend? Foe? Animal? Machine? Vegetable? Spiritual? Or all of those?'

It was possible the thing didn't understand her now they had broken their esoteric communication.

'Farris, how do we question this thing?' Corinna asked, striding purposefully back to where the boy was sitting. In the light of the lamp, she could see, beneath the rubble of loose rocks, that the floor had once been smooth. She looked up quickly. Perhaps part of the roof had fallen in.

'It only shows pictures,' Farris said. 'You can't ask questions.'

'Mmm. Does it show the same pictures all the time?'

Farris shook his head. 'No, I've seen many lives.'

'What about the walls. Did you see the walls? The lines and all that? Where are they now?'

Farris looked confused. 'I don't know,' he said. 'Only the pictures.'

'Have you seen any recent pictures?' Corinna asked. 'Like the one about the flyer crash?'

'No.'

'Hmm.' Corinna paced up and down to think. 'How about their initiation into being Greylid. Did you see any of that? You know, it was almost, well, sexual.' She felt embarrassed mentioning it to Farris, but it was essential to establish whether she had imagined that.

Farris merely stared at her.

Corinna sighed, cleared her throat self-consciously, and looked at the light where it hung a few feet away, seeming to observe them curiously. She felt fairly sure it was absorbing everything that was happening, but was it sentient? She wondered why she had been so terror-stricken the first time she had visited the cave, and also why that sense of panic had left her. It had been so definite at the time, an almost tangible thing. Elements of what had apparently happened to Mollen resonated painfully with certain things Corinna had experienced herself; invasion, mutilation. She realised she felt an affinity with the dead Mollen because of this, even though she knew it was really quite senseless to identify with her, because Mollen had been an entirely voluntary subject. Nevertheless, the feeling of empathy was still very real. Was that significant? Could it be that the reason she had been singled out for the Presence's attention was because of her past experiences? Corinna couldn't decide. It was so hard to be objective. She needed a confidante to discuss this with, a sounding board.

'Farris, we have to understand what's going on. Will you tell me everything you've experienced and seen?'

Farris looked furtively away. He shook his head. 'I don't want to.'

'Why?' Corinna squatted down beside him and touched his arm.

He turned his head to look at her hand, distantly.

'Farris, I was very scared when I first came up here. It made me ill. I need to understand why. I don't give a damn right now about anybody else; what Freespace wants, or off-worlders, or anyone. Just me. I have to know.'

Some genuine urgency in her voice made him look her in the eye. She dropped her gaze. 'There are things about me that no-one knows,' she said. 'Sometimes I'm not sure how they've affected me. I'm hoping what's happening here will help me understand.'

Farris was still regarding her warily. 'If I tell you things about myself, you must swear never to repeat it.'

'I swear. I promise.' Her expression never wavered as he told her. There was no judgment in her eyes, no amusement, just genuine interest. 'It would have hooked on you, I think,' he concluded. 'Because you were the first living person with the right...' He struggled for the correct term. 'Feeling, I suppose, to enter the cave, but you weren't right in other ways.'

Corinna pulled a face. 'This is beginning to make sense,' she said. 'I think.' Now she turned her head away. 'Farris, I might as well tell you - and this, as well, is not to be repeated, but I'm kind of unsexual. Something happened to me that made me that way. If the presence here is related to that kind of feeling, I'm not surprised it made me sick!'

'It attempted to communicate with you using a language your body couldn't translate,' Farris said.

Corinna was surprised by this eloquent deduction. 'Seems so. But where does Zy Larrigan come into this?'

Farris shrugged. 'I think he may have, or be, something the Presence can use. I don't know why. At first, I thought he was some kind of miracle, a wish made real. For me. Now, all that glamour has been taken away. You and your scientific analysis!'

'Am I supposed to apologise?' She couldn't help smiling.

Farris wrinkled his nose, shook his head. 'No. It's OK. I prefer to be objective now.'

'Has Larrigan... reacted to you in any way?'

Farris sighed. 'Hard to tell. He's not like us. The Presence made me do something weird in front of him. He probably thinks I'm a freak.'

'Something weird? Like what?'

'Oh, my mother was going to tell him everything, about this cave and what's been going on, and I was more or less pushed into the room to stop her. It must have looked very... mysterious.'

'You can communicate with this thing from Freespace, then?'

'I wouldn't call it communication exactly. I can't work out what it wants. It thinks we're more intelligent than we are, I suppose. It thinks we know already.'

'Does the process work two ways? Have you told it things about yourself?'

Farris nodded. 'That's why I thought it was touching me in that way. I told you, I thought it was granting a wish.'

'Perhaps it was! We should look at things from all angles.'

'You ask it for something then. Experiment. Be scientific!'

'Alright. I will.'

Corinna closed her eyes. The first picture that came to mind was of Carmenya, which she banished instantly. No. This is an investigation. Be sensible. Considering her immediate desires, she visualised something harmless; the farm at Vangery, a home, the stilt-house in the marsh. It was pleasant to think of that and reconstruct it in her head. She had to concentrate hard to remember all the details. It was sad how much of it she had forgotten already; where the rickety board had been on the back ramp, the exact arrangement of the pulleys under the belly of the house.

After a while, she opened her eyes. Was there a chance now that, when she walked out of here, she would find herself back in the marsh, and that all of recent history hadn't happened? Could anything be that powerful?

She shook her head, deciding the time had come to eat. She broke off a chunk of bread from one of her loaves, which she handed to Farris. 'There's meat and salad too. Eat.'

'Seems you've thought of everything.'

'Still think I'm a pain?'

Farris grinned, but didn't reply. He bit into the bread.

'Would you be prepared to let the presence touch you in front of me?' she asked, trying to make that sound like a normal request.

'Why?'

'So I can get aroused second-hand of course!'

Farris shook his head and laughed. 'I don't believe you.'

'Good. I was lying. I just want to see what happens, that's all. Perhaps you're being changed into a Greylid.'

'Goddess, I hadn't thought of that!'

'See how useful I am?'

'I'll think about it. I don't know you that well, Corinna. It would be very embarrassing.'

'No, it wouldn't. I told you, I can't feel anything in that way. It'd be like doing it in front of a tree!'

'If you believe that, you're mad,' he said. 'But I'll think about it.'

Chapter Twenty-Five
Carmenya

After Corinna had left for the cave and Freespace had more or less settled, if only temporarily, back into its usual routine, Carmenya went to see Alouine Crestick again. Nobody had felt any easier when they'd heard what Zy had to say. They all wanted to know why and how the flyer had been influenced to crash nearby. Larrigan's unintentional suggestion that the agency responsible might be mechanical, rather than supernatural, had certainly opened a few eyes. It was also, perhaps, the evidence they'd been fearing that the unknown presence in the cave was not a benign force. Perhaps Alouine could shed more light on the subject, even though her view was bound to be even less objective than Larrigan's, who at least had the benefit of greater experience with technology. Carmenya was aware, however, that just as much could be learned from an alternative opinion, no matter how uninformed it was. Alouine might have noticed things that Larrigan hadn't, before, during or after the crash. Carmenya also felt compelled to ask the woman for her story, simply because she didn't think anyone else had bothered to talk to her.

'You look better,' she said, as she entered the room.

Alouine was sitting up in the bed, propped by pillows. 'Yes, I am, thank you ma'am. The people here are kind.'

Carmenya waved a dismissive hand. 'No ma'am here. I lost my rank the moment I fled the city.' She looked around the room. 'You've got a better deal than your friend, Mr. Larrigan, believe me. The Tendaughters have one of the best residences around here.'

Alouine tried out a painful smile, and Carmenya went to sit on the bed, helping herself to a cup of fruit-juice from a jug on the table nearby. 'Want some?' she asked.

Alouine shook her head. 'I've been thinking,' she said. 'I admire what you people have done. Nobody thought you would, that you'd survive. I suppose Zy - Larrigan - told you what's been going on; the tourist resorts and all?'

Carmenya finished off her drink and put the cup down. 'Yes. Quite a joke, isn't it?'

Aouine nodded. 'We questioned the wisdom of it. Somehow, finding this community, separate from the city, and thriving, makes me see things in a new light. It doesn't seem such a far-fetched idea now. Silven Crescent and the sister cities aren't the only settlements on this world any more. We can't feel so possessive about it now, can we?'

'No, you... *we* were wrong ever to have done so. It's surprising how things fall into perspective once you're away from... well, you know.'

'Entirely.' Alouine sighed and raised her eyes to the ceiling. 'Goddess, I wish Welma was here. She'd have loved it. She was getting so used to being out in the wilds. You should have seen her...'

Carmenya thought of the excavated grave and shivered. 'It's a tragedy, and a mystery too.'

'Yes, the priestess Meera has been to see me. She explained a little of your problem here. One thing wasn't explained though... Your position as regards the city knowing where you are. I suppose you'll be reluctant to let us return.'

'Can we count on your silence?'

Alouine pulled a painful face. 'Mine, maybe so. But Larrigan's a business man. He's prospecting, and Freespace has boundary rights or something. He was talking about that before, asking Welma if she thought there were refugee settlements anywhere. You have rights, ma'am, believe it or not. Silven Crescent might not be able to touch you, now they're operating with these off-worlders. There are inter-planetary laws about the rights of settlers and so on.'

Carmenya considered this and then said, 'haven't I said don't call me that? I've renounced that privilege.'

'Have you?' Alouine asked dryly. 'I expect you're still wielding power here though, aren't you?'

'Hardly. The Freespacers have little love for those of us who were once part of Yani Gisbandrun's dictatorship. At best I'm regarded with suspicion, at worst as a scapegoat, although I'm being useful to them at the moment.'

'And you've never wanted to come back to the city?'

Carmenya glanced away. 'Never.'

'There are obviously greater things in life than power, then?'

'You talk as if that comes as a revelation. I hope not.'

'Those who have power rarely regard it as a necessity. To those without, who are subject to the power of others, it seems the only path to freedom.'

Carmenya laughed uneasily. 'When you are well, take a walk around this little shanty town, Alouine. It may well enlighten you.'

'I intend to.' Alouine paused, cast a furtive glance in Carmenya's direction. 'May I ask you something?'

'Go ahead.'

'Is L'Belder here with you people?'

Carmenya stiffened a little. 'I'm surprised you ask that. No, he is not. As far as we know, he never left Silven Crescent.'

'As far as *we* know he didn't, but then he was never found either, alive or dead. He disappeared. Naturally, some of us assumed he'd followed you people north.'

Carmenya frowned. 'I can see why you'd think that. None of us knew what was happening. To this day, I'm not sure what I saw on that last night in the city, Alouine. Something happened, that's all I can say. A madness came, from which I ran. I never met L'Belder. He is not my messiah. If I am here with the people you consider to be his, it is only because attaching myself to them was the only option open to me at the time.'

Alouine did not appear interested in Carmenya's sudden confession. She pulled herself up off the pillows. 'But do they have his power?' she asked.

Carmenya drew away from the almost greedy urgency in Alouine's voice. 'The only power we have here is... that of our hands and hearts and minds,' she answered. 'If L'Belder really did have some kind of extraordinary strength, it was not something he bequeathed to us.'

'I am not so sure,' Alouine said. She flopped back down onto the bed, breathing fast.

'You think I'm lying?'

'No.' Alouine closed her eyes. 'You're not lying, but I'm still not sure. I keep wondering about how Larrigan and I were brought here, and why. It seems such a coincidence that we've run into the people who once had connections with L'Belder. It's too much of a coincidence.'

'He is not here, Alouine. Don't look for such demons under your bed.' Carmenya smiled. 'Look, you've exhausted yourself. Get some sleep.'

In the night, Carmenya woke up frantic and afraid. It took a few moments to reorientate herself. For a crazy second or two, she was convinced she was back in her bedroom at the house in Silven Crescent. She had even smelled it; wood and polish. Impossible. Outside her shack, the light was turning towards dawn, birds were beginning to sing, while she lay alone in her narrow, makeshift bed, far from her old home.

Groaning, Carmenya swung out of bed and padded naked to her water supply; three buckets, one already rather stale. She hadn't been home much recently, if this place could be called home. Dipping a mug into the nearest bucket and taking a long swallow, she sought to identify what had woken her. A bad dream? It had involved L'Belder, she was sure, and it had been horrific. A feeling of insecurity was still with her. Alouine's words must have stuck in her head. She'd scared herself. Corinna Trotgarden had also figured in the dream somewhere. That certainly wasn't a novelty. Corinna often haunted Carmenya's dreams, appearing as a pale waif of a girl, much as she'd been when Carmenya had last seen her in the city; wounded innocence, a face hollowed by betrayal. Carmenya did not like to think about Corinna, not for the reasons Corinna suspected, but because it made Carmenya feel dirty. She knew, more than anyone, how badly she'd let the girl down. Corinna hadn't even wanted to go to the city. It had been Carmenya who'd forced the issue, using her influence with Dannel, knowing Dannel was slightly afraid of her, making out it was some kind of honour. What it had been was lust; pure and simple. She'd wanted Corinna as a concubine and had had her. Lost her too. No, lost wasn't the right word. Carmenya had abandoned Corinna, given her up to Fate and the cruelties of Yani Gisbandrun.

During the first few months of the journey north, Carmenya had repeatedly dreamed of the night when she'd delivered Corinna into Gisbandrun's custody. She'd seen the different options that had been open to her, the multitude of opportunities she'd had to help Corinna get away, but fear, and an instinct for self-preservation, had forced her to obey orders. At the time, she'd called it survival, which had fitted well into the space in her spirit left by self-disgust. Travelling north, she had recognised her actions for what they'd really been; those of cowardice. She hadn't been able to face Corinna after that, and had avoided her as much as possible, even though her cold indifference must have been driving a crippling knife deeper and deeper into Corinna's soul. Now, Corinna despised her, and rightly so. Too much silent time had passed for them ever to begin speaking naturally now.

Carmenya threw the mug into the bucket, satisfied by the angry rattle it made. *That's my soul*, she thought, *a metal cup rattling around in a bucket of stale water*.

A hard core inside her still insisted that Corinna had asked for what had happened to her. She had helped L'Belder, sought out the rebels and joined them. The consequences had been her own fault.

You can't blame yourself for that, Oralien.

No, but if I hadn't taken her to Silven Crescent in the first place...

Oh, what's the use of worrying about it now? It's an old argument. Perhaps both views of it are true.

Carmenya went back to lie down on top of her bed. It had been weeks since she'd thought about any of this, and she'd hoped it would eventually be forgotten entirely. History had no place here.

Don't kid yourself, said the cold, inner voice. *They hate you here. They won't let you forget.*

This was true. Other members of Silven Crescent's military had followed her out of the city to freedom, and every one of them was now invisible within Freespace's community. But not Carmenya Oralien. The war criminal's crimes were too great to allow her serenity. Freespacers were liberals. They allowed her sanctuary, but shunned her friendship. Even her old comrades kept their distance now, fearing taint. Only Trotgarden's gelding ever had any time for her, and old prejudices meant she could never feel comfortable in his presence. She was aware that Shyya pitied her, and that made her angry. She was also furious with herself because of the way she responded to his sympathy; with helpless gratitude, as a dank might to the praising hand of its rider. Nauseating! What had happened to her? Perhaps that was why she was glad Alouine Crestick was here. Poor Alouine, still calling her ma'am, still trapped in the empty barrel of Gisbandrun's dictatorship. Nevertheless, it was flattering when Alouine spoke to her with respect. She'd needed it for a long time. The old Carmenya had thrived on admiration.

She glanced down at her body, which was leaner than ever, and still boyish, despite the encroachment of age. It was perhaps the only thing that still gave her pleasure.

Unconsciously, Carmenya let her hands stray over its firm contours, drawing up her knees when her fingers reached the core of delight and letting, for the first time in years, Corinna's face supply the fantasy to her lonely desires.

In a few hours, she would accompany the Trotgardens to the valley. In a few hours, she'd be facing the real Corinna, but there would be no soft smiles, no brief caresses. All that was confined to the realms of fantasy. Carmenya knew that the innocent girl she had once desired so much was dead. The woman, whom Carmenya had secretly grown to love and respect in her own right, was very much alive.

It is a pity, Carmenya thought, *we are so far from each other's grasp, it really does not matter whether either of us are alive or dead.*

In the morning, she would not believe she could think such a thing.

Chapter Twenty-Six
The House

Meera protested bitterly when she arrived at the Trotgarden cottage, only to be informed by Meonel that he didn't think it would be a good idea for her to go up to the cave with them.

'Other people have opinions as well as yourself, Meonel Trotgarden!' she said. 'You know damn well I should be there. Why are you stalling?'

'Today, Carmenya Oralien and Gick will be going up with Shyya and myself,' Meonel said. 'As you know, Carmenya was chosen at the first meeting to visit the cave with me. We haven't been able to do that yet. Perhaps you can go up tomorrow.'

'You are making a mistake in edging me out,' Meera said, her voice dark with meaning.

'That is not my intention, Meera, of which I think you're aware. If you want my advice, I think you're becoming dangerously intense about all this. Lay off for a while. It makes people nervous.'

Meonel watched the priestess march off, back to her dwelling. Perhaps he *was* making a mistake.

Not long afterwards, Hollis Backwater watched the little group leave the Trotgarden house and ride off on dank-back, heading towards the cave. He was perched on the Tendaughters' roof, helping Sander finish off the chimney. Hollis knew he should have volunteered to go with them; after all, he'd offered to before. Somehow, the whole business was beginning to feel unreal to him. The eagerness with which his fellow Freespacers were embracing all these wild theories made him uneasy. How could any of it be possible? Perhaps it was all in their imagination, and Corinna really was losing her mind. Deep down, he was also wary of visiting the site, because he was sure Corinna would barely acknowledge him, devoting all her attention to the Oralien woman. It wasn't something he was sure he could stomach.

Sander caught him staring after the group, and said, 'When are you going to let that matter drop? You're wasting your time there.'

Hollis was stung by that, embarrassed that his feelings for Corinna were such common knowledge throughout the community. 'I have let it drop,' he said gruffly. 'I was thinking about something else, such as, are people heavily deluding themselves around here?'

'Course you were!' Sander laughed good-naturedly, and patted Hollis' arm. 'Join the clan.'

Hollis remembered Sander himself was another of Corinna's rejected suitors. Embarrassing, embarrassing. He didn't want that kind of pity. He shuddered. 'Don't you wonder though, Sander?' he asked icily. 'Isn't this all getting rather far-fetched?'

'I keep an open mind,' Sander replied. 'Whatever happens will happen, whether I believe in it or not. Right now, this chimney needs finishing.'

Hollis took the point and renewed his work more vigorously. Let them all pursue their wild fantasies. He'd just get on with the business of living, as always.

As they urged their animals up through the thick forest, Meonel found himself riding beside Carmenya, and telling her about Meera's visit earlier. 'The sooner we get all this sorted out the better,' he said. 'It worries me, all this bickering and craziness. We have more important things to concern ourselves with.'

Carmenya brushed away a low branch from her face. 'Trotgarden, whatever Corinna says about Freespace having no leaders, you're surely up there somewhere. I don't think we'd have survived without you.'

Meonel was surprised by this unexpected opinion. 'I would never have thought to hear that from you, Oralien.'

Carmenya shrugged, and pulled her dank's head out of the clump of fern it was trying to eat. 'I'm not shy to admit I've had to change a lot of my opinions. Goddess, do you remember that day I came to Vangery, asking Dannel if Corinna could come to the city?' She laughed coldly. 'You were so different then, a petulant boy! And what was I?'

'I'd prefer not to answer that.'

'You were a *bitch*, Carmenya,' Shyya's voice came from behind.

'Still eavesdropping like a slave, boy?'

Shyya snorted. 'If you'd listened more to your slaves, you might not have found yourself in that mess back then.'

'True, and now they wouldn't avoid me as if I was a social pariah!'

'Carmenya, you *are* a social pariah!' Meonel said.

'Yet riding knee to knee with one of Freespace's brightest stars,' Shyya said. 'That's quite an accomplishment for an outcast, isn't it?'

'Enough of that,' Meonel said. 'All I do is talk.' He pulled his dank to a halt. 'Ah, here we are. Think this trail is too steep for mounted beasts? Perhaps we'd better dismount.'

Corinna had been to the mouth of the cave several times to see what time of day it was. She was anxious to speak with Meonel and Shyya - to try and get some perspective on what she had learned. Over the last day, she'd experienced sporadic visualisations, which had granted her information about three, separate Greylid lives. Although this had been interesting, it hadn't divulged anything concerning the present, whether the light had been active since ancient times or whether it had recently been reactivated. She really needed to know how to interrogate the thing herself. Was it caprice on the light's part that it kept its mechanisms concealed, or ignorance on her own that she didn't know the correct procedure to access them? The answer to that would make a big difference to how they approached the problem.

Yearning for company was not the only reason she had sought the open air. She hadn't really expected Farris to comply with her rather personal request, concerning his intimate relationship with the presence - or the shadow-lover, as he referred to that aspect of it. She couldn't really blame him. All the assurances of an entirely neutral stance wouldn't have made much of an impression upon her either, if she'd been in Farris' position. They'd lain awake for most of the night, talking. Certain barriers had been breached; Farris was allowing himself to get to know Corinna. She had to admit he was an attractive person, in character as well as physically, once he let his defences drop. He had been quite open about the way he felt regarding Freespace, and had even confessed he'd once had a crush on her. The fact that he referred to this in the past tense made her feel distinctly wistful.

'I've changed so much in such a short time,' he said. 'It's like I'm caught up in a great wind, that's moving so fast.'

'Things can happen that way,' Corinna had replied. 'Life changes aren't always gradual.'

The conversation had meandered quite naturally back to the subject of Zy Larrigan. 'How can I tell if it's desire?' Farris had asked, a genuine question. 'I've never felt that for anybody.'

'I'm not the best person to give advice on this,' Corinna reminded him. 'But you may as well face it; you have to form relationships with people one day, or remain celibate until you die. Meonel told me it's always better for men to sleep with men first, rather than women, because it's less stressful. I can't vouch for that advice, but it's all I know. If you like Larrigan, why not get on with it?'

'I don't want to make a fool of myself, Corinna. He's an off-worlder. Our ways are probably as alien to him, as the

Presence is to us.'

'Well, if he doesn't fancy you, he's mad,' Corinna decided, settling herself more comfortably under her blanket. 'And not worth bothering with.'

There was a moment's silence while Farris considered her advice. Then he said, 'Corinna?' His voice had changed.

'What?'

'You wanted to see, didn't you? Oh, Goddess!' The words trailed into a groan.

Corinna fumbled for the lamp, turned up the flame. 'Farris? Farris, what's wrong?'

He didn't answer. His body had become luminous. The presence was nowhere to be seen. She realised it was, in fact, inside Farris' skin. Instinctively, she flinched away, drawing up her knees, hands to her mouth. She could only watch. Whatever was happening to him, it did not look or sound pleasurable. It was like some kind of fit, his body writhing beneath the blanket.

Finally, his cries subsided and the glow faded away, leaving him damp and panting in the dim light of the lamp.

Corinna could not speak.

Farris wearily turned his head towards her. 'You wanted to see. Now you have done,' he said. 'I had no choice.'

Then he turned his back on her.

Whether it was the conversation they'd had about Larrigan, or a response to her query, or simply whim on the part of the presence, Farris' shadow-lover visited him several times during the cold hours of the night.

Eventually, Corinna could stand it no longer and went outside. The air was chilly and damp, the trees below rustling eerily in the grey predawn light. Someone from Freespace would be here soon, surely? Corinna thought longingly of the Trotgarden cabin; warm food and comfort. She'd brought a blanket with her and now pulled it more firmly round her shoulders, her knees hunched to her chin as she sat waiting for company.

Meonel was first onto the ledge, and Corinna jumped up to embrace him. 'Goddess, am I pleased to see you!'

'You look positively disturbed' he said, his humorous tone barely disguising concern.

'No, I'm just bored. And hungry and cold.' Corinna greeted Shyya and Gick and then noticed who was with them. 'Oh, hello, Carmenya.'

There was a moment of tense stillness.

'So!' Meonel said brightly to break the chill. 'Let's have a look inside then, shall we?'

'Er - no,' Corinna said. 'I mean, I've been cooped up there all night and could do with a walk. Why don't we show Carmenya and Shyya the valley?'

Corinna didn't feel it would be fair for people to go barging in on Farris, who was feeling exhausted and drained, and who might also be in the throes of a further bizarre experience. She also felt uncomfortable about anyone else getting close to the presence just yet.

'OK, we'll go for a walk,' Meonel said carefully, giving Corinna a significant look, to show he wasn't deceived and that he suspected her motives.

They unloaded what provisions they'd brought for Corinna and, leaving the danks hobbled together on the ledge, went back down to the forest. Corinna led the way down the wide, stone steps, linking her arm through Shyya's. 'Well?' he hissed, bending his head to her ear.

'Well, what?' she hissed back.

'What's going on that you don't want us to see?

'Farris is having a wet dream in there. Honestly! Well, it's more than that, but no one should go in there just yet.'

Shyya drew in his breath. 'I see. And what have *you* learned?'

'Nothing like that.'

Shyya suddenly remembered what Dannel had told him. He wondered whether he should mention it.

Corinna began speaking, obviously to change the subject.

'It *is* Greylid in origin, Shee. It seems Meonel was right, and there was a community here once. I think the light is some kind of artificial intelligence. It showed me some choice bits of Greylid history, but it's more open with Farris than me.' She sighed. 'Hell, I promised him I wouldn't tell, but...'

'Secrets kept,' Shyya said, touching his lips, nose and eyes.

'OK, but you'd better! He'd kill me if this got out!'

Shyya listened with intrigued amusement to Farris' story. 'How lurid!' he said, when Corinna had finished telling him. 'Perhaps it's a machine fuelled by venal force!'

'And what's that?'

'Sexual energy.'

Corinna pulled a grimacing face. 'If that's so, the possibilities are endless! We could utilise it in building the town. We could have a power supply, electricity. However, I don't think Freespace would react favourably to a hundred grunting individuals powering up their generators in that way, do you?'

'No, but that wasn't exactly what I meant, C'rin.'

'Then what did you mean?'

Shyya shrugged. 'It was just an idea. The Presence has to be doing all that to Farris for a reason, doesn't it? I can't believe it's just for his benefit. Well, it's just a wild guess, but I wonder whether it's not feeding off him at those times.'

'That's pretty ghastly, Shee.'

'That remains to be seen. We don't know if there are any side effects yet. Hmm. It lures him to the cave and feeds off his energy, then you come along...'

'Precisely. Then I come along. What does it want with me? After all...' Corinna pulled herself up short, closing her mouth with an audible snap.

Shyya tugged her arm. 'After all, what?'

'Nothing.' Her voice had become terse.

Shyya squeezed her flesh. 'Oh Goddess! I get it. Listen, C'rin, I *know*. You don't have to say any more.'

Corinna knew Shyya well enough not to question him and

see if they meant the same thing. She simply asked, 'How do you know? I don't believe for a minute your acute, psychic powers can see right through my trousers!'

Shyya sighed. 'You won't like it, C'rin.'

She sighed too. 'I don't expect to.'

'Well, Elvinia found out when she examined you the other day. She told Dannel.'

'And Dannel told you, and Goddess knows who else! Wonderful!'

'No, just me. I promise.'

'Not Meonel?'

'Not even Meonel. I'm sorry your secret's out, but it's safe with Dannel and me, I swear.'

Corinna pulled him closer, and rubbed her cheek on his shoulder. 'Thanks, Shee. I'm kind of sensitive about it sometimes, but well, I suppose you understand that.'

'Painfully so!'

'It's typical though, isn't it? You can't keep anything secret round here.'

'You've done a good job up till now. I never guessed. Did it happen at the same time as your face, or don't you want to talk about it?'

'I don't want to talk about it now, no, but I will one day. It did happen round about the same time though, you're right.'

'Oh, C'rin.' Shyya put his arm around her shoulder and kissed her cheek. 'I love you, you know. Why the hell didn't you talk to me?'

'Because you love my step-father more,' she said and kissed him back. 'It's alright Shee. It's no problem.'

'Was I that preoccupied?'

'Yes. I told you, it doesn't matter. Forget it.'

'I can't! You must have needed to talk so much, and I was all dewy-eyed, gawping at Meonel! Goddess, I'm so sorry.'

'Shut up! The others will hear. I forgive you, OK? Let's just talk about the original subject, shall we? Let's suppose you're right, and the light is feeding off Farris in the way you think.

We have to work out why it seems to be interested in me. I'm about as sexual as a dead dank.'

'Physically maybe. Mentally? Sexuality is more than physical, C'rin. You're suppressing your sexual identity, yes? Or let's say, you have the inclination, but no way to express it. Wouldn't that simply intensify it? Perhaps you're a walking power house!'

'Hmm, an interesting concept,' she said wryly. 'This is all getting very personal, Shyya Trotgarden. I'm not sure I should be discussing this with my step-father's lover.'

'Might as well keep it in the family.'

'Talking of which, there is one other question we haven't asked ourselves.' They had near to the bottom of the steps, and the others were drawing closer.

'What's that?' Shyya asked in a low voice.

Corinna walked out onto the grass and then turned to face him. 'What about you, Shee? Why hasn't it summoned you? If anyone has the psychic ability to communicate with that thing, you have. And, if what you said about me is correct, then doesn't that apply to you too?'

Shyya stroked Corinna's face with a light finger. She seemed to see him with a greater clarity; his long, tawny hair, lit with subtle, lighter shades, his lovely face, the perfection of his flesh beneath his loose shirt. He was an icon, maybe, nothing more. She knew the answer he would give her, even before he spoke. 'Poor little C'rin,' he said. 'The reason for that is obvious. I'm blissfully happy, aren't I? Contented and fulfilled.'

'You think I'm not?' She wished she didn't sound so pathetic.

Shyya smiled and drew away from her as Meonel came alongside. Corinna watched as her step-father slung an arm around Shyya's shoulder, seemingly a careless gesture, but the proprietorial air was unmistakable. She did not need a spoken answer to her question.

By the time they reached the edge of the meadow, the sky

was pink and gold with dawn, and birds were singing vigorously. A herd of rock antelope, grazing in the valley, bounced away in alarm when the five people walked out into the grass.

Carmenya had overtaken the others in the trees, and was now in the lead. 'This is wonderful,' she said, 'but what the hell is that?'

Her companions pushed forward to take a look, following the direction of Carmenya's pointing arm.

'Goddess! How did that get there?' Meonel exclaimed. 'C'rin?'

'I... I'm not sure.'

A short distance away, virtually on the banks of the stream where it widened into a small pool, stood a stilted building.

'Where did it come from?' Gick asked, rhetorically.

The group advanced cautiously towards it.

Corinna uttered a nervous laugh. 'Doesn't it look sort of familiar?' she said shakily.

'In more ways than one,' Shyya confirmed.

The stilts were wooden. Why would a building be raised above ground level in this place? It was, of course, the way everything had to be built on the marsh.

Goddess, look!' Meonel cried. 'It's Larrigan's!'

Above the stilts, they recognised metallic parts that had once belonged to Zy Larrigan's flyer. The legend "Speed Lady" could plainly be seen on one of the walls. Wood and metal had been fused together into a bizarre kind of building block. Without a doubt, however, the structure was a crude representation of the old Trotgarden farmhouse at Vangery. It was too much of a coincidence.

'The light built this,' Corinna said. 'In a way, I suppose I told it to.'

'How?' Meonel asked sharply.

'Don't ask me! Farris told me yesterday to think of something I desired, so I thought of our old home. Isn't that something we all want - a proper home? I didn't take it seriously, though. Goddess, perhaps I should have been more specific!'

'I hope you're not suggesting we should actually live in something like this!' Meonel said.

Corinna shook her head. 'I didn't say that. I was just giving an explanation.'

'And did you tell your luminous friend to do this?' Carmenya called out, from the other side of the building.

The others strolled round to investigate what she'd found. The whole structure was cleverly glazed with a thick, glossy lacquer, but everyone was appalled to discover it had not been built entirely of local wood, stone and cannibalised bits of flyer. The raw redness of what could only be Welma Barbarel's half-eaten bones shone barbarically from lintels and window-frames, still dressed in the rags of a Silven Crescent military uniform. Her head grinned out from above the main door, one lidless, staring eye preserved perfectly by the lacquer.

Corinna turned away abruptly; sick to her core.

Meonel swore beneath his breath.

'It's just too gross,' Gick said, shaking her head. 'Horrible.'

'Goddess,' Carmenya murmured inadequately. 'This is no dream house. More like nightmare.'

'How did it *do* this?' Shyya asked.

Corinna still faced away from the house. 'I dread to think what we might find inside. I don't want to look.'

Meonel crouched down to examine the ground. 'Look at this. The grass is churned up in places. I don't think the flyer dragged itself to this spot, do you?'

Carmenya was squinting up the valley, shading her eyes with her hand. 'There are faint tracks in the grass if you look carefully,' she said. 'It looks like they lead from the cliffs themselves.'

'Maybe there are machines stored in there or something,' Corinna suggested shakily. 'The light must be able to activate and use them.'

'You did say it was very... active with Farris last night,'

Shyya said.

'This is all very well, and very clever,' Meonel said. 'If we can learn to communicate with this thing, the possibilities are clearly enormous, but think about this: what kind of conscience does it have to be happy about making houses out of *dead* people?'

'I can't question it,' Corinna replied hurriedly. 'It transmits pictures, and it obviously takes information from me,' - she gestured towards the house without turning to face it - 'look at *this*! But I don't know how to speak to it directly. It only responds to the thoughts it wants to.'

'You have to bear in mind you are not a Greylid,' Shyya pointed out. 'It goes without saying that human beings must think in a different way. Perhaps the light doesn't understand human thoughts, only their energies.'

'That's possible,' Corinna admitted, unconvinced.

Carmenya paced around the building, looking up at it. 'Well, this certainly puts the lid on all poor Meera's hints of divine manifestation, I must say!'

Nobody was very keen to climb inside the building and investigate further for the time being. There also seemed no easy or obvious way to retrieve the human remains from the structure and bury them. One thing the group agreed upon unanimously was that others should be kept from the site. The elders of the Freespace community, such as they were, must be called together to discuss the matter, but a general meeting of the people would inspire only panic and fear.

As the group walked back towards the wood, Corinna told the others all she'd learned, omitting any mention of Farris' personal experiences. 'It seems to me the intelligence is not fully operational,' she said. 'Remember what I said about the circuitry in the walls? Perhaps, if we could get the thing running properly...'

'This is very ambitious, Corinna, and probably a good idea,' Meonel said, 'but who in Freespace has a working knowledge of such advanced technology, if that's what it is?

Most of us have only heard about computers and such like. Only those of you who've lived in Silven Crescent have ever seen one, never mind used one.'

'And it must be said, Silven Crescent facilities are primitive to say the least,' Carmenya said. 'I know that, because I had the privilege of studying what information the palace archives contained about the past. Yani discouraged the use of technology, we all know that. I've worked on the small databanks in the city, but they were nothing like this! I wouldn't even know where to start!'

'Aren't we looking at this in rather a narrow way?' Shyya said. 'Isn't the light trying to work out how to use us, as much as we want to get it running properly? It seems to me, both sides are working towards the same end, but I'm not sure who will benefit the most when it's accomplished!'

'You lot are so dumb!' Gick said, not having been asked for her opinion. 'Haven't we got just the person on our doorstep at present, who might know what he's doing, if he took a look at this thing?'

'The off-worlder. Larrigan,' Meonel said.

'Precisely!' Gick confirmed.

Corinna didn't look sure. 'But doesn't the light want him, in some way, too? We'd be playing right into its... hands... if we took him up there. What would it do to him?'

'Well, we could at least ask him,' Shyya said. 'Put him fully in the picture and see what he suggests.'

'There's one other consideration, though,' Meonel said. 'Inconvenient to our enthusiasm as it may be! If Larrigan finds out about this, won't he have his wretched tourist company crawling all over the place as soon as he can? Even to me, it looks like a major find, and I know next to nothing about these things. We must face the fact we're risking total exploitation, if off-worlders get wind of this. We've seen some of this device's power already, and I suspect that's merely a foretaste. It might be that Freespace would have to move after all; not because of imminent danger, but just for some privacy!'

'We'll just have to see what the others think,' Carmenya said.

'I think that's best,' Meonel said. 'I don't want to take responsibility for involving Larrigan, although I think Gick is right, and it's the only way we'll make any progress. We're stuck in a corner here, I'm afraid. What we've seen here today put a rather more sinister light on everything.'

With this rather glum thought hanging over their heads, they pushed back through the forest.

Once they had reached the ledge outside the cave, Meonel said to Corinna, 'Are you going to insist we wait awhile before confronting the Presence with any more people, then?'

Corinna nodded. 'For the time being, yes. Farris and I are doing all we can.' She avoided Shyya's eye.

'So how long are you both planning on staying up here?' Shyya asked.

Corinna wrinkled her nose. 'Oh, only till tomorrow, I think. Maybe I'll come home tonight. I could do with a rest, and I don't think I'm going to make any more progress until we've thought of a new approach. Have that meeting and send someone up to tell me what's happening.'

'Would you like me to stay with you?' Carmenya asked.

Corinna was so surprised by this, she didn't have time to calm herself sufficiently, and a hot blush invaded her face, displaying her feelings to all present. 'Er... no, it's OK. Like I said, I don't think it's a good idea for anyone else to confront the thing yet. I'll be fine. It's better than reading a book, all these Greylid histories! I'll be fine.'

She stood on the ledge to watch them leave, waving until they disappeared from sight. *I'm so good at giving advice,* she thought. *Now, why can't I follow it myself?*

Chapter Twenty-Seven
Socialising

Elvinia had decided Zy was well enough to sit outside for a while. 'The air will do you good,' she'd said, and installed him in a makeshift wooden chair packed with blankets, which Zy suspected some member of the family had hastily knocked together especially for his use. The Windteasels had begun to cultivate a patch of earth behind their tent. Zy sat gazing over a dozen rows of feather-leaved winter-root, to where Quality and Softly were working on the new house. Maybe, when he finally returned home, he'd suggest the Freespacers should be taken on as a work force for building holiday villages on Artemis. It was obvious they were true artisans. Freespace itself could be an attraction. He visualised off-world tourists strolling through the streets of the town; it would have streets by then, of course, although it would be essential to keep them unpaved. People would exclaim in delight at the quaint crafts being demonstrated around them; house building, ore-mining, natural healing. The latter could certainly be a money spinner.

Zy could find no complaints with the way Elvinia and her family had treated him. There was no infection in his wounds, and the herbal drugs they had dosed him with had certainly accelerated the healing process. And yet, as he recuperated, his muscles seemed to be hurting more. Zy realised this might be caused by a certain amount of Mangine withdrawal - he had been using it a lot lately - as well as by the battering his body had received during the crash. No position was truly comfortable at present, but at least it was restful to sit out in the sun. Zy had quickly become bored with his surroundings inside. There were no holovids to watch, no senstims to plug into, not even a book to read that he could see. The Freespacers appeared to have little leisure-time; they worked till they dropped. He watched them going about their business, contemplating their industrial lot, and idly munched some freshly-shelled nuts that Elvinia had given him. He could believe this was a holiday if he tried.

Elvinia had told him a lot about the community; how it had begun, how it had survived. It was a fascinating story. He wondered what Alouine Crestick thought about it all. As soon as he felt capable, he would go and visit her. At some point, they might have to discuss how they could leave this place; sweet though its diversions were. There had been no sign of the danger Meonel had hinted at, so Zy could only assume it had all been a fabrication to keep him cowering in Windteasel care, and prevent him from making an escape bid. Elvinia's talk of an 'alien thing' seemed no more than mere superstitious nonsense. Freespace was as mundane a place as it was possible to find. It was important to remember these people were not as advanced as those he was used to.

'Zy, you have visitors.' Zeta Windteasel had poked her head round the side of the tent.

Sometimes, Zy confused her with Farris, they were so alike; gypsy tans and wild, black hair. Zeta, however, liked to wear colourful skirts, which he presumed Farris had no taste for. 'Me? Who?'

'The Queen of the Mountain, of course!' Zeta grinned at his puzzled expression. 'Actually, it's two of the Trotgardens. Are you decent?'

Zy shrugged, indicating his blanket-huddled body.

'Good.' Zeta disappeared and, shortly, Meonel and Shyya strolled into sight.

Since Elvinia and her daughters had explained Meonel's role in the community, Zy couldn't help but feel rather in awe of him. A natural leader, obviously, no matter how they tried to deny it. Zy considered it inevitable that such tribal people as he thought the Freespacers to be would have chieftains of some kind. It was amusing how they declined to acknowledge this, claiming they had achieved a non-hierarchical, advanced society. But then, in comparison to Silven Crescent, it undoubtedly was quite advanced. It was hard to believe either Meonel or Shyya had ever been a slave, and harder still to imagine Shyya's disabilities. (Barbaric practices! Castration! Silas and Kitzuki wouldn't believe it!) Would Shyya speak with a feminine voice? Zy wondered.

'A good day for sitting outside,' Meonel said, towering over the invalid's chair. 'You are fortunate the weather has cleared.'

Zy stared in fascination at Meonel's ears; bones, feathers and beads were threaded through the flesh on wire.

'Yes, it's a lovely day.'

Meonel settled himself cross-legged on the ground, and Zy noticed he shot Shyya a glance to indicate he should do likewise.

Ah, Zy thought, *First we discuss the weather, then they try to put me at ease. What comes next? Probably an enquiry about my health. Or else the offer of a peace pipe!*

'You appear to be mending swiftly,' Meonel said. 'But then, you were lucky; Elvinia did point out you and Alouine Crestick were both plastered in spore dust when we found you? We use the dust as antiseptic. Anyway, how do you feel?'

'Achy.'

'I expect you're anxious to get away from here.'

Zy shifted uncomfortably. 'Not really. I'm content for the moment. It only makes me anxious when I think about how you might not want me to leave.'

Meonel nodded. 'That's understandable.'

'Some enlightenment would be appreciated.'

Meonel raised an eyebrow. 'You are not a prisoner here, Zy Larrigan.'

'Aren't I?'

'No. How would you like to come for breadlemen at the

Trotgarden estate this evening?'

'That's very considerate of you!' Zy did not trust Meonel's apparent innocence of intent.

'Not at all. We'd like to talk to you. In fact, you may be able to advise us.'

'Oh? What about?'

'I should imagine you want to know, as much as we do, why your flyer crashed in the way it did.'

'Naturally, but I've already told you as much as I can about that.'

'True, but we haven't told you as much as *we* can.'

'I suspected as much.'

Meonel smiled widely. 'Are you well enough to get over to our place later on?'

'You'd better ask my consultant.'

Meonel frowned. 'Elvinia,' Zy added.

Elvinia, who Zy thought would object, readily accepted the Trotgardens' proposal. 'I feel too weak,' Zy protested, after they'd gone.

'You'll be fine,' Elvinia told him. 'Zeta can give you an aromatic rub this afternoon. That should put some life in your bones.'

Zy's cosy image, of being artfully massaged by dextrous female hands, was effectively shattered by the pounding Zeta put him through. Initially, Zy beamed expectantly at the array of essential oils she laid out in a row, and made comments of interest as she mixed them with balm-nut oil in a wooden bowl. She held the concoction up for him to sniff. 'Heaven,' he said and lay back to enjoy the pampering.

His mistaken belief was short-lived. The girl passionlessly removed the night-shirt Elvinia had given him, partially covered his body with rough towels, and then got to work. She silenced all his complaints with the remark, 'You're too soft. You don't know what's good for you.'

'You're supposed to be healing my bones, not breaking

more!'

'Quiet! I can't concentrate with you whining!'

Halfway through the torment, Farris arrived back home and came to investigate the pitiful cries issuing from his bedroom. He lounged in the doorway for a while, arms folded, a faint smile of his face. To Zy, he looked utterly exhausted. There were dark rings around his eyes, and his skin looked waxen. The Freespacers worked too hard. Zy wondered what gruelling labour Farris had been involved in all day.

'What are you doing, Zeta?' Farris asked.

His sister didn't look up. 'What does it look like?' she snapped.

'Killing... killing me,' Zy gasped. 'Make her stop.'

'He's a mass of hard nerves,' Zeta said, digging her thumbs into the muscle of Zy's right thigh. 'Too tense. It'll slow his progress.'

Farris shook his head, and Zy dared to hope he might offer to take over. 'I'll be in mother's room,' he said. 'I'm dusted flat.'

'Yeah, you look it,' Zeta agreed. 'How's it going up there?'

'Deep, it's going deep,' Farris replied, and shot Zy a curious, furtive glance.

'I hope you know what you're doing,' Zeta said, pausing for a moment from her task and looking up at her brother. 'Goddess, Farris, you look terrible! I think I'd better give you a massage next.'

Farris just smiled and let the door-curtain drop.

'What is he doing, then?' Zy asked.

Zeta slapped his thigh. 'Working hard,' she replied. 'Will you just relax, please? Put your head back down.'

The Trotgarden 'estate' was a simple, long, low cottage, built on the edge of a plaisel grove, which had been partially felled. A fenced clearing was home to the family's small herd of danks, which were all serenading the evening in their mournful yet comical voices. Smoke issued from a squat chimney on the roof of the house, filling the air with the scent of burning sap. Zy, reclining in the back of the Windteasel family conveyance - a rough, dank-drawn cart - had to admit he was feeling livelier this evening. Zeta, for all her bullying, had apparently assuaged some of his pain. The evening promised to be a time of bliss.

Lights glowed comfortingly through the dusk, cosy, homely sounds issued from the tents and cottages, and the air was full of natural perfumes. Also, Farris was driving the cart, having been included in the invitation.

Farris pulled the dank to a halt outside the Trotgarden cottage and jumped down from the driving seat. He had not spoken to Zy throughout the journey, and now ignored him for a few moments longer as he loosened the dank's harness. Zy could hear him making soft whistling sounds to the animal.

'Are you going to leave me here all night?' he asked, feeling it was about time one of them broke the ice.

Farris began pulling back the bolts that held the side of the wagon in place. 'You won't have to climb,' he said. 'Can you sit on the edge?'

Zy wriggled over, his face creasing in pain, some of which, he had to admit, was rather exaggerated. He made one or two anxious noises. Farris hesitated for a moment and then put his hands under Zy's arms. 'Put your wait on me.' Effortlessly, he lifted Zy out of the wagon as if he weighed no more than a child.

'You people are all made of steel wire,' Zy said. He was unsure whether his legs could support him; the world was swaying ominously.

'You're unnaturally light,' Farris replied.

'We're made differently, you see. I'll explain it to you, if you like.'

Farris smiled.

Zy was encouraged by the fact that Farris hadn't let him go, even though he was holding him at arm's length. Perhaps he was reluctant to enter the cottage.

'I suppose you think we're all aliens,' Farris said.

'No. I'm the alien here, Farris.'

The door to the cottage opened, and a teenage boy came bounding out, curtailing any further exchanges. Zy was disappointed; things had been promising.

'You need a hand there, Farris?' the boy asked, laughing.

'I was managing,' Farris said. He gave Zy an exquisitely piercing glance, before offering his arm. 'You'll need this. Why didn't you bring a stick, or something, to lean on?'

'But I did,' Zy replied. 'I brought you, didn't I?'

'Everyone's waiting,' the Trotgarden boy said. 'We heard the cart arrive.' He tucked an arm through Zy's other elbow. 'I'm Orblin Trotgarden, Meonel's son. Come inside.'

The opportunity for Farris to respond to Zy's provocative comment was, thus, instantly lost.

Zy let them virtually carry him over the threshold.

Inside, the cottage appeared packed with people; the Trotgardens were not just a family, but a tribe! Only once he'd been settled, did Zy realise there weren't more than half a dozen people or so. Everyone was introduced; again most of the names escaped him. A heavily cushioned chair had been provided for him at the head of the table; perhaps a privileged position.

Meonel looked relaxed and sensuous in an oversized, home-spun woollen; his hair tied back, but dripping loose tendrils. Beside him sat a person Zy recognised; the girl with the scars. Of course! He realised where he thought he knew her from. The city. But he'd been thinking of Layna Minnders, he could see that now. The scarring was almost identical. She was dressed in scuffed leather; every inch a relative of Meonel's. It would surprise Zy later when he discovered they weren't related by blood.

'I hope you're hungry,' Dannel Trotgarden said, lowering herself into the seat at the other end of the table.

'It smells wonderful.'

'It is. I made it.' A striking, black-haired young woman was carrying a huge pot over from the stove, which she dumped on the table. 'Guests first,' she said, licking her fingers. She ladled a fragrant stew onto Zy's plate.

'Thank you,' Zy said. 'Er... I'm sorry, I can't remember your name. I have a terrible memory for things like that.'

'Bolivia,' said the woman, handing him a fork.

'Bolivia. There used to be a country on Earth called that.'

'Did there now! How fascinating.' She began to fill the other waiting plates.

'Yes. I studied Earth history a lot when I was younger. Bolivia was a place famous for its harmful leisure drugs.'

Orblin Trotgarden started to laugh, causing Bolivia to lash out at him with the serving spoon. 'What a fount of knowledge you are, Zy Larrigan,' she said.

Zy wondered whether he'd said something wrong.

Throughout the meal, the Trotgardens asked him questions about life beyond Artemis. He was happy to oblige, telling them more anecdotes about his profession and Plate life. Dannel wanted to know if he had any family, and he was slightly ashamed of the fact he didn't tell them about Silas and Kitzuki. He knew such relationships were just as common among the Freespacers, but he was conscious of Farris sitting there, and didn't want to appear unavailable. 'No, I'm alone now,' he said.

Dannel pulled a forlorn face. 'You poor thing!'

'You don't look like the sort of person who'd be alone for very long,' Bolivia drawled, in what he suspected was a half-seductive manner. 'You must have lovers, surely.'

'Livvy!' Dannel admonished. 'Don't be personal.' She smiled placatingly at Zy. 'You'll have to forgive us, Mr Larrigan. We Freespacers tend to be very open, and it might be a little strange to you.'

'On the contrary,' Zy replied. 'I'm all for openness myself. In response to your question, Bolivia; I have no lovers here, and as this is where I'm living at the moment, it's all that's important.'

Bolivia smirked appreciatively and inclined her head.

'Perhaps I'd better introduce the subject of why we asked you here,' Meonel said dryly, 'Before the conversation declines into propositions!'

Everyone laughed, and Meonel succinctly took control of the entire gathering. 'First of all, I'd like to introduce my stepdaughter, Corinna, who is instrumental in what I have to tell you.'

Zy and Corinna nodded politely at each other. 'Just how open-minded are you, Mr Larrigan?' she said.

A response was required. Zy displayed his palms. 'Please. Try me. I'm a good listener.'

Meonel smiled. 'You might find what we have to say hard to believe.' He began a concise, yet detailed, description of all that had occurred in Freespace since he and Corinna had discovered the cave.

Zy tried to keep a straight face, although he did smile inside, when Meonel described all the so-called supernatural experiences people had had. It sounded more like group hysteria to him. Corinna mentioned that the community priestess thought they were undergoing some kind of religious awakening. Perhaps some of the Freespacers had taken that to heart.

'And so you think this light you have found forced my flyer to crash,' Zy said, when Meonel had finished speaking.

Meonel gave him a hard look. 'I anticipated your scepticism.'

Zy shrugged. 'I'm not accusing you of lying. But there may be natural explanations. Gases, for example. On some worlds, natural gases can be hallucinogenic, and luminous. It may be a similar thing.'

'That does not explain my visions!' Corinna said.

'Visions,' Zy repeated flatly.

Corinna looked away. 'They were very real. They corroborated a lot of what we already know about the Greylids.'

'Precisely. What you already know. If you think about it,

it's quite possible your own imagination conjured up the visions. You believed the light to be of Greylid origin.' He tapped his mouth with his fingers, frowning. 'However, I am interested in what you have to say about the Greylids. I did wonder, on the way north, whether they were a real phenomenon or not. How many of you have actually seen one of these creatures?'

'Meonel and I,' Shyya said. His voice was not at all squeaky, but more like a faceful of cold water. 'And yes, it is quite possible we were hallucinating.' He smiled, with an acid sweetness.

'I'm not criticising any of you,' Zy said, 'But you have to be realistic.'

'Can you explain how your flyer crashed, then?' Corinna asked. 'Don't you think it's a coincidence we should discover this thing at the same time? And what about the fact that it showed Farris and I where to find you? Still think that's an hallucination?' She sounded defensive.

Zy shrugged. 'Listen, as I said, I'm not trying to criticise you. Someone has to ask the obvious questions. Of course I don't know the answers, but I think it's a mistake to jump to conclusions. I'm just being devil's advocate.'

'Why not come up to the cave yourself?' Corinna said. 'See for yourself. I think you'll be surprised.'

'Well, I would love to, but I can't walk very far at present.'

'Can you ride a dank?' Meonel asked, and addressed Farris. 'You're the only healer we have here. What do you think?'

Farris narrowed his eyes at Zy. 'If he took it slowly, maybe. It's up to him, really, whether he feels he can make it.'

'I think we need your advice on this,' Corinna said grudgingly.

'Alright,' Zy said. 'I'm game. It's too intriguing an event to miss!'

'We'll dose him up with painkillers,' Farris said.

Zy smiled thinly, hoping he wasn't making a mistake.

He and Farris left the gathering soon afterwards, Farris urging the dank to a swift pace between the cottages. Zy felt that the jolting movement, and the pain it provoked, was a grim foreboding of the forthcoming journey to the cave. He was enjoying being outdoors, though. The small, pungent tent-room he'd occupied for the past few days had become oppressive.

'Do we have to go back yet?' he called to Farris. 'Won't you take me for a drive?'

Farris pulled the dank to a halt. 'You're not tired?'

'No. Let's get away from civilisation. Show me some wilderness!'

'Alright.' Farris smiled, and turned back to the dank, clicking instructions so that the beast increased its pace.

They headed out along the mireway, water flying up in plumes behind the wheels. Zy gripped the sides of the wagon and gritted his teeth. Under normal circumstances, the ride would have been exhilarating.

Eventually, Farris pulled the dank up again and leaned over the back of his seat. 'This is killing you!' he said. 'Why didn't you say?'

'Hurting, yes. But I was still enjoying myself. I'm sick of being cooped up in that tent. It stinks of your dirty feet!'

Farris let the dank lower its head to graze on the mire-tufts and nimbly vaulted over the seat. He squatted at Zy's side. 'My feet are not dirty,' he said. 'And be thankful you have my bed!'

'Oh, I am.' Zy grinned a handful of meanings into the words.

Farris leaned back. 'You don't believe us about the cave, do you?'

Zy shrugged. 'I think it might have a simpler explanation than you think, that's all.'

'You don't know half of it!'

'Look Farris, people in a culture like yours often like to put... well, more mysterious meanings into things. It's quite natural.'

'What do you mean: *a culture like mine*? You make us

sound like primitives!'

'I didn't mean...'

'I know what you meant!'

'No, you don't. Please understand, Farris, and I don't intend this to be insulting in any way, the people of Artemis are - well - quite backward in comparison with many other worlds. I'm not saying you aren't intelligent, don't get me wrong, but in a way, the Artemisians are throwbacks to a much earlier period in human history.'

'What do you mean?'

'Well, at one time, human beings actually lived in caves. They were very much like animals. Then they evolved. That means they learned things, became more...'

'I know what that means!'

'Of course. I'm sorry. Anyway, what I'm trying to say is, the Freespacers remind me of an early, almost prehistoric community, yet strangely melded with fragments of a much more advanced culture.'

'You've made quite a study then, while you've been here.'

'Yes, I have. It's most fascinating. I'm sure people back on Africa Plate will be very interested in what I have to tell them.'

Farris stared across the mire-way, blinking hard, squatting against the wagon side, his long, tanned arms stretched out along its rim, knees raised and poking through rips in his threadbare trousers.

Zy wondered what the boy was thinking. With his bare feet, scratched brown ankles and tangled black hair, he resembled some kind of elfin aborigine. Zy wished he still had the holocam from Speed Lady to capture the moment. A glorious evening sky provided a spectacular back-drop to this idealised portrait. The decoration these people used on their clothes, their primitive jewellery, all spoke of a distinctly tribal culture. It was exquisite. Freespace had developed its own racial identity from the ruins of its old home. Quite a feat. Zy found it all entrancing. 'You are, as I said, quite a beautiful person, Farris,' he said, in a coaxing voice.

Farris glanced back at him. There was no welcome there; his expression was agitated. 'I suppose you're thinking of making Freespace into one of those theme villages you told us about, complete with authentic dumb natives!'

'What do you mean, Farris?'

'It means I understand you, Zy Larrigan.' He mimicked Zy's speech. 'I understand where you're coming from!' He hunched down so far, his knees were virtually round his ears.

'I can't help but be honest. I don't know why you're offended. You can learn as much from me as I can from you.'

'And I'm supposed to be grateful for your superior knowledge, am I?'

'Now, Farris, don't over-react. I told you; I'm not trying to insult you. I think you people are wonderful, and I must admit, I had hoped we could be friends, you and I, well, more than that actually.' He hoped he wasn't being too forward, but then it was probably necessary to spell it out.

Farris did not react favourably. 'It would be a bit of fun for you, would it, to amuse yourself with a primitive? Then you could tell all your sophisticated, weightless, intelligent friends about it when you get home! In fact, you could make it a feature of your tour packages. Make love with animal people! Except I don't suppose you call it that, do you. What do you call it: relief exchange, removal of unwanted pressure?'

'Farris, I'm puzzled as to why you're saying these things. I find you attractive. Where I come from, such feelings are resolved expediently and without fuss. Come back here. I'll show you.' Clearly, some severe social education was required.

'No!' Farris scrambled back into the driving-seat. 'Less stressful indeed!'

Zy did not understand that last statement, and Farris clearly did not intend to expand on it. He whipped the dank up into a brisk lope, and wheeled the wagon back in the direction of Freespace. Zy bounced around in the back, clinging on stoically and wondering what he'd done wrong.

Chapter Twenty-Eight
Zy Larrigan Investigates

Half an hour out of Freespace, Zy wondered whether it would have been more comfortable for him making the journey up to the valley on foot. The dank's swaying motion jostled his torn muscles, causing his chest and neck to hurt unbearably, despite the herbal pain-killers Elvinia had given him, and the firm strapping of his arm up against the injured collarbone. Ahead of him, Meonel expertly urged his animal up the sheer slope, clicking instructions, moving obscuring branches from his line of sight. 'You OK back there?' he called, not looking round.

'Surviving,' Zy replied, hoping that was true. Behind him, Shyya, Corinna and Farris were keeping an eye on his progress. Farris was being extremely surly with him, and wouldn't even meet his eye. Zy told himself this didn't bother him, and had even made a show of flirting with Zeta, when they'd returned to the tent last evening. At first, she had seemed puzzled by his attentions, but had eventually mustered up some enthusiasm; at least more than her brother had done. Zeta was a sensible sort. She would not fly into a temper if he spoke his mind, he was sure. Zy did question why he was making such an effort in this respect with the Freespacers. Usually, he kept aloof from local people. Admittedly, they were an extremely attractive race. He admired their wiry wildness, their forest-haunted sensuality. Even their old folk seemed unbowed and regal. A pity about Farris, but then, Elvinia had already hinted that all was not right with the boy. Shyya's voice broke into Zy's thoughts as he urged his dank up alongside. 'Are you sure you're alright? We could stop for a while if you need a rest,' he said.

'No, I want to get this over with. I want to lie down,' Zy replied.

'Perhaps we're being unfair, dragging you up here so soon.'

No, it's quite alright. I wanted to come.'

'Well, if you're sure...'

Zy tried to ease his limbs into a less agonising position. 'Tell you what. Take my mind off the pain. Tell me more about the Greylids.'

'You mean my *hallucinations* of Greylids.'

Zy groaned. 'You wouldn't believe how often I'm rubbing people's fur up the wrong way around here. I'll suspend disbelief, OK? Just tell me.'

Shyya related how he, Meonel and Elvon L'Belder had sought out the Greylids in the forests of Ire and Penitence, east of the marsh. He explained how, prior to this, L'Belder had virtually washed up on Vangery's shore, escaping from the city. Dannel had taken him in, and given him a new identity. 'But he would not give up his cause.' Shyya said. 'You have to understand that the rest of us had grown up with tales of the Greylids. As adults, we no longer believed them; they were stories for children. But L'Belder thought no such thing. He was convinced the Greylids really existed, and wanted to seek them out, ask for their help. He thought they'd be as worried about Gisbandrun's behaviour as he was but, when he finally found them, he discovered they weren't interested in the lives of humans on Artemis. After all, the Artemisians' reluctance to go beyond their own boundaries meant the Greylids could carry on living in peace and quiet.'

Zy was stunned. 'You could understand them, then, and speak their language?'

'They spoke ours,' Shyya explained. 'Many people, who'd left the cities over the years, had gravitated towards the Greylids and joined them. They had become Greylid.'

'What do they look like?'

Shyya shrugged. 'Humanoid, I suppose. They cover themselves up. I can't say what they *really* look like. Elvon somehow persuaded them to make him like them. Greylids *do* have power, you see; a power we can't understand. Elvon wanted to use it against Gisbandrun.'

'Did you see any of their technology?' Zy asked. 'What about the place they lived in. What was it like?'

Shyya sighed. 'If they have technology, it's up here.' He tapped his head. 'They live in a place called Vez'n'Kizri, a sort of ruin, deep in the heart of the forest. They are like ghosts, in that place. It's covered in moss and creepers.' He pulled a face. 'Dead, you might say.'

'Did you witness L'Belder's... mutation?'

Shyya shook his head. 'No. He left us. The Greylids also offered the change to Meonel and I, but we weren't interested. We left the forest and rode to Silven Crescent. We saw the flames...' Again, he sighed. 'Corinna came to meet us on the road, and we headed north, gathered our people, and fled the marsh. We never saw L'Belder again. Only the result of what he did.'

'It sounds as if he must have been quite a guy.'

'He was. And yet, just a man, for all that, until...'

'Do you think he's still alive?'

Shyya shrugged. 'If he is, I doubt very much if he's still the man we knew.'

'That's an incredible story!'

'I know. You still think I hallucinated it all, Zy Larrigan?'

They had come to the edge of the glade. Meonel had broken off a long stick from one of the threadwoods on the way up. His dank had a tendency to be stubborn at times. Now, he used his makeshift whip to point out the steps up to the cave. 'That's where the cave is, up there, but first, I want to take you to see what's happened to the remains of your flyer.'

'What does he mean?' Zy hissed at Shyya.

'We decided it would be better to show you than tell you,' Shyya said. 'After all, you really weren't very accommodating last night.'

'I can't help it. All this sounds so outlandish. Someone has to be sceptical.'

'Wait and see,' Shyya said. 'Then be as sceptical as you like!'

Riding some distance behind, Farris had been unburdening himself to Corinna, telling her about what had happened the previous evening. 'Corinna, Zy Larrigan is inhuman, I swear it!' Farris concluded. 'He has no idea how to behave. Or is everyone like that?'

'No they are not!' Corinna replied. 'Sounds to me as if he's *over* civilised. I suppose you still fancy him like mad?'

Farris pulled a face. 'I don't know. I don't know what I think. Things have gone quiet; you know? I don't feel as if the Presence is breathing down my neck as much, especially since last night. Perhaps Larrigan is right, and it *has* all been in our imaginations. I thought he was brought here for me, but I can't believe that now.'

'Farris, he doesn't know what he's talking about! How can it be in our minds? You haven't seen the house it built in the valley! I don't believe for a moment I did that through the strength of my imagination!'

'He's taken all the magic from it, though,' Farris said. 'Gases! Hallucinations! Primitive cultures! Agh! I wish he, and the light, would both go away!'

'Just let him try and come on all superior with me!' Corinna said, darkly.

Wind rustled through the long grass of the meadow, making it bend and shine, so that it rippled like water. Large clouds, bright at the edges with sunlight, passed rapidly over the cliffs. They approached the building at a brisk trot.

'I hope you're not squeamish,' Meonel said, leading the way round the other side of it.

'Not particularly,' Zy answered carefully. However, when

he saw the remains of Welma Barbarel emblazoned across the wall of the house, he had to turn away quickly, fighting a profound nausea as it surged through him. Who, or what, could have done that? 'Has anyone been inside?' he heard himself ask. He had no desire to dwell upon what he'd just seen.

'Are you alright?' Meonel said.

'Yes, yes,' Zy answered, and asked again, 'Has anyone been inside?'

'We were unsure whether it was safe,' Meonel replied. 'The whole thing might collapse under our weight. It is only an approximation of Vangery, after all.'

'I don't know,' Zy said, painfully dismounting from his dank, 'but it looks pretty sturdy to me.'

'Be our guest, then,' Shyya said, 'Go inside.'

'Alone?'

Meonel looked at the others. 'Well? Any offers?'

Farris shook his head meaningfully and Corinna screwed up her face. 'I'd rather not,' she said. 'It's eerie, disturbing... I just don't want to face any more body parts.'

There was a moment's silence, during which Meonel wondered whether he would have to be the one to volunteer. Like Corinna, the house gave him a bad feeling that was more than just because of the obvious – the use of human parts in its construction. Simply the fact it looked so like Vangery made it seem more obscene, somehow.

'Oh, Goddess!' Shyya said into the silence. 'I'll go with him. This is ridiculous!'

'Well, shout if you need any help,' Meonel said. 'We'll be just outside.'

'If we do need any help, just don't take too long making up your minds who's going to come after us,' Zy said, pointedly.

Shyya shook his head, rolled his eyes behind Zy's back and followed him to the front of the house. It looked as if the stairway to the main door had been partly constructed from the flyer's access ramp.

'You say it just appeared here one morning?' Zy asked Shyya as they climbed.

'Yes. Do you think *we* did this?'

Zy looked at the intimate fusing of wood and metal. 'I really can't see how,' he said. 'But someone did.' He thought there was something very ominous about Speed Lady being chewed up and reconstructed in this way, something malevolent, but didn't say so aloud. His scepticism concerning the Freespacers' story was decreasing all the time.

The front door was slightly open. Shyya and Zy entered together, cautiously.

'It's very much like Vangery,' Shyya said softly.

They investigated all the rooms. Zy was amused, as much as he was frightened, by finding parts of Speed Lady's computer and engines alive and working, now ready to perform new functions. Perhaps they would operate household gadgetry, such as air conditioning, central heating, or appliances for cooking and bathing.

In the kitchen, which, like the original at Vangery, hung from the belly of the house in a basket of beams and pulleys, he discovered the flyer's coffee dispenser. On idly pressing the power pad, he had to stop himself from leaping back in surprise when the machine began to hum, and illumined its 'ready for operation' light. 'Amazing!' he said. 'Where's the power coming from?'

'We only had a conventional generator back home,' Shyya said. 'I can't hear one running here, can you?'

Zy shook his head in perplexity. 'No. Perhaps Speed Lady's energy reservoir packs have been used, but thinking back to our hell-ride from the edge of the marsh to this place, I can't imagine them having much in store. What have you got here? Little house spirits?'

'Something more sinister, I think,' Shyya said. 'Well, sinister in as much as we can't understand it.'

'Mmm. Maybe.'

In one of the main salons, they came across part of the flight console including the light-screen and voice-control system of the computer. Both Zy and Shyya were tremendously relieved not to have found any more of Welma's remains.

'I wonder...' Zy said, reaching to touch certain pads.

'Do you think you should do that?' Shyya queried apprehensively, backing towards the door.

Zy laughed. 'What are you expecting? Assault cannons swinging from the walls? Come on, it's a flyer's computer. It might tell us something, if it still functions.'

'Very well, then.'

'Come here. Watch.'

'I'd rather...' Zy dragged him over, finding, not really to his surprise, that it was really quite pleasant hanging on to Trotgarden's boy. 'Watch. If this does anything, you'll have to learn it, won't you?' He was surprised, though, when the screen reacted to his commands, blooming with light. Vocal instructions, however, were not quite as successful. The lights remained stupidly dumb. 'Obviously voice command is out,' Zy said, thinking aloud, 'If we're talking alien intelligence here - and I think we are - it may no longer understand me. The function pads might do something, though. Let's see.'

At the stroke of a pad, one of the windows creaked open with a shudder. Their companions could be seen outside, backing away across the grass in alarm.

'Interesting,' Shyya said, sarcastically.

Zy let him go, to concentrate on the controls. Within a few minutes, he'd activated the heaters and coolers, and all the windows were open. 'It's certainly rearranged everything,' Zy said, 'Speed Lady's brain must have been totally fried. Can't expect anything more, I suppose. The crash couldn't have done much for her self confidence!'

'At least we haven't discovered any more pieces of your unfortunate companion,' Shyya said. 'It's a pity about those bones out there. This place would be quite habitable otherwise.'

Zy smiled. 'Look a little further, my friend. If your light-creature is real, and can do this, it can also build houses for any one of your families. You just have to find out how to communicate with it.'

'Have you had experience of alien life-forms, Mr. Larrigan?'

Zy shrugged. 'I've never slept with one.' He grinned.

Shyya did not appear amused.

'Well, I've seen all I want to for the time being,' Zy said, flexing his limbs to remind Shyya he was a thing to be pitied. 'Perhaps we should go and take a look in the magic grotto now, huh?'

'Yes. Let's do that,' Shyya said stonily.

Because of what Farris had told her, and also because of the way Larrigan had covertly mocked her the previous night, Corinna was prepared for antagonism. She strode quickly up the steps to the cave with Farris, leaving Meonel and Shyya to fuss over the off-worlder's tentative climbing. 'I think he's awful!' she told Farris. 'So patronising.'

'Mmmm,' Farris answered. He did not sound convinced, and was now prepared to be charitable. 'I think he's just out of his depth here. It must be so different to what he's used to.'

'I hope we *are* right about the Presence,' she said. 'I couldn't bear it if *he* was!'

'He can't be right,' Farris said. 'What about the house? Now he's seen it, he can't possibly call that a hallucination, neither can he say we did it ourselves.'

Corinna pulled a rueful face. 'True. But that means, if we are right, Larrigan might well have been dragged here for your benefit. Your wish come true; like the house was mine, maybe.' She snorted derisively. 'And good luck to you, Farris Windteasel! I don't envy you.'

When the others arrived at the ledge, Corinna led the way inside. Everyone paused in the outer cave to admire the rock formations, and to allow Zy to get his breath back. Farris had begun to look distinctly edgy. Corinna felt herself bristling when Zy hobbled over to her.

'Well, you're the guide, I take it?'

She was conscious of the man's furtive examination of her facial scars. He'd been staring at them the previous night, too. She pushed back her hair self-consciously, almost able to hear him think: tribal marks, rites of passage, primitive. Let him think that if he liked. 'I'll lead the way, yes,' she said frostily.

'I hear you're rather a local heroine,' he said.

'Locally, I've done nothing heroic, actually.'

'Weren't you involved in that civil war shambles, though?'

Corinna thought she recognised the same tone in his voice that had been present in women's voices, when she'd first arrived in the city from the marsh. Like him, they'd considered they were talking to an idiot peasant. Larrigan obviously looked on all the Freespacers that way; condescendingly confident he could solve their problems. She decided the best action was to play upon that, and ignored his last question. 'You know, I really believe it's the voice of the Goddess here,' she said in an awed voice. 'I can feel it in the walls, can't you? She speaks to me.'

'Really.'

'Yes, she says the off-worlder is not such a god from the skies as he thinks he is. And although we're not over-run with computers and star cruisers, we are not stupid.'

'She has a sense of humour, then.'

'She laughs wildly, actually, and is quite convinced the man from the sky ruined his last commission because of his overwhelming lack of tact and his insensitive manner. Also, that his seduction routine is not all it might be.'

'The man from the sky performs an obeisance and inserts his foot in his mouth accordingly. Was I that bad?'

Corinna turned and looked at him then, realising, with some surprise, that it was possible she might end up liking him. 'I'm afraid so,' she said.

He sighed. 'Oh dear. I stand admonished.'

'Your sincerity needs working on, too. Come along. This

way!'

She offered Zy her arm as he struggled up the steep slope to the back of the cave.

'So, what are your honest opinions on what's in here?' he asked. 'And that *was* sincere, by the way.'

Corinna smiled. 'Well, I'm convinced it's some kind of artificial intelligence - you see, I'm not totally devoid of jargon - definitely used by Greylids at one time, and probably constructed by them. I'm still not clear on this 'One God' business, though.'

'Yes, Meonel mentioned that last night. Can you just run over it again?'

She explained about the visualisations she'd experienced. 'I've made notes about everything. It would make a marvellous history book of Artemis. But it's not the past that I'm interested in. I want to know what its function is now, and why it's interested in us. There must be some way to interrogate it. We're hoping you'll be able to find out how.'

'What's Farris been doing up here? Has he been receiving this data too?'

'He's been receiving something, yes,' Corinna answered. 'I feel it's up to him to tell you about it, if he feels it's necessary.'

'How intriguing!'

The passage to the inner cave was now lit with lamps. 'There are other tunnels leading off, further on,' Corinna said. 'I've gone a little way down some of them, but whatever chambers I've come across are empty, and many of the passages are blocked by rock-fall.'

'What you told me about circuitry in the walls sounds interesting,' Zy said. 'I think we should try and confirm your theories that it is an AI, and then concentrate on powering it up somehow, access its memory.'

'You think you can do that?'

'I don't know yet. It's possible.'

'You said your computer in the Vangery copy worked,' Corinna said. 'Is there any way we could use that?'

Zy shook his head. 'I'll have to take another look at it, but I've lost the manual.' She looked at him sharply, and he shrugged. 'I'm not that competent.'

The light was visible from where the passage straightened out into the final stretch to the next cavern. 'It's very bright today,' Corinna said. 'It must know you're coming.'

'Let's hope I'm welcome, then,' Zy replied. He was beginning to feel slightly faint, and wasn't convinced his legs would hold out for much longer.

What he saw in the inner chamber took his breath away.

'Tell me that's luminous gas,' Corinna said triumphantly. 'Go on, tell me.'

'If that's an AI, human technology is pure clockwork!' Zy exclaimed. It was a ziggurat of energy, a spinning sphere, a mathematical equation, a bursting cosmos of polymorphic stars. Holographically, it illustrated theorems that were utterly alien; glyphs and ideas poured from its substance in a flickering stream, too fast to take in.

'Well, it's certainly putting on a display for you,' Corinna said.

Meonel, Shyya and Farris had just come in behind them, both Shyya and Meonel making exclamations of astonishment.

'It's printing data,' Zy said excitedly. 'That's what all that gibberish is, don't you see? Printing it into the air, into reality! It's amazing. If only we could record it somehow, translate it!'

'I can almost feel it thinking!' Meonel said.

'Can you touch it?' Zy asked.

Corinna shrugged and looked over her shoulder. 'Farris, can he touch it?'

Farris just looked sick. He shrugged. 'If you think he can.'

Corinna pulled a face at Farris behind Zy's back, and pointed to the ground by her feet in a 'get over here at once' gesture. Reluctantly, Farris slouched to her side.

Zy didn't wait for Corinna's opinion, but approached the light and held out his hand. He hadn't expected the phenomenon to be so visible. The light abruptly contracted to a small, spinning core and retreated a little way, pulsing rose-pink. 'It seems wary,' he said.

Farris pushed past Corinna, hands in pockets. 'It doesn't know you,' he said. 'Look.' He extracted a hand and held it out, palm upwards. It was as if the light was drawn to him. It spiralled down to hover over his hand, a dense ball the size of a clenched fist. Zy gently reached out towards it, and a shock went up his arm. It was not electrical. He gasped, dizzy for a moment.

'That was me you tasted,' Farris said, without looking at him.

Zy dropped his hand, and the light flew up to the jagged roof. 'I'm... I'm sorry,' he said, clutching his hand. It felt icy cold to the touch, yet burned as if scalded.

'Don't be,' Farris said. 'The Presence doesn't know how you feel about primitive natives like me.'

Corinna made an anguished sound, and moved between them. 'I did try to tell it about the house,' she said. 'You know, how we felt about bones being in it? I'm not sure it understood me. Perhaps it thinks I'm ungrateful.'

'You talk as if you think it's alive,' Meonel said.

'You tell me it isn't!' Corinna replied. The light zipped towards her face in a tantalising manner. She laughed and rubbed the tip of her nose. 'Believe me, it's alive!'

'I'd like to have a look at the walls,' Zy said, still gazing spellbound at the hovering light. 'Can you show me where I should start, Corinna?'

'Over here.' Corinna walked to the wall and laid her hand upon it. 'It's actually quite smooth. I've had a lamp on it, though, and I can't see anything. Part of the wall has come away up there. Perhaps it was damaged.'

'Have you looked in the rubble?'

'Yes. Nothing.'

'Mmm.' Zy peered closely at the wall. 'I can't see anything either. Are you sure that thing's not dangerous?'

'Isn't that what we're asking you? It hasn't harmed me

while I've been here. I've a feeling it gets frustrated because we can't understand it. Perhaps that's my imagination.'

'Maybe, but in view of what I've seen so far, I'm not so sure. This is beyond me, Corinna, it really is. You'll have to get expert help.'

Meonel and Shyya were being shown around the other side of the chamber by Farris, who was pointing out various tunnels they'd investigated on earlier visits. Before Corinna could respond to Zy's suggestion, Meonel came over to join them.

'I think you'll agree we are not hallucinating now, Mr Larrigan,' he said. 'Have you seen anything like this before?'

'No, never.' Zy admitted. He shook his head, one hand poised outstretched, a few inches from the wall. 'I must be honest here; I'm amazed. If it really is part of an alien culture, I can't urge how strongly I think you'd be safer seeking off-world help. Get people here who have experience of this kind of investigation, who might have the knowledge to deal with it.'

'We can't do that,' Meonel said. 'At least... not yet.'

'Why not? Are you still afraid of the city?' Zy made an exasperated gesture. 'This world doesn't belong to those Silven Crescent people any more. It's part of the universe. It belongs to everybody. Even they don't realise that yet. You, as leaders of this community...'

'We have no leaders,' Corinna interrupted.

'OK, you, as part of the *executive committee* of this community, have to be made aware you have rights; boundary rights, land rights, habitation rights, even the right for a certain amount of aid from the Central Development Resource. That's an organisation that provides funding and support for developing cultures. There are many people throughout the galaxy like yourselves who are trying to set up communities. CDR helps them get started. You could apply for grants for building, technology, computer hardware. You could have representatives on the coordinating body of the CDR itself.

Don't you understand? It's about time you all woke up and realised Artemis just joined civilisation.'

Corinna and Meonel were stunned. Such possibilities had never entered   their minds. They looked at each other. 'Are you sure about all that, the grants and such?' Meonel asked, knowing he was speaking for both of them.

'Yes, quite sure. Once CDR hears your case, and how you people were oppressed, they'll fall over themselves to help you. It's the kind of positive publicity they'll break limbs for! Your beautiful, virgin world might soon be crawling with off-world industry and tourists, but there'll be benefits for the taking, too.'

'I had no idea.'

'Oh, come on. I've tried to tell you people this. Elvinia thinks I'm delirious, I'm sure. She's still convinced that once the city people find out where you are, you'll be invaded, and I know she's not alone in thinking that. But you've got to realise there's no risk of that now.'

'Doesn't this all rather depend on you getting back to civilisation, as you call it, in one piece?' Meonel asked daintily. 'Perhaps you'd better think about how you too might be at some risk from the city women now. They won't exactly leap up and down with joy at your proposals, I'm sure.'

Zy shook his head grimly. 'Is your planet stuck in some kind of dark age nightmare or what? I'll just have to be careful. When I get back to the city, I'll call people for you, get things moving.'

'Are you really that concerned about us, Mr. Larrigan?' Corinna asked. 'I've heard a whisper you have plans of your own for Freespace, concerning a tourist village. You haven't mentioned any of these wonderful benefits before. Have you changed your mind about that?'

Zy drew in a sharp breath and held it, embarrassed. 'As you rightly pointed out, Corinna, I'm apparently not as good a salesman as I thought I was. Maybe I *have* changed my mind.' He indicated the chamber and its glowing occupant. 'All this would change anybody's mind. Anyway, it's really immaterial whether I'm concerned or not. It's just common sense. Any creditless bum off the street could tell you this, on other worlds.'

The light had come to hover just behind them at shoulder-height, as if listening to their conversation. Corinna turned to look at it and held out her hand, towards which it glided like a bird. 'It may sound crazy to you,' she said, 'but I'd still rather solve this myself if I can. You've seen a little of what this thing can do. I want to know more about it before I hand it over to somebody else. Anyway, Freespace will get swamped when your galactic authorities find out about this, won't it?'

Zy sighed. 'Listen, you haven't got a chance of cracking this problem yourself. It's even beyond me, I told you. And what selfish purposes can you use it for? Start a new religion, so you can all come up here and space out on visions? If you can't use it yourselves, you should bring in people who can. Won't you be as bad as the city women if you don't? Think about progress.'

'To be perfectly frank with you, I think I'd rather it was used in the primitive way you suggest, than lose Freespace,' Meonel said.

'Certainly,' Corinna agreed vigorously. 'We happen to like it here, Mr. Larrigan, and we came a long, long way to find it. Oh, you can't appreciate...' She broke off. It was pointless. The Freespacers' efforts and troubles would mean nothing to this man, who crossed light-years of space as part of his job. Crossing a few hundred lope-leagues of marsh and mountain would mean nothing to him.

'Look, I do understand,' Zy said, 'and I'll do all I can to help, but you mustn't blind yourself to the realities.'

'We appreciate your observations, Mr. Larrigan,' Meonel said, 'but what is your reality needn't necessarily be ours. Now, I think we should all get back to the town. This phenomenon isn't going to go away, is it?'

Chapter Twenty-Nine
Evening

A brisk wind started up as the investigating party began the descent to Freespace. Zy shivered in a skin of chilly sweat. His head was pounding, and the aches in his body were so bad, he felt he was remaining conscious only by immense effort of will. But the exertion had been worth it. He wished he still had Speed Lady's recording equipment. A holovid of the light in the cave would come in useful when he got home. He wondered whether the thing really had been responsible for Speed Lady's crash. If so, why? Accidental interference? It seemed the only answer. He did not give credence to the dark hints of some great purpose for his being brought to Freespace. Over his head, the tall threadwoods hissed and moaned; clouds scudded impatiently across an overcast sky. His dank skidded awkwardly down the slope, each stride conducting a symphony of untold agony in his body. The thought of the Windteasel tent was a tantalising balm he couldn't wait to reach.

The Trotgardens accompanied Zy and Farris back to the tent-house, where Meonel helped Zy to dismount. It was clear to everybody that Zy was in a bad state, and had perhaps over-stretched himself riding up to the cave. Meonel began to apologise, but Zy wearily waved him aside. All the Trotgardens looked rather surprised when Farris just led the danks off without offering to help Zy inside the tent. Meonel delivered him into Elvinia's hands with the platitude, 'You get some rest. I'll come over and see you tomorrow.'

'Please think about what I said,' Zy said. It wasn't very

persuasive, but all he could manage at the time.

Meonel nodded thoughtfully. 'I'm sure you think you know what's best,' he answered.

Elvinia shook her head, frowning, as she arranged Zy on the bed. 'You overdid it,' she sang. 'Why did you have to go rushing around like that! Riding a dank indeed. What difference would waiting a couple more days have made?'

'Don't nag me, Windteasel,' Zy responded weakly, the nearest he could manage to repartee.

'Nag you! I should smack your ass!' She tucked the blankets around him furiously.

'Yeah, that'd be good.' Zy tentatively wriggled himself into the least uncomfortable position he could find. It felt as if his kidneys were about to burst.

Elvinia handed him a mug of water with more balm pellets to swallow. 'You stay here for at least two days now,' she said. 'Take it easy.'

'I will. I will.' Zy groaned and covered his eyes with his free arm. 'Elvinia, "alien thing" didn't come into it. There's something truly amazing up there in that cave.'

'Not worth killing yourself for, though!'

Zy uncovered his eyes. She was standing there, arms folded, looking mulish, mouth turned down at the corners. 'What does Farris do up there?' he asked. 'Do you know?'

'Sees things,' she answered bluntly. 'That's what. Unhealthy. Why does he do that, Zy? What is that thing, really? How can it affect our minds the way it's done, and why?'

Zy shook his head slowly on the pillow. 'I'm not sure what it is, or how it works,' he replied. 'Farris does seem to have a kind of empathy with it, though.'

There was a moment's silence and then, as if she'd been wondering whether to speak, Elvinia said abruptly, 'I wish you'd talk to him. It worries me, the way he is.'

'Why me? I'm an outsider. Whatever I say to him offends him.' Zy wondered how much he should confide in Elvinia.

After all, she was Farris' mother.

'I think he'd listen to you,' she said. 'You've lived a different life to us, and perhaps see things with a wider eye. He has to respect that.'

Zy wondered just how well Elvinia knew her son. He couldn't imagine any attempt at a man-to-man talk would be taken well by Farris. 'I don't think I know him well enough,' he said. 'I'm sorry, but I'd rather not get involved.'

Elvinia shrugged. 'It was just a thought.' She sighed. 'Goddess, you're exhausted. Get your head down. Don't worry yourself about our problems.' She strolled to the window-curtain, lifted it, and squinted outside. 'Bad weather on the way. I can feel it.' She began to tell Zy about the winter storms on the marsh, the great spears of ice that fell from the skies, the floods, the sheer chaos of it. Her words lulled him into a shallow sleep, where dream fragments of whirling wind drifted in and out of a consciousness that was fraught with apprehension. Greylids. Zy remembered interviewing the girl on the marsh, and it was as if he was living her story. A tall figure stalked stiffly towards him as he stood knee-deep in water, a sickle hook in his hand. Elvinia's words had infiltrated his dream. The weather was awful; pelting, freezing rain. The figure halted in front of him. He had to squint through the driving water to see it. Grey robes smudged with moss concealed the body inside.

'Who are you?' Zy asked. 'Do you come from Freespace?'

The Greylid held out a long, thin hand, but there was no gift to be accepted. Zy slipped his own hand into the creature's grip. It seemed the right thing to do. He felt sinew and bone, flesh and warmth. The Greylid threw back its hood and a man stood there, smiling at him. The rain had stopped.

'Are you confused?' asked the man.

'Yes. What's happening? Tell me the truth.'

'Well, that is simple,' said the man. '*Everybody* is right.'

'That's not an answer. That's a riddle.'

The man shrugged. 'It really *is* quite simple,' he said.

'Is it? Then what's my part in all this? What's simple about that? I don't belong here. It's not my world.'

The man laughed. 'You're a prospector,' he said. 'Define your territories.' And then he was gone.

Zy woke up quickly, opening his eyes to an empty room, feeling as if the echo of spoken words had just died away. He shivered. *I don't like this*, he thought. *It's getting too tight.*

The shadow-lover had woken up. Its call had become strident, nagging. Farris, lying on his parents' bed, was busy praying. He wasn't sure who he was praying to, or even what for, but the urge was strong in him, simply to *entreat*. Since returning from the cave, he'd felt very cold, sick and weak, as if mirroring Zy Larrigan's condition. He was sure there was something important he'd forgotten to do, something he hadn't been looking forward to.

'Please,' he whispered, 'Please, please.'

Simply that. His energy was exhausted. He felt sucked dry. If only there was some way he could ignore the call; block his ears, numb his mind, sleep. But it reached right into him, straight to the brain; there was no escape. *Let me rest!* he thought fiercely. *I've had enough.*

And it seemed as if a voice replied insidiously, 'Oh, but you haven't even started yet. Remember what you have to do?'

'No,' Farris responded. 'I don't. I've forgotten.'

'Then I'll remind you.'

The touch, when it came, was so real and sudden, it nearly made him vomit. He resisted strongly; the first time he'd ever done that. 'No! You're not real! You don't exist!' His body flared with pain.

'Why are you resisting me, Farris? Haven't I always brought you pleasure? Melt to my touch. Go with it; attune, absorb.'

'No.' Farris writhed in discomfort. Something was inside him, a physical living thing, opening him up like a flexing fist.

He felt himself begin to tear apart. Panicking, he pulled himself into a sitting position, feeling for the walls of the tent, which swayed behind his head. There was nothing to grab.

I must cry out, he thought. *Someone will hear. My mother will come.*

But, as in a nightmare, he could force no sound from his throat.

The voice was perfectly reasonable inside his head. 'Farris, Farris, just comply. Do it. Relax. Then you will see.'

Farris hung over the side of the bed, and crumpled to the floor. *When will this end?* he thought miserably. *Oh Goddess! Help me!*

'It will end when you decide to end it,' the voice reminded him primly, 'and it's no good calling on Parthenos. She can't tell you anything different.'

Farris lay on his back on the floor. He could feel the coarse rugs pressing into his skin. The tented ceiling seemed very high above him. Sweat bled from his body, his body pulsing to the pain. He wondered whether he might die. For a moment, he let go, too weary to protest any more, and the instant he did, the Presence had him. Pain was transformed to pleasure like the opening of a bud to the rays of the sun. It flared, golden and piercing, before being withdrawn, almost simultaneously.

'I only wanted to remind you,' it said.

'I want to rest,' Farris murmured.

'Soon,' said the Presence. 'Don't make me be cruel to you, Farris.'

Meera was meditating in her cottage. It was hard to gather her thoughts, she was feeling so distressed. *I've let everybody down,* she thought. *I've made a fool of myself.*

Corinna Trotgarden had touched on a painful truth when she'd reminded the priestess there were no leaders in Freespace. Hadn't she, Meera, tried to take that role on?

But it was selfless, she told herself, I just wanted to get things organised. We *need* leaders. Someone has to make the decisions.

Yes, but shouldn't you have waited to be asked?

We'd have to wait forever then! she answered herself angrily. Parthenos, why did you come to me only to desert me again? Why?

Meera opened her eyes, reaching to turn up her single lamp and fill the cottage with light once more. It was clear she'd get no peace of mind today. Better get on with something mundane and physical. Her hand touched the warm metal of the lamp. Familiar, worn.

She gasped.

A swift needle of cold shot through her fingers. The light began to glow icy blue. *What?*

She pulled her hand back, sucked on it, shook it. Her room was filled with the eerie glow. Meera tried to stand. She was afraid. For a second, she thought about how she might have been wrong all along, and now the Greylids, or whatever they were, had come to mock her, to prove to her just how wrong she'd been. Then the simple room was filled with musical laughter.

'So easily discouraged?' said a low, warm voice. 'Sister, please!'

Meera turned round, her fingers still in her mouth.

Behind her, against the door, stood a tall, solid, naked woman, wreathed in soft, floating hair. Her eyes were stars, her smile the knowledge of aeons. The woman held out her hands. 'Tonight,' she said, 'I will call you.'

Meera squinted, confused, disorientated. 'Who...?' she whispered. 'Who *are* you?'

The woman laughed again, a sound of Spring, so poignant it brought a fragrance of cut petals to the air. 'I am your Goddess,' she said, and vanished.

The evening was hot and close, the sky a blaze of colours, yet still the perfume of storm electrified the air. Hollis Backwater had heard how Corinna was back at home and, ignoring the carping voices of his pride and better judgment, called in at the Trotgardens after breadlemen. It pained him how pleased he was to see Corinna again; doomed pleasure, he was sure. Trying to keep his complaints of how little he'd seen of her recently to a minimum, Hollis persuaded Corinna to go for a walk. She could produce no good reason to get out of it. Hollis countered her feeble excuse of tiredness with the argument that some fresh air would do her good. 'You've been cooped up too long in that damp, dark cave,' he said.

'OK,' Corinna agreed resignedly. After all, Hollis was a friend, wasn't he? The days when they'd worked together, laughed together, seemed a long way off now. The Corinna who'd experienced them seemed nothing but a dim, dark memory. Odd. Had she changed that much so quickly?

Hollis suggested they walk out over the mireway, in completely the opposite direction to the dam and the valley. Corinna wondered whether that was deliberate.

'Do you think I've changed?' she asked, as they walked along. The mireway was glinting red and silver in the twilight, between splashes of dark shadow where the tussocks lay.

'How would I know?' Hollis answered sharply. 'You never let anyone get to know you anyway.' He drew in his breath, plucked a long twig from a threadwood and attacked the tussocks angrily. 'Yeah, I suppose you have changed. That's the nearest to a personal thing you've ever said to me. I've missed you, C'rin.'

'Hollis!' Corinna made her voice dangerous, trying to frighten away whatever he might come out with.

He threw his stick into a puddle and jumped into her path, so she had to face him. 'Am I that ugly?' he asked.

Corinna tried to step past him, but he wouldn't let her. 'I don't know what you mean. No, you're not ugly. Persistent maybe, but not ugly. I don't want to sleep with you, Hollis. I think I should say that, before this conversation wastes any more of our time.'

'You think that's why I came round, to ask you something

like that?'

'How should I know?' she mimicked. 'OK, deny it.'

'I can't. Not really, but it's not a cold and calculating desire like you make it sound. I... think a lot of you. I suppose you know that.'

'Hmmm.'

'Orblin tells me it's a bad idea to let you know, but I can't see the point of lying. Will you tell me something? Is it still Carmenya you want? Is that why?'

Corinna said nothing.

'I'd like to know. It would make me feel better. I've been trying to attract you for months.'

'I don't want *anybody*, Hollis.'

'That's not natural! I don't believe you! You're flesh and blood: real. A passionate creature if ever I saw one...'

'Hollis, for the Goddess' sake!'

'Shut up. Listen. What I mean is, celibacy doesn't go with the rest of your personality. It doesn't make sense. Understand me?'

Corinna felt suddenly warmed, flattered. 'Yes, I understand, and you're probably right, but there are reasons for my peculiarities I can't talk about with you, Hollis. Respect me and drop it, will you? The reasons are strong ones.' She could tell he still took that as a rebuff, even though she hadn't meant it that way. 'Look, if I could, I'd have glorious, explosive affairs with Carmenya and you both, OK?' She laughed, in an attempt to lighten the atmosphere. It didn't work.

'Then why don't you? What is it, C'rin? *Talk* to me.'

'No.' She put her hands lightly on his chest, took them off again sharply, then put them back. She was aware of a faint growling in the air, a heavy tension. Hollis' bony face looked like a stone carving in the dim light, his eyes deep set and invisible. Without thinking why, or analysing her reasons in any way, Corinna stood on tiptoe and kissed his mouth. Soft. Hard. A brief kiss. She stepped back. *Goddess, why did I do that? Why do I complicate things?* She found herself looking round to see if anyone else was about, if anyone could have seen. She laughed nervously.

Hollis just stood there like a statue.

'I'm sorry,' Corinna said. 'I don't know why I...'

Inevitably, perhaps because she'd been waiting for it, he reached out awkwardly with his hands, enveloping her in his arms. She wondered for a swift moment whether some subconscious part of her, unaffected by superficial neuroses, was experimenting. The words 'self-imposed exile' flashed across her brain. Was it?

He set about kissing her, somewhat fiercely, which the cool inner Corinna identified as recklessness and shyness combined. It was not frightening though, or threatening, but strangely exhilarating. Her response, she found, was entirely cerebral; heady, like drinking too much or smoking hag-moss. It was rather a disappointment when he let her go.

'I can wait,' he said. 'But it's not just sex I want, honestly.'

'I know.' She felt dizzy with the realisation that, for so long, she'd denied physical comfort from other people, simply because of some weird inner compulsion to punish herself for what had happened to her. It made sense, didn't it? Her mind was daring to think, *Can I tell him? Can I? If he loves me, as he's hinted, would the foulness change that? If it didn't bother him, we could still be lovers, like Meonel and Shyya. I could still have so much, even if I couldn't have it all. Someone to share with; the closest of friends. I can't ever imagine being able to tell Carmenya, but Hollis...? Dare I? Dare I?*

Perhaps now was the opportunity, but she couldn't make herself begin.

'I'm worried about the effect all this nonsense with the cave is having on you,' Hollis blurted furiously, interrupting her thoughts.

Corinna was relieved and regretful; the opportunity had passed. 'I'm alright,' she said lightly. 'I suppose we'll end up doing what Zy Larrigan suggests. It's a shame. I've got quite fond of that thing in a way. I think it likes me too.'

'Corinna Trotgarden! You tell me I've got nothing to worry about? You're mad.'

'How can you say that? You've never even seen the light.'

'Is that a pun?'

Corinna laughed. 'Maybe it is.' She took his hand. 'Come up with me sometime.'

'You're taking unfair advantage of me. How can I refuse anything you ask?'

'Well, you shouldn't make judgments on hearsay, should you? Will you come?'

He was silent for a while. 'I'm afraid it's all getting too big. Sometimes I think it's all rubbish, people's imaginations, other times...' He sighed. 'I'm scared it will change us all completely.'

'That needn't necessarily be a scary thing.'

'You're braver than most people.'

Corinna dropped his hand. 'No, I'm not! Don't *you* come out with dank shit like that, Hollis, please! I don't like being thought of as some kind of heroine. It's such a responsibility living up to a reputation like that.'

'But all you went through...'

'Goddess! You don't *know* what I went through! It's not how you think.' She was aware she was punctuating her remarks with hand gestures that were a little too vigorous.

'Then how is it?' Hollis asked.

There was a moment of intense quiet, as if even the night animals had paused to hear her reply. 'Hollis,' Corinna said in a faltering voice, 'You might not like me in quite the same way if you knew, and I don't want that.'

'Corinna.' He took her hands once more. 'For what I want between us, there can be no secrets. I want to know, whatever it is, whatever you did or didn't do.'

'I've never told anybody, apart from Gick, and I trust her. If I tell you, I'll end up with everyone knowing.'

'No!' Hollis began hotly, but Corinna shook her head and didn't let him carry on.

'Yes, Hollis. I don't mean you'll run round telling

everybody, but I know, deep inside, that when I break the silence, it's broken for good.'

'Then perhaps it's time for that anyway.'

She pulled her face into a wry grin. 'My, that's metaphysical for *you*, Hollis! OK.' She turned to face the town, visible now only by its lights. 'Might as well begin in a sensible way. Hear this, Freespace...'

It surprised her how good it felt to speak her thoughts aloud, how cleansing it was. She virtually forgot about Hollis standing quietly just behind her. She could not see his face, did not want to. It was like telling a story; she even took pleasure in relating the details correctly. And there, emblazoned against the deepening sky, were the images that haunted her like hungry vampires: the house in Silven Crescent, the smell of it, the feel of it. Could Hollis smell it too? Were all of Freespace, at this moment, living her history with her? She felt the images were too real to be witnessed by herself alone. She spoke warmly of her life at court. It *had* been enjoyable. She spoke about the friends she'd made, Carmenya's careful wooing and ultimate seduction, and finally, the end of blissful ignorance; the accidental insult to Yani Gisbandrun, incurring her displeasure and scrutiny. After that, Corinna had befriended Meera more intimately, persuaded the priestess to reveal what she was involved in - the rebellion - and had naively involved herself, in a storm of righteous outrage against Gisbandrun's hypocrisy. Ignorance. It hadn't been real, she hadn't fully understood the risks, believing herself protected by Carmenya's reputation. And then: her arrest, the interrogation, her attempts at being clever, the silly sense of triumph when they did not torture her for information. If only that dumb girl had known then her silence didn't matter. The punishment was still waiting; relentless, undiscerning, the same for everybody. She gulped air as she saw again the Rooms of the Red, those sumptuous chambers whose atmosphere reeked of ruin and despair, the home of Yani Gisbandrun's elite group of personal 'attendants'. Not a privilege, no. Every girl in that place was serving a penance, forced to swallow regret and anger until her stomach turned numb from the bitterness. Knives. Mutilations. Savage reminders. Faces flickered rapidly before her mind's eye; scarred faces. And the bodies: missing fingers, toes, ears, eyes, noses, sometimes whole arms, breasts - and then, those mutilations that did not show so blatantly. Like her own. There was a face, crazier than the rest, evidence of a personality totally destroyed. The face had a name: Last Light. The last person with whom Corinna had experienced any sexual contact. Raped by a woman before the knives came. Is that sick enough for you, Hollis? Telling the rest of it, about when L'Belder came, and the consequent flight from the city, was easy in comparison. All this time, she'd told herself it was the lies about her so-called heroism that had angered her. That wasn't true. It simply didn't matter at all. It was always the knives, at the back of it, always that, and Last Light's face, grinning mindlessly, in a cold tower room, where Corinna had lain, spread-eagled on a surgical table, waiting for the knives.

'I hate them!' Corinna screamed, meaning everything, herself, the city, the Rooms of the Red, bodies in general, and every deity that had ever been given a name by humankind. She did not weep, though.

When she'd finished talking, she and Hollis stood in silence, still not facing one another, maintaining a distance. They were both utterly motionless, but for the breeze lifting their hair. Then Hollis put his hands on Corinna's shoulders. He whispered, 'Thank you,' so quietly, she could barely hear it. She felt his lips briefly touch the back of her neck. He cleared his throat.

'Now you know,' she said, and strangely it did not hurt her, or make her feel ashamed that he did.

'Yes,' he said. 'But I didn't need to hear as much as you needed to tell me.' He squeezed her shoulders. 'It's out now, up there in the air, blowing away.'

'You're quite a romantic really, aren't you!' She turned to face him. 'But, doesn't it make you feel sick, what's been done to me?'

He shook his head. 'No. Why should it? I feel sad for you, but I can't see why you thought someone knowing your past would make them feel differently about you. Not me, certainly. It's the personality inside your body I love. After all, I was never confident enough to believe you'd ever let me touch you.'

'Then we were both wrong.'

'And we can both congratulate ourselves on being very courageous this evening!' He laughed. 'Come on, we're out here for a walk. Let's walk.'

She took his hand. They walked.

Chapter Thirty
The Night

Zy threw off his covers, groaned, tried to toss in the bed, but it was too hot. And they think winter's coming! he thought, painfully rearranging his limbs. His body ached with more than the pain of his bruised muscles. He'd been woken by the after-image of more disturbing dreams; of a lucid kind which tricked the sleeper into believing he was awake. He'd dreamed of home, yes, and his lovers; but the later dreams, heavy with the silky callisthenics of good sex, had not included them. Zy had woken, gasping for fresh air in the staleness of the tent, feeling frustrated, lonely, and far from home.

Normally, when working, he could divert all thoughts connected with relaxation, and its attendant pleasures, away from his conscious mind. What was it about Freespace that made this technique impossible? Trying to centre himself and regain control, he conjured up a visualisation of Africa Plate, as if he was approaching it from space. The sprawling orbital cosmopolis tumbled gracefully in the void, forever bathed in the acid glow of the star Thelema 23. It was a busy hive of excitement and stimulating leisure palaces. Just about everything a person could lust after could be found somewhere on the Plate, waiting to be discovered by those brave enough to look beneath its sleek and glittering surface. Zy was well acquainted with the sub-life of the place. Over the years, he'd trained himself never to seek involvement with the people he met on far worlds. First, because he always, inevitably, had to leave them and second, because it could only interfere with what he had to do, and delay his return to the Plate. His

relationships with Kitzuki and Silas were casual, true, yet
ultimately consistent. Kitzuki: the high-powered executive,
cruel and adventurous in bed, a sharp-witted conversationalist
and cosmetically engineered for maximum beauty. And Silas;
androgynous, languorous, skilled at pampering, a highware
bum, making a living selling para-reality to the desperate.
Neither of these people resembled anyone on Artemis, and Zy
knew he loved both Kitzuki and Silas deeply, in his own way.
They were *his* people, who made him feel comfortable, who
shared his realities. They did not demand commitment and did
not expect to have to give it. If he called them up, fine, they'd
give him a good time, as long as they were free. He knew both
of them would be there for him in a crisis, if he needed help.
Wasn't that what true relationships were all about? Now, if he
dared to probe this painful thought, he was beginning to
wonder whether they gave him enough. Wasn't there
something missing, something that breathed from the very soil
of this backward world? Passion; heartfelt, mindless passion,
unchoreographed, howling, and full of colour. Even when he'd
first met Kitzuki, and had begun the dance-sequence that
would end inevitably in her bed, he'd not been fearfully
excited, but just quietly contented she found him as attractive
as he found her. There'd been little challenge, because to Plate
people, sex was something that friends just *did*. Asking
someone to make love was as common as asking them if they'd
like to go out to a restaurant or a club, and probably just as
meaningful. Last evening, someone had said 'no' to him,
actually said 'no.' This was a first to Zy, and more of an affront
than Farris could ever guess, or that Zy would admit to himself.
He'd been making the offer of friendship in the way he
understood, and it had been refused. His natural instinct was to
withdraw his interest immediately. This should have been a
simple manoeuvre; a conscious decision. Why was it proving so
difficult?

I am going out of my head! Zy thought furiously, dragging
himself into a listing sitting position in the bed. His erotic

dreams had been haunted by the presence of Farris. Why? Despite his physical attractions, the boy was so *weird*, a primitive throwback and abnormally naive for his age. If Kitzuki met him, she wouldn't even touch him until he'd been in a rehabilitation retreat for at least a month. Zy could hear her voice reciting a list of Farris' possible neuroses. He couldn't stop the fantasy. It went this way: For some reason he'd ended up taking Farris back home with him. Kitzuki was worried and enthusiastic at the same time, bringing brochures for various retreats round to the apartment, while Farris shrank and glowered like an exotic wild cat in the corner, unable to understand her Plate patois and frightened of her robotic perfection.

Afterwards, she'd call Silas and say something like, 'Get over there, Si. If he needs a man, make it *you*. That boy is *dangerous*, crawling with badpsych. Zy will *revert*, I just *know* it!'

Silas would then slink round and terrify Farris to death.

Zy could envisage no happy end to this nightmare. It was senseless to pursue it. No doubt there were individuals who looked just like Farris living on Africa Plate right now, who could be uncovered with a little time and effort.

He lay back down again, his perplexity unresolved, wishing he had some Mangine, wishing he had company. Out of all these people, why Farris? Surely the Trotgarden girl was more his type, or the cool, stripy-haired Shyya, who was purported to be psychic, and whom Zy could envisage adapting quite freely to Plate life. Why Farris? Zy closed his eyes.

If only you could sleep again, he thought. *Sleep without dreaming. Get better and leave this place. Everything would be alright. These crazy thoughts are happening just because you're sick. Take control, Zy Larrigan. Come back to yourself. Careful now. Breathe deep. That's it. Long and slow. Think of soothing oceans, vast skies, distance and weightlessness. There, that's better...*

He sighed; a long, shuddering breath. An endless vista of a dimly-lit shore bloomed before his inner eye. He began, in his mind, to walk along it. A soft breeze caressed his skin, full of gentle murmuring. The shore-vista was his own; private and unassailable. And then, a vision of Farris Windteasel walked up the sand towards him. 'You are a prospector,' he said. 'Define your territory.'

Like Zy, some distance away, Corinna couldn't settle. Outside her curtains, the night was close and humid; inside the air was stale and motionless. She couldn't relax enough to sleep, reliving in her mind the evening walk with Hollis, flashing back again and again to the moment they had touched. And the purging, the release of all those rotten, festering words. Shouldn't she feel cleansed and refreshed now; hopeful? Hollis had made it clear her mutilation meant nothing to him, so why this lingering agony? *Because it's not enough!* she thought. Bitterness welled up inside her, like poison spilling from a morbid wound. *I want it all, like before the bitches cut me. I want the soft eyes, the laughter, the dance of desire, that rises, slowly, slowly, to the ultimate consummation of love. Not just the surrender, but the sweeping pleasure, that infinite feeling of oneness, the sense of magic. But I can't have it, no, they stripped me of that!*

She was too angry even to weep. Grief had gone beyond that. Wriggling around in her bed, wrestling with impotent, vengeful thoughts, she tried to find a comfortable position, but the bed was too soft; it felt wet. Across the room, Bolivia's breathing seemed far too loud; a further irritation. Corinna thought of the peace and solitude of the cave, albeit dark and hard, and knew she wanted to go back there now, this instant. She needed to speak to the light, tell it what had happened. Oh, she wouldn't get a tangible response from it, she knew, but it would be comforting to know it stored her knowledge. Corinna was sure the light was sympathetic to her, even if they hadn't learned how to communicate properly. She didn't get an outright call from the cave as Farris did, it was more subtle with her than that, but she felt the desire to return there always involved more than just her own decision.

Thinking of the cave and the light had soothed her anger, so much so, she didn't even notice when it left her. Instead, her mind had wandered onto more meditative paths. She wondered what the presence in the cave wanted of her. Could it be fascinated by her mutilation and the way such suffering had scarred her mind? Was it simply studying her? *Will we ever know what it wants without off-world help?* She felt there had to be a way to understand the presence without resorting to that. *Goddess, why can't I see the answer? I feel it's so simple, yet...*

She remembered all the Greylid lives she'd been shown; vivid, but carefully devoid of any useful information. She'd seen Greylids acting out religious rites, walking across the face of Artemis, working on mechanical and electrical equipment she could not quantify, but there were no real answers. She hadn't found out *why* the Greylids had happened, and only a little of how. Was it possible she and the other Freespacers were unwittingly flirting with the possibility of being similarly altered themselves? Was the light itself the agency that caused the change? She shuddered and, in a blindingly-honest flash of insight, thought, *Maybe I want that change. I don't want half a life with Hollis, or anybody else. If it means being different, then I don't care. I just don't want to be this anymore. I'm going to enter the light, like Farris did. I'm going to will it to change me. Elvon did this. Elvon did it. Maybe, I'll even find him again this way.*

She was out of bed and pulling on her clothes before she'd even finished thinking. Breezes arose from the east and hurried through the make-shift lanes and alleys of Freespace, pushing aside the hot, damp air, fingering the sleepers, bringing dreams.

Alouine Crestick moaned and tossed in a nightmare where Welma's dead face peered in through the reedpad window panes, and Welma's fingerless hands thumped repeatedly on the thin membranes, requesting entrance.

In her cottage nearby, Meera had fallen into a restless, shallow sleep, while sitting upright on her bed, waiting for the Goddess to come to her. She dreamed a woman had come to lead her and now she was following her out of Freespace, only to wake and find she'd merely dreamed. This happened several times. Meera became unsure of reality.

Rosanel, meanwhile, awoke convinced Elvon L'Belder had been shaking her and calling her name. She was filled with joy. Tonight he would return. She got out of bed and dressed herself, quite calm, combed out her smoky hair, painted her eyes with charcoal dust. Now, she looked more like the Rosanel of old, the one Elvon had left behind in Silven Crescent to pursue his quest for freedom. He would welcome her, wouldn't he? It would be like the old times, wouldn't it? The door to her hut opened behind her. She could see nothing in the fragment of mirror she faced and had to turn around. 'Elvon, is it you...?' No, the hut was empty; beyond the door she could see the threadwoods swaying in the rising wind. She shivered - the air had gone cold - and went to close the door. A fantasy...? No! Borne on the night wind she heard a sound: a voice, her name. Just once.
'Rosanel!'
She hurried outside. 'Elvon?' she whispered.
Only the wind, the furious trees. Clouds were gathering, obscuring the moons, boiling busily around the sky. *Power is coming*, Rosanel thought, and shut the cottage door behind her, giving herself up to the direction of the wind.

Farris, by this time, had already left the settlement, heeding the call he could not ignore. He walked in his sleep, his footsteps guided up through the forest towards the cave.
Come to me, whispered a voice in his head, *and I will tell you the secrets, I will give you my heart.*
Farris climbed, through the wind-lashed dark, with his eyes closed.

Corinna almost fell over the hunched form of Zy Larrigan at the base of the cliff. He was leaning against the grainy, red rock, his hair blowing across his face, looking seriously ill. Annoyed at this distraction, Corinna wanted to hurry right past him, but decency compelled her to stop and see if he was alright. 'What are you doing out here?' she hissed. 'You look terrible!'

'I'm not sure,' he answered, trying to straighten up and push the hair from his eyes. 'I... I don't know where I am.' He looked confused, as if he'd just woken from sleep. His face was damp with sweat, and sickly pale.

Corinna was moved to sympathy and took a firm hold of his unbandaged arm. She was surprised at the heat of his flesh through his clothes. 'Come on, Zy. Everything's fine. I think you're feverish. Don't worry; I'll take you back to Windteasels.'

He tried to pull away, stumbling against the rock-face. 'No. I can't go back there.'

Corinna narrowed her eyes, trying to see his expression in the poor light. 'What do you mean?' She thought she knew the answer to that.

Zy tried to crane his neck upwards, his nostrils fluttering, as if he was summoned by a strong, irresistible scent. 'There,' he said. 'I have to get... *there.*' He blinked, his good hand groping for the rock to pull himself along.

You too, Corinna thought. *It was all dreams, Zy Larrigan, that talk of investigation and understanding. It could only ever come to this. The time has come. A summoning. You were brought here. Inevitable. And now, the night is here. The only possible night.*

'Goddess, you're in a bad way,' she muttered, attempting to shoulder his weight. Like Farris had been, she was surprised by his lightness. He made a feeble cry, scrabbled in her arms a little. 'Sssh, be still. Don't worry. I'll help you.'

'Up there!' His head jerked back.

'Yes, I know,' she soothed. 'You won't make it alone. You're too sick.'

'Doesn't matter. I have to... try.'

He was now leaning against her. She could smell his hair, redolent of antiseptic rinse. 'I know. I know you do.'

'You're going... *there* ?' he asked.

'Yes.' She tightened her arm around him. 'You too. Come on.'

He broke into a bitter laugh, ragged at the edges. 'You know, I'm not sure I'll make it.'

'Me neither but, as you said, you have to try. It won't let you rest otherwise.' For a moment, she considered turning back to fetch a couple of danks, but whether because the presence was too impatient to allow it, or the physical struggle to reach it was part of the process, her mind swiftly rejected the idea without conscious reason.

Together, she and Zy walked slowly along the length of the cliff, and the lights of Freespace faded behind them. They were alone with the muttering air. Peering through the darkness, Corinna led them past the rock-face, over peaty soil where a mountain stream slowed into a pool. Then they began to head upwards, through the plaisel groves, where the slope grew steeper, and the tall threadwoods snarled in a wind not felt at ground level. No stars were visible in the sky. Zy leaned drunkenly against her shoulder, his fingers digging into her flesh.

It's tonight, she thought. *This is it. Goddess. Tonight.*

They had to pause for a while. Corinna wasn't sure how far up the forest they were; it was too dark to recognise landmarks. She eased Zy down onto the bank of a steeply-falling stream. The noise of its waters was somehow soothing. She wet the edge of her shirt in it and dabbed at the man's face. It occurred to her he might be killing himself attempting this climb, but she knew neither of them could do anything to stop it. The call was too strong. In her heart, she knew he would not die before he reached the cave, but afterwards?

As if reading her mind, Zy grabbed for her arm, and asked, 'What does it want with me? Tell me, Corinna. I have to know!'

'I can't! I don't know what it wants with any of us!' She slapped his hand away, helplessness at his predicament making her angry.

'Are we in danger?'

'It's just happening. We have to follow it through. There's no point in thinking anything other than that.'

As Corinna dragged him to his feet, Zy too was wondering whether he was going to die that night. It seemed entirely possible, but strangely, no longer important. It was as if his whole existence centred upon reaching the cave; nothing else mattered. His life so far had been nothing but symbols of the journey from Freespace to the Presence. Every triumph he'd ever lived through had been a presentiment of this thick stand of thorns successfully passed, that rock-fall negotiated. Every hurt he'd experienced before had been a metaphor for the current jarring of his torn muscles and injured bones. This time had been waiting, in his future, from the moment of his birth. It was the place where his life-path had always led. If life ended now, it didn't matter, because he couldn't live beyond it in his imagination. His existence on Africa Plate was a fantasy; this was real. It had all seemed so clear when he'd woken up in the tent such a short time ago. The only possible action was to reach the cave. He had defined his territory.

When they reached the sheer, thorn-garlanded slope leading up the cave mouth, Corinna paused again to catch her breath, leaning down to press her face into the cool, fragrant soil. Zy knelt beside her, gasping, one hand holding onto her for support. She could feel him trembling. 'Not... far... now,' she said, reaching up to pat his hand. It seemed such a ridiculous thing to say. She could offer no comfort to this man, this alien man, caught up in something neither of them could possibly understand.

Zy pressed his forehead against her shoulder. 'Farris is here, isn't he,' he said, his weak voice muffled by her jacket.

'Yes,' Corinna replied. 'He's here. He's always been here.' She shivered, unable to pull her jacket closer round her body because of Zy hanging onto her.

'Is it him calling us?'

'No. It's more than that.' She pulled him against her as if he was a child. She stroked his hair. Poor man.

They struggled onto the ledge outside the cave mouth, Zy a dead-weight in Corinna's arms. Here, the wind was pure and cold, its voice a strident song. Corinna laid Zy down on the ledge, scraped hair from her eyes, and gasped. Before them, the outer chamber of the cave was now filled with light. It shone like a cathedral lit up by a thousand devotional candles. 'Goddess!' she breathed. 'Look, look...' She could not see the source of the light.

Zy was lying on his belly, panting. He raised his head weakly. 'All decked up for a festival,' he said, and rested his face on the rock again. 'It's no use. I can't go on. I'm too wrecked to do anything. I can't move.'

Corinna squatted down beside him, put a hand on his heaving shoulders. 'Just rest a minute or two,' she soothed. 'You'll be alright.' She reached for his hand, which was damp and trembling, and squeezed it. 'Something is happening,' she said. 'Can't you feel it? You can't stop now. You know that really.'

Zy lifted his head again and blinked at the shining cave. 'I'm nervous of this,' he said. The subsequent shaky laugh was unconvincing.

'We both are,' she answered, although inside, she was more resolute than she'd ever been. 'It will all be over soon.'

Zy nodded painfully. 'Corinna, if you... if you ever get out of this, and I don't...'

'Hush, don't talk that way.'

'No, please listen. All I said to you was right. You must contact CDR.'

'That's irrelevant now!'

He shook his head. 'No, no it isn't. Promise me!'

'Alright.' She was lying, and felt he knew that, really.

'Help me up,' he said.

Once he was standing, he seemed to pull himself together. Some of the weakness left his limbs, as if for a final burst of energy. 'Corinna,' he said. 'If it's possible, will you stay with me... until... Well, I'd be grateful if you didn't leave me alone.'

'I won't.'

Together, they walked into the radiance.

Far below, the huts, the tents, the half-constructed houses, opened their doors to the elements, as if moved by unseen hands. Freespacers rose from their beds, from late night conversations, and went outside to look into the wind. Felids and danks were silent, children did not cry. Only the wind gave tongue, speaking in a language the people could nearly understand. It was more than moving air; it was alive with intention. And yet, for all its strength, nothing was blown along before the wind, no rags, no brush, no loose tools. There was no sound of falling things, but only the bugling elemental voice. People blinked and watched, sheltering against their homes, waiting.

And then; a sere radiance. All around the edges of the town, plumes of blue-white light sprang up, fizzing sentinels, no taller than a human being.

Hollis Backwater stood in the doorway to his family's cottage, with his arm around his mother, and said, 'What are they?'

'We will see,' his mother answered, and took a step forwards.

All fears had been extinguished by fatalistic resignation. In every brain: acceptance. This was the time; simple as that. And every soul, too, experienced a real excitement, that resonated with the energy sweeping over the settlement.

Dannel Trotgarden led her family outside the cottage. Bolivia held onto her arm.

'Corinna's not here,' Orblin reported, not really to anybody's surprise. 'What's going to happen, Meonel?'

Meonel had no idea how to answer his son's question.

'We'll see soon enough,' Shyya said. 'We'll be told.'

He saw Carmenya Oralien wandering round the huts with a puzzled expression on her face and waved to catch her attention. She walked over to the Trotgarden group, far from reluctant to seek their sanctuary.

'Are these Greylids?' Carmenya asked in a vague voice.

As if in response, a huge crash announced the bursting open of Meera's cottage door. The priestess herself could be seen in the doorway, limned in a blaze of radiance that seemed to emanate from inside the building. Her arms were held aloft; her face appeared wild and exultant. Searing blue-white light poured round her body, accompanied by billowing clouds of what might have been steam or smoke. The priestess' body was drawn up onto tiptoe as if someone had grabbed her arms from above and lifted her bodily into the air. She screamed joyfully, 'Goddess! Goddess!' before being hurled away from the radiant building to land face-first in the dirt outside, her limbs akimbo. The smoky vapour continued to pour over, past her, out through the cottage door, filling Freespace with an electric sweetness.

Rosanel stepped forward from the confused crowd. She went to kneel beside her friend, and helped her to rise. Meera's face was turned towards the soaring, red cliff beyond the trees. It seemed an even greater light was burning there, high above the trees, in the place where the valley lay. All eyes followed her gaze and, soon, the Freespacers began to walk that way too.

Chapter Thirty-One
The Inner Chamber

Corinna and Zy didn't rest for long in the outer chamber of the cave. Whatever waited for them would be found in a deeper place. Corinna made a short examination of the walls, squinting up to where the crystal straws hung down from the roof, but could not find out where the sizzling light was coming from. It simply *was*, a living radiance, and it appeared to have filled all the tunnels at the back of the cave too. Corinna thought it best they proceeded at once to the place where she had always communed with the Presence. She suspected the light was feeding Zy some kind of sustenance because he wasn't hanging so heavily on her arm. His eyes, however, were unfocussed, the pupils dilated. There could not be much time left for him, in this state.

The brightness was so intense once they reached the cave's inner chamber, it was impossible for Corinna and Zy to see whether anyone else was there before them, or even where the light-core of the Presence itself might be. Corinna called out, without much hope of response, 'Farris? Farris, are you here?' She was aware of a deep, humming sound, like the purr of a gigantic felid.

'Do you hear that buzzing?' she asked.

Zy nodded slowly. 'Is it in the walls?'

'I don't know. I can't see anything.' She led them into the centre of the chamber, and never had light seemed such a solid, sticky substance to her before. It was like trying to push their bodies through mud. Her hair was full of static, and her teeth had begun to ache.

'What shall we do?' Zy asked.

'I think we should just sit and wait,' Corinna replied. She wasn't sure whether the Presence was with them or not. 'This can't take long. Everything's happening now.'

They crouched down together on the stone floor. The air was warmer than it usually was in there and pungent with a strange, bitter odour. Corinna felt as if she'd gone blind. Her head was full of the white light; she wasn't sure how long she could stand it.

Perhaps they waited mere seconds, perhaps minutes, perhaps hours. Neither Zy nor Corinna could be sure. Eventually, Zy jerked against Corinna's side. 'We can't just wait!' he said. 'We're being shaken apart. The Presence isn't here.'

Corinna could hardly see his face; a few dark lines before her eyes suggested the hint of features. 'But what else...?'

Zy was trying to get up. Corinna could hear his feet scrabbling. And then, abruptly, the light contracted, dimming down swiftly to an orange glow. Corinna yelped in surprise. For a few moments, she was just as blinded as she'd been before. Then, Zy Larrigan's face began to materialise before her eyes. He looked ghastly; haggard and waxen. Even the astonishment in his eyes was weary.

'What now?' Corinna said, under her breath.

Zy struggled into a kneeling position. 'We move, I think. There are passages over there. Look.'

'They've always been there,' Corinna answered. 'They're impassable.'

'Are they? I can see light down them.' Zy tried to pull himself to his feet. 'That's where we have to go.'

'No, wait!' Corinna said.

He shook his head miserably at her. 'I can't,' he said.

Those two words meant so much. Corinna got up and stood beside him. Which way, then?'

Zy wobbled as he turned his body, looking intently at the passage-mouths. There were three of them. He made a decision. 'That one. On the left.'

'How do you know?'

He shook his head. 'You tell me.'

'Well, let's go, then.'

He paused, reached out an unsteady hand to touch her arm. 'Are you sure you want to come with me?'

Corinna sighed and crossed her arms. 'Didn't I make a promise to you, Zy Larrigan?'

He smiled weakly. 'I know. I was just being polite.'

She took his arm. 'Well, come on, then!'

Corinna felt as if she was entering the throat of some gigantic animal. The passage they'd chosen turned a sharp corner almost immediately, which she was sure hadn't been there before, but then, it was difficult to remember exactly. The appearance of the rock had changed. There were translucent spots above their heads; a visible source of the dim light. Also, the stone appeared to have been worked in some way, carved and smoothed into fantastic shapes, uncannily suggesting bone and muscle formations. Fluted ribs arched over their heads, vaned with crystal-thin transparent membranes from floor to roof. Was this Greylid architecture, or had, at some time, this place really been a living organism? Perhaps it still was. Corinna could hear a vague gurgling sound, almost beyond perception. It made her think of blood, living juices. 'It's warmer down here,' she said, comforted by the sound of her own voice. 'Look, Zy, the walls.'

There were faint threads of light running through the rock, very similar to what she'd seen in her earlier visions.

Zy did not answer or even try to look, as if he could only concentrate upon his destination, wherever that might be. His face was dripping sweat, his brows knitted with determination.

The passage sloped gradually downwards, and the walls and floor became increasingly organic in appearance. Corinna felt as if they were being swallowed whole, slipping down some vast, living neck into a maze of convoluted tissue and bone, where they might be dissolved completely and absorbed.

The rhythmic pulse that had filled the rock ever since they'd entered the cave had become deeper, more resonant. *It is a heart*, she thought. *A beating heart.*

The passage began to curl; the walls were damper, and the odour of the place almost overpowering. It was a carrion smell, a gut smell. More than ever, Corinna was convinced they were walking about inside the body of a living creature. And yet, even when thinking that, there was no true fear. She felt tranquillised, drowsy, and beyond panic. When she spoke, her voice sounded sluggish and muffled. 'Zy, Zy, stop a minute. Look, what are they? Could they be doors?'

The passage had become lined with pursed slits in the oily rock, lipped like mouths.

Zy would not pause, weakly trying to drag Corinna onwards. 'Not... for... us...,' he grunted.

'None of this was here before,' she said faintly. 'I'm sure of that. Farris and I investigated all the tunnels. Every one of them ended in rubble. It's all been cleared out, opened up.'

Zy didn't comment on her observations. He pulled her over to one of the slitted orifices. 'Here...' he said.

'Here? What for?'

Zy blinked madly. 'Through it. Here.' He tugged on her arm.

'But how? How do we get through?' For the first time, Corinna experienced an aversion to carrying on. For a split second, she considered pulling away from Zy Larrigan and fleeing back up the passage. It was short-lived.

Zy dug his fingers into her arm. 'End of journey,' he said and swallowed deeply, his face creasing as if even that caused terrible pain. He staggered away from her to touch the passage wall. 'I can... feel the source,' he said. 'It's here.'

Corinna tentatively reached out and ran her fingers over the wall. It felt greasy, warm. 'Closed,' she said. 'Closed tight. Oh!'

The wall opened up so suddenly, both she and Zy fell through it. They landed, in virtual darkness, on something soft and yielding. To Corinna, it felt like flesh. As her eyes adjusted to the even dimmer light, allowing visibility to about a metre in front of her, she could see that it looked very much like flesh too; dark and contused. She looked up but could not see the walls of the place. However, she could sense space around her as if they were in a large, high-ceilinged room. The air now smelled oily and resinous. 'Where are we?' she wondered aloud. There was no answer, however rhetorical, from her companion. She crawled over to him, feeling the way with her hands. Zy was lying on his face. She shook him a little. 'Zy, are you alright? What *is* this place?' She could hear the panic in her own voice.

The door had closed behind them and was now invisible. They were trapped. No-one knew they were here. This was the night. *Accept it. You cannot flee. You cannot fight. Fear is a waste of energy. Acceptance is the only course.*

Corinna rolled Zy onto his back. There was shiny wet darkness around his mouth. 'Oh Goddess,' she whispered. 'Zy, talk to me!'

Was he dead? She patted his face sharply, suddenly terrified of being left alone. No, thank the Goddess, not dead. His eyelids fluttered, his lips worked on silent words. She could see his tongue, red-black, the foam of blood and saliva between his teeth. 'Zy,' she said, helpless. 'Don't die on me. Don't leave me. I don't know where we are. I don't know what will happen. Zy...'

He managed to reach out for her blindly with his free hand. The fingers flexed, clutching air. Corinna took them in her own, and squeezed them hard. She remembered the time she'd come rushing up to the cave, convinced her family were inside, being led into danger. She remembered suddenly coming to her senses and wondering what she was doing there, how she could have believed such a senseless thing. It felt like that now. Whatever influence had drugged her mind was wearing off. She could feel fear. How cruel, at the last moment, to do this to her. Maybe they wouldn't have to wait too long.

She hoped there'd be no pain. She hoped it would be quick, whatever happened.

Fool! You galloped up here wanting this!

Zy's hand trembled in her own. He must hold on! She pressed his fingers against her chest, desperately willing some of her own strength to pass into him. He sighed. 'Don't worry, I'm here,' she said

Chapter Thirty-Two
The Freespacers

Freespacers poured up through the forest, silent, separate, as if ignorant of each other's presence, aware only of the seductive call reaching them from the valley cave, its promise of wonderful surprises that would change their lives forever. Like children lured by the offer of sweets and toys, they climbed in trusting innocence, all constructions of ego, practicality and scepticism put aside, left behind in the town where doors hung open to the night.

Will-o-the-wisp vapours flanked their passage, flickering through foliage, filling the tumbling streams with inner radiance, turning black stone to crystal. Wind howled through the trees, high up, above the Freespacers' heads, leaving them to scramble through briars and ground-vines as if in an airless void. It was like a parade of the dead. Freespace settlement, a single entity, climbed in eerie silence, broken only by panting breath.

There were the Trotgardens, still roughly in a bunch, their faces blank and stony. There, the Windteasels; Elvinia wearing only a belted robe, which flapped open, revealing her cold, goose-pimpled legs. Everyone was there, even the sick; Alouine Crestick struggled up with the others, her expression one of mindless determination.

Carmenya marched strongly, her eyes alight as if she was filled with a stirring, inner song.

Children climbed on hands and knees, their attention quivering like leapdog pups', ever upwards, heads tilted back, mouths open in wonderment.

Meera and Rosanel led the way, some distance apart from each other, and their faces were those of people who have glimpsed beneath a shroud of great mystery. They smiled in rapture; and climbed.

Everyone began to gather in the outer chamber of the cave system and, here, they seemed to wake up a little. A murmur filled the cathedral hall of the place. What is this light? What is this hint of song? Lovers sought each other's hands, children their families' shelter. Yet every face was still filled with awe.

Meera and Rosanel faced the crowd. They spoke with one voice. 'Wait here,' they said.

The crowd murmured its assent and the two women turned to face the passage that led to the inner chamber. They looked at each other and their expressions held hints of shyness, fear and hope. Then they went inside.

Meonel held Shyya in his arms, settling himself for the final period of waiting. Dannel stood close behind him, holding onto Bolivia and Orblin as if they were still small children. Like everyone else, Meonel freely accepted that the people of Freespace had been summoned here to experience some undreamed-of revelation. The mysteries that had puzzled them would soon be explained; everything would become clear. It was a situation that both thrilled and frightened him. Although he realised just how helpless they all were, unable as they'd been to ignore the summons, he did not feel they were being physically threatened. For once, no-one had turned to him for reassurance. 'Are you afraid?' he murmured in Shyya's ear, kissing his cheek. He expected Shyya to reply with soothing words and insight into what was happening. He was unprepared for the response.

Shyya's flesh seemed to ripple in his arms. 'Meonel, I hurt,' he murmured weakly. 'It hurts me.'

Pain? Here? In this light, this radiance? How?

'Hurt? Where?' Meonel asked.

Shyya shuddered deeply. 'No, not again,' he said desperately. 'It's forgotten, this pain.' He looked bewildered, searching his lover's face for answers that only he, Shyya, could possibly know.

'What pain?' Meonel asked raggedly. 'Where?'

'You never hurt me,' Shyya said and then cried out, crouching down, clutching himself.

'What is it?' Meonel looked round wildly, seeking Elvinia or Zeta, but it was impossible to find individuals in the crowd of people. It seemed no-one could see what was happening, as if only he and Shyya were awake.

'Take me inside!' Shyya gasped.

'Where?'

'The chamber, where the light is. Meonel, please! I have to!'

Meonel had never heard fear in Shyya's voice before. 'Is Corinna there?' he asked.

Shyya just shook his head angrily. 'I don't know! Just take me there! Now!'

'Why?'

'It's Elvon! Elvon's here!' Shyya cried and, pulling away from Meonel, began to stumble, almost bent double, into the passage by himself.

Parthenos was waiting for Meera in the inner chamber. She manifested as a naked woman, taller than average, with blue stars for eyes. Meera sank to her knees. 'Oh how beautiful!' she breathed and reached for Rosanel's hand, who was in a half-crouch beside her.

'Yes,' Rosanel whispered. 'Much more so.' She gazed at the tall figure, tears rolling unnoticed down her face. She gazed into the face of her lost lover, Elvon L'Belder. He was robed in silver-grey, his arms held out to her; a tall, lean man with shaggy brown hair.

'Elvon,' she said. 'I never doubted.'

The figure smiled, its expression full of love. 'Perhaps you should have done. Doubt makes you question things.'

'How could I question you?' Meera cried.

The Goddess shook her golden head. 'How like children you are. Was I ever like this? It is so...' she laughed, 'lovable!' She extended a hand to each of them. 'Follow me, sisters. I'm glad to have done this. It is now time.'

Rosanel took the hand of Elvon L'Belder and let him lead her off down one of the passages. She had eyes only for him and did not see whether Meera was with them or not. She wasn't. Meera had taken the hand of Parthenos and was led a different way. It was, ultimately, still the same path.

Chapter Thirty-Three
Gods Touch

Zy didn't know how long he'd been lying there, Corinna's hand clasped in his own. There was no pain inside him anymore. It seemed as if his body no longer existed. He could not move it.

The girl was looking down at him anxiously, stroking his hair with her free hand. 'Everything will be fine,' she said, defiantly.

He closed his eyes. Will it?

After a moment, she said, 'Zy,' and he opened his eyes once more. 'It's getting lighter,' she said. She let go of him and stood up. 'Yes... I can see... There are... *things* over there. Can you see them?'

He could neither speak nor move, and she had disappeared from his line of sight.

'Goddess!' he heard her say. 'What is that?' She didn't sound frightened. What had she found? She came hurrying back and began hauling at his body. 'You've got to see this!'

He must have been a dead weight. She groaned from the exertion, apparently unconcerned whether she might be damaging him further or not.

'Look!' She'd hauled him up against her kneeling body, supporting him beneath the arms, his head against her breasts. He could feel her heart beating, the outline of her ribs. 'Look!'

The walls were of some brownish-red material, vaulted with arching ribs from which greasy membranes stretched to the floor. Everything was vibrating; Zy's flesh crawled. The place was enormous. Ahead of them, a jumble of complex machinery blended with organic-looking structures that glistened as if smeared with oil. A tangle of serpentine, dull-metallic coils, streaked with crusty corrosion, bristled from the walls, piercing the floor, the machinery itself, flexing slightly as if alive. Zy croaked. It was the best sound he could manage.

"That's... fantastic!' Corinna said, her voice awed, fascinated.

It's revolting, he wanted to say.

A light began to bloom within the machine itself, revealing a cluster of large, transparent, yellowish bladders clinging to its side, high above. These were laced with darker threads that were like networks of veins and arteries. One of them was glowing especially brightly. Within it, something moved.

'Oh no! What is that in there?' Corinna breathed. 'No, it can't be!'

She eased Zy off her body, and he managed to stay propped up on his elbows, able to watch her advance cautiously, like a stalking smoom, towards the snaking coils and bulbous vats of the machine. He wanted to shout, 'No! Don't go too close!' but could only manage a faint squeak, which she either ignored or did not hear.

The glowing bladder trembled, as if sensing her approach. It wobbled as if it was filled with liquid. Then with a smooth jerk, it seemed to detach itself entirely from the machine. It hung for a moment uncertainly, and then floated up and out towards her. Only when its inner light illumined the coils behind it, could Zy see the bubble was still connected to the machine by a sinuous mechanical arm. Perhaps terror warped his perception, but it looked as if the arm's metal joints were ligamented with glistening, living muscle. He had a crazy fear the thing was going to fall on Corinna, absorb her, and tried to cry out a warning, but it was unnecessary. The bubble ignored her, passing right over her head. Zy could see her face bleached in its light as she looked up at it, open-mouthed. Sick realisation puddled through his mind. It's coming for me! He was the victim, not Corinna.

All considerations of pain and injury fled his mind, as he tried to scrabble away from the looming mechanism/organ sweeping towards him. Its slow, leisurely approach was almost insulting, as if it was well aware of his incapacity and mocked him. Just as he was spotlighted, helpless and crawling, by the bladder's inner light, something slashed up through the fleshy floor. He heard it rip, and then dull metal coils were curling around his body. He was pinioned, supine, blinking into a painfully blazing light. This was a nightmare! He would wake up soon. This couldn't possibly be true! Yet he could feel the ridged, warm surfaces of the coils pressing tightly against his flesh. Not too tightly. It did not hurt. This was restraint, not torture.

The bladder hung directly over him now, its inner glow plainly revealing what was contained within it. Hair, long, black hair, floating in liquid; limbs, an open hand. He could see it all. The body of Farris Windteasel was curled foetally inside the bladder. It was pierced in more than a dozen places by devices protruding, via the bladder, from the extended, supporting arm. Bio-metallic fingers and pads invaded the boy's eyes, mouth and ears. Other coils had delved deep into the flesh above his collar bones, and through his abdomen and hips. He was so hideously permeated by these bizarre mechanisms, it seemed he was simply part of the machine itself.

Zy wanted to turn his head away; the vision was abominable! But he could not move. His stomach clenched, bile rose to scald his throat, but before he could vomit properly, his mouth was filled by something soft and tongue-like. It sent warm, living threads down his throat and into his windpipe. His body convulsed in vain.

Corinna came rushing over, freed from a stasis of shock. She was making unidentifiable noises, tugging at the metallic coils, trying to prize them from Zy's body. She pushed her fingers into his mouth in an attempt to dislodge the damp, slippery tube disappearing down his gullet. Her mouth shaped anguished words, but he could not hear them. She beat at the coils with her fists, tried to tear at them with her nails, finally, in utter desperation, leaning down to bite them.

For a moment, the machine seemed ignorant of this treatment. Then, it apparently identified her as a minor nuisance. One of the coils lazily unwound from Zy's body, lifting itself like a snake. It appeared to examine Corinna through its tapered end for a second, and then smacked her smartly out of the way. Zy heard her yelp, and then a dry thud as she hit the floor, some distance off. The bladder still swooped gracefully, slowly, towards him. It was the last thing he saw before his eyes were covered. Flashing colours spurted across his vision, and he had a horrible suspicion needles were being inserted into his eyes, even though he could feel nothing. Sound condensed and dulled as the bladder enfolded him, sealing him inside it and closing with a sphincter snap.

He was wrapped in warmth; soothing uterine fluid lapped his skin. He sensed the pulse of a living creature and knew he was inside it, part of it. Any residual fears were soothed away by a voiceless sigh that told him all he needed to know.

I am holding you close, close; protecting you. Nothing bad can reach you here. See how safe you are, how comfortable? No pain here. No pain at all.

Zy experienced a slight ache, as the machine slid its tapered fingers into his groin and neck, but the discomfort was short-lived. A delightful languor spread throughout his body; better than a Mangine rush, better than sex. He relaxed into it, only dimly aware of movement, things progressing, outside himself. The unknown drug caressed him, body and mind. He could feel it travelling through his blood, sense its icy, fiery passage. It gripped him like a lover. He felt as potent as a god, an icthyphallic god, erect and throbbing with the desire for release.

Now the visions began, archetypal and vivid, eclipsing the grotesque reality of his position. He was the Primal God, striding over the virgin ground of Mother Earth, aeons past.

The land was so unbearably green, its air milk sweet. He was alone, crossing mountains in a single leap as if jumping a ditch, scaling down in size to walk the wide meadows, in the shape of a man. He knew he was seeking his temple and that he could not rest until he found it. There was something he had to do when he got there, but he could not yet recall what it might be. He would soon remember; his mind contained the knowledge of the universe.

Now the Goddess herself had come to stride beside him. She reminded him vaguely of Kitzuki, dressed in a metallic-blue gown that rustled as she marched. They crossed continents in a single step, paddled oceans, ankle deep. Their brows crackled against the skin of the world's airy mantle.

'Fire and water, you and I,' said the Goddess. 'A heavenly steam we make. The heavenly creation; but remember there are others. The marriage of fire and air. An alternative creation.'

And there was the temple before him, so unbearably white and pure; a forest of glistening columns, crowned by cloud. He stood alone. The Goddess had left him to his destiny. Now, the temple portals swung wide, bidding him enter.

Inside, it was dark and cool, fragranced by subtle vapours. He sensed vast space, and came to be walking between two rows of columns that were so high, they disappeared into a misty murk. A simple, marble shrine appeared before him, lit by a soft, rose light. Flowers lay on its altar; the only offering. It was framed and curtained by thick veils of incense smoke, which tumbled incessantly from bowls of carved bone high above.

'I am the secret god,' said a voice.

Zy paused before the altar. Was this his shrine? Who worshipped here? And then a breeze fretted the heaps of flowers on the stone; they shifted and tumbled, liquefying, spurting out jets of intensely sweet perfume. Before his eyes, they took on a new form, those treasure-mounds of petals, shaping themselves into the semblance of a human body. Naked, it lay there, its breast rising and falling, still dusted by a final snow of falling blooms. Its eyes were closed.

'Farris,' Zy said, and reached out to touch him. He, as a God, could give this body life. He could wake it. His fingers were glowing with a soft pearly light as he placed them over the place where Farris' heart beat invisibly beneath the skin. He directed his will into the flesh beneath his hand, conscious of a vast, untapped reservoir of strength shifting like a tide inside him. 'Wake,' he said, without sound.

But even as the boy opened his eyes, Zy felt a sharp, rending tug. The vision before him shattered as if painted on glass. Colours flew around his head, spears of red and blue and violet, shrieking with a terrible, grinding voice. He raised his arms to shield his face, crying out in bewilderment and terror. Then, darkness. Silence.

He hung in eternity; a fraction of time. Universes gave birth, flung themselves out to forever and died, in the space of time he hung there. It was but a second. Was there a body attached to this consciousness? Was there? He felt as if he was simply the essence of a man; all that is male, an abstract principle beyond the edge of reality. Then, as this abstraction, he felt himself seized and engulfed. He had become his essential purpose; simply that. There was no touch of caressing fingers, no seeking mouth, in that un-ness of being. It was the juxtaposition of basic components; life-force to life-force, exhilarating because of its utter, passionless precision. It was a building process, a rush of unhallowed ecstasy. It was conception, but of a type never before, in that world, experienced by man. Here, now, an explosion of energy creates life. Something from nothing. Time from no-time. Space from void. Light spins out from the source in the seconds after creation. It is the first event. Others follow, catalysed by the first. Gods bloom and die. Gods become merely men.

Zy became aware of himself as a separate entity; a mind, a body. He sensed the ebbing, the fading howl, of immense energy. In its wake was the knowledge that he had been, if only for a short time, a god. Maybe death now. Maybe that. He did not resent this possibility for he had learned there was no true dissolution; only transformation. But he did not die.

New substances entered his blood, soothing him into a dreamless sleep. The fronds invading his flesh now tuned themselves to a different function. All light within the bladder grew dim. Humming maternally, it veiled itself in darkness, and began to withdraw towards the main body of the machine, taking Zy with it.

Chapter Thirty-Four
Reacquaintance

Corinna crouched shivering on the floor. Her shoulder ached from the impact of her fall, but she was otherwise unharmed. She had curled, face covered, into a tight ball. Zy was lost to her. She had tried to save him, but it had been no use. He was gone. She was alone. After a few minutes, she'd dared to uncover her face.

Overhead, the bladder hummed and glowed. She could see both Farris and Zy within it, like insects caught inside a carnivorous flower. What was that thing doing to them? Were they dead? For a while, everything was motionless, but for waving hair, then the mechanisms within the bladder had begun to glow and its occupants were revealed more clearly; tortured bodies. Corinna thought of corpses festooned with carrion vines; it looked like that. The bodies jerked; it was hideous. At that point, Corinna had hidden her face again. Farris had been right. Zy Larrigan had been brought here for him, but not for love. Their bodies were conjoined, true, but through the third agency of the machine, and for what purpose? Was it merely that the Presence supposed it was helping Farris to achieve his desires? No, there was more to it than that, she was sure. Farris and Larrigan were being used for a specific purpose. And what part had she yet to play?

Eventually a slight noise, intensification of a visceral hum, caused Corinna to lift her head again. The bubble glided smoothly overhead. She watched it pass, unable to see inside it any longer. It had become utterly opaque. The place on the floor, where Zy had been imprisoned by the coils, was unmarked; not a single filament remained. Glancing around herself, she wondered whether it was safe to move. Could she try and find the entrance to this place and get out, or would that simply remind the Presence she was there, and initiate a fate similar to Zy's? Goddess! She pressed her fingers into her eyes. *How do I get out of this?*

Gone were thoughts of a Greylid Change. Was that what had happened to Zy? She just wanted to escape, even if it meant abandoning Zy and Farris to whatever destiny the machine had decided on for them. She would run all the way back to Silven Crescent to escape this place. The fears that had claimed her, on her first visit to the cave, had been justified. She'd been seduced into ignoring them - for this!

'Goddess, let me out!' she whispered.

'Corinna.' A weak call.

'Zy?' She looked up, hardly daring to hope. 'Is that you?'

'No, it's me. Farris.'

He was only a short distance away from her, leaning against the convoluted sides of the machine, dwarfed by its mass. Corinna wondered whether it was safe to trust him now. Maybe he was no longer human, but part of this thing, totally absorbed; perhaps dead in the true sense. His body was wet. He was naked and shivering, the flesh yellow-pale, red marks visible where the machine had inserted its tendrils into him. He tried to stand, wobbled, and then carefully made his way down a short slope to where Corinna was crouching, holding her breath. The shaky movement, the vulnerability of his naked body, was absurdly, comfortingly human. Corinna exhaled in relief, and knelt upright, leaning towards him.

'What happened?' she asked. 'Are you alright?' It was such an understated question, she began to laugh. Thank Parthenos, she was no longer alone. Farris was alive! Thank Parthenos!

His teeth were chattering. He managed a smile. 'Yes. I'm alright. Just cold.'

Corinna took off her jacket, held it out to him. 'Here. Put

this on. Are we safe?'

He slowly wrapped himself up and nodded. 'Yes. It's over, C'rin.'

'Is it?'

'That part is. I'm glad. I was... *worried* about it.'

Corinna pulled him towards her, which he submitted to bonelessly, and inspected his face. He looked normal enough; tired out, enervated, but without doubt the Farris she was familiar with. 'How do we get Zy out? Is he still alive? How do we get out?'

'We can't take Zy. Not yet. Yehhuk is repairing him.'

'Yehhuk?'

Farris looked confused because she didn't understand him. 'Yes. The Presence.' He gestured with a shaking, wet arm. 'All this.'

'Yehhuk. What does it want?'

'Nothing. It's what we want.'

'Did you want that?' She pointed at the dark, throbbing machine.

Farris closed his eyes. 'It was necessary.' He looked at her. 'You saw?'

She nodded. 'I saw something. What did it do to you?'

Farris rubbed his face. 'It... conjured energy from us, drew it out, somehow. The energy gave Yehhuk life.'

'It's disgusting! A parasite!'

'No it will give life to you too!' Farris insisted.

'You look terrible! I don't want to look like that.'

'It can repair your body,' Farris said, gripping her arms.

'You know nothing...'

He silenced her, raising a hand, cocking his head on one side as if straining to hear something.

'What is it?' She hissed. 'What do you hear?'

'Ssh. Yes.' Farris nodded. 'Yes, I see.' He pulled away from her and stood up.

Corinna gazed up at him stupidly.

'Yehhuk can talk with me now.' He held out his hand,

which Corinna stared at for a moment, before reluctantly placing her own within it. 'Come on.'

She stood up. 'Where?'

'To an old friend,' he said.

The inner chamber was almost in darkness when Shyya and Meonel reached it. Light from the passages fell into it, but there was no longer any direct source of illumination.

'Where now?' Meonel asked. 'Which way?'

Shyya raised his hand. 'That way...' His arm felt long enough to touch the far wall. Grey, shadowy shapes clustered round them.

Meonel said, 'Greylids,' sensing movement, but Shyya answered, 'There's nothing here.'

The shadows dissipated. He straightened up, and Meonel noticed the grimace of pain had faded from his face.

'Are you OK now?'

Shyya nodded. 'It was never a real pain. I wonder why it came, what it was supposed to signify.'

'Perhaps we're in more danger here than we think.'

'We have no choice but to go on.' Shyya led the way into one of the passages, and Meonel was reminded of when they had travelled through the forest of Ire, seeking Elvon L'Belder whom the Greylids had taken from them. It had felt like this; fearful resignation, a conviction that the only way was forward, no matter what danger awaited them.

Shyya seemed confident of which route to take, pausing only briefly when they reached a junction of the tunnels and, on two occasions, stopping to cross similar chambers to the one they had left. At first, Meonel tried to take careful note of the directions they followed but, after a while, became confused. It would not be easy to get out of here in a hurry. He wondered what had happened to Rosanel and Meera. Were they still here somewhere? Were they safe? Or... No, surely not, the summoning had felt so kind, so motherly. Could it be true, what Shyya had shouted in the outer cave? Had it been

L'Belder here all along, playing some kind of outrageous joke on them? Meonel could only be sceptical about that. He'd always believed L'Belder couldn't possibly have survived, in his original form, what had happened in the city. He remembered the foaming light in the sky above the Palace Hill, and Corinna's later garbled words of L'Belder appearing, transformed into a being of light, and engaging Yani Gisbandrun in some kind of elemental combat. The Greylid change had been so recent for L'Belder when he'd taken that battle on; how could he have been strong enough to live through it? It was possible the Greylids had come for him, taken him back to their mossy stronghold of Vez'n'Kizri, in the floating forests. But, even if they had, the identity of Elvon L'Belder, rebel leader, had surely undergone drastic change. The Greylids were unconcerned with humanity, considered it nothing worse or better than an ephemeral nuisance. If Elvon was with them, he'd share that philosophy now.

Eventually, Shyya stopped with purpose outside a closed door. It was quite a normal-looking door, in comparison to some of the bizarre sphincter openings they'd passed, appearing rather like a giant, oval reed-pad membrane, in a frame of carved wood. He looked briefly over his shoulder. 'Here,' he said.

'What is?' Meonel put his hand on the door. It was warm and had the feeling of tough, knobbly, reptile skin.

'Some of the answers, at least,' Shyya replied, and tapped upon the door, an absurdly prosaic thing to do. It made a sound like someone banging a drum.

In response, a slit in the centre of the door elongated and peeled open.

Shyya stepped boldly through into the room beyond, Meonel following more tentatively.

Inside, artificial light resembled that of the suns outside. The chamber was circular, its ribbed walls dark and glistening, its soft floor littered with foamy lumps, which were evidently organic cushions. Two people occupied the room, both of whom Meonel and Shyya recognised instantly. One was Rosanel Garmelding; the other, without doubt, looked exactly like Elvon L'Belder as they remembered him.

'So he did go back,' Meonel said softly, to Shyya alone.

'We don't know what we're looking at yet,' Shyya replied. He advanced towards the relaxed figure on the cushions. 'Who or what are you? Why have you brought all our people here? What do you want from us?'

The L'Belder figure stood up, and held out its arms. 'Shyya, beautiful Shyya, is this the way to welcome me?'

Shyya rigidly endured the embrace. He was not sure whether what held him was a man, or not.

'Relax, little mystic,' L'Belder whispered in his ear. 'Remember the attic room in Vangery, how we touched each other there. Can you deny that you know me?'

Shyya pulled away. 'Elvon L'Belder is no more,' he said. 'At least that's what we were given to believe. If he exists now, it is as something other than his original form. Forgive me, but you look just like the real thing.'

L'Belder scratched the back of his neck; a familiar gesture. 'And how do I convince you? Change my shape?' He laughed. 'I can be whatever I like. Greylids taught me the talent.' He crossed his arms. 'You both look well, if a little green in the face. Meonel.' He took Meonel's stiff hands in his own. 'How well you've done; you took control. Good! I always knew you'd make a good pioneer, if I kicked your ass often enough.'

Meonel looked flinty, unconvinced, even though the affectionate insult was characteristic of the man he'd once known.

L'Belder clapped his hands together, glanced back at Rosanel, who was still sitting demurely pale upon the cushions. 'They don't believe it's me,' he said to her, smiling, raising his arms.

'It is,' she said to them.

'Why don't you just explain what's going on around here,' Shyya said. 'It doesn't matter whether you're L'Belder or not, does it.'

'I will, I will. Corinna is on her way here. Everything shall be explained then. Believe me, something great has happened tonight. You are very lucky people, very lucky indeed.'

Meonel was impatient with the mystery. He wasn't sure whether to trust his eyes or not. It was all like a bizarre dream. Were they really standing here talking to Elvon L'Belder, or was this all a hallucination? 'Where is Meera, Rosanel?' he asked.

The woman's eyes were glazed and unfocussed, as if she'd been hypnotised or drugged. She was smiling, gently, in an unpleasantly lunatic manner.

'Your priestess is safe,' L'Belder answered for her. 'She is listening to Parthenos, somewhere else.'

Meonel glanced at Shyya to signify the answer did not satisfy him. 'Where's Corinna?'

'I told you. On her way here. Now, no more questions for the time being, please. Would you like refreshment?'

'No thank you.'

'Then please, sit down.'

'I'd prefer to stand.'

L'Belder laughed. 'Ready for a quick getaway, eh? You're most suspicious, Meonel, a life-saving trait, I suppose.' He sighed. 'I wish I'd been with you people, all this time. You've accomplished so much. It must have been such an adventure.'

'If you are L'Belder,' Shyya said, 'your life can't have been that dull either. Where did you go to, Vez'n'Kizri?'

'For a while,' L'Belder answered vaguely.

'But you are one of them, one of the Greylids?'

'You make it sound so sinister.'

'Only as sinister as the fact you won't answer us.'

'I want everybody to be together before I reply to your questions.'

'Everyone being?'

'You two, Rosanel and Corinna. The boy too, I suppose, although his part is recent.'

'The boy?' Meonel asked. 'Farris Windteasel?'

'He is quite remarkable. A power-house. Ah...'

A section of the far wall peeled back to reveal Corinna and Farris on the other side, standing in a dark, vaulted passage. 'Come in, come in,' L'Belder said.

Hardly even sparing L'Belder a glance, Corinna ran to Meonel and Shyya. Meonel wondered what bizarre sights Corinna had recently confronted for her to run past a vision of L'Belder so carelessly. Had she already known he was here?

'Goddess, there is some real weirdness happening around here!' she said, embracing them both. She did not seem to be hurt or confused. 'Is that really who I think it is? On the way here, Farris dropped me a few hints about what to expect, but I don't believe it's really him. It's not possible, is it?'

'Your guess is as good as ours,' Meonel answered. 'We'll have to wait and see.'

'He looks just the same, though,' Corinna said, glancing round.

L'Belder had Farris' chin in his hands, apparently examining the boy's eyes. Farris stood there patiently, submitting to the inspection.

'The L'Belder who came to the city was nothing like that,' Corinna added.

'Will you all sit down now please,' L'Belder said, pushing Farris gently down onto one of the cushions, apparently satisfied by his examination. 'You have nothing to fear.'

Shyya, Corinna and Meonel swapped wary glances, before Corinna shrugged and sat down. Meonel and Shyya followed suit.

'I know you view me with mistrust and suspicion; that is only to be expected,' L'Belder said, still standing, 'but perhaps, once I have explained a few things, you will not feel so threatened. In a way, your suspicions are well-founded. I...' he gestured towards himself, '...as I stand here, am not the man you once knew. His personality is a component of my psyche, yes, and I am frequently motivated by his personal ambitions, but you must look upon me as more of a composite being. I am Greylid, and part of Greylid, but choose to appear to you here as Elvon L'Belder, because I know that you are comfortable with his form. L'Belder did return to Vez'n'Kizri, as you've guessed, and his essence gravitated naturally towards the more outspoken element of the Greylid community.' He frowned and tapped his lips. 'Let us say now, that some part of the Greylid consciousness wanted to reclaim knowledge that had been lost to us for a long time. As L'Belder had been an innovative man, he became the cohesive and active force within this segment of the community, and reactivated a branch of investigation long neglected.'

'Well, that's a comfort,' Meonel said sourly. 'Sounds as if L'Belder didn't change at all!'

L'Belder smiled widely, unaffronted. 'Anything that comforts you at this moment is good,' he said. 'Now, allow me to continue. Over the centuries, individuals from the human community have found their way, by design or accident, into the Forests of Ire and Penitence, and have been absorbed by the community in Vez'n'Kizri. Although the majority of our being is against interaction with the outside world, more recent elements of the Greylid consciousness stressed the need for advancement, and perhaps interaction with the race that has come to live here on Artemis - humanity. Greylid has, for too long, been a word synonymous with mystery. We have achieved an advanced state of evolution - a miracle - yet nothing positive has been done since, because the evolutionary process has not been properly completed. The Greylids had begun to stagnate a long time ago; we were in danger of passing from corporeality altogether. The new element was bitterly opposed to this. You know how humankind have cursed themselves with wars, disharmony and oppression these last few hundred years. Perhaps none of this would ever have happened if the Greylids had not shunned contact with them. However, that is now all in the past, and cannot be undone. What *can* be undone is the problem that was caused by aborting our evolutionary process, the abandoning of the Lord of Rocks.'

'And who or what is the Lord of Rocks?' Meonel asked.

L'Belder extended his arm. 'Basically, all this, what you see around you. As a principle, it may be seen as Activity, Progression and Chaos. The Greylids abandoned it in favour of the Moss King, which is the principle of Passivity, Covering and Order. Synchronicity brought you, the Freespacers, to this spot where the Lord of Rocks lay sleeping. Corinna, when you, with your frustrated and bitter self-reproach, set foot in this cave, you unconsciously reactivated the Yehhuk. It was merely boosted by the consequent arrival of Farris with his pent-up desires. You were both living batteries from which Yehhuk could power itself up; wells of depthless energy, constantly recharged by your own life-force, and that of this planet - which your priestess calls Parthenos. Parthenos and Yehhuk are probably, in essence, the very same thing. Yehhuk was not manufactured, but harnessed, by the Greylids. The light and the caves within these cliffs are merely accommodation for the living energy which is Yehhuk.'

'So it isn't a machine,' Corinna interrupted.

'Yehhuk isn't, no. The machines are its prosthetic limbs, the light its communicating organ. Yehhuk is the predominating evolutionary force that seeded Greylid. It is, as the old Wanderils termed it, the One God. It operates solely on the principle of entropy, manipulating conditions so that the remotest possibilities become attainable. It is a force encountered by every living race once they reach a certain level of neurological development. In Greylid, it perhaps overestimated its subject matter. There are pockets of tranquillity to be found within the ripple of Yehhuk, temptations if you like. These are the province of the Moss King. Utopia. But stagnant. The Greylids embraced this ambience and abandoned what they felt was a disruptive force. How much easier to bask in the endless stillness of the Moss King and not have to deal with that lively, chaotic maelstrom called the Lord of Rocks! Well, it was their choice, but in their flight, they forgot that Yehhuk had willingly come to inhabit the body they had made for it, and because it had devoted itself so intimately to their development, remained trapped in the mechanisms when they abandoned it. The task was not completed. Yehhuk could not move on without being released by the Greylids themselves. Once the process has started, it has to run through to its conclusion. Yehhuk had allowed itself to be disabled by permanent location, adapted itself to be vitalised by the life spirit of Greylid. What else could it do but wait here patiently for the opportunity to reactivate, complete its task, and move on?'

'And it needed other intelligent beings to charge itself,' Farris said, speaking for the first time. 'Us. Freespace.'

'Well, yes, but more precisely, you.'

Meonel was far from comforted by L'Belder's explanation. 'If the Greylids abandoned this thing, I'd say it must have been for a good reason,' he said. 'What makes you think we won't reach the same conclusion? If this Yehhuk is so disruptive, perhaps we'd be wiser to leave this place right now - all of us. You can help it finish whatever it wants to do!'

L'Belder shook his head. 'No. You people must not make the same mistake as the Greylids did. Humanity is a very vital species, perhaps more suited to what Yehhuk can do. Greylids are innately passive. We became indolent, introspective, content to travel only through our limited personal realities, and retired from the physical world. That is not the way to get the best from Yehhuk. Being mystic is all very well, and part of what every individual should wish to attain, but we have our physical selves too. They must not be neglected.' He paused, scratched his neck and grimaced. 'Oh, perhaps we have pushed the issue on you too summarily. I know the excuse it's for your own good won't impress you that much, but we have the well-being of Yehhuk at heart too. It needs to work. If you work with it, you will attain, not only for yourselves but the entire human race, the access to your next evolutionary form. This is not the frightening and grotesque physical mutation you fear. I know the Greylids appear to have particularly bizarre forms to you, but that is only our interpretation of physical perfection. You don't have to choose that way. All you have to do is allow Yehhuk to help you become acquainted with your own higher psychological circuits. Once that state is achieved, a being such as Yehhuk will not seem to be a potent, alien force, but simply a kindred spirit. It does not seek power over you; that is not its function.'

'I think we need to know more about what this will involve on a mundane, day-to-day level,' Meonel said. 'What does Rosanel think?' He eyed the vacant-faced woman sceptically.

'She embraces the idea more than any of you,' L'Belder said. His body rippled as if seen through moving water. 'My outer form is only what you perceive it to be - as with any material thing. See for yourself.' The rippling ceased.

Rosanel Garmelding stood before them now, robed in grey. The cushions where she'd been sitting were empty. 'Do you see?' she said. 'I am reunited with Elvon.'

'You have renounced your individuality!' Shyya gasped, appalled.

'No.' A manifestation of L'Belder appeared on the other side of the room. 'Don't be so narrow, Shyya. We simply have a more efficient means of communication than words or gestures.' He walked to Rosanel's side.

'I didn't hesitate,' Rosanel said. 'It took only an instant for us to be one, all of us. Yet I can project individuality at any time. It's a wonderful thing. You just can't appreciate how much.'

'You are playing with us,' Meonel said, his skin crawling.

'A little,' L'Belder admitted. 'What Rosanel chose is probably far from what you and your people would want - yet. I have been preparing for our reunion since I left the city, so the assimilation is a kind of marriage, I suppose.' He smiled at her. 'The best I can offer.' His attention returned to the others. 'It is up to you to discuss with Yehhuk what ultimate result you wish to achieve. It will, of course, take generations to be fully accomplished, but smaller, immediate effects may also be realised. Your bodies are not the tyrannical masters you seem to think they are. You must learn to work body and mind together.' He looked hard at Corinna and Shyya. 'And I'm speaking to you two in particular here.'

Corinna and Shyya exchanged a glance, which L'Belder intercepted, despite its brevity. 'You doubt?' he said. 'Listen friends, if you are willing to jump forward, now, your wildest dreams can be realised. To Yehhuk, flesh is just another building block.'

'So we'd noticed!' Corinna said abruptly, recalling the gruesome materials incorporated into the house in the valley. 'Are you offering what I think you're offering?' She didn't dare to hope, revulsion mingling with fearful joy.

'It isn't an offer, Corinna, it's a choice. Your choice. That simple.'

'I'm not sure I'm ready for miracles,' Shyya said.

'I know. You are comfortable with your disabilities. If you discard them, you are proving to yourself that all I say is true. And that frightens you, doesn't it. Foolish. You could walk out of here to your people as perfect in body as the day you were born - more so. Yehhuk doesn't despise the body in favour of the mind. It knows they are both the same thing, ultimately.'

'I don't think I can make a decision quickly,' Corinna said, and Shyya shook his head to agree with her.

L'Belder extended his hands. 'Think about it, then.'

'Why all the dramatics?' Meonel asked. 'Why tease us as you have done, only to reveal yourself and your purpose now? Do you think we're so easily frightened we'd have run screaming from you if you'd just come and knocked on our cottage door?'

'The atmosphere had to be moulded,' Rosanel said. 'You needed a shake-up. I, as Rosanel, was only near grasping the truth in that I felt L'Belder was returning. You thought it was the Greylids, Meera that it was Parthenos. We were all right. Parthenos is a spiritual visualisation, created by the collective unconscious of the population, and energised by the planetary life-force. If you like, She is the personality human beings have invented for Artemis. Because humans don't realise the power of their own thoughts, they are unaware that they create their own gods. Parthenos is far more human than Yehhuk, simply because humanity gave her birth. But she is still part of the energy force of the universe; a single thread, identifiable from the weave, but still essentially of the whole. Yehhuk's stirrings acted like a magnet. The planet power condensed here because of it and, empathising with Yehhuk, helped it to communicate.'

'As Greylid is in tune with the planet force, it was through Parthenos that I learned you'd settled here,' L'Belder said. 'Synchronicity. What a happy coincidence!' He laughed loudly.

Meonel was not amused. 'So, are you going to tell us what it was that happened here tonight, that we're so lucky about?' he asked. 'Is it simply that you've told us the truth?'

'Not exactly,' L'Belder answered. 'In order to reactivate Yehhuk entirely, it required a special formula of polarised energy. An ignition, if you like. As you probably know already, the energy of living beings is one of the most potent forces of the universe. Farris, and the off-worlder Zy Larrigan, provided the boost Yehhuk needed. It was a special elemental fusion. No combination of native essences could have achieved the right effect, and for the purpose of this event, it was necessary to initiate a di-masculine conjunction; that is, the positive and negative charges of masculinity. Yehhuk is all things, of both polarities, but has been trapped here in an essentially feminine expression. It is regrettable the accident with Larrigan's flyer occurred when Yehhuk was trying to bring him here. Yehhuk was having to operate blind for the most part, and the fact that Larrigan tried to wrestle control away caused the miscalculation that resulted in the accident. It was planned to bring the flyer down in the valley out there.'

'Miscalculation? Accident?' Corinna cried indignantly.

'Somebody died for that! Alouine and Zy were horribly injured.'

'Which Yehhuk is well capable of repairing and has, in fact, already finished with the man. The dead woman's consciousness was pacified and reprogrammed for her next phase of existence, to prevent her suffering the trauma of sudden and violent death. Yehhuk can tidy up quite well after itself.'

"How convenient!' Corinna sneered.

'It is, isn't it? A convenience you will be able to make good use of, I'm sure. Corinna, this area is packed with Greylid hardware they put aside once they embraced the Moss King. All of it is at Freespace's disposal now. As I said, the choice is yours. Do you begin now and put right the wrongs that were once committed against you? The Greylids showed me what happened to you in Gisbandrun's palace. I knew, yet was powerless at the time to prevent it. It would give me great satisfaction if I could do something now. Trust me, Corinna. Elvon L'Belder is not as far from you as you think.'

Corinna looked at Shyya. Was this possible? If she went along with L'Belder could she be made whole once more?

Shyya took her hand. 'Back in Vez'n'Kizri, this offer was made to me once before,' he said. 'I knew if I chose to benefit from it, I could never go back to being Shyya as I knew myself. I declined.'

A strange relief pervaded Corinna's mind. Shyya was telling her not to accept, wasn't he? It seemed so long ago - yet it was only hours - since she had rushed from her family's home, brave enough to face the challenge of being altered in some way, simply to escape from her mutilated form. What was holding her back now?

Shyya seemed to guess what she was thinking, and shook his head. 'No, C'rin, don't misunderstand me. The Greylids who made me that offer were the ones L'Belder has just told us about, those who preferred the domain of the Moss King. I don't think the Greylid we see here is of the same type. I think he can do the things he promises.' He gave Corinna's hand a squeeze. 'It's not a question of believing it's possible, it's a question of whether we can handle something we've tried hard to come to terms with as irreversible. We must take down our own defences, which, even though necessary, might leave us terribly vulnerable. After all, our lives have been very uncomplicated, in a sexual sense. There were no choices for us, until now.'

'Spoken, as always, with clarity and insight!' L'Belder declared. 'You are right, but Yehhuk can help with the psychological problems involved too. It will be the first step. Something your people will need as proof. The injured woman, Alouine Crestick, will be healed as well. Yehhuk is anxious to correct that mistake.'

'It sounds as if we can look on any kind of physical disability as a thing of the past,' Meonel said, still sceptical.

'Yehhuk will have to train you to accomplish these effects yourself, but yes, what you say is right.'

'It's all too much, too much of a good thing.'

'And naturally, you distrust it because you are conditioned to expect the worst and the least of everything. Give up your self-imposed restrictions. Be free. Fly. Do anything. Are you really too timid to take hold of this power?'

'And what is the price?' Farris asked. He had been very quiet. 'There will be a price, won't there?'

L'Belder turned to look at him. 'Yes, you're right. Everything has a cost. But you are assuming it is a price you are not prepared to pay.'

'And if we don't take up this offer?' Corinna asked. 'Will you go away and leave us, or can we expect the choice to be withdrawn, and something more demanding to replace it?'

L'Belder considered her words. 'To be honest, I have made no plans for the possibility of you rejecting this chance.'

'And why is that? I thought you were so prepared.'

L'Belder smiled. 'Why? Because I know you won't reject it.'

Chapter Thirty-Five
Morning

Meera the priestess came back to normal consciousness. She sat for a moment on the floor of the simple, dimly-lit room where Parthenos had brought her, and considered what she had learned.

'Why did you look for some kind of Divine Arrival?' the Goddess had asked. 'Don't you know that I *am* you, forever part of every living thing? You made me real.'

'But the visit...' Meera had said, wanting to make amends for what she sensed as disappointment in the Goddess' voice. 'I had never felt you so clearly before.'

'Wrong. You thought you had only come closer to humanity here in the north. That proves, in fact, that you were closer to me than you've ever been. I am not separate, Meera, never have been, never will be, can't be. Yehhuk can stimulate your consciousness so you can visualise me more easily, but it only amplifies the symbolism, the realities that are already within you. When I came to your cottage that night, what you really found was yourself, just as you are now speaking with yourself through me. I am your inner flower, the spark of life. It is a sidetrack to kneel and worship me at your altars, because then you are simply externalising an aspect of yourself that you should seek to integrate fully.'

'Parthenos, Lady, are you real, or am I hallucinating?'

The Goddess laughed, sending out a spray of light. 'Meera, what you are saying is like asking, are the stars shining in the night sky? Do you understand? They look so close together don't they, hanging there in splendour, but your logical mind also tells you that they are billions of light-years apart. However, to you on Artemis, they are close, because that is how you perceive them. Therefore, they are both. That is the answer to your question.'

At some point, Meera realised she was no longer communicating with an entity outside of herself, and found she was alone. For the past few minutes her conversation had been entirely internal. She became aware of sight and sound; the hum beyond the walls that spoke of vast machinery, the soft quality of the illumination that seemed to seep through the ceiling.

What a waste of time it was, worrying about spiritual training, teaching people to carry out the same old rituals, she thought. *How wrong too to see myself as some kind of martyr, a vessel for the truth.*

She thought about how, since leaving the city, the Freespacers had come to flow and ebb with the land, absorbed comfortably into the seasonal cycle; this, more than anything, proved that spiritually they had advanced way beyond the ritualised city worshippers. She thought of Shyya Trotgarden and the Windteasels, the witches of the community, whose magic was taken for granted and rightly so. They were part of the structure. If Freespace could be looked upon as an individual, then the healers, the shapers, were its imagination, the capacity to dream.

And what is my function? she wondered piously, only to be presented with the thought *the elimination of waste,* which caused her to laugh aloud. Of course.

She stood up. It was time to rejoin the others.

Carmenya Oralien found herself standing next to Hollis Backwater in the crowd. For a while, they studiously ignored each other; Carmenya, because Hollis was just another male member of Freespace who despised her, and Hollis, because Carmenya was a person Corinna loved, which made him jealous.

Hollis knew Corinna was somewhere deep inside the cave

system. He had faced the loathsome possibility she might never emerge again, and also the equally unpleasant one that he might not either. No-one knew why they were here, only that the compulsion to congregate in this place was impossible to ignore. He wondered if anyone would leave here to take up their lives as before, or whether, in the morning, Freespace would be an empty shell, as desolate as if it had never been occupied. Was it possible that, one day, southerners or off-worlders might find it, abandoned and reclaimed by the land? Wouldn't they wonder what had happened to its inhabitants? Another mystery for this strange, secretive world. He thought of fairy-tales from his childhood; old, old stories of people who disappeared, led by fairy temptation into the heart of the mountain, never to see the sun again. Would the rocks soon close against the Freespacers, sealing them inside? What would happen then? The fairy-tales never reported beyond the closed and silent rocks.

Hollis shifted uncomfortably, accidentally treading on Carmenya's foot. She made an irritated noise, and they were forced to communicate. Hollis could see Carmenya was afraid, and he guessed intuitively it was because she thought some kind of divine judgment was awaiting her. Everyone knew the story of how she had once betrayed Corinna. Hollis could see the pain of that betrayal reflected in Carmenya's face. Oh, she knew what she'd once done, alright, and had never been allowed to forget it. She and Corinna should have put aside their pride, and discussed it all long ago, laid its ghosts to rest. If Corinna showed she had forgiven Carmenya, then Hollis was sure the rest of the community would too. Perhaps, it was too late for that now; perhaps, they'd never have the chance.

Moved by a surge of compassion, he nodded at Carmenya and said, 'Corinna still cares for you, you know'.

Carmenya stared at him steadily, perhaps thinking he was mocking her.

He smiled. 'I mean it,' he said. 'I feel you should know that now.'

She smiled back, warily.

It surprised him how much easier it was to feel sympathy for this woman, rather than hostility. Carmenya did not comment on his words, but Hollis sensed there was now peace between them. 'It must soon be morning,' he said.

'Yes,' Carmenya answered huskily. 'I can't turn round and look at the sky. Can you?'

He tried, but it was as if his will-power was concentrated solely on the back of the cave, where the tunnel mouths glowed. 'No,' he said.

'This is crazy,' Carmenya muttered. 'Look how many of us there are!'

'So?'

'We must all look back,' she said. 'We can't be dominated by this. It's crazy. We're like stupid danks!'

She began to push through the crowd. Hollis could see her red head disappearing between the ranks of people in front of him. He followed her, not wanting to lose sight of her. He heard her shouting out, 'Look at the sky! All of you, look at the sky!'

'Carmenya!' he called after her, wondering whether the woman had gone utterly mad.

A wave of muttering, like a rising wind, eddied through the crowd, so tightly packed. Carmenya had reached the back of the cave, and had clambered into a cluster of stalagmites. She was still facing the tunnels, but had raised herself into everybody's sight. Hollis could see her struggling to turn, as if physical bonds kept her facing the rock. He lunged forward and grabbed her ankle. Her face was twisted with effort. She had gone mad. What was the point of this?

'Carmenya,' he hissed. 'Come down, it'll be alright. Come down.'

'Alright?' she answered. 'Will it?' And with a surge of strength, hauled Hollis up behind her. 'Let's look. Let's see,' she said. 'Can we manage it together?'

They clasped hands.

'Maybe,' Hollis said.

Carmenya smiled. 'Of course we can!'

Slowly, they turned and faced the dawn, unaware of the multitude of white faces looking up at them.

'It's beautiful,' Hollis said, and Carmenya echoed, 'It's beautiful. Look. Everyone, turn and look.'

With a groan, the great body of Freespace turned to face the sky. It was radiant with the promise of sunlight, and limned against it, huger than the sky itself, was the welcoming figure of Parthenos.

'Now you can see me,' the Goddess said, and Freespace began to move its many limbs towards the ledge. It snaked towards the stone steps, flowed down them, across the glade still dark with night, and through the silent, sleeping forest, until it splashed like a tide out into the valley meadow, where the house of Vangery stood resurrected, its metal parts catching the first light of the suns. The black cliffs shone with crystal, mimicking the night sky, and the long grass stirred with the first breeze of morning.

On the steps of Vangery stood Corinna Trotgarden. She wore a grey robe and was holding onto a banister for support. Weariness showed in her face and the stoop of her body, but her eyes were alert and bright. Carmenya and Hollis, still holding each other's hands, pushed through the mumbling crowd of Freespace.

'It's her!' Hollis cried, and Carmenya needed no prompt to run.

'Is she... is it really Corinna?' Carmenya asked, both eager and afraid of facing the young woman on the steps.

They sidled through the group of children standing at the front of the crowd.

Corinna saw them. There were tears on her cheeks, whether of joy or pain or sadness, they could not tell. She said, 'Please. Come to me. I cannot walk too well yet.'

Freespace had fallen silent. Both Hollis and Carmenya experienced a slight wrench when they broke away from the crowd.

'Corinna,' Hollis said, at the foot of the steps. 'Are you alright?'

She nodded and began to cry, trying to wipe her eyes and nose on her sleeves, which fell right over her hands. 'Yes,' she said and looked at Carmenya. 'It doesn't matter anymore. The past, that is. It's resolved. It didn't happen.'

'What do you mean?' Carmenya bounded up the steps and put a protective arm around Corinna's shoulders, a gesture that brought an ache of memory, and a sweetness of new dawn.

'I'm the same as I was,' Corinna said. 'Can't you see? Look at me.'

Hollis had pushed up beside them. He and Carmenya looked into Corinna's face, and she laughed through her tears. 'Can it be you've forgotten already?' she asked. 'My face, look!'

'The scars!' Carmenya gasped.

'What scars?' Hollis said, and the three of them embraced.

Somewhere in the middle of the crowd, Dannel Trotgarden stood with her other two children. She had no immediate urge to run to her younger daughter. All the fear, mistrust and worry had been left behind. She had dropped it somewhere between this place and the day before. Bolivia and Orblin crept closer to her sides, and she was conscious of her size, of her capacity to enfold and nurture. Dannel put her arms around her children. 'I think,' she said, 'that today will be a holiday.'

L'Belder was waiting for Shyya when he emerged from the healing bladder he'd entered, nervously, only a short time before. Around them, the vast chamber was empty, and Shyya felt as if they must be alone within the caves, that everybody else was now outside. He shivered, and L'Belder offered him a robe. Shyya had not realised he was naked. For the first time in years, he'd remained utterly unselfconscious of his body in the presence of another.

'Well?' L'Belder said.

'I can feel it,' Shyya said, fighting the overwhelming urge to lean down and examine himself in detail. 'Maleness. But it's overlaid on my emasculated state. I feel both. Is that right?'

'You can either merge it or keep it separate, as you wish. Personally, I would merge it, but then merging has become a lifestyle for me.'

'Is it... will it... work?'

L'Belder laughed. 'Shyya, you have been restored. Experiment as soon as you get the opportunity, but just remember that Meonel will have to get used to the change as much as you, so be careful.'

Shyya tentatively ran his hands down his body. 'It was only after the mutilation I became what I am, if you know what I mean. Will I have to lose my Sight now?'

L'Belder shook his head. 'Still obsessed with sacrifice, Shyya? Come on, dress yourself. Meonel is waiting for you.'

'I can't believe...'

'Don't. Just accept.'

Shyya shrugged himself into the voluminous cloth and followed L'Belder across the living floor. Before they went out into the passage beyond, he laid a hand on L'Belder's arm and said, 'Tell me, now, the truth. Is there any of Elvon left at all, or is there nothing more than this image you've adopted to assuage our fears?'

L'Belder smiled. 'Doesn't that amount to the same thing?'

'I don't care. I want an answer. An old-fashioned, black and white answer. Save the conundrums for our 'training', or whatever. I want to know, as human to human, if you are the man I once knew.'

'L'Belder melded with the Greylids, Shyya, so he can never be the isolated creature he once was. That is the Greylid way, perhaps extreme to you, but what he opted for nonetheless. L'Belder's personality was strong. We can bring it out whenever we choose, as you have seen. I can tell you everything that happened between yourself and Elvon, but part of me did not experience it firsthand. Freespace will not choose this way. They will be wiser perhaps, or just different.'

'So the answer is no, you are not the man I once knew.'

L'Belder sighed. 'If you insist.'

Meonel was waiting in the room where they'd first encountered L'Belder. When Shyya followed L'Belder through the door, he stood up anxiously, perhaps afraid Shyya had been changed irrevocably, forever.

Rosanel was with him, or an image of her. Shyya was still slightly appalled that she could have rushed into such a drastic change so quickly. Would she regret it later, or was the human part of Rosanel, who'd feel things like that, already dead?

Meonel looked too worried to move.

'I'm alright,' Shyya said. 'Don't look at me like that! Has our friend here given me an extra head or something?'

'Success!' L'Belder announced, beaming, and raising his arms dramatically. 'Not that I had any fear to the contrary, of course!'

'You will have to be flexible,' L'Belder told them, before they went down to the valley. 'Zy Larrigan will scurry back to his people and spread the word. It's likely they will greedily flock here to see how they can use what you've found. You may have to perplex them in order to defend yourself. Yehhuk will show you how. Defence is far easier without the shedding of blood or resorting to violence. Look upon the off-worlders as ignorant children, and treat them gently because of that. You must send representatives from Freespace to Silven Crescent as soon as you feel you're prepared. I feel Alouine Crestick should be among those emissaries. You have to face the fact that, through your assimilation with this planet, you are, to all intents and purposes, alien beings to the Silven Crescent people now. Alouine has experience of both. She can be your voice.'

'That brings something to mind,' Meonel said. 'If we make comparisons, I suppose the Freespacers are like the Greylid community, while the Silven Crescent people are like the old Artemisians who perished. Is that right?'

L'Belder looked thoughtful. 'To a degree, I suppose.'

'Does that mean whoever doesn't join with us will be wiped out, then? After all, there aren't many old Artemisians left around to tell the tale, are there?'

'The Old Artemisians, as you call them, hardly resembled the Silven Crescent people. They had their own problems, which do not concern you. Put aside any fear that Yehhuk destroyed them. They destroyed themselves. Only those of them who guessed the truth survived, and they are now part of Greylid.'

'What did happen to the old race, then?'

'They lost their hope. Life became mechanical for them, spirituality was utterly lost, and thus all meaning drained from their existence. Can you understand now why it is so important for humanity to work with Yehhuk?'

'It becomes clearer,' Meonel said carefully. He sighed. 'Goddess, we thought our life-work would be how to get a town on its feet, how to mine resources, build up our own technology. The responsibility for that has been taken from us, hasn't it! Those things aren't really problems anymore.'

'What about the Greylids in Vez'n'Kizri?' Shyya asked. 'Will they join with the life on this world now?'

'Some will,' L'Belder answered. 'My...our... other parts. They will come to work with Yehhuk once more. Those who live in the domain of the Moss King will stay there, I expect. That is nothing to do with any of us.'

They had come to the outer cave, where the wind ushered in the perfume of life from the forest.

'Aren't you coming down to the valley with us?' Shyya said, when L'Belder hung back near the passage mouth.

'It is not my place,' he replied. 'The joy is yours. I'll be around, though.'

'Can a Greylid come down and sit at a humble table and take breadlemen with the Trotgardens?' Meonel asked. 'I know Dannel would like to see you, Elvon.'

L'Belder cocked his head on one side and glanced at Shyya, who was thinking of their earlier conversation. L'Belder could never come to share a meal, because he no longer existed, not really. Shyya kept his silence. There was no reason why that should be known. It made no difference really.

'Tell Dannel to lay an extra place,' L'Belder said, cheerfully. 'I'll not neglect my old friends - any of them.'

Meonel nodded. 'Thank you. For everything.'

'You doubted me once, Meonel. Look on this as my sublime, egocentric attempt to prove you wrong. I've succeeded, haven't I?'

Meonel smiled wryly. 'I have to admit you have,' he said. 'I wouldn't have done what you did back in Vez'n'Kizri, but I suppose someone had to.'

'Someone already had,' L'Belder answered enigmatically, and disappeared into the inner caves.

In a room with curved and gnarled walls, like the inside of an enormous hollow tree, Farris Windteasel watched the sleeping form of Zy Larrigan. L'Belder had directed him there while he was busy with Corinna and Shyya. Zy had not woken. He was sleeping peacefully, his face smoothed of cares, his hair damp and hanging over his face. He lay on a raised platform, covered from the chest down by a sheet that looked like an enormous, yellow-brown leaf. Farris sat on the warm floor with his knees up, biting his fingers nervously. He was afraid of what would happen should Zy wake up. They had been close, but not in the way of lovers. The purpose for his being there was fulfilled; there was nothing more to add. An end to dreams.

Farris cursed his own cowardice. If he was brave, he'd wake Zy himself; with a kiss, or a caress. With confidence. He couldn't.

Farris shivered, as if a breath of cold air had passed over him. He glanced quickly over his shoulder and saw the figure of Elvon L'Belder standing there, just inside the room. He didn't know what to say. Was this the creature he'd been communing with all this time? If so, L'Belder knew everything about him; his deepest fears and desires. It was not a comfortable thought. He'd never wanted his shadow lover to become real, in this sense.

'You are alright,' L'Belder said.

Farris wasn't sure whether that was a question or not.

'Yes,' he answered.

L'Belder leaned down, and placed a long-fingered hand on Farris' shoulder. 'I want to talk with you again,' he said.

'What about?'

L'Belder hunkered down beside the boy. He glanced at Zy Larrigan, who stirred slightly in his sleep, but did not wake. 'Your friend Zy will soon leave here,' L'Belder said, without preamble.

Farris lowered his head, his face bleak. 'I know that,' he said. 'I didn't expect anything else.'

'Farris, Farris, why do you try to lie to me?'

Farris looked up. 'You tricked me! You lied to me! I don't understand why you did that. I trusted you. Why did you make me want him so much?' Farris felt dangerously close to tears, and gritted his teeth. Breaking down would achieve nothing but further humiliation.

'You had the choice, Farris. You denied him. Remember the night you drove Zy back from the Trotgardens...'

'Was that all it was supposed to be, then? Hurried groping in the back of a dank-cart. Am I expected to be thankful for that?'

L'Belder looked perplexed. 'It was not my intention to hurt you. I can see now I was clumsy. You are a sensitive soul, aren't you? You wanted to be wooed, cherished. I'm sorry...' He reached out and briefly squeezed Farris' shoulder. 'There is an answer, you know. You could still have all that you want and need.'

'How? By forcing Zy into staying here? More manipulation?'

L'Belder shook his head. 'No. That's not what I meant. It is simply that, when he leaves Artemis, you must go with him.'

'Me? How?' Farris asked, his voice cold and defensive, but

his face betraying a wretched hope. 'I can't. We are so different. He doesn't...'

'Hush, hush,' L'Belder interrupted. 'He will take you with him if you want to go. You are right; there are vast differences between you, cultural differences, and because of that there has been rather a problem in communication, but it is not insurmountable.'

Farris shook his head. 'I would embarrass him on his world. It would be terrible.'

'Well, I won't deny it will be hard for you at first,' L'Belder agreed. 'But you are not stupid, Farris. And don't underestimate Larrigan's feelings. After what happened tonight, he will need you. There is also another reason you should go.'

'I feel this must be the real reason,' Farris said dryly.

L'Belder shrugged. 'As you like. Anyway, I feel it's important your people have eyes and ears in Larrigan's affairs. The reasons are obvious.'

Farris sighed. 'I can't do that. I'd just make a mess of things, I'm sure.'

L'Belder smiled. 'Oh, how you underestimate yourself! Not just your innate strength, but also the hold you will have over this man. He will not want to lose you, Farris. When he wakes up, this will all become clear. That he will take you away from here is inevitable. I'm just preparing you for it.'

Farris sighed glumly, looking around at the glistening, ribbed walls of the room. 'Then I have been given what I wanted, just like Yehhuk promised, but there is a price too, isn't there.'

L'Belder put his arm around the boy's shoulder. 'Not a price, just a consequence,' he said. 'And we all have to live with those, don't we?'

Chapter Thirty-Six
Last Light

In Silven Crescent, Layna Minnders walked past the barred doors to the old apartments of Yani Gisbandrun, on her way to a meeting with the Council. She was surprised by a sudden thought of the off-worlder Zy Larrigan - his face came right into her mind - and she wondered how he and the women were getting on. They were due back any time now. She realised that, in a way, she was quite envious of Alouine and Welma, mainly because they had the courage to face what lay beyond the familiar. It surprised her to find that she wished she'd gone with them now. Larrigan had made her the offer, too. If only she'd been brave enough to take him up on it. What would she have seen and learned by now?

Something caught her attention, and she glanced down the galleried passage to where the great dark-wood doors concealed and restrained the presence, however tenuously lingering, of Yani Gisbandrun. Layna shuddered. It hurt her to remember those times. Terribly. Luckily, she'd disciplined herself not to dwell on the past, although, because some inner compunction forced her to gaze upon those doors, her hands strayed unconsciously to her chest, her flat, scarred chest. She had lived there once, down that passage, through the doors, and beyond, beyond, in the place called the Rooms of the Red.

No, don't think about it. There's no point. Walk past. Hurry. The meeting is waiting. Don't think. Artemis is out there, wide and beautiful. We are going to meet her soon. The past is dead.

Layna choked on an uncontrollable, whining sob. 'Let me go!' she hissed, wondering, for a panicked instant, whether there really were ghosts in there, coming to claim her, take her back.

No, her logic insisted. *Elvon L'Belder, the shining man, gave you back your sanity, and closed the doors to that place for you forever, even if he could not give you back what had physically been cut away.*

She found she was clutching the wall carvings, her faced pressed painfully into the stone. The doors; they weren't barred at all! They were opening! She was coming back! No!

Layna struggled desperately to move, but her limbs were held rigid by an unseen force. In her mind, she screamed for somebody to walk by, someone who could shake her from this terrible stasis. Around her, the palace was unnaturally still. She could see shadowy movement by the doors. Oh no, Goddess, please...

The shadow detached itself. A figure, robed in red, uncompromisingly solid, was swaying up the gallery towards her. It seemed drunk, its hands pawing air for support. Layna's heart contracted into what felt like a small, hard stone. The figure was so familiar.

'You're dead!' Layna whispered.

She knew what she was seeing couldn't possibly be real, and yet, it was. There was no mistiness, no transparency. That was a real woman staggering towards her.

The figure was very close to her now. Layna could see the tired, crazy face, the deep-set eyes, the shorn head. It seemed to see Layna for the first time, and tottered to a standstill. It rubbed its face, screwed up its eyes, swaying as it peered at her. 'Can you... can you tell me if there's a way out of here?' it asked her.

Layna could smell alcohol and the sickly sweet aroma of Gisbandrun's favourite drug, Eema's Itch. Her jaw had locked solid; she could neither speak or scream.

'Oh, you're not real, are you,' the figure continued, nodding to itself. 'Can't you tell me something, though? I got this far!'

Layna gulped air into lungs that felt as if they'd turned to dry paper. 'No, go back!' she managed to rasp. 'You don't belong here. You belong in there! Go back!' Her body had begun to shake.

'Is that the truth?' asked the figure, wistfully. 'I belong in there? Forever? Is that all there is?' It held up its hands and inspected them, bending the white wrists backwards. And Layna was given a flash of insight, of memory.

She remembered a drunken night, when she'd been intoxicated enough to walk right out of the Rooms of the Red. She hadn't been trying to escape really, hadn't possessed the volition to. She realised now that she must have been seeking extinction, a guard to make her turn back, who she could have disobeyed. She could have walked into the blade of death, and it would have been freedom. There had been no guards, however, but in her wretched madness, she'd come across a shining, beautiful woman, whose face had been comfortingly familiar, and had asked her the question 'Is there a way out of here?' She hadn't meant a physical way, even in her stupor. The figure had been an angel. She'd asked for enlightenment, a pitiful clarity seeping through her defence of insanity. The angel had given her peace, albeit forgotten almost instantly on a conscious level, but somehow deeply retained, for just this moment.

The angel had said, 'You will be free. You will be cleansed. Last Light, go back. Go back and wait.'

Later that night, L'Belder had come.

Layna faced the awful vision of her past, the ghost of herself, and said, 'You will be free. You will be cleansed. Last Light, go back. Go back and wait.'

Time and space jumped around her. Evening light fell softly into the passage, and Layna realised the doors to Yani Gisbandrun's apartment weren't black and cold as she'd thought, but living wood, warm and golden in the late sunlight, and closed and barred. She was alone. She could move.

Layna straightened up, smoothed her dress, and walked

down the passage to the doors. She lifted down the heavy bar, and opened them wide. Then she went to her meeting, aware of the fact that she had been her own salvation, and that she was alive, and that she was grateful to the entire universe for that existence.

A few days later, Alouine Crestick landed a sleek new flyer on the palace roof, and reality had to be realigned for everyone. But the doors to the chambers of horror were never barred again.

Chapter Thirty-Seven
The Teacher

Kitzuki was putting finishing touches to her make-up, an air pencil poised in one hand, the other smudging her brow. It was the eve of yet another company reception, this one to celebrate the annual anniversary of D&K's inception. It was destined to be a large affair, thronged with celebrities. Kitzuki pursed her lips at her holo-image, blew herself a kiss. She inspected her nails critically and then turned on her stool.

'Darling! If I see that face once more this evening, I swear I shall scream!' She swooped over to where Farris Windteasel was sitting dejectedly on her sleeping couch, and planted a kiss in the air above his cheek. She did not, after all, want to smudge her make-up. 'Come along, Farris, Zy and Silas will be here soon, and I did promise I'd help you get ready.'

'I *am* ready!'

She observed his clothes, immaculate, and chosen by her especially for the occasion, his faint cosmetics, which she'd artfully applied, his glossy hair, which she'd persuaded him to tie back. So far, all her entreaties to have it styled had been repulsed. Still, it was early days yet. 'You certainly look ready,' she said, tapping her cheek with a lacquered talon, 'but, you're not. What is it?'

'Do I have to go?'

The enquiry was so plaintive, Kitzuki was actually moved to give him a real kiss. 'Of course! People are dying to meet you!'

'I won't know what to say, though. I'll look stupid.'

'Then say nothing, dear. Be mysterious and silent. You

look so beautiful, no-one will mind.'

He sighed resignedly. 'Alright.'

Kitzuki put her head on one side. 'Are you homesick? Is that it?'

Farris smiled - oh, what charm! - and shrugged. 'A little. I'm still not used to this place. Sometimes, I get wobbly and sick.'

'That will pass, Farris, honestly. Just keep away from observation galleries, like I told you.' She sat down beside him and patted his hand. 'Zy wants to show you off. We all do. People will want to get to know you...' She couldn't help adding dryly. 'We all do.' Zy had been uncommonly possessive about this one. Kitzuki, being the person she was, in no way resented Zy wanting to bring a new person into their relationship, especially such an exotic one, even if it did extend the partnership somewhat beyond conventional limits. However, Zy had made it abundantly clear that he did not want either her, or Silas, making any propositions to Farris. He refused even to discuss it with them. She supposed the boy needed time. No doubt Plate relationships were rather strange to him. She also knew intuitively that Zy needed something only Farris could give at the moment. It was still rather a mystery exactly what had happened on Artemis. Sometimes, Zy seemed like a stranger.

Farris was giving her a very keen look. Quite often, she felt he could read her mind. She patted her hair self-consciously. 'Well,' she began, trying to think of something to say.

Farris interrupted her. 'You don't resent me being here, do you?'

Kitzuki smiled widely. 'Of course not! How could you think such a thing! Don't be silly!'

'I have changed things a lot for you though, haven't I?'

She raised one shoulder expressively, pulled a face. 'We-ell, a little, but I don't mind. Whatever Zy wants, I want.' She glanced at him quickly. 'You're very special to him, I can tell.'

'How much has he told you about what happened in

Freespace?'

She laced her hands in her lap. 'Everything. About the accident and how your family healed him.' She paused, frowned. 'That *is* everything, isn't it?'

Farris stared at her for a moment.

Her heart nearly stopped. 'He is... he is *alright*, isn't he?' she asked.

'Yes, he's fine.' Farris looked strangely relieved.

Silly boy! He'd been afraid she was jealous of him 'Then there's nothing for either of us to worry about, is there!' She stood up and smoothed her dress. 'The party will be fun, Farris. We'll drink and drink and be very happy. Maybe later, the four of us can come back here, get to know each other a little better. What do you think?' She turned back to the holo-screen, as if to examine her face. Unbelievably, her heart was racing. He probably wouldn't even understand the question.

There was a sound of movement, although faint. She felt his presence behind her rather than heard it. She laughed nervously, oddly reluctant to turn round, and had a dreadful feeling her face was actually red.

Farris put his hands on her shoulders, bent to kiss her neck. She jumped. 'Farris!' Another laugh. Where had this assertive creature come from? It was most unnerving but, she had to admit, exciting too. 'I would like to teach you,' she said softly. 'I know you've never had a woman, Farris. I can give you so much.'

He smiled wryly. 'You'll be surprised,' he said, 'what I can teach *you*.'

Chapter Thirty-Eight
Yehhuk

Yehhuk could be playful when the mood took it. Corinna suspected that Yehhuk was playing all of the time, and found it rather hard to behave seriously, which was what humans felt comfortable with, when involved in such life-defining work.

Sometimes, Yehhuk manifested in the form of a child and would accompany Corinna on her tasks around Freespace. One day, they rode danks out to the boundary fence, to the place which Corinna and Hollis had fixed up all that time ago. Three seasons had passed, and the fence had come loose again.

Sighing, Corinna hopped down from her dank and began to unstrap her tool-case from the saddle. Seeing this place made her feel nostalgic. Back then, she would never have dreamed any of the things that had happened to her since could be possible. Now, she had a family of her own, which was well on the way to expanding. Two moons-arc after the Cave Time, she had moved out of the Trotgarden residence and into the one she and Hollis were building, up in the valley. They'd used much of Yehhuk's machinery, but nearly everyone in Freespace still felt more comfortable using their own hands to construct things. Mind-power could be exploited later, perhaps generations later. Freespace did not want to rush things; they wanted to complete their community as they'd intended, in the manner they'd intended, and as themselves. For now, the power of Yehhuk would be used mainly for healing, as such power always had been, in modest amounts. It was decided the intake of knowledge would be gradual, and natural. They had had enough of upheaval. Still, things were changing on

Artemis, and changing fast.

True to his word, Zy Larrigan had contacted CDR, and representatives had come to offer support, and also to investigate the phenomenon Larrigan had told them of. Yehhuk had been presented as an advanced form of artificial intelligence, but the bulk of its abilities were concealed. Larrigan had been sick; he must have hallucinated a lot of what he'd reported. The CDR representatives could only agree on that, although they still had a couple of operatives up at the cave, examining data. Freespace was tolerant; it would let them play in its back-yard, if they wanted to.

New settlements were springing up, some distance off, and the government in Silven Crescent had descended for a meeting with the people of Freespace. Keeping straight faces, the Freespacers had respectfully and humbly accepted the political pardon Eugenia Gulding bestowed on them. Carmenya Oralien had even been offered a new position in the city, which she'd gracefully declined. Her life, she'd said, was in Freespace now.

A short while after Corinna and Hollis had moved into their new home, Carmenya had joined them. Corinna had discussed it many times with Carmenya before the final move was made. She could not countenance being a lover to Hollis and Carmenya separately. They must be together, as a loving family, with all that implied, or not at all. They agreed upon a trial period. Carmenya was frankly terrified of getting close to a man. She and Corinna had had many conversations about it, Corinna guiltily aware of how she was applying a subtle pressure on Carmenya. Hollis had become a good friend of Carmenya's, but she found it difficult to look upon anything male as physically attractive. Corinna persisted in her persuasions, but they had all harboured doubts whether the situation would work. However, mainly because Hollis had remarkable patience, and they'd all had a genuine desire to make it a success, the trial hadn't been that at all, but a wondrous time of discovery for all three of them. It had also been a time of great creativity, and in more than one way. Carmenya had fallen pregnant first, Corinna following only a moons-arc afterwards. They had so much to share, so much to look forward to.

'What are you doing?' Yehhuk asked, settling itself onto a nearby boulder to watch. 'You don't need a fence anymore.'

'I built it,' Corinna answered. She unconsciously put her hand protectively over her swollen belly as she picked her way across the mire-tufts. 'I like to keep it intact.'

'Fences, boundaries!' Yehhuk chided in a mocking tone. 'Just when are you going to grow up, Corinna?'

'Look, this isn't a symbol or anything. It's craftsmanship, art if you like. Look at these bindings, these joints. My skill, OK? This fence is my sculpture. Now shut up and hand me some nails, will you?'

Yehhuk hopped down off the boulder, and watched in silence as Corinna repaired the fence, handing her the nails when she needed them'

I don't know,' Corinna said, 'you'd think a mega-entity like yourself would know how to mend a fence!'

'I know everything you know. You were the one getting all possessive about your 'art'.'

'Know what I know, huh? Doesn't it bore you being with such an undeveloped creature as me?'

Yehhuk shook its curly, blond head. 'Sometimes, Corinna, I don't think you've realised what I am. I'm disappointed. I thought you, of all people, would know.'

'OK, what are you? All the gods that ever lived?' She laughed and shook her head, knocking in another nail.

'Silly! Gods! Haven't you learned that lesson yet? I'm you.'

'Sure. Gods come from ourselves, blah, blah, blah.'

'No. That's not what I meant. Yehhuk is a teacher, yes? An advanced form of consciousness and being?'

'Yes. I know. You keep telling us.'

'But where do I come from?' Yehhuk was now positively bouncing up and down with excitement, for all the world appearing like any normal, eight year old girl.

'I don't know. You tell me. Some other primitive race you brought up to standard?'

'No. Guess again.'

'The end of the universe.'

'No. Again.'

'A clue, then.'

'The original Artemisians were a future form of humanity.'

'What? What do you mean?' Corinna put down the hammer. Was this another joke?

When she looked round, Yehhuk was wearing the form of Parthenos, a manifestation it reserved for serious issues. 'It's true. In one reality, at least.'

'I don't understand. How can they be? We came after, thousands of years after!'

'Yes, but the original Artemisians were colonists too. Human colonists. They were much more advanced than you, and understood about time. You'll get there one day, and reach that understanding. When they colonised this world, they went back to a time in its evolution when there could be no risk of a competitive sentient species. They often did that.'

Corinna shook her head. 'None of this makes sense to me! It's hurting me trying to work out what you mean! Please, be quiet. I don't want to know.'

'Yes, you do!' Yehhuk insisted, having become a child again. 'The Greylids were the future form of the old Artemisians.... so... what comes next?'

'I expect you're dying to tell me.'

'Don't you want to guess?'

'I give up.'

'Oh alright, I'll tell you. Yehhuk is the final evolutionary form of humanity. It is eternity too. The future, the past, the present. Beyond reality and all realities. Now do you understand?'

'No. Neither do I want to!'

'Why do you say those things, Corinna Trotgarden?'

Yehhuk asked, coming to clasp Corinna's knees and raise a sweet, smiling face up to her. 'You're a very curious person. You do want to understand. I know you do.'

Corinna sighed. 'OK, you're trying to tell me that you are, in fact, us, or at least a future form of ourselves, who can manipulate time as well as space. Is that it?' She was still thinking it must be a joke.

'Corinna,' Yehhuk said, shaking its head. 'Don't you realise? Even now, I am you, part of you, at least. Whatever I teach you means you're only teaching yourself!'

'Hand me a nail!' said Corinna Trotgarden, and promptly wiped the memory of the conversation from her conscious mind.

The knowledge did not resurface until two generations later, in Corinna's female grand-child, who experienced it as a revelation. By which time it was not a surprise, or maybe it was. There are many realities to choose from.